The Righteous Blade

...book was originally published in Great Britain under the title *Quicksilver Zenith* ...004 by Voyager, an imprint of HarperCollins Publishers.

...E RIGHTEOUS BLADE. Copyright © 2004 by S. J. Nicholls. All rights reserved. ...nted in the United States of America. No part of this book may be used or repro-...uced in any manner whatsoever without written permission except in the case of ...rief quotations embodied in critical articles and reviews. For information address ...HarperCollins Publishers, 10 East 53rd Street, New York, NY 10022.

HarperCollins books may be purchased for educational, business, or sales promotional use. For information please write: Special Markets Department, HarperCollins Publishers, 10 East 53rd Street, New York, NY 10022.

FIRST U.S. EDITION

Eos is a federally registered trademark of HarperCollins Publishers.

Library of Congress Cataloging-in-Publication Data

Nicholls, Stan.
   [Quicksilver zenith]
   The righteous blade / Stan Nicholls.—1st U.S. ed.
      p.   cm.—(The dreamtime ; bk. 2)
   Originally published in Great Britain under title: Quicksilver zenith. 2004.
   ISBN-13: 978-0-06-073891-4 (pbk.)
   ISBN-10: 0-06-073891-X
   I. Immortalism—Fiction.   2. Utopias—Fiction.   I. Title.

   PR6064.I179Q533 2005
   823'.914—dc22

                                                    2005044206

06 07 08 09 10 NMSG/RRD 10 9 8 7 6 5 4 3 2 1

Books by Stan Nicholls

The Covenant Rising
The Righteous Blade

The Righteous B

BOOK TWO

OF THE

DREAMTIME

STAN NICHOLLS

This b
from
to ac

This
in 2

TH
Pr
d
b

An Imprint of HarperCollinsPublishers

For their love and inexhaustible support, *The Righteous Blade* is dedicated to my dear mother-in-law, Eileen (Paddy) Booth, my sister-in-law, Janet Calderwood, her partner, Owen Sutherland, and my delightful, frighteningly bright nieces, Anna and Elaine Kennedy.

The story so far . . .

The world is saturated in magic.

Its influence is felt in every stratum of human culture. It acts as technology, currency, and as an instrument of control. Its possession and quality denotes social status. It can manifest in many ways, including sham lifeforms, universally referred to as glamours.

The magical system is the legacy of a long-vanished race known as the Founders. Their era, the Dreamtime, flourished before the dawn of history. But why it came to an end is a mystery.

Rival empires Rintarah and Gath Tampoor, equally matched in arms and sorcery, now dominate most of the globe. The island state of Bhealfa sits between them like an egg in a vice. A colony of both empires at various times, it currently bears the shackles of Gath Tampoor.

Bhealfa's sovereign is Prince Melyobar, a puppet ruler obsessed by death, which he sees as an animate being. In order to outrun his fate, Melyobar has created at vast expense a magically impelled travelling court; a floating palace that is literally never still. The thousands of camp followers it attracts effectively makes the court a nomadic city.

The brutality of the empires has bred an opposition movement, active within Gath Tampoor and Rintarah themselves, and their many dependencies. At the heart of this opposition is the armed Resistance.

The paladin clans are principal enforcers of the empires' oppression. Mercenaries in all but name, the clans' self-seeking precepts allow them to serve both sides. They are as wealthy and powerful as any imperial institution bar the governments.

Reeth Caldason's hatred of paladins is legendary. A notorious outlaw in the eyes of the authorities, Reeth is a Qalochian. The Qalochians, a warrior race indigenous to Bhealfa, are scattered and nearing extinction. They have suffered betrayal, massacres and discrimination. Caldason himself was one of only a handful to survive the slaughter of his own tribe, and is looking for vengeance. He also seeks a cure for a unique, and unexplained, malady.

Grudgingly at first, he befriends Kutch Pirathon, the young apprentice of a sorcerer he hoped to consult, but who was killed by paladins. Caldason shocks Kutch with his antagonism towards the magic everyone else takes for granted, despite wanting its aid. Even more alarming are the berserk fits of rage Caldason suffers, and the bizarre visions that plague him.

The pair cross paths with Patrician Dulian Karr, a dissident politician opposed to the colonial rulers. Karr offers to put Caldason in touch with Covenant, a secret order of sorcerers who might be able to lift his misfortune. Caldason agrees to accompany the patrician and Kutch to Valdarr, Bhealfa's largest city.

In Merakasa, capital of Gath Tampoor, Serrah Ardacris leads a special forces unit of the Council for Internal Security. During a raid on a gang trafficking ramp, an illegal narcotic, one of her unit is killed. As he was the scion of an aristocrat family, there are political repercussions. Serrah is unjustly blamed for his death and pressured to make a public confession. Although subjected to harsh treatment, she refuses.

Serrah's daughter, Eithne, died aged fifteen of a ramp overdose. Eithne appears to Serrah, apparently brought back from the dead. But Serrah recognises this as a cruel magical ruse, designed to break her spirit. Close to despair, she's rescued from captivity by a Resistance group. She escapes from them and manages to get out of Gath Tampoor on a ship bound for Bhealfa.

En route, she overhears stories of a warlord, Zerreiss, who has risen in the barbarous northern wastes. Known to his people as the Man Who Fell From the Sun, Zerreiss has some unknown power which enables him to conquer neighbouring lands.

Clan High Chief Ivak Bastorran, hereditary leader of the paladins, and Gath Tampoorian Imperial Envoy Andar Talgorian, although mutually antagonistic, co-operate on organising an expedition to find out more about Zerreiss. They are spurred by the suspicion that Rintarah is planning a similar mission.

Devlor Bastorran, nephew and protégé of Ivak, and heir to leadership of the clans, is obsessed with killing or capturing Reeth Caldason. His uncle urges him to caution, revealing that the paladins have to follow certain unspecified rules in respect of Caldason. Rules imposed by the highest authority.

Tanalvah Lahn, a state-sanctioned courtesan, and a Qalochian, has never known any other life than working in the brothels of Jecellam, capital of Rintarah. But everything changes when her best friend, another prostitute, is murdered by a client. Defending herself, Tanalvah accidentally kills the man. Terrified of the consequences, she takes her friend's two young children and flees. Securing passage on a ship, they sail for Bhealfa.

Kinsel Rukanis, a Gath Tampoorian, is one of the empire's leading classical singers. A pacifist, he covertly supports the Resistance. Rukanis encounters Tanalvah and the children in Valdarr docks, being chased by watchmen and a paladin. Serrah Ardacris, having arrived at the same harbour, saves Kinsel and the others, killing three of their pursuers in the process. Kinsel takes the women and children to a Resistance safe house.

Reeth Caldason, Kutch Pirathon and Dulian Karr arrive in Valdarr. They meet Phoenix, the head of Covenant, who appears in the guise of a churlish ten-year-old girl. In reality an elderly wizard,

Phoenix has studied what little remains of Founder lore, and uses this advanced magic to adopt a variety of guises. Caldason also comes upon Quinn Disgleirio, a representative of the Fellowship of the Righteous Blade. A martial order long dormant, the Fellowship has recently been revived to fight for Bhealfa's independence.

The Resistance, Covenant and the Blade Fellowship have formed an alliance to fight the empires' tyranny – the United Revolutionary Council. Karr confides that the Council has something more radical in mind than mere revolution. Their aim is no less than the founding of a free state, at a location yet to be chosen.

The full extent of Caldason's affliction is revealed. He is partially immortal, in the sense of being extremely resilient rather than indestructible. If wounded, he heals remarkably quickly, and he ages hardly at all. His condition dates back to the time his tribe was massacred, over seventy years before, though he has no idea how he achieved this state. The visions and rages he endures make him fear insanity.

Phoenix believes the Founders left a fund of knowledge, dubbed the Source. The Source is associated with the legend of the Clepsydra, said to be a device for marking off the eons to the Day of Destruction. If the stories are true, the Source could provide the Resistance with a powerful weapon against the empires, and Caldason with a cure. Covenant research indicates the Clepsydra's possible location, and Caldason is desperate to investigate. The Council promises to mount an expedition, but it will take time.

Phoenix also thinks that Kutch could be a latent spotter. Possessing an incredibly rare, natural talent, spotters can look beyond the falsity of magic and distinguish illusion from reality. Kutch agrees to let Phoenix train him and bring out the skill.

Reeth and Kutch's lives entwine with those of Serrah Ardacris, Kinsel Rukanis, Tanalvah Lahn and the children, who have been given Resistance protection. Shortly, Kinsel and Tanalvah become lovers, and set up house together with the children. But Tanalvah is worried that Kinsel is running too many risks through his Resistance work.

Devlor Bastorran identifies Kinsel and Tanalvah as having been at the centre of the brawl at the docks. He orders them to be watched, and bides his time.

A special operations band is formed, headed by Caldason and Serrah. Their mission is to penetrate a secret government records office and destroy its files. On its shelves, Caldason finds a file bearing his name, but all the pages have been removed. The depository is razed. Fleeing the scene, Caldason is confronted by Devlor Bastorran. A furious duel ensues, leaving the paladin severely injured.

Taking refuge in a temple, Serrah runs into Tanalvah. A follower of the benign goddess Iparrater, Tanalvah persuades Serrah to ask the temple oracle a question. The answer pitches Serrah into a deep melancholy.

Inflexibly convinced of his cause, Prince Melyobar devises a scheme to exterminate the entire population of Bhealfa. His plan is to deprive his great enemy, Death, of the masses he hides among.

Kutch tells Caldason that he, too, has started to see visions. When the apprentice describes their content, Caldason realises they are sharing the same dreams.

Overcome by misery, Serrah tries to commit suicide, making for little jubilation when Dulian Karr announces that a location has been found for the rebel state . . .

1

There had been no reprieve for reality. It remained in abeyance.

The night-time city was smothered by a dense fog that choked sound but only dimmed the constant discharge of magic. The gleam of sorcery pulsed and sparkled. Phantasms were on the wing, apparitions walked abroad.

A young man shuffled through the damp streets. He was bundled against the autumnal chill, collar up, battered cap pulled well down, a few unruly wisps of blond hair poking from underneath the brim.

He couldn't see. His eyes were covered by a contrivance resembling a leather mask, with two round patches, tied fast. Behind each patch was a coin, wrapped in wadding.

In one hand he held a cane, and used it to tap his uncertain way. In the other he grasped a leash, tightly coiled. This was attached to a halter girdling the shiny black carapace of a millipede – a creature the size of a large hunting dog. It moved sinuously, huge insectoid eyes set in an unblinking gaze, its multitude of twiggy legs rippling in unison.

The youth was anxious. He reckoned he was in a less than salubrious quarter, and he'd lost track of the time. Rapping his stick left to right, he walked falteringly, as though newly sightless. The millipede strained at its leash, probing, snuffling, guiding its charge around obstructions. The young man tried to hurry.

Had he been able to see, he would have regarded the blizzard of magic on every side as of little account. It was too ordinary. But another sight might have given him pause. Ahead of him, a pair of lights bobbed in the murk, and they were getting closer.

He was aware of a sound. Tugging the millipede to a halt, he stopped and listened, head tilted to one side, his eye patches like dark hollows. He heard the steady crump of boots on cobblestones. A small group, marching in unison. Coming his way.

His sense of unease increased and he thought of hiding. Lifting a hand to his mask, he made to peel it off.

'You, there! Don't move!'

The rasp of blades being drawn underlined the warning.

Breath stilled, the youth froze. The millipede scuttled back to him, brushing his calves as a frightened cat might do, for solace.

From out of the swirling, yellowish mist came a band of men. Foremost was a three-strong watch patrol in grey uniforms. Beside them, his scarlet tunic contrasting with their drabness, strode a paladin clansman. The patrol's requisite sorcerer brought up the rear, dressed in tan robes and bearing an ornamented staff. Two of the watch held charmed lanterns, bathing the scene in a soft, magical glow.

'Drop the weapon!'

He realised they meant the cane, and let it slip from his fingers. The clatter it made was all the louder in the taut silence.

They approached him warily.

'Don't you know there's a curfew?'

The speaker was the watch captain, grizzle-faced and lanky.

Despite the cold, his arms were bare. One was tattooed with a rampant, fire-spitting dragon, emblem of Gath Tampoor, the prevailing empire.

Still masked, the youth said nothing.

'Lost your tongue too, have you?'

'I'm sorry, I . . .'

'You're breaking the curfew,' the paladin barked. 'Why?'

The young man swung towards the new voice, swallowing hard. 'I . . . misjudged the hour. I thought –'

'That's no excuse,' the watchman snapped.

'Any more than being blind,' somebody added gruffly.

'But I'm –'

'Ignorance is no defence,' the paladin recited. 'The law's the law.'

Someone elbowed his ribs, making him wince. 'What're you doing here?'

'Where're you from?' asked another, breathing the fetid odour of cheap pipe tobacco.

'Who brought you?' rasped a third, his mouth unnervingly close to the youth's ear.

He reeled under the barrage of questions. Floundering, he tried to answer, tried to placate them. But they were as bent on harassment as interrogation.

The captain eyed the millipede. 'Where did you get a glamour this expensive?'

'It was a gift,' the young man lied.

'And who would *you* know with that kind of wealth?'

He didn't reply.

'Can you prove ownership?' the clansman pressed.

'As I said, it was –'

'Then we have the right.'

The clansman nodded at the sorcerer. Gravely, he produced a long-bladed silver knife, embellished and fortified with spells, and offered it hilt first. The watch captain took it.

'If you can't prove,' the watchman said, 'you can't keep.'

'Please, don't . . .' the youth implored.

The millipede looked up with doleful eyes.

Stooping, the captain raised the knife, then plunged it into the creature's back.

A myriad cracks appeared on the insect's husk. It bled light. Thin needles at first, piercing the gloom in all directions. A second later, shafts; intense as summer sun and just as dazzling. The millipede turned translucent, no more than a hollow outline, before melting into a silvery haze which flickered briefly, and went out.

The glamour died.

A little inrush of air filled the vacuum it left, and the leash the young man clutched hung slack, its collar vacant.

His persecutors mocked him with laugher.

'There was no need,' he protested weakly.

'You can't account for yourself and you're in violation of the curfew,' the paladin told him. 'We're taking you in.'

'C'mon.' The watch captain laid a rough hand on the youth.

'I won't!' the young man blurted, trying to shake himself loose.

'You *what*?'

'I mean . . . it was just a mistake. I didn't know I'd broken the law and –'

The watchman cuffed him, hard. It was enough to make the youth stagger.

'You speak when you're spoken to.'

A red welt coloured the youth's cheek, a trickle of blood snaked from the corner of his mouth. He braced himself for another blow.

'And you address us with the respect we're due,' the watchman added, raising his fist again.

'Take your filthy hands off him.'

A figure emerged from the fog. He was tall and dark. His flowing cloak made him look like some kind of giant winged beast.

The watchman swung to face him. 'Who the hell are *you*?'

Forgetting their captive, they all turned their attention to the newcomer.

'Stand aside,' he said. His tone was even. Calm.

'Who in damnation do you think you're giving orders to?' the paladin thundered.

'I said stand aside.'

'Who are you,' the watchman repeated, 'to be out in curfew and obstructing the watch?' Stupefaction tinged his building rage, unaccustomed as he was to having his authority defied.

'The boy's coming with me.'

'Is that so? Well, *we're* in charge here.' He sliced air with the sorcerer's knife to stress his words. 'If he's going anywhere, it's with us. And you with him.'

The stranger came closer. His movements were unhurried, almost leisurely. But now that he stood in the lantern's glow they saw that there was something disturbing about his eyes.

'No we're not,' he said.

The watch captain glared at him. He took in the man's brooding features. The somewhat angular structure of his face, the slight ruddiness of complexion, his long raven hair.

'Should have known,' the captain sneered, turning his head to spit contemptuously. 'We've got ourselves a real lowlife here, lads.'

His comrades laughed again, united in bigotry, if a little uneasily this time. The paladin stayed silent, and so did the sorcerer. Bewildered, the youth's head swung from side to side, trying to make out what was going on.

'Reckons he can insult his betters,' the watchman grandstanded. 'We'll show him the price of that.'

The stranger moved forward. He only stopped when the tip of the watchman's raised knife touched his chest. It didn't seem to bother him.

They locked gazes. The stranger didn't blink, or move a muscle. The captain's knuckles were white.

A flock of oversized butterflies fluttered past. They were garishly coloured and appeared to be made of hammered tin. A faint squeaking emitted from their beating wings. Nobody paid them any mind.

'We can settle this peacefully,' the stranger said. 'Give me the boy and I'll let you go.'

'Let *us* –?' The captain seethed. He applied more pressure to the knife. 'It'll be a cold day in hell when we bow to your sort.'

'I can arrange for you to check the temperature person- ally,' the stranger offered, and smiled. There was nothing comforting about it.

Perhaps there was a glimmer of realisation in the captain's features, a suspicion of what he might be facing. The shadow of a doubt darkened his face. He half whispered, 'Who *are* you?'

'A man who doesn't like being on the business end of a blade.'

There was a blur of motion, an action so quick and fluid the others couldn't follow it.

Now the stranger had the knife. He held it by the blade, hilt up. Dazed, empty-handed, the captain gaped at him.

'I think this belongs to you,' the stranger said, and just as swiftly lobbed it. But his target wasn't the watch captain.

The knife winged to the sorcerer. It punctured his chest, driving deep. Whiskered mouth in an O of surprise, the wizard gawked, bewildered, at the blade quivering in his breast. He went down in a swirl of robes.

What had been a glacial scene instantly thawed.

Everyone bar the stranger seemed to be shouting. There was a confusion of movement. Weapons were deployed, lanterns discarded.

'What is it?' the youth pleaded, twisting in the chaos. 'What's happening?'

The stranger shoved him aside. The youth tottered, and fell.

From beneath his billowing cloak the stranger quickly drew a pair of swords. Then the patrol moved in to engage him.

On hands and knees, head low, the young man scurried away from the sound of ringing steel. Bumping into a wall, he huddled with his back against its coarse surface, making himself small.

A watchman circled the stranger to seize him from behind. He met the smartly delivered backward thrust of a granite-hard elbow. There was the audible crack of a breaking nose. Palms to face, the watchman reeled clear. The stranger resumed fencing with barely a pause.

He faced the captain and the third patrolman. His most dangerous opponent by far, the paladin, knelt beside the sorcerer. He was feeling the wizard's neck for a pulse, but his eyes were on the fight.

Anger rode the captain. It made him unruly. He fought with wild swings and a reckless stance. His companion was more sober. He came in with measured passes and well-aimed strokes. The stranger met both with equal vigour, his twin blades flashing smoothly from one to the other.

The alley was lit by an eerie gleam from the cast-off lanterns. It threw enormous shadows of the duellists onto the wall behind the cowering youth. The shades of frenzied giants, performing an eccentric ballet. Until one of them stopped.

An expression of consternation was etched on the captain's

face. A blade jutted from his chest. The stranger tugged it free in a gush of crimson. Knees buckling, the captain dropped.

His cohort, momentarily stunned, battled on with renewed ferocity. The man with the broken nose, bloodied and ashen, recovered enough to join in. They tried to overcome their opponent with sheer force but he held them off with ease, dodging swipes, side-stepping thrusts with sure dexterity. Nothing they did slowed his attack. Then he took an opening.

The young man, cringing at the wall, had his hands covering his bowed head, fingers splayed. Half a dozen paces to his left was a sealed window. A grey-uniformed body hurtled into it, crashing through the wooden shutters. It came to rest half in, half out, legs dangling. The youth whimpered.

With Broken Nose out of the picture, the stranger turned to the remaining watchman and fell on him like a ravening wolf.

A slash of glistening arterial blood sprayed across the brick-work above the youth. Flecks splashed him, warm drops spattered his head, hands and shoulders. He quailed.

The stranger had no further interest in the downed watchman. His attention was on the paladin, still kneeling by the wizard. They stared at each other. The paladin was young, robust; his turn-out immaculate, with hair and beard neatly trimmed, in common with his kind. He slowly rose. With measured tread he advanced, drawing his sword as he came. For his part the stranger re-sheathed the flatter of his blades, leaving him with a rapier.

The paladin asked, 'Why do that?'

'So we can meet equally.'

'Gallantry from a savage?' he scoffed. 'Only a fool throws away an advantage.'

They'd begun to circle each other slowly.

'We'll see,' the stranger replied.

They moved simultaneously, and fast. Their blades met,

pealing, and for a moment locked. Disengaging, both men pulled back and commenced their duel in earnest. Exchanging stinging passes, hacking and chopping, they set up a rhythmic beat of pounding steel. The paladin was a skilful fighter, and disciplined, but no match for his opponent.

The end came when the stranger parried a stroke and deflected his foe's blade. The follow-through ruptured a lung and brought the paladin down.

Rivulets of blood fed the lane's rain gully, colouring the sluggish flow.

The stranger looked around and saw the youth huddled at the wall. Ramming his sword into its scabbard, he swept to him, cloak flapping.

'Get up,' he said.

The young man didn't move, aside from trembling.

'On your feet!'

Still the youth didn't stir. The stranger took him by the scruff and roughly hoisted him.

'Now take that thing off.'

'No. I can't, I –'

He was slammed against the wall. 'Take it *off*!'

'I daren't.'

Brutally, the stranger ripped the mask from his face and flung it aside. The freed coins bounced across the cobbles.

The youth kept his eyes screwed shut.

'Open them,' the stranger demanded. *'Open them.'*

With some effort, and timorously, he did as he was told.

'How is it?'

The young man blinked and looked about sheepishly. 'It's ... it's all right, I think.'

'There's no need for this. It's stupid and dangerous, and –'

'No need? You know what I've been seeing. How can you say –'

There was a groan close by. They turned and saw that the

watch captain was feebly breathing. The stranger drew a knife.

'No,' the youth begged. 'Can't you just leave him?'

'We don't take prisoners. Any more than they do.'

He moved to the dying man and quickly finished him. The youth couldn't watch.

Wiping his blade on a scrap of cloth, the stranger said, 'You think I'm cruel. But this is a war. Maybe not in name, but that's what it amounts to.'

The youth nodded. 'I know.'

'Come on. It won't do to linger here.'

They set off together through the fog.

Something that looked like an eel swam past them. It was candy-striped and had a pair of wings far too tiny to fly with. As it made its serpentine way it left a trail of orange sparks.

In a voice much gentler, Caldason asked, 'How are you feeling?'

'I'm scared,' Kutch said.

2

Dawn was near. The fog was clearing.

Valdarr, titular capital of the island state of Bhealfa, began to stir. People were coming out to mingle with the magic that never slept.

As in all great cities, areas of wealth and deprivation sat cheek by jowl. Likewise, there were districts neither prosperous nor impoverished; unassuming quarters where the dwellings and their attendant glamours were humble.

A closed carriage travelled at speed through one such neighbourhood. It was drawn by a pair of jet-black horses, and its driver, swathed head to foot, was unrecognisable. Rattling along narrow, waking streets, it pulled up outside a row of spartan buildings. Most were private homes. Others served basic needs, with paltry wares and tawdry charms stacked outside on rickety tables.

The carriage's passenger alighted. He wore a tightly wrapped cloak and his expression was sombre. The driver immediately cracked his whip and the carriage moved off. As the sound of its departure faded, the passenger paused for a moment, looking up and down the deserted street before crossing to the open door of a bakery.

Loaves, pies and sweetmeats cooled on wooden racks, waiting for customers. For now, there was only an old woman, standing at a worn counter. They exchanged nods. Without a word, he squeezed past and went to the back of the room, where he descended a stone staircase. This led to a sturdy door, which he rapped on, and once checked via a spy-hole he was let in.

He was hit by the warmth, and the smell of baking bread. The kitchen was long and low, with a curved ceiling, all in unadorned brick. There were sacks of flour, barrels of dried fruits, bushels of salt. One wall held three ovens. Each consisted of two sets of iron doors; the oven itself and a massive grate below. Sweating men, using tongs to unlatch the doors, fed the hearths from pyramids of wood blocks. Bakers in white aprons hefted long-handled, flat paddles, bearing dough shapes to the ovens.

The visitor was recognised and greeted. He shed his cloak, dropping it across the only chair. His appearance was distinguished, and his clothes were of good quality. He had silvering hair, overly long, and an intellect that shone through tired eyes. His age was not as great as wear made it seem.

He walked to the last of the three huge ovens and the workers clustered around.

'I'm getting too old,' he decided, half to himself. Louder, he asked, 'Would you be so kind?'

'Glad to oblige, sir,' the master baker replied, signalling. He was plump and sheened with perspiration.

A man came forward and split the oven's belly. The blast of heat was like a punch. Roaring flames erupted.

Two muscular workers took hold of the visitor. Hands behind his knees, and at his shoulder-blades to steady him, they raised him in a chair lift. With practised ease they swung him back and forth, working up momentum.

Then they tossed him into the furnace.

The blaze seemed so real, and the heat was searing. He nearly cried out, despite knowing.

Instantly he broke through. From intense light to relative dimness. From withering heat to the welcoming cool.

He landed on a heap of sacks stuffed with yarn, but still had the breath knocked out of him. Seen from this side, the glamour he'd passed through was a window-sized square on a wall. It was filled with muted colours, gently swirling, like oil on water. There was no illusion of flames, and certainly no warmth.

'On your feet, Patrician.'

Dulian Karr looked up. A woman of middle years towered over him. She was well built, though more muscular than flabby, and she had a mordant face. As always, she toted a thick wad of documents, currently tucked under one arm. Her other hand, surprisingly callused for an administrator, was held out to him.

'Goyter,' he said, by way of greeting, and allowed her to pull him to his feet. As he rose he made a sharp little air-sucking noise through pursed lips. 'My aching bones,' he complained.

'Rubbish,' she snorted briskly, 'you're not that much older than me. I suggest you stop feeling sorry for yourself and do something useful around here; that usually improves your mood.' Her piece said, she turned and marched away.

Karr had to smile as he watched her bustle off to harass somebody else.

There were plenty to choose from. This particular hideout was much bigger than the bakery he'd just left. It consisted of the cellars of several adjacent buildings, knocked through, and at least a score of people were working here. He dusted himself off and started a tour of inspection.

One section was given over to manufacturing glamours. Men and women, wearing cotton gloves, sat at lengthy tables, gingerly tinkering with magical ordnance. Under the cautious gaze of supervising wizards, stocks of illegal munitions took shape: mirage pods, dazzlers, mendacity flares, odour grenades, stun poles, eavesdropper shields disguised as necklaces and bracelets.

He swapped brief greetings and wandered on to look at the firing range.

An area several hundred paces long and perhaps thirty wide had been devoted to testing occult weaponry. Given the dangerous nature of the spells involved, the zone was sealed inside a protective screen. This was almost entirely transparent, except for a faint tint of rainbow colours, not unlike a soap bubble.

A number of dummies were propped up at one end of the range. Essentially elaborate scarecrows, they were lashed to timber frames. At the other end, a line of testers took aim.

Energy bolts flashed from staves, decapitating their targets in explosions of straw. Other glamoured devices engulfed them in glutinous ectoplasm nets, or peppered them with ice needles. One of the testers raised a brass horn to his lips and blew. But instead of a musical note, it discharged a cloud of minute, winged lizards with barbed talons and razor teeth. The swarm soared to a dummy and began ravaging it, shredding cloth and wood.

Another tester held a combat wand. It was snub and black, and it joined to a handgrip with leather tendrils that looped around her fingers and wrist. When she pointed, the wand belched apple-sized fireballs. The flaming orbs burst on contact, setting the manikins ablaze. Some missed and bounced around the range before detonating. Falling short of its target, a fireball glanced off the paving and ricocheted towards Karr. It struck the near-invisible shield directly in front of his face, erupting in a brilliant red and yellow flash. Instinctively, he recoiled, though he knew he couldn't be touched.

The tester gave him a contrite grin. He thought how very young she looked.

Goyter appeared at Karr's side. 'We're working on their stability,' she said, nodding at the wand. In a lower voice, she added, 'It's not like you to be so jumpy. Everything all right?'

'I'm fine. Just . . . tired.'

'Hmm.' Looking unconvinced, she went back to her chores.

Karr stood with eyes closed, massaging the bridge of his nose with thumb and forefinger.

In the shadows of a nearby recess, something stirred. Slowly, it dragged its bulk into the light. The creature was powerfully built, and its massive shoulders were broad. It was covered in abundant dark fur, with short, red-brown hair on its paler chest. Its face resembled old leather; its nose was flattened, its eyes black. Moving with a rolling gait, knuckles almost brushing the floor, it made for the patrician.

Alerted by the sound of its shuffling approach, Karr turned.

'What do you think?' the gorilla said. It gave a lumbering pirouette, an unconscious parody of an arthritic matron displaying a new gown. 'It's a bit bulky, but much more comfortable than that little-girl persona. With a few adjustments it should –'

'For the gods' sake, spare us,' Karr interrupted wearily.

'What?'

'I preferred the child.'

'Oh.' Insofar as it was possible, the gorilla looked deflated. 'Why?'

'Because you keep chopping and changing. At least we knew where we were with her. Irritating as she was.'

'The time seemed right for a change.'

'We have enough change to cope with as it is, don't you think?'

'That's rich, coming from you.'

'You can have too much of the wrong sort. Look, I find debating with an ape a bit beyond my present mood. So, if you wouldn't mind . . .'

The gorilla held up its palms in a mollifying gesture. 'Point taken.' It swung around and loped back to its nook, arms dangling, legs bowed.

There was a commotion in the half light of the alcove; a flickering of intense radiance, a honey-coloured haze and the whiff of a pungent, sulphurous odour. A moment passed, the furore died down. Then a lanky man emerged from the cranny.

He was old and grizzle-faced, but his back was straight and his stride steadfast. His apparel consisted of a simple blue robe held fast by a cummerbund, and gold braided slippers; a style favoured by the sorcerer classes. As he walked he smoothed down errant strands of his grey hair and copious beard.

'I have to say your attitude's more than a little acidic today, Patrician,' he observed.

'I'm sorry, Phoenix. It's a fraught time.'

'You're exhausted, man.'

'The pressure's on. With the move so near –'

'You can't bear the weight of the world on your own shoulders. You look as though you've got a foot in the grave. You have to learn to relax.'

'*Relax*? How can I relax? The preparations, the logistics, the number of people involved; the sheer scale of what we're trying to do is staggering.'

'Even so, you should let go a bit. Delegate.'

'Did you know,' Karr replied, ignoring this advice, 'that half a dozen homes of colonial administrators went up in flames last night?'

'I heard.'

'That wasn't our doing. People are starting to take matters into their own hands.'

'That's good, isn't it? The more blows the regime suffers, the better for our cause, surely?'

'Armed rebellion's not the plan, you know that. We harry them, yes, but we don't want outright confrontation. Everything we're trying to do is predicated on the fact that we couldn't win that way.'

'There's nothing we can do about it, Karr. If the populace feels aggrieved enough to hit out, who are we, of all people, to say they can't?'

'We don't need anarchy.'

'I'm not sure I agree with that. The clampdown's increased recruitment, if nothing else.'

'And it's all my fault.'

'What is?'

'Three months of worsening repression. Curfews, innocents rounded up, torture, summary executions; all sparked off by the raid on the records office. I should never have authorised the mission. It was a mistake.'

'No, it wasn't. We hit them where it hurts, and we knew there were likely to be repercussions. This constant blaming of yourself is getting tiresome.'

'Anything we gained has been outweighed by the consequences. The paladins have been given their head. Such small freedoms as we had are even smaller. Why shouldn't I blame myself?'

'Because it isn't your fault. Or is your self-regard so great that you can't see you're no more of a cog than the rest of us? You're not alone in trying to steer this scheme, you know.'

Karr looked chastened. 'I suppose I deserved that. I guess what's troubling me is that I hoped we'd have more control at this point.'

'Control's an illusion, you should realise that by now. The best we can do is ride the surge. Don't lose faith, Karr, not now. Not when we're this close, and when our destination's causing so much strife.'

'Strife's too hard a word. Some have still to be convinced, that's all.'

'Not hard to see why, is it?' The wizard crossed his arms. 'I mean, of all the places to pick –'

'Don't start that again, Phoenix, please. The refuge was agreed by all of you in Covenant, and by the full Council.'

'I know, I know. I'm just saying it's an . . . unusual choice. And that's not a rare opinion among those who know about it.'

'The issue's settled. There's no turning back now.'

'All I'm doing is reminding you that the decision isn't universally popular,' Phoenix pointed out, a testy note creeping into his voice.

'Then you're saying nothing that hasn't already been said.'

Just as they reached a stalemate, Goyter appeared with a pair of new arrivals. One was tall and hardy, his garb black, his eyes dark and penetrating. In his wake came a youth, nearly a man; not shaven like his companion but striving for whiskers, and acting coy.

'Morning, Reeth,' Karr greeted the older man, glad of the interruption.

Caldason nodded.

'And how are you this day?' Karr inquired of the youth.

Kutch Pirathon said nothing, looking instead to the Qalochian.

'It's been happening again,' Caldason explained.

'The visions?' Phoenix asked.

'And his way of trying to avoid them.'

Kutch stared at his feet.

Phoenix sighed. 'We have to get to the root of this.' To Caldason, he added, 'It would help if we knew more about what he was seeing.'

'I've told you all I can about that.' The response was frosty enough to forbid further questioning.

'Come on, Kutch, let's see if we can talk this through.' Phoenix took the boy's arm.

'Just a minute,' Karr said. He indicated Kutch's blood-speckled jerkin. 'What's that?'

'What do you think it is?' Caldason returned, casually defiant.

'How many times do I have to tell you about your brawling?'

'You can say it as often as you like. It won't stop me acting as I see fit.'

'The last thing we need now is to lose somebody like you, and we can certainly do without drawing attention unnecessarily.'

'A watch patrol caught me,' Kutch volunteered, 'and Reeth –'

'It was necessary, Karr,' Caldason cut in. 'Or perhaps you'd prefer the boy was captured and made to talk?'

'I was being stupid,' Kutch admitted, eyes downcast.

'And reckless,' Caldason added.

The boy looked up. He almost whispered, 'I don't think I'm the only one guilty of that.'

Caldason was going to say something, but checked himself.

It was Karr who spoke. 'This isn't a time to be playing the fool.' His gaze flicked from man to boy. 'Either of you.' Goyter and Phoenix loitered at the fringe of the conversation. He addressed them. 'By the look of him, the first thing Kutch needs is sleep. See he gets some. Then do what you can, Phoenix.'

The wizard nodded and made to leave. Then he noticed Caldason staring at him. 'What is it? What's wrong?'

'I think I preferred the ape.'

'Hmmph.' Phoenix turned on his heel.

Kutch gave one glance back before he and Goyter followed into the maze of cellars.

'The boy worries me,' Karr confessed as he watched them go.

'He should,' Caldason replied. 'I know what he sees.'

'And we're no nearer grasping how you came to share these illusions.'

'I've spent years trying to work out why *I* have them, and what they might mean. I feel as though I've . . . infected him in some way.'

'We can only hope Phoenix and Covenant come up with a solution.'

'If they don't make things worse.'

'Your attitude towards magic's understandable, but it hardly accords with reality. You'd have us turn our backs on the only possible remedy for the boy. Not to mention the many other benefits.' He nodded towards the firing range.

The first batch of dummies, charred beyond recognition, had been dragged away. Now the testers were working on destroying a new group, some of them dressed in the distinctive red tunics of the paladin clans. Eye-aching miniature lightning bolts crackled from the testers' wands. An arrow was loosed. Bound with a chicane spell, it appeared to be dozens of identical shafts. The glamour bolts imploded on impact and vanished; the real arrow pierced its target. Projectiles hurled from slingshots exploded at the manikins' feet in a green flowering of crazed venomous snakes.

'I'll take cold steel any day,' Caldason said.

'It's not what Kutch needs.'

'He did tonight.'

Karr slowly shook his head and laughed softly. 'We're never going to see eye to eye on this, are we?'

'Probably not.' Caldason regarded him. 'You said Kutch needed rest. That goes double for you. You look worn.'

'Everybody's been telling me that lately.'

'Then listen; they can't all be wrong. You're bearing too much.'

'It'll soon be a little less, I hope. I'm resigning my patrician-ship.'

'You've said that often enough.'

'This time I mean it. It's a move I should have made long ago.'

'Good. When?'

'A matter of days. It's going to feel strange after serving for so long.'

'I don't believe politicians achieve that much. Even the few decent ones end up tainted. You're better out of it.'

'I've come to think that way myself. And that maybe I've wasted all those years.'

'No, not wasted. I didn't say politicians don't achieve *anything*.'

The patrician smiled. 'From you, that's quite a concession. But I'm ready for the change, though it's going to take away what little protection the status affords me.'

'So do what you're always urging Rukanis to do; go underground.'

'I'll have to think about that. Disappearing after I quit could just confirm the authorities' suspicions about me. It might be best to keep some kind of public profile for a while. But I have a more awkward task before I make that decision.'

'What's that?'

'A social gathering, and a very prestigious one. It's a ball, in fact, so it combines two things I don't much care for: official functions and masquerades.'

'They're not exactly to my taste either, but it doesn't sound that bad.'

'You haven't heard the worst of it. It's hosted jointly by the Gath Tampoorian diplomatic corps and the clans. I'll have the pleasure of the company of Envoy Andar Talgorian, and no less than Ivak Bastorran himself.'

'I'd pay a good price for a few minutes alone with that one myself,' Caldason returned grimly. 'But if it's such a trial, don't go.'

'Protocol wouldn't allow that. Particularly as it's where my resignation's due to be announced.'

'Then you'll just have to smile through it.'

'Yes, and after that I can concentrate entirely on our plans for the refuge. Talking of which . . .' He altered course with a politician's deftness. '. . . I'm having a meeting soon with the owner of the location. I'd like you there.'

'What could I contribute?'

'Something very valuable, perhaps. I can't go into details now, but will you come?'

'Some idea of what you expect of me would help.'

'Possibly a service to the new state. Perhaps nothing beyond attending the meeting.'

Caldason thought about it. 'All right.'

'I'd like Serrah in on this, too.'

'The meeting?'

'This could concern your unit, and she is a member.'

'Who hasn't been on a mission for three months.'

'I'd like the option of her being included. We can't afford to have somebody with Serrah's experience stand idle, not when we're this stretched.'

'I'd like to have her back. She's moved on a lot since she tried to kill herself. But she's still . . . unpredictable.'

'She's lost so much, Reeth. Her child, her job, her country, all she believed in. I think that entitles her to be a bit erratic, don't you? I'm not convinced she's ready for mission duties yet, but we should at least consider the possibility.'

'As I said, I'd like her back.'

'Excellent. I'll get word to her.' He looked around the bustling cellar and spotted Goyter returning. He waved her over.

'Any idea where Serrah is this morning?' he asked.

Goyter licked a thumb and consulted one of her numerous pieces of parchment. 'She's with Tanalvah Lahn.'

'Ah, good. Tanalvah's steady. She'll keep Serrah out of trouble.'

3

Serrah Ardacris was in trouble.

Horrified, Tanalvah watched as her charge was driven back towards a wall by the two sentries still on their feet. They had pikes, giving them the advantage, and they were enraged. Serrah fought like a rabid thing, hacking at them savagely with her blade as she retreated.

To Tanalvah the situation looked dire. But Serrah seemed to be laughing.

Three of the sentries' comrades were down. One was groaning and trying to rise. Another sprawled unconscious. The third lay very still in a widening pool of blood. The bench they'd been using as their checkpoint was overturned, and scraps of parchment fluttered in the chill morning breeze. On either side of the wagon that served as a roadblock a small crowd had gathered.

A loud crack brought Tanalvah back to earth. Serrah had chopped clean through one of the guard's pikes. Its bearer was disbelieving for a second, then narrowly dodged her follow-up swing. Discarding the useless halves, he quickly pulled back, fumbling for his own blade. She turned her grinning wrath on his companion.

He had a simple strategy: herding her like swine until he could bury the pike in her chest. Serrah thought him unimaginative. She spun at him, using the momentum to hurry along a low stroke. He recoiled, avoiding it by a hair's-breadth. Her next blow scoured his fist, biting deep. Wailing, he let go of the pike with his injured hand, upsetting its balance. As he botched correcting it, she went in again. He took the full force of her blow, toppled backwards, and landed flat-out, arms and legs akimbo, the pike rolling clear.

From where she stood, pressed into a doorway thirty paces distant, Tanalvah could swear she heard a hefty smack as he hit the flagstones.

Head thrown back, her long blonde hair falling loose, Serrah was laughing. Partly in triumph, but mostly from some darker impulse.

The remaining sentry charged, bellowing to mask his dread. She stood her ground and met him. Their swords crashed together in a discordant note nobody failed to hear. Then their blades took to chattering; a brittle, malevolent discourse in steel.

The intensity of her attack began to overwhelm him. He longed to abandon the fight. It was in his face. In his eyes. Even Tanalvah saw it, a good stone's lob away. But there was no break, and their clamour grew more frantic. The sentry hammered and slashed, while Serrah wielded her blade like a scalpel. He tried to overcome her with force and bluster. She fenced.

And in a split second, struck. Her blade raked his cheek. He cried out and slapped a palm to the wound. Crimson ribbons dribbled from between his fingers. In pain and fury he rushed at her, brandishing his sword, yelling hoarsely. She swept aside his blade and cut him down. He sank rather than fell, ending on his knees, head lolling. She was already moving away as he pitched to the ground.

Tanalvah slipped from her hiding place and dashed to her friend. She found her smiling.

'Come on! We have to get away!'

Vacantly, Serrah stared at her.

Tanalvah grabbed her wrist. 'We can't stay here. *Come on!*'

Smile fading, Serrah focused. She glanced down at Tanalvah's hand. 'You're shaking.'

'You're the one who should be.' She squeezed Serrah's arm and implored, 'This is crazy. They'll be others here soon. We've got to *go.*'

The small crowd watched them silently.

Serrah looked about, as though seeing her surroundings for the first time. Something of her old self emerged. 'Yes. Yes, you're right.' She nodded at the main thoroughfare. 'That way.'

They ran.

A smattering of cheers rose from the crowd, and several people shouted encouragement. Others began yelling abuse. As the women jogged away, a shoving, ill-tempered commotion broke out; a scaled-down version of the divisions that plagued Bhealfa as a whole. But Serrah and Tanalvah weren't pursued. Not by anything human.

They'd covered a block when Tanalvah tugged at Serrah's sleeve. 'Look!' She pointed back the way they'd come, and up.

Serrah turned without breaking step. She saw something above, flying at rooftop height and closing in on them. Its vast wings flapped in a slow, leisurely rhythm. Though everyone knew it didn't really need wings at all.

A shadow fell across the fleeing women. The creature circled overhead, and they could see it more clearly. It was some sort of hybrid, mostly bat with insect traits, the latter providing it with three sets of spindly legs. The effect was not unlike a housefly, albeit one the size of a hay cart and sporting coal-red eyes.

'I don't think it's a hunter-killer,' Serrah judged, scowling irritably, 'just a damn snoop.'

'Then any minute it's going to start shouting about where we are.'

They were trotting now, with the tracer glamour hanging over them, keeping pace. There weren't many people on the streets this early, but those that were began taking an interest.

'Alert! Alert!' the glamour screeched. *'Felons sighted! Summon the watch!'*

Tanalvah mouthed, 'Oh, no.'

People were stopping to look.

'Fuck this.' Serrah's hand went to her belt.

Wheeling, the glamour continued its hue and cry. *'Fugitives! Insurgents! Here! Here! Here!'*

Serrah tugged out a short-bladed throwing knife.

'Alert! Alert! Anti-social elements at large! Summon your . . .'

Arm drawn well back, she lobbed it with all her strength.

'. . . local militia or —'

The blade struck the creature's fuzzy underside, and seemed to be absorbed into it. At once the glamour froze. Its serrated wings stilled. Yet still it hung in the air, impossibly.

What looked like a circular red stain appeared at the spot where the knife had entered. It began to expand. Resembling fire spreading across paper, it started to turn the creature's apparently solid flesh not to ash, but countless silver motes. Racing faster, the corruption riddled the glamour's body, veined its wings and stripped its bristly legs. The illusion of ebony tissue dissolved into a mass of tiny radiant pellets.

They fell as silvery hail, gently popping on the pavement below. What was left drifted down as a soft rain of shimmering pewter, dusting the streets and early risers before vanishing.

Serrah's knife clattered to earth somewhere, heard but unseen.

'Good shot,' Tanalvah whispered, plainly fearful.

'A good knife lost,' Serrah complained.

They took to running again.

Their flight was more artful this time. They used alleys and back ways, narrow lanes and covered passages. When they caught sight of the main thoroughfares they saw mounted militia heading in the direction they'd come from.

'Slow down,' Serrah panted. 'Running attracts attention.'

'And killing people doesn't?' Tanalvah retorted.

Serrah shrugged.

'Are you *trying* to get yourself caught?'

'*No.*' Serrah regarded her with hard eyes. 'That's never going to happen again. I'd rather die.'

'Ah, so that's it.'

'What do you mean?'

'You have to *ask*? You're too volatile, Serrah. What you did back there was . . . insane.'

'I won't be treated like shit.'

'It was all unnecessary. You should have just shown them your identity documents. The forgeries are good enough to pass.'

'You're missing the point, Tan. They disrespected me. I'm not a piece of meat to be abused.'

'What price respect if they'd killed you? Or captured us both? And who knows what would've happened to us then.'

It wasn't only Tanalvah's agitation that had passersby staring. Her jet hair, light tan complexion and slightly angular features attracted glances too. She had enough experience of casual prejudice towards Qalochians to ignore them.

'As I said,' Serrah replied coldly, 'I won't be taken.'

'What about me?'

'I wouldn't let it happen to you either.'

'Really? How?'

'If there was a chance of you being captured I'd cut your throat.'

'That's a comfort,' Tanalvah returned sarcastically. 'Your actions have consequences, Serrah, and not just for yourself.'

'You think I don't know that?'

'You act as though you don't.'

'I do what I have to do.'

'And relish it, if that fight you just started was anything to go by.'

'In a way, yes. There's nothing like being near death to give life some kind of meaning.'

'I suppose that's an improvement. Not that long ago it was only death you wanted.'

'Keep moving,' Serrah urged, blanking her.

As they hurried on, Tanalvah muttered, 'Gods, you frighten me sometimes.'

They were nearing the city centre, where the streets were much more crowded. It was a crisp morning, and weak, autumnal sunshine burnt off the last of the night's haze.

The fog had cleared but the magic was thick.

Wherever people congregated in numbers, the magic naturally tended to be more abundant. In the plazas, markets and boulevards of Valdarr's hub, it was already dense, despite the hour. And its variety was as diverse as the populace.

For the rich, magic was the agency for parading their wealth. They strolled in the company of glamoured escorts, exquisitely beautiful and uncommonly repulsive. They summoned flocks of living doves made of ice, which melted as they flew or shattered into a thousand fragments on touching the ground. They conjured herds of pink fawns, and fireflies the size of pigeons that throbbed with blinding light. They caused talking bears to roam abroad, and produced cockerels that sang rather than crowed the hour.

For the poor, magic was the balm that soothed their misery. In side streets and dingy turnings, unwashed children made do with cheap clown glamours that flickered and slurred through their performances. Or tumbling acrobats in washed-out colours that faded in and out of focus. The youngsters' gaunt elders, dressed in rags, wrung subsistence out of begging. They used rudimentary spells, counterfeit or stolen, to materialise basic musical instruments. Glamoured pipes and fiddles, suspended in empty air, tooted and scraped simple melodies. Passersby flung the odd coin into the paupers' upturned caps.

There were glamour beggars too, collecting for benevolent leagues that eased poverty, or affected to. These glamours, in clean rags and with scrubbed, smiling faces, were idealised versions of their human counterparts. Consequently their caps overflowed while the real poor were ignored.

Everywhere there were glittering illusions and cunning phantasms to deceive the senses. New glamours were constantly appearing, while others, expired or dismissed, were snuffed out.

Another day of infinitely malleable reality, and it wasn't mid-morning yet.

Serrah and Tanalvah took it all for granted. They were much more concerned with the level of security on the streets. Watch patrols and militia mingled with the crowds, as was to be expected, but in recent days their numbers had greatly increased. And now there were army regulars at every corner too, and the distinctive scarlet tunics of the paladin clans could be seen on all sides.

Tanalvah did everything she could to avoid attracting attention. She prayed Serrah would do the same.

'There's a rumour they're going to ban weapons in private hands next,' Tanalvah confided.

'How could they do that? You listen to too much gossip, Tan.'

'Kinsel overheard something about it at the concert hall. From a couple of high-ranking administrators.'

'People wouldn't put up with it. They'd resist. If anybody tried to take my blade off me —'

'You're doing it again. Seeing everything as solvable by violence.'

'How else would you stop them? Honeyed words and garlands?'

'What I mean is –' Tanalvah looked around and lowered her voice. 'What I mean is that this isn't the time to be taking any kind of risk. Not with the move so near.'

A wraith-like entity flew past, travelling at speed. Looking vaguely female, it seemed to be clothed in something gauzy that flowed behind it like a tangle of spider webs. It showed no interest in them. Tanalvah guessed it was a messenger glamour.

'As I've been allowed no part, I can't really do anything to endanger it, can I?'

'But I'm sure they will. Involve you in the move, that is. With your talents –'

'Yes,' Serrah replied cynically, 'of course they will.'

'Oh, Serrah . . . We need you. Whether you have a role in the exodus or not.'

They reached a crossing of two main thoroughfares. Grand carriages swept by, drawn by zebra, stags, panthers, grotesquely large swans and lizards; any of a hundred different exotic beasts the horses had been charmed to resemble.

'I'm going back to Karr's place,' Serrah decided.

'I'll come with you.'

'No. I'll be fine.'

'I'm worried about you.'

'There's no need.'

'Well, I am supposed to be at Kinsel's. Sure you'll be all right?'

'I can manage.'

'If you come across any more roadblocks . . .'

'I promise I'll restrain myself.' She flashed a fleeting but genuine smile, turned and moved into the throng.

Tanalvah watched her for a moment, then set off in the opposite direction.

It was a short walk to her destination. But Tanalvah took a convoluted route, just in case.

The neighbourhood where she now lived was affluent. It had wide, clean streets and substantial, well-maintained buildings. The magic on display was tasteful and costly, and there were no beggars. Everything about the place seemed designed to make her feel guilty.

When she entered the villa, Tanalvah's lover was waiting for her.

They embraced, and he said, 'What's the matter, Tan? You look troubled.'

'I've been with Serrah.'

'Ah.' It was all Kinsel Rukanis really needed to know. He'd been there when Serrah gave way to despair, and he'd seen how she was since. Nevertheless he asked, 'What happened?'

'Nothing she hasn't done a dozen times before. Not that that makes it any less frightening.'

'No. But we mustn't forget that if it wasn't for Serrah –'

'We wouldn't be here. I know. If it hadn't been for that, I'd say to hell with her.'

'She needs her friends more than ever now. Attempting suicide wasn't the end of her troubles. Far from it.'

'At least she hasn't tried it again.'

'Really? Don't you see her reckless behaviour as just another way of achieving her death wish?'

'I don't think it's that simple. Well, maybe it's partly that. Mostly I reckon she's . . . pushing boundaries. It's like she has to have control, even if it means creating situations where she's most likely to lose it.' She shrugged. 'I don't know.'

'We don't need a problem like this at the moment, Tan. Not with the move imminent.'

'I told her that. She might have taken it in, I couldn't be sure.'

Kinsel sighed. 'The Council has enough complications to deal with, seeing as our destination's causing so much controversy.'

'That's not your concern, dear. Let others take the decisions. Don't fret about it.'

'I do rather, don't I?' He smiled, almost shyly. 'But it's only because I care passionately for the enterprise. I wouldn't want anything to endanger it.'

She smiled back. 'I know *that*. Even if we don't see entirely eye to eye on the place the Council's chosen.'

'I think it's an inspired choice.'

'In some ways it is. But it has bad associations for many in my former profession. It's never been that popular with whores.'

'I wish you wouldn't –'

'We can't change what I was, Kin. I thought we'd agreed to be honest about it.'

'We did. I just don't like you referring to yourself that way.'

'It's only a word. A description of something I did, not what I am.'

'Of course it is, my love. And as far as the haven's concerned we can expunge its history and build something better there. But it doesn't matter where the refuge is. The important thing –' he leaned forward and kissed her '– is that we share the same dream.'

'Yes, darling.'

'I only wish I could do something more constructive to help bring it about.'

'This is your day for worrying, isn't it?'

'Well, there's not much call for a pacifist in a resistance movement.'

'Idiot,' she teased. 'You've done invaluable work for the cause, and risked your life in the process.'

'I think you're pitching it a bit high, Tan. Anyway, since Karr pulled me from intelligence gathering I feel like a fifth wheel on a wagon.'

'I'm glad he did. It was getting far too dangerous. Now you can concentrate on your real talent.'

'The singing? It seems frivolous at times like these.'

'It brings people respite. Don't underestimate the value of that, my dear.'

'If anybody's getting respite, Tan, it's the wrong people; the rich, the influential, the occupiers and their followers. What I do never seemed more irrelevant.'

'So make it relevant.'

'What do you mean?'

'You have a gift from the gods. It's a sin not to use it. Take your voice to those who wouldn't normally hear it. Let the poor have the benefit for once.'

'I've always tried to perform for as wide an audience as possible.'

'Yes, but what does that amount to? A few seats for charity cases. That's not your fault, Kin; it's the system you're part of. What I'm thinking of is something big, and cheap enough for people to afford. No, forget that. *Free*. Free and open to everyone.'

'In one of the city's open spaces. A park, perhaps.'

'Right.'

'It's a good idea, Tan. But . . .'

'What?'

'We're in a state of emergency, remember. Martial law. The authorities aren't keen on large gatherings.'

'You have connections. Use them. Pull strings.'

He brightened. 'I could try, I suppose.'

'Sell it as a mollifying event. You know, a way to turn people's minds from the troubles.'

'Bread and circuses.'

'If you're not taking this seriously, Kin –'

'No, no.' He laughed and hugged her. 'I said, it's a good idea. Thank you, Tan.'

She could see he was taken with the notion. It was good to set his mind on something other than brooding about the move.

There was a clattering on the stairs, and shrill, excited voices.

Kinsel grinned. 'Here comes trouble.'

Two minor hurricanes burst through the door. Teg, nearly six, had a shock of ginger hair and freckled cheeks. His sister, Lirrin, going on nine, sported a long blonde mane nearly as pale as her milky complexion.

The children rushed to enfold themselves in outstretched arms. Amid a flurry of caresses and laughter, Kinsel ushered the youngsters into the parlour. Tanalvah hung back, watching them. Lirrin, wearing her habitual, slightly serious expression, even when she should be free of cares. Teg, mercifully still too young to comprehend the full horror of their mother's murder.

And Kinsel. A little on the short side, well built, with a classical singer's drum chest, cropped black hair and a close beard. On his hands and knees, blissfully happy in horseplay with the children. Like a child himself. Trying, perhaps, to bind the unexplained wound that blighted his own childhood.

Tanalvah's family. The only one she'd ever known. Miraculously arriving in her life ready-made: another gift from the gods.

Let there be something better for them, she thought. *For all of us. In our new home.*

She shivered as though a chill wind had blown in from the unrealised future.

If we ever get there.

4

In common with every other land, there were locations in Bhealfa that people tended to avoid. Dangerous, unsettling places, such as the Great Chasm at Murcall, that legend said had opened up to swallow a warlord's invading horde. Spots like the forest of Bohm, with its curious ruins that many believed dated from the time of the Founders, and from which few travellers returned. Or the Starkiss valley fracture, where at intervals a geyser spewed raw magic, despite a thirty-year effort to seal the breach.

There were undesirable sites for urban dwellers, too. Lawless quarters, debtors' prisons and the re-education camps figured high on the list. But one was shunned above all others. A place where people were more often taken than chose to visit.

The headquarters of the paladin clans in Valdarr was a forbidding redoubt. Doubly so as an autumnal dusk fell. A large and imposing complex of grey stone structures, it existed behind high walls and heavily guarded gates. Black pennants flew at the tops of its many watchtowers.

That the compound stood in such a prime position was testament to the clans' overweening power. As soldiers of fortune, to use the polite term, they fought for both Gath Tampoor and Rintarah, and professed to see no conflict of loyalties. Their constitutional position was unique. They were deemed stateless, a legal nicety they'd wrung from grateful clients on opposite sides of the divide.

If an ignorant person were to ask what the paladins did that regular forces didn't, the answer would be everything and anything. Consequently their wealth and influence were considerable.

As the light began to fail, a man walked the spotless paths bisecting the rows of neatly maintained buildings. An observer would have put his age at around twenty summers. He was blond and clean-shaven. The tunic he wore was black with triple lines of red piping at the wrists and a circular red patch on the left breast. Markings that indicated his function was administrative rather than combative, and that he served the clans without being fully *of* the clans. He had an oilskin document pouch tucked under one arm. Back straight, he moved smartly, free arm swinging military style. Watchful human eyes followed his progress, and eavesdropper glamours hovered above.

His thoughts centred on the secrets harboured by his stern surroundings. Their secrets, and his own.

He came to a long, low, single-storey building that was in fact a wing projecting from a much larger central edifice. This was the core fortress, its sloping walls dizzyingly tall and dressed with crenellated defences. The wing was an infirmary, reserved for the highest ranking.

A pair of sentries guarded the door. Their tunics were crimson, indicating full clan blood. They didn't salute him, but did stand aside to let him pass. He nodded and went in.

The interior consisted of a central corridor with doors off to either side. The room he wanted was at the far end. Just before he reached it, the door flew open.

An elderly man stumbled out. His robes marked him as a physician, and he was in a state of agitation. No sooner had he cleared the door than a china jug flew out, barely missing him, and shattered against the opposite wall. He pushed past, ashen faced, and fled.

The young man took a breath, knocked, and stuck his head into the room.

'I said *stay out*! Oh, it's you, Meakin.'

Devlor Bastorran, heir apparent to the clans leadership, lay in an oversized bed. One of his legs was plastered from thigh to ankle and suspended by a pulley. He was coverd in scars and abrasions and his closely trimmed black hair had a small shaven patch, revealing a laceration that was still healing.

He put down the porcelain bowl he was about to throw. 'Well, don't just stand there, man. Come in!'

Lahon Meakin entered. 'If this isn't a convenient time, sir . . .'

'Time's one thing I have plenty of at the moment.' He nodded at a chair. 'Sit.'

The aide shut the door and did as he was told, placing the folder on his lap.

Bastorran turned to look at him, and winced through clenched teeth. 'Damn leg!'

'Can I summon assistance, sir?'

'Absolutely not. If that last healer's anything to go by, I'm better off without their ministrations.'

'Sir.'

'Now report.'

Meakin started to leaf through the contents of his folder.

'And keep it brief, will you?' Bastorran added. 'Just the basics.'

'Yes, sir. I have a summation here.' He fished out a sheet of parchment and cleared his throat. 'Let's see. Accounts for today are still coming in, of course, but we have most of Valdarr's figures for the last twenty-four hours. There were fourteen instances of public disorder serious enough to warrant our attention. Five cases of arson directed at government or imperial property. An attempt was made to steal a consignment of arms in transit, which proved unsuccessful, though there were three fatalities. Regrettably, two paladins lost their lives in other incidents. As did eleven members of the watch and a licensed sorcerer assigned to one of their units.'

'Detentions?'

Meakin consulted another document. 'Er, seven hundred and twenty-two, sir.'

'That's up again.'

'Yes, sir. And thirty-one of those resulted in summary execution, as allowed for by the new emergency regulations.'

'Excellent. Things are certainly looking up now we've been allowed to take the kid gloves off.'

'The Clan High Chief must be very pleased, sir.'

'My uncle?' Bastorran's face clouded.

'As he's campaigned for so long for tougher measures against the insurgents, sir,' Meakin hurriedly added.

'Ah. Yes, Uncle Ivak's a pig in shit at the moment.'

If Meakin thought that was disrespectful, he knew better than to say so. 'Do you want the details, sir?'

'What?'

'Of the arrests. I can break them down into –'

'Details weary me. You should know that by now. The only important thing is that we're consigning more of these criminals to prison or to the block. But that isn't the reason I wanted you here.'

'Sir?'

'I want you to meet someone. I'm doing this because you might have to liaise with this person if I can't. But you have no need to know what task they're performing for the clans. Nor do you have to know more than necessary about this visitor.'

'I understand, sir.'

'Understand this, too.' He spoke emphatically, his gaze unblinking. 'Everything to do with this person is to be regarded as secret. Any breach of security will have grave consequences. You're comparatively new to my service, so let me underline the importance of the oath you took to the clans, and your personal oath to me. Break it and you know what the consequences will be.'

'Yes, General.'

In a slightly softer tone, Bastorran went on, 'You've made good progress in the paladins, Meakin. I might say remark-able progress given that you weren't clan-born. That's rare. And not everybody approves of your rise. So see this as a test of your loyalty. Serve me well and you'll not regret it.'

'Yes, sir. Thank you, sir.'

'There's just one thing I should tell you about our visitor. She's a symbiote.'

Meakin found it difficult to hide his surprise. 'A meld?'

'I believe that's the common term for a very uncommon . . . relationship. But it might be better not to use it in front of her.'

'Of course not, sir.'

'I expect you to extend the same courtesy to her as you would anyone else acting on our behalf.'

'I've never seen a symbiote before, sir. Not insofar as I'd know it, anyway.'

'Very few people have.There can't be too many around, after all. It's not a pact many would willingly enter into.' There was the sound of movement in the corridor. 'I think you're about to have your first encounter, Meakin.'

Somebody rapped loudly on the door.

'Come!'

Their guest entered, accompanied by a guard whom Bastorran curtly dismissed.

The person standing before them was an arresting sight. Her appearance was androgynous. She had straw-blonde hair cropped so short it could have been shaven. Her skin was white like marble, and she had thin, bloodless lips. Meakin found her eyes frankly disturbing. They were inordinately large, and their irises were blacker than any he'd ever seen on a human, stressed the more by unusually milky surrounds. She was trimly built, yet her frame implied a well-disciplined strength.

There was something slightly odd about the geometry of her face, as though every line was one percent out of true. She was neither ugly nor beautiful. What she possessed was a severe elegance; like a glacier made flesh. The overall effect was alarming, and somehow mesmeric.

She was completely at ease, and returned their stares with a brittle gaze of her own.

At length, Bastorran said, 'Welcome.'

The woman barely acknowledged his greeting.

'This is my aide,' he continued, 'Lahon Meakin. Meakin, say hello to Aphri Kordenza.'

Nods were exchanged. Hers was slight, disinterested.

'In the event that I'm not able to deal with you myself, Kordenza, you're to liaise with Meakin here. Meakin and no other. I trust that's clear.'

'Yes.' Something about the timbre of her voice set the small hairs on Meakin's neck tingling.

'There's no point in you lingering here, Meakin,' Bastorran decided. 'You may go.'

He didn't seem to hear. He was staring at her.

'*Meakin.*'

'Sir!'

'Get out. And make sure we're not disturbed.'

The aide gathered his papers, then quietly left.

The bed-ridden paladin and the glamour symbiote studied each other.

'Mind if I demerge?' Kordenza asked.

'Mind if you do *what*?'

'Sharing with a glamour pair gets uncomfortable when we're both in at the same time. Makes me feel like I've eaten too much. I'm hoping to make our cohabitation less unpleasant in future. Until then . . .' she thumped her flat chest with a black-gloved fist, '. . . better out than in, know what I mean?' She smiled, though her face wasn't made for it.

'Just remember I have men outside that door. If you even think of –'

'Calm yourself, General. We should trust each other; we're in a business relationship. Besides, if we wanted to kill you, you'd be dead by now.'

He felt a little confused by her use of 'we'. 'So go ahead.'

What took place next was no less startling for happening fast. Aphri Kordenza simply stepped to one side. But an outline of herself remained in the space she vacated. It hung in the air like a slender rope, mimicking her shape. Within its contours a kaleidoscope of particles churned and vibrated. They coagulated and clarified, and within seconds came together to form something that looked human. The emerging figure appeared to be Kordenza's twin.

Bastorran saw that an almost invisible membrane, a viscous, cobwebby lattice, attached Kordenza to the conjured glamour. The filmy web grew taut, snapped and was immediately re-absorbed by the twin.

On closer inspection, Kordenza's double proved not entirely identical, though its clothes were.

It, too, was androgynous, but with definite masculine features. Nor did it look completely human.

Kordenza was stretching, elbows back, head rolling. Unwinding after a weight had been removed. Next to her, the glamour twin did the same. They unconsciously mirrored each other, like a well worked-out piece of choreography.

Straightening, expelling a breath, Kordenza declared, 'Anything you have to say can be said to both of us.'

'We work together,' the glamour added. Its voice was a giveaway, if one were needed. It had the timbre of sorcery; a little hollow, a touch lifeless, a hair away from humanity.

Bastorran regarded the pair silently, as though he were weighing whether to deal. At last he said, 'What do I call you?'

'Aphrim,' the glamour replied.

Aphri leaned against a dresser, arms crossed. The glamour, which Bastorran was forcing himself to think of as 'he', adopted a similar pose by the hearth.

'Let's get on with it,' Bastorran prompted. 'You're aware of the nature of the commission.'

'We only accept one kind,' Aphri said.

'All we need to know is the target,' her twin finished.

'When you do, you might think twice about taking the job.' The pun had been unintentional, but neither of his guests seemed aware of it.

'We always appreciate a challenge,' Aphrim told him.

'It keeps us on our toes,' Aphri explained.

'Your problem,' the glamour ventured, 'is connected with your present state of health, yes?'

'You want vengeance,' Aphri reckoned.

'Not just for your injuries . . .'

'. . . but for the terrible public humiliation you suffered.'

Bastorran found the way they shared speech as provoking as what they said.

'A stain not only on your reputation . . .'

'. . . but on the clans as a whole, and –'

'*All right!* I'm close to having you *flogged* for impertinence.'

'You might find that a little hard in my case,' the glamour commented.

'Looks like we were right in our assumption, Aphrim,' Kordenza said.

'Yes,' Bastorran confirmed, 'it's Caldason. I want him . . . *destroyed*.'

'Hmm. He's a notorious bandit.'

'A hard man to kill.'

'Some say he *can't* be killed.'

'That's superstitious nonsense,' Bastorran snapped.

'Perhaps,' Aphri conceded. 'Nevertheless, such a commission would require a substantial fee.'

'That needn't be a problem. Providing your demands aren't too outrageous.'

'We all know that outrageous is the going rate for this job, General. As to the form the payment takes; we want coin, naturally, but we'll take the bulk of it as magic. Is that a problem?'

'For the clans? Of course not. But why?'

'Our relationship's very magic hungry.' She looked to Aphrim. 'Particularly as my partner needs all his strength to interact with humans.'

Bastorran raised an eyebrow.

'All right, to kill them,' she amended.

'Money, sorcery; take your price any damn way you want. Just get Caldason for me.'

'I don't want to talk ourselves out of a job,' Aphri said, 'but why can't you do this yourselves? With all the resources the clans have –'

'There are certain restrictions placed on how we can engage with the Qalochian.'

Her oversized eyes widened a little more. 'The mighty paladins, limited?' There was more than a hint of mockery.

'Just technical niceties that don't concern you. All you need know is that we've decided to contract out on this occasion.'

'How do we find him?' Aphrim wondered.

'You mix with the dregs; don't tell me you have no sources. In addition, I'll see you get any clan intelligence that might help. And of course I can offer some measure of protection while you go about your work.' He was growing testy. 'Do you want this commission or not?'

'One thing,' Aphri asked. 'Does the Clan High Chief know about this?'

'I'm the only authority you need worry about,' Bastorran returned icily. 'My uncle's a busy man. I don't trouble him with routine trivia.'

The twins exchanged meaningful glances.

'Be clear,' he continued harshly. 'Fail in this, or be indiscreet, and I'll have you –' he pointed at Aphrim '– *negated*. While you –' he indicated Aphri '- will be making the acquaintance of my master torturer. And be assured that only when you're completely ruined will he put out your eyes.'

'Sounds tasty,' Aphrim mouthed quietly.

'I think we understand each other.' Bastorran favoured them with a chill smile. 'And forget about my uncle. As I said, he has more than enough to occupy him at the moment.'

5

After their brutal taking of Bhealfa, the conquering imperialists of Gath Tampoor demolished the triumphalist structures left over from rival empire Rintarah's occupation. They replaced them with buildings grander, taller and more opulent..

Few were as magnificent as the vast construction the Gath Tampoorians erected in central Valdarr. Within sight of the clans' headquarters, it was in sharp contrast to that baleful pile. Where the paladins' base appeared grim and brooding, this was celebratory, its every line glorying the authority of its builders. It was a monument to triumph and might. A building that bragged.

There was magic in its architecture, literally. The stones it was constructed from were charmed, and enchanted dust had been mixed into the very mortar. Pigments used to decorate its splendid stained-glass windows were rumoured to include a concentrate of demons' blood, the ground bones of trolls and desiccated unicorns' mane; notwithstanding that such creatures no longer existed, if they ever had. The upshot was that it permanently shimmered with magical energy, and on the ample expanse of its outer walls inspiring images could be conjured at will – the likenesses of imperial heroes and statesmen, explorers and merchants. Icons to hearten the populace, or to remind them that they were vanquished.

The Gath Tampoorians saw no irony in naming it the Freedom Hall, and it was proclaimed as a palace of the people. Though naturally common folk were rarely permitted to enter, except as menials.

This evening, fleets of carriages jammed the surrounding streets, delivering an army of grotesques. The comely and the hideous, the fabulous and the whimsical, climbed the stairs, wide as a city block, to the massive doors. Once inside, they were ushered into a series of elegantly appointed reception rooms, then through to the great hall itself.

The enormous chamber was lit by a score of magically illuminated crystal chandeliers. Each the size of a haystack, they hung beneath the vaulted, gold-inlaid ceiling with no visible means of support. The light they threw made the room's accoutrements glitter and sparkle. Gold again, lots of it, along with flashes of silver and the crisp glint of gems; precious metals and exquisite jewels were moulded into the decor and furnishings. Beautiful tapestries adorned the panelled walls. Underfoot, the carpets were rich and plush.

It wasn't only feet that padded over them. Paws, hooves, claws and suckers walked them, too. Dreams made flesh. And nightmares. People with eagle, goat and locust heads. Revellers who chose instead to transform their bodies, and who wore elaborate masks. Humans in the guise of demons and cherubs. Or cats and cockroaches, large as men. The best body magic money could buy.

Genuine chimeras mingled with the humans. Pure glamours in numerous exotic forms, brought as companions and pets, or just for effect. Impossible to tell from flesh and blood, they reflected their owners' natures. A few were angelic. Most were incarnations of base instincts, ugly and venal.

The masque was well underway. A glamoured orchestra played. Liveried flunkies weaved through the dancers, pewter trays held high. Secure in the knowledge that they were above the law – indeed, many present were servants *of* the law – the revellers behaved as they saw fit. They imbibed grape and hop, some recklessly. Others sampled the pleasures of cuzcoll, viper sting and pellucid, or stronger narcotics like sabre cut, red frost, and even ramp.

In a quiet corner, a rat and a serpent were engaged in earnest conversation.

'I'm not saying I *sympathise* with them, for the gods' sake,' the rat protested. 'It's just a question of methods.'

'You always were inclined to be too soft on these dissidents,' the serpent snorted.

'I resent that! I loathe them as much as you do. We differ only in how best to address the problem.'

'All a bit academic now, isn't it? Word's come down from on high and it no longer matters what we think. Or are you questioning your superiors' wisdom?'

'No, no. Of course not. I'm just saying that honey catches more flies than vinegar. I've always believed that stealth's the best policy when dealing with these misfits.'

'Mollycoddling them, you mean.'

The rat's whiskers quivered irritably. Before he could respond, a drunken satyr barged between them.

'Let's sit,' the serpent said, nodding towards an empty table.

Once they'd settled, a servant brought them drinks. Wine for the rat, brandy for the serpent.

The rat wore a plump, copper-coloured medallion. He ran his thumb over it, dismissing the mask. It evaporated to reveal a clean-shaven man of middle years. His velvet skin and silvering, coiffured hair indicated one who lived by talk rather than deeds.

Following his lead, the serpent wiped away his own disguise. He was older, and his face was weathered from a lifetime of doing. In his hair and beard, close-cut military fashion, he was further along the road to silver than his companion.

'You have to admit, Clan High Chief,' the one-time rat continued, 'that the unrest has got worse since the emergency regulations were brought in.'

'There's always a period of turmoil after measures like that are introduced,' Ivak Bastorran told him as he lifted his draught of brandy. 'It'll calm down once the hotheads know we mean business.'

Gath Tampoorian Ambassador Andar Talgorian thought the paladin sounded typically self-satisfied. He took a sip of wine and kept that to himself. 'Far from abating, reports reaching the diplomatic corps indicate dissident activity's spreading like wildfire.'

'I wouldn't say things are that bad. We've had our successes against these terrorists, and it's in their nature to retaliate.'

'There, you admit it. Your heavy-handedness is making the situation worse.'

'I didn't say that. We're stamping out a pestilence. There's bound to be bloodshed before we're through. It's a case of holding our nerve.'

'Let's hope the rebels blink first. For all our sakes.'

'You give these people too much credence, Talgorian. Not least in dignifying them as rebels. They're criminals, chancers, vandals. Scum. I'm proud the clans are at the forefront of eradicating them.'

'It must be very gratifying to have a free hand at last,' the Ambassador commented dryly.

'I've made no secret of my views on public order. And it seems I'm not alone. You know as well as I do that Rintarah's cracking down hard, too. That proves the canker's everywhere.'

'So the insurgents *are* organised, then? You can't have it both ways, Bastorran. Either this is an outbreak of random disobedience or a movement.'

'They're as organised as any other bandit gang, and their aims are no more noble.'

'We shouldn't allow ourselves to be hampered by too rigid an outlook,' Talgorian replied pointedly, 'or we'll miss seeing the true nature of the problem.'

'Nonsense. The truth is both empires are applying stricter sanctions because lawlessness is endemic if you let the mob have its head. East and west have been too soft. It's past time to redress the balance.'

'Throw oil on the flames, more like.'

'And what would your remedy be? Soft words? Yielding to their insolent demands?'

'I'd apply a little balm. Toss the people a few concessions. Repeal one or two petty laws, perhaps a small easing of taxes; and allow the poorest better access to basic provisions. They'd not be so easily stirred up if they had full bellies.'

'Sounds like appeasement to me. Why give them what they haven't earned?'

'You asked for my opinion. I think artfulness has its part. A carrot to entice the donkey.'

'Carrots,' the paladin sneered. 'What about the rod?'

'Don't make the mistake of thinking me squeamish. My way, we'd isolate the ringleaders and make examples of them. Single them out for assassination even, as the Council for Internal Security does back home.'

'Then we're in accord. The clans believe in eliminating the agitators, too. It's just that where you see a few rotten heads in a field of corn, we see them all as infected.'

'And cut down the lot.'

'If need be. But you'd do well to leave such considerations to us, Talgorian. You're too much of a worrier.'

'It's what they pay me for.'

'Like this warlord you're so obsessed with,' Bastorran ploughed on. 'You fret about him unnecessarily, too.'

'Nothing's happened to make me believe Zerreiss is any less of a threat,' the Ambassador returned indignantly. 'Everything we hear suggests he's continuing to make inroads.'

'I don't know why you get so worked up about it. If the barbarians want to make a sport of slaughtering each other, that's their affair. They can never offer any danger to the empire.'

'Again I hope your optimism proves well founded.'

'You won't have to rely on my opinion alone. The northern expedition should be reaching its destination soon. Then you'll see this Zerreiss for what he is. Any word, by the way?'

'None. And according to our agents, nothing's been heard from the Rintarah expedition either.'

'Communication's always poor from the barbarous lands. Everything gets delayed coming that far.'

'I suppose so.'

'There you go again with the anxious face.' He took a gulp of his drink. 'Trust me, Ambassador; you'll see that all this is just a rash of pinpricks.'

Talgorian's attention was on the far side of the room. He nodded that way. 'Talking of pinpricks . . .'

Bastorran looked, seemed uncertain for a second, then spotted the mark. 'Ah. Dulian Karr.' There was no warmth in the recognition.

Karr stood with his back to a wall. It bore the ubiquitous emblem of Gath Tampoorian rule: the dragon rampant, scales shimmering, belching gouts of glamoured flame. Karr was conversing with a small group, but it was obvious even from a distance that he wasn't really engaged with them. He wore a simple black cloth eye-mask, contrasting with the elaborate facial decorations all around.

'That speech he gave earlier,' Talgorian recalled, 'wasn't far short of a disgrace. All that guff about sympathy for the so-called dispossessed . . .'

'Close to seditious, if you ask me. Sentiments almost worthy of your own.'

The Envoy's face darkened. 'I do *not* appreciate that kind of comment. As I keep stressing, it's only in methods that we –'

'Yes, yes, I know. Take a jest, man. Your views are simply misplaced; Karr's border on treachery.'

'I'll take that as a back-handed compliment,' Talgorian replied coolly. 'At least you appreciate the difference between my concerns about strategy and Karr's flirting with anti-social elements.'

'You know it's more than flirting. We've suspected him for years, and so have your people. He's a sympathiser, a fellow traveller. Maybe more than that.'

'Suspicion's one thing, proof's another.'

'Circumstances have changed. We have a freer hand, remember. And in a couple of weeks he'll be stepping down from his patricianship. That office gave him a measure of protection. Once he goes, the restrictions go.'

'He's not a man to underestimate. It takes a certain cunning to sail so close to the wind all these years.'

'He'll be given every opportunity to stumble, believe me. If he has so much as a hair out of place –'

'He's seen us.'

Skirting the outlandish dancers, Karr made his way to them. They greeted him with sham smiles and hollow salutations.

'Patrician,' Talgorian drawled. 'An excellent speech.'

'Very enlightening,' Bastorran echoed.

'Thank you.'

Talgorian indicated the spare chair. 'Please, take a seat.'

'So,' the diplomat said, 'you're finally retiring from public service. After . . . how many years is it?'

'Too many, it sometimes seems.'

They gave expedient, empty laughs.

'And how will you fill your days?'

'I expect I'll have plenty to occupy me, Clan High Chief.'

'No doubt your passion for the downtrodden will continue to find expression,' Talgorian suggested. 'Perhaps in the form of charitable works?'

'I hope I'll always find time for the less fortunate.'

'I see you're showing solidarity with them tonight in your choice of dress,' Bastorran commented, in reference to Karr's plain, unglamoured mask.

The patrician smiled thinly. 'I think it behoves the more privileged to set an example.'

'By looking impoverished ourselves? You're to take no offence from that yourself, of course.'

'Of course, Ambassador. The example I had in mind was one of modest consumption.' He saw their puzzled expressions. 'Look about you.'

Bastorran sniffed. 'I see men and women of substance. The example *they* hold out is the possibility of a better life for all.'

'Prospering under the wing of the empire,' Talgorian added, almost piously.

'How many here have earned it?' Karr wondered.

'Ever the controversialist, eh, Karr? Public life will be the poorer for the lack of your witticisms.'

'I don't think the destitute are laughing too heartily.'

'Your beloved downtrodden,' the paladin leader came in irritably, 'would be best employed improving their lot through honest hard work.'

'Most would like nothing better. Assuming work existed, and they didn't risk being arbitrarily rounded-up and brutalised every time they stepped onto the streets.'

'If they've done no wrong they have nothing to fear.'

'They'd say they're treated as enemies of the state regardless.

Not all of them are necessarily insurgents, you know.'

Bastorran fixed him with a hard stare. 'You'd be surprised who is, Patrician.'

'I'm sure your sentiments are commendable, Karr,' Talgorian interjected, 'and we can all applaud your humanitarian instincts. Let's charge our glasses and toast your retirement.' He made to beckon a waiter.

'No,' Karr replied. 'Thank you, but . . . it's been a long day and I have others to see before I can leave.'

'You are looking a little out of sorts, if you don't mind me saying.'

'It's nothing. Overwork. You know, trying to clear everything before I retire.'

'It wouldn't do to jeopardise your health,' Bastorran said, an unmistakably barbed edge to his words. 'Retirement was a wise decision. Now you can lay down your burden and let others worry about the welfare of the people.'

'Indeed.' He gave each a small nod in turn. 'High Chief. Ambassador Talgorian.' Then he left.

As they watched him moving through the crowd, Talgorian breathed, *'Scandalous.'*

'Wouldn't so much as take a drink with us. As for his views . . . Free expression's all very well, but –'

'He looked ill, don't you think?'

'I'm a great believer in the inner man determining the outer. Nine times out of ten it's a guilty conscience that brings about the appearance of poor health.'

'At least he's abandoned what little power his position gave him.'

'Doesn't mean he'll stop fighting for lost causes. The man's a born meddler.'

'You'll be keeping an eye on him, then?'

'Oh, we will, Ambassador, we will. As no doubt you will yourself.'

Talgorian leaned closer. 'You are aware that there have been attempts on his life?'

'More than a few, I understand. And with all the hall-marks of being officially sanctioned.'

'Not by my people. Or any of the other departments of state that I'm aware of.' His voice dropped to a whisper. 'I suspect they were the work of the CIS.'

'There'd be no mishaps if the paladins were given the job.'

'No doubt. My point is that the CIS aren't supposed to operate beyond Gath Tampoor's shores. Legally, that is. But I've been hearing rumours that their methods might be exported to the protectorates.'

'What's your meaning?'

'Should Karr be the victim of assassination, my superiors, your employers, could hardly kick up a fuss when one of their agencies has been trying the same thing.'

'Interesting. I'll bear it in mind.' He surveyed the bizarre throng. 'We're neglecting our duties. Better get back to it.' The touch of a finger against his medallion re-formed his mask. An elongated snout appeared, the eyes grew slitty, yellow-green scales formed.

'Excellent guise,' Talgorian commented.

'It is rather fine, isn't it?' Bastorran admired himself in a nearby wall mirror.

The Ambassador reactivated his own mask. Grey fur erupted, the nose blossomed, whiskers sprouted.

Bastorran glanced at his companion. 'I meant to ask.'

'Hmmm?'

'Why a rat?'

'Irony.'

6

Recently imposed public order laws tended to operate as a
two-tier system. Gath Tampoorians resident in the Bhealfan
colony simply ignored them. A similar laxity was allowed
citizens of Bhealfa who enjoyed power and influence.

The same licence applied to enforcing the curfew. Those
of wealth and rank were free to dally.

The weak and insolvent had law-keepers on their tails.

As the hour of prohibition drew near, the streets swelled
with people trudging homewards. In a manufacturing quarter
of the city, the human surge broke against the prow of a
building that stood at the confluence of two main roads.
Outwardly, it was an administrative block, a hive for bean
counters, and anyone entering would have found this to be
the case. Now its clerks and scribes had joined the exodus,
and it was deserted.

Its several floors were in darkness, and one, cunningly
fashioned from loft space, was hidden. Gaining entry to it
from within was complicated, not to say potentially lethal,
given its glamoured defences.

A small group was gathered there.

'Where the *hell* is Disgleirio?' Caldason grumbled.

'Probably held up by the crowds,' Karr told him. 'He'll get here no quicker for your pacing. Join us.'

Sighing, the Qalochian took a seat opposite Karr at the large wooden table. At one end sat Kutch, looking uncomfortable and fiddling with a pair of his makeshift eye covers. Serrah was present too, but isolated from the rest, her chair set well back. The expression she wore was unreadable.

'While we wait,' Karr said, 'I've got something you might find interesting.'

He pushed a finger into his right ear. For a second he twisted and dug with it. Then he brought out a tiny object, held between thumb and forefinger. It resembled a pearl, and had a similar milky white sheen. He flung it at the nearest wall.

The little globe didn't bounce or shatter. It stuck as though resinous, and immediately began to flatten and spread. When it matched the size of a large serving platter it stopped expanding. At that point it opened, like the petals of a flower. Having doubled its diameter it opened again and again; more and more petals rapidly unfolding until the wall became a shimmering, pearly white screen.

'A much more detailed schematic,' Karr explained. 'Better than anything we've had before.'

Lines and contours, dips and bumps came into focus. A three-dimensional representation of an island formed. It was roughly kidney shaped, only a kidney that had been gnawed at one end by a hungry dog. Its outline showed cliffs, sandy beaches, inlets and bays. Offshore, in the rippling ocean, reefs and rocky outcrops appeared.

The island had two harbours, on its western and southern sides. There were green pastures, hills and woods. A river snaked from the east, branched and rejoined the sea on the north-eastern shore. Tracks criss-crossed, and more substantial roads sneaked from the ports. A scattering of buildings was visible here and there, and near the island's centre was what could have been a town.

'The hope of the world,' Karr announced. 'Batariss.'

Serrah stirred from her introspection. 'What?'

'It's the proper name for the place. Though not many seem aware of it.'

'I remember when that's all it was known as,' Caldason said.

'You would,' Serrah told him. She probably meant it humorously. He decided to take it that way.

'Our thought was to rename it,' Karr revealed; 'call it something that has more relevance to its new status. Perhaps after one of the Resistance martyrs, like Sab Winneba, Kryss Mirrall or –'

'I'm sure they're deserving,' Caldason cut in, 'but face it, Patrician; nobody's going to call it anything but the name that's stuck.'

'The Council feel this would be a good opportunity to honour someone who made the ultimate sacrifice for the cause.'

'Very commendable. But don't you think we should concentrate on getting there first?'

Kutch broke the ensuing silence. 'I always assumed it was named after its shape or something.'

'No,' Karr replied, 'its function.'

'I didn't know they actually mined gems there.'

'They don't. It's called the Diamond Isle because of the wealth it generated.'

'So how come we got the chance to buy it?' Serrah asked.

'It's been in decline for years. It was at its height as an attraction when Reeth here was a child. If it still produced riches on that scale we wouldn't be in a position to buy it. As it is, the present owner's had enough and is looking to retire.'

'How can an island that size be private property? I thought only the empires' rulers had the kind of clout needed to own real estate on that scale.'

'The island's status has always been an anomaly. Way back, a century or more, it was as much a pawn for Rintarah and Gath Tampoor as Bhealfa is today, or any of the other states they squabble over.'

'What happened to change that?' Kutch asked.

'Both sides came to feel it was too insignificant a prize to shed blood over. Then somebody, probably one of the old bandit clans, came up with the idea of turning it into a pleasure retreat. That was during one of the empires' virtuous periods, when gambling and prostitution were frowned on. Batariss filled the need. Another factor, of course, is that it's not officially in anybody's territorial waters, though it's nearest to Bhealfa. But in practice, the island operates because whichever empire happens to be in control of this part of the world has let it.'

'Why would they do that?'

Karr scrutinised his tiny audience. 'You must have heard all this before.'

Serrah shrugged.

'It fills the time until Disgleirio deigns to show himself,' Caldason remarked.

'I don't know any of this,' Kutch said. 'I think it's fascinating.'

'All right,' Karr went on. 'Why have the empires left Bata – the Diamond Isle to its own devices?' He took a reflective breath. 'Well, there's some evidence that in the early days, when the place was much more exclusive, the empires' favoured supporters were sent there as a reward. Later, when it got easier for more people to go, the official view seemed to be that it served as an outlet for the masses' pent-up resentments. Or at least it did for those who could afford it. And they tended to be the well-heeled, educated classes, who might organise opposition; the sort the rulers wanted to keep sweet. Then again, it's rumoured that the authorities take rake-offs from the island. Unofficial taxes, some call them. Who knows why the Diamond Isle's been left alone? I think it's probably just unfinished business.'

'They'll finish it quickly enough when we start moving over in droves,' Caldason warned.

'Not if we do it artfully. And once there's a sufficient number of us on the island . . .'

'I know. We'll make it too costly in blood to recapture. It's a hell of a risky strategy.'

'Of course it is. But we've planned meticulously. If the move goes as it should –'

'That's more likely to happen if you've got everybody behind you.'

'I know the island strikes many in the Resistance as an unlikely choice –'

'Oh, I don't know,' Serrah contributed, 'a pleasure resort seems no more insane than anywhere else you might have picked.'

Karr ignored the gibe. 'Look at it.' He nodded at the gleaming map. 'It's perfect. About a tenth the size of Bhealfa, easily big enough to support a substantial population. It's got fresh water and ample wood. There's plenty of arable land. And it's defendable. In time, we can make it completely self-sufficient.'

'In time,' Caldason echoed. 'It'll be a race, and if you think Gath Tampoor's going to sit on its hands while you do it –'

'It's a gamble. We know that. The whole plan's predicated on us beating some long odds. But what would you have us do otherwise? Give up and let our conquerors roll over us? Abandon any hope of ever throwing off their shackles?'

'Nobody's saying that,' Serrah reminded him. 'Anyway, is this the time to be going over it all again?'

'You're right. The owner's going to be here any minute, and we have to show a united front.'

'You'll get no dissent from me,' Caldason promised.

'It would be nice to believe that.' Karr smiled. 'Phoenix himself has cloaked this place against eavesdropping. You're our second line of defence, Kutch. I wouldn't have asked you to do this, except for the chronic shortage of spotters. Particularly with the . . . difficulties you've been having lately.'

'Are you saying this meeting could be dangerous?' Caldason asked.

'No. But let's not lose sight of the kind of man we're expecting. Are you all right about this, Kutch? Because if you'd rather . . .'

'I want to help. But if I do sense something, what do I do?'

'Just shout out loud,' Caldason told him, 'we'll do the rest.'

'Does our visitor know what we want the island for?' Serrah wondered.

'I don't think he cares,' Karr replied. 'Though he's not stupid. A shabby opportunist, yes; but not stupid.'

'Can't wait to meet him.'

Above a set of robust doors at the loft's far end, a glamoured crimson orb began flashing.

'You could be about to get your wish.'

With a rattle and creak, the doors swung open.

The man who entered was perhaps thirty years old, sported a clipped moustache and had a hardy countenance. His garb and easy confidence spoke of an adept swordsman.

'Forgive me,' he said, unlacing his cape. 'The streets were choked and I was against the tide the whole way.'

'Some of us started out early,' Caldason offered.

'Not all of us had that luxury.'

The Qalochian and Quinn Disgleirio, apostle of the Fellowship of the Righteous Blade, held each other's gaze.

'Don't mind Reeth,' Karr advised, 'he's in a fractious mood.'

'When isn't he?'

'You've missed nothing, Quinn,' Karr hastened to add. 'Our guest hasn't arrived yet.'

'Yes he has. He's on his way up now.'

The patrician's manner was instantly businesslike. 'All right. Weapons in plain view, as agreed.' Disgleirio, Serrah and Caldason, with some reluctance, unsheathed their various blades and laid them on the table. 'Kutch, put those blinkers of yours out of sight.' The globe above the doors started to flash. 'All of you; keep in mind that our visitor's both smart and unprincipled. But remember that he needs us as much as we need him.'

The doors were thrown wide, crashing against the walls.

A small entourage entered. There were four bodyguards, dressed alike in black leather jerkins, trews and boots, with leather wrist and headbands. One was a woman, flame-haired, green-eyed, and no less hale than her masculine cohorts. All were extravagantly armed. They were clustered around their employer, and for a moment it looked as though they were carrying him shoulder high. As they fanned out it became obvious that he was held aloft not by muscle power, but sorcery. He sat on a large, padded disk, with a backrest similar to a chair's. His legs dangled over the edge, and a thick safety belt girdled his waist.

Those who had never seen Zahgadiah Darrok before, but knew his reputation, might have expected an individual wracked by sloth and debauchery. They didn't anticipate someone looking as fit as an athlete. Nor did they count on him being handsome; the possessor of a finely chiselled face, adorned with a neat blond goatee and dominated by quick, china-blue eyes.

The only jarring note came when he spoke. A brisk order to his escort, to give up their arms, revealed a gravel voice that seemed out of keeping with his appearance. It had an inflection more often associated with an habitual pipe smoker or drinker of coarse liquor.

As Darrok's bodyguards laid down their weapons, Karr made introductions. Then the attendants withdrew, but stayed watchful from a distance. Darrok guided his floating dish to the table and descended to hover at sitting height.

'Can we offer you refreshments?' Karr asked, indicating stone-bottled wine and sweetmeat platters.

'I don't believe in tainting business with frivolity,' Darrok grated.

'As you please.'

'I suggest we get straight to the matter of the final payment.'

'That's what we're here for.'

'You can get the money?'

'Of course.'

'In gold?'

'In gold, yes.'

'And you can deliver it, as I specified?'

'We can meet all your requirements. But naturally we need to be sure you can satisfy ours.'

Darrok showed a flash of annoyance. 'You had my word.'

'We're not trying to offend you. But it's vital you understand the necessity of making the handover as smooth and as secret as possible.'

'I could ask why you feel the need to be so clandestine if your aims are lawful.'

'I'm sure we all have private matters we'd prefer to keep that way,' Karr said. 'In fact, I should remind you that a slice of the not inconsiderable price we're paying is supposed to ensure confidentiality.'

'And you'll get it. My guarantee.'

'I'd like your bond on another matter, too.'

'Oh?'

'As you know, some of our people will be arriving on the island soon as pathfinders. We have to be able to count on you co-operating with them.'

'We've agreed all this, Karr.'

'It's as well to underline its importance.'

'Yes, yes, we'll do as you ask. Now about the gold –'

'It would save us a lot of trouble,' Disgleirio suggested, 'if payment could be made here on the mainland.'

'Now who doesn't understand the agreement? The deal was that the balance of the money went to the island for onward movement.'

'So we take the risks and you reap the benefit.'

Darrok shrugged. 'It's a sellers' market.'

'We'll keep our end of the bargain,' Karr promised. 'You keep yours and we can have the shipment there in a matter of weeks.'

'You'd do well to send it with as much protection as you can muster.'

'Naturally we'll take precautions.'

'You might need a little more in the way of precautions than you're contemplating.'

Disgleirio regarded him suspiciously. 'Why?'

'There's a certain amount of . . . unrest in my home waters.'

'What kind of unrest?'

'We have a few problems with privateers.'

'You mean *pirates*?' Kutch blurted out.

'I'm not in the habit of answering questions from a child.'

'Then try answering a man,' Caldason told him, his manner threatening.

Darrok adopted a dismissive tone. 'I'm not accustomed to explaining myself to the hired help either.'

The Qalochian rose, toppling his chair. Then Serrah was on her feet. Darrok's bodyguards began to move in.

'*Enough!*' Karr thundered. 'We're here to talk, not to fight. Now calm down. All of you.'

There was a frozen moment, each side eyeing the other, fists balled, muscles tensed.

Karr nodded at his people. 'Sit.'

Darrok waved away his bodyguards.

Caldason righted his chair and Serrah sank back into hers. Both moved reluctantly, and kept their gazes on the escort.

'So, you have trouble with pirates,' Karr recapped.

'I think they prefer to be called merchant adventurers,' Darrok corrected.

'To hell with what they call themselves; why didn't you tell us before?'

'I'm telling you now.'

'How big a problem is it?' Disgleirio wanted to know.

'Until recently it was manageable; no more than a minor irritation. But that's changed.'

'Why?'

'Traditionally, the privateers were disorganised. As ready to fight amongst themselves as to plunder travellers that came their way. Now they've got together and formed an alliance.'

'That wouldn't have happened without a leader of some sort,' Caldason reasoned. 'Who rallied them?'

'You're more perceptive than you look. Have you heard of a man called Kingdom Vance?'

Serrah mouthed, 'Oh, shit.'

'I take it you have,' Darrok said.

Karr scowled at him. 'Who hasn't? Given that he's the most infamous, cold-blooded freebooter ever to cut a throat. And you're telling us *he's* organised this alliance?'

Darrok nodded.

'He must have held out a prize tempting enough to bring them together,' Caldason decided. 'A prospect bigger than their differences.'

'That he did. He offered them something they've wanted

for a long time.' Darrok paused and scanned his hosts' faces. He saw that one or two had already guessed. 'A land base. A country they can call their own.'

'They want the island,' Disgleirio whispered, realisation dawning. 'You bastard, Darrok! This borders on treachery. What are you after? More money? Is that it?' He was on his feet.

'There's no deceit on my part.' Darrok gestured at his restive bodyguards, checking them. 'All I'm asking for is the final payment.'

'After dropping this on us? Forget it.'

'I think you'll find the pact we have stipulates no full payment, no deal. And I get to keep what's already been paid.'

Disgleirio swung to Karr, red with anger. 'You agreed to this?'

Before the patrician could speak, Darrok answered. 'There isn't exactly an abundance of islands for sale. Like I said, it's a sellers' market. Take it or leave it.'

'Karr?' Disgleirio pressed.

'He's right. We're not in a position to dictate terms.'

It was Serrah who broke the ensuing silence, and in contrast to Disgleirio's outrage, she seemed almost amused. 'Well, you could cut the tension in this room with a knife,' she said. Glancing at the surrendered weapons, she added, 'Anybody like to try?'

Karr stood, signalling for calm. 'All right. *Everybody.* Let's keep things civil. We can sort this out.'

'Always the conciliator, eh, Patrician?' Serrah gave him a smile that fleetingly looked half demented.

'He's right,' Darrok intervened. 'You might have rivals for the island. So what? They're small in number compared to you, judging by the set-up you have here. You can deal with it.'

'You make it sound trivial,' Disgleirio remarked, still seething.

'No, I make it sound like it isn't my problem. My only concern's spending the money you'll be giving me.'

'So you can buy more toys like that?' He jabbed a thumb at the hovering dish.

Darrok made it rise, lifting him to the height of a man standing. 'This is more in the way of a necessity than a luxury.' He rapped his knuckle against one of his legs, then the other. The hollow ring attested to their being artificial. 'Kingdom Vance,' he explained starkly. 'That's why it's not my problem.'

When that had soaked in, Karr told him, 'We have to think on this.'

'I'll be in Valdarr a few more days. You know how to reach me.'

Zahgadiah Darrok motioned to his retinue. The bodyguards came forward to collect their weapons, then gathered about their paymaster and followed as he glided to the exit.

The doors slammed resolutely behind them.

Karr turned to face the others. 'We're not going to let this get in our way.'

'Really?' Caldason said, making no effort to hide his cynicism.

'Yes. Too many people are relying on us. We owe it to them.'

'I can't believe you struck such a deal with that man,' Disgleirio complained. 'Isn't the task we've set ourselves hard enough as it is?'

'It's done, Quinn. And Darrok was right about it being a sellers' market. We're over a barrel.'

'So what do you propose we do about it?'

'For a start, the band Reeth's leading with the consign- ment of gold needs to be beefed up.'

'Just a minute,' Caldason cut in. 'Asking me to deliver the

gold's one thing. Expecting me to take on a pirate alliance is a different proposition.'

'Surely you can see –'

'What I see is that I'm no nearer reaching the Clepsydra, despite your promises. Now you're enlisting me for a war that's none of my making.'

'But the plan –'

'Is your problem, Karr. Find yourself another dupe.'

He headed for the door, snatching up his blades as he passed.

'*Reeth!*' Kutch yelled.

'Let him be,' Karr advised as the doors slammed one more time. 'He'll come round. And if he doesn't . . .'

'Don't look at me,' Serrah said. 'I can't be trusted enough to go, remember?'

Kutch slumped, despondent. Disgleirio was buckling on his sword, still incensed.

Karr expelled a weary breath, shoulders sagging. He stared for a moment at the radiant map spread across the wall. Then he snapped his fingers. The map instantly compressed, became pearl-sized again and dropped to the floor. It bounced, just once but high, and arced his way, dropping into his outstretched palm.

He took the hope of the world and stuck it back in his ear.

7

There was only silence. A downy white haze enveloped him. He was cold, and felt weightless.

Slowly, he gained a sense of self. But there was no awareness of who he might be. Or where. Then he became conscious of rushing air. It prickled his skin and tousled his hair; it stung his eyes and made them water. A tingling rippled the pit of his stomach. Blood pounded in his ears.

He was falling.

The clinging whiteness disappeared. As he tumbled, he saw that it had been a cloud, high above him now. Then a glimpse, higher still, of blue velvet powdered with stars. Spinning, twisting, he caught sight of the earth, so far below he could make out its curvature. He plunged headlong, serenaded by the whistling wind.

He had no control over his descent, yet it seemed he began to move with purpose. No longer did he simply fall. He flew.

The land beneath him grew, its features becoming more distinct. Snow-dusted mountain peaks, silvery rivers and verdant pastures. Sweeping plains, lush valleys, the emerald froth of mighty forests. Diving ever lower, he saw, here and there, the hand of Man. Land ploughed and cleaved into meadows; granite farmhouses, wooden lodges, the scars of roads. A giddy swoop took him down to one such track. Flying higher than the tallest trees, he followed it.

A large group of riders came into view. Armed men, galloping hell for leather. He shadowed them, negotiating the road's bends and turns with no effort on his part. In this way he kept pace for many miles. Then it dawned on him that they weren't the only ones travelling in that direction. Something else moved in the riders' wake; something that flew as he did, but at a greater altitude and to his rear. It wasn't chasing the horsemen. It accompanied and drove them.

Whatever it was that traversed the troubled sky could be sensed but not seen. Perversely, it was both a pack and a single intellect. He knew this, without knowing how he knew. As sure as he felt the malignant force it radiated. A wave of menace that beat at him and kindled the purest dread.

His fear acted as a spur. A swift acceleration took him forwards, outstripping the riders and the horror trailing them. He moved with jarring speed, the landscape beneath passing in a blur, a daze of green smudged with brown. Lakes like mirrors, patchwork fields, copses that drank the light. Until he came at last to a remote region where the land was untamed, and he slowed.

He hung above a clearing in a wood. It was occupied by four or five straw-coloured bubbles. A moment went by before he realised they were roundhouses, thatched and built of timber. A handful of people tended the camp. Somebody was hauling a bucket from the well, while another cut logs. Most stood guard. Some livestock was corralled, and several horses were hitched to a post. There was a nagging familiarity about the place. And when he started to sink down towards it, helpless to resist, his unease increased.

His coming to ground was gentle and noiseless. He expected to be challenged. But there was no turning of heads, no rushing guards. He could see, but not be seen.

The first thing he saw was that these people were of his kind.

A scream rang out. It came from a smaller hut, set apart from the others. No one in the camp looked that way. Instead, they snatched up their weapons and nervously scanned the surrounding woods. The scream came again, high-pitched, more drawn out. He made for its source; unseen, as though a ghost.

The interior of the hut was in semi-darkness, lit only by the soft radiance of hooded lanterns. As his eyes adjusted he could make out a small group, huddled together around something on the earthen floor. Two were matriarchs, wise women, with a novice serving them. The remaining person was an old man of indeterminate race. He, too, seemed strangely familiar.

He went further into the hut, and saw that they ministered to a woman of his ilk, stretched on rude sacking. Her woollen shift was gathered at the waist, revealing the ripe swell of her belly. Strands of lustrous black hair plastered her sweat-sheened forehead. Her pearl-white teeth were exposed, clenched in exertion. Even contorted by pain, even in the half-light, he thought she was beautiful.

He watched mesmerised as they tended her. But almost immediately it became obvious something was wrong. The woman's writhing grew more intense, her screams more prolonged. Her attendants exchanged anxious glances. Their efforts became increasingly frantic. Powerless, a disembodied observer, he could only look on as all their midwifery skills were applied.

Once delivered of her boy child, the woman fell back and was silent. A silence more ominous by far than her cries had been. The babe itself was no less quiet; a small, seemingly broken thing, it took no breath of air. As the women worked to stem the mother's copious flow of blood, the old man lifted the baby. Swiftly, he cut the cord with a silver sickle, as tradition dictated. Then he hoisted up the blue-tinged youngster, dangling it by an ankle, and slapped its hindquarters. He did it twice more before the child gulped air and started to wail.

There was no rekindling of life for the mother. She lay inert, already beginning to pale with the chalky whiteness of death. Her mouth was slack, her eyes glazed. The despair of her helpers was palpable, and it gripped him, too. A clamp fastened on his heart.

His veins coursed with ice. Feeling a sense of loss far greater than the sorrow of a mere onlooker, he moved nearer.

He was stopped by a chorus of shouts from outside. The old man clutched the new-born tighter to his chest. With fearful expressions the midwives turned their heads to the door. The shouting was louder. He stared at the occupants for a second before leaving the hut.

Outside was all commotion. Men running, yelling. Some throwing saddles onto horses; others already mounted and wheeling, churning mud. Through the trees he glimpsed the riders he'd seen on the road. A multitude, closing at speed. The men of the camp, hopelessly outnumbered, scrambled to face them.

A few gazed at the sky. It was filling with a presence, a brooding. But only he could truly see the malevolent horde of black wraiths gathering overhead.

The old man came out of the roundhouse. He held the child, wrapped in a bloodied blanket. Pausing for an instant, he surveyed the scene, and looked ruefully to the ominous skies. Then, hugging the bundle, he sped with surprising agility into the woods, away from the attackers.

Suffused with a blistering radiance, the shadow beings loomed overhead. They were malleable, assuming an infinite variety of grotesque forms. As they dived, blinding currents flowed ahead; terrible energies that rent the air itself. Bolts of fire sloughed from them, and lethal radiances pulsed. They fell as a living rain of death.

And as above, so below. The horsemen were sweeping into the clearing. They came with dreadful cries and scything blades. Few as they were, his kinsmen stood ready to meet them. From the land and from the heavens, battle was joined.

Flame and steel rolled in to engulf him.

He came to, biting back a scream.

Someone's hand was on him. He snatched their wrist and held it like a vice.

'*Ow!* You're *hurting* me!'

Caldason blinked into focus. 'Kutch? What the *hell* are you doing? Don't you know it's dangerous to –'

'You were shouting fit to bring the house down. I heard you from upstairs.'

'I . . . I'm sorry.' He let go.

Kutch rubbed his wrist, looking pained. 'What was it? Another one?'

'Yes.' He sat up and shook his head to clear it. 'A . . . dream, or whatever they are.'

'Sounded bad.'

The Qalochian nodded. 'And different.' A thought struck him. 'What about *you*? I mean, did you see anything? Were you –'

'No, I didn't share it. Not this time. It's happening less now I've stopped spotting so much.'

'You still think there's a connection?' He swung his legs off the cot and stiffly rolled his shoulders.

'Well, it started when I began training as a spotter. I can't think of any other way I've changed.'

'You've changed in lots of ways since we came here, Kutch.'

'Have I? How?'

'Mostly for the better.' He put on a weak smile.

'You said it was different. The dream.'

The smile faded. 'Yes. Some of it was familiar. *Too* familiar. But there was something new.'

'What?'

Caldason stood and walked past him to the window. It was early light, and Valdarr's streets were already bustling. For the most part, genuine humans milled below. But there was much of the phantasmal, too. Many illusions were obvious. Others might be mistaken for flesh and blood by a casual observer. Bursts of light marked the appearance of new glamours. Equally numerous were the implosions of non-light indicating their demise. A flock of birds flew across the grey sky. Perhaps they were real. He couldn't tell.

'Reeth?'

'The visions have shown me my death many times,' Caldason said, his eyes still on the scene outside. 'Well, what should have been my death. Now there's something else.'

'Whatever it was, you seem pretty shaken by it.'

'I think I saw how I came into the world. And how my coming into it killed the woman who birthed me.' He turned to face the boy. 'I was responsible for my mother's death, Kutch.'

High above, the birds flapped lazily towards the rising sun.

8

Thousands of birds darkened the watery sky.

They circled an area that had a comparatively sparse population, despite being in central Bhealfa. What drew them in such vast numbers was easy pickings. Not just the countless worms churned up, but the profusion of refuse left by the cavalcade they followed. For the birds, it was a never-ending banquet. Although it was not without its dangers. Wild dogs and feral cats were attracted by the feast, too. And the humans in the great procession used hawks and archers to reduce the flocks, and for sport.

The birds' other rivals were the armies of scavengers living in the convoy's wake. These men, women and children existed in a hierarchy as rigid as that of the wider society that shunned them. The lowliest, the dung gatherers, roamed on foot, their carts and wagons being employed to carry the valuable fruits of their labours.

The niche above them was occupied by the rag pickers. Notwithstanding their job description, they ferreted out anything of value from the general detritus. Fuelled by stories of discarded coins, and even jewels, many pickers had the mentality of gold panners.

Occasionally, they came across a dead body. These were the result of execution or exile, which amounted to the same thing if the accused was cast out from one of the convoy's higher places. Some were suicides of people who came to prefer death to the regime's haphazard cruelty. Once stripped, the bodies were left for the carrion crews. Spurned by everyone, these motley bands contained many outcasts; sufferers of unsightly diseases and the mentally unstable who could find no other employment. They survived by selling the corpses back to their often aristocratic families for decent burial.

The travelling artisans considered themselves far superior to the scavengers, pickers and body snatchers. Carpenters, builders, thatchers, wheelwrights, blacksmiths and a dozen other trades made up their ranks. Their bread came from offering to make good the damage caused by the passing of the procession. A handful of sorcerers of dubious repute were loosely affiliated with this group, promising the afflicted charms to avert such disasters in future.

Being more prosperous than the baser camp followers, the artisans could afford magic, if largely rudimentary. Glamoured bird scarers were part of their cache, and every so often they let one off to have a few minutes' respite.

So it was this brisk dawn. A hex ignited an ear-splitting salvo. Flaming, multicoloured tendrils jabbed the sky, dispersing their squawking targets. The birds escaped to higher reaches, to regroup.

One scavenger took the racket as a signal to straighten his aching back for a moment. He raised a hand to mop his sweaty forehead, despite the morning chill. Grabbing a breath, he gazed at the source of his livelihood, perhaps a mile distant, and felt the familiar *thrump-thrump-thrump* through the soles of his feet as it slowly moved away. He never ceased to be awed at the spectacle, the chaos. Or to be grateful that

it fed him. It was a miracle, a gift from the gods. This clandestine economy built on the foolishness of one man widely
considered insane.

Some likened Prince Melyobar's roving court to a sow
nurturing her incalculable litter. The less benevolent saw it
as a bloated leech gorging on the blood of all around it.

Melyobar's palace was a capricious affair. Huge, as befitted
the ego of its master, the structure expressed his aberrations,
too. It was a rare angle that struck the eye as true. There
was an over-abundance of towers and spires. A host of statues
stood on its battlements, uniformly freakish or alarming. It
bristled with defences and scaling obstacles. Everything was
embellished, carved, tinted, bedecked and overlaid with
precious stones and valuable metals. The impression was of
a spiky cake iced by a demented chef.

The palace-cum-fortress had never been still. It floated,
under direction, and was powered by stupefyingly expensive
magic. Its sole purpose was to accommodate the Prince in
his craving to outpace Death, and thus cheat death.

In this endeavour he was alone, but not unaccompanied.
To maintain their stature the aristocratic families had travelling palaces built too, though they were careful to make them
less opulent. The guilds did likewise, along with various
courtiers of influence and great wealth. All vied to squander
their fortunes in the cause of keeping up appearances.

There were magically powered auxiliary structures to
serve the Prince's needs. The Royal Guardsmen, quarter-
masters, armourers, fletchers, administrators, scholars, diviners,
sorcerers and a dozen other specialist groupings had their
own transports.

Lesser functionaries and camp followers, who were legion,
had to make do with more conventional ways of keeping up.
The number on horseback were uncountable, including
several detachments of cavalry and an entire division of

paladins. Wagons, carriages, coaches, gigs and chariots were present in hundreds. Their occupants had a relatively easy passage compared to those on foot, who numbered many thousands, and who had to rely on an elaborate system of horse-drawn sleeping rigs to take their rest. For the only rule was that the cavalcade stopped for nothing.

There had been suggestions, not entirely frivolous, that Melyobar's nomadic folly should be officially recognised as a city.

Any such thought was far from the mind of the Prince himself. He was focused wholly on a scheme to defeat his deadliest adversary. To that end, he stood with a detachment of militia on a parade ground abutting one of the palace's highest ramparts.

As monarch, Melyobar was automatically named Supreme Commander of the Combined Armed Forces, although the title was honorary, since Gath Tampoor effectively ran things. For no apparent reason, today the Prince chose to disport himself as Lord High Admiral of the Fleet, as was his right. His dark blue, shoulder-padded uniform jacket was smothered in gold braid. The coat didn't quite meet over his paunch, so the gold buttons were undone. Breeches with gold stripes down the sides, and shiny, knee-high boots disguised his puny legs. He wore a tricorn hat with a white plume. Strands of greying hair poked from beneath the rim, giving his ashen, puffy face a cracked-egg impression. He had a splendid sword to wave about.

'Now send over another one!' he demanded, his voice too high-pitched to command respect in itself.

'Sir!' A sergeant smartly clicked his heels and, to his credit, maintained a granite expression. He marched off to bellow orders.

'Over there!' the Prince yelled. '*That* way!' He pointed at a distant farmhouse gradually drawing level. '*Hurry!*'

A unit was manning one of the large siege catapults lined up near the parapet's edge. Frantically, they wound back the arm, accompanied by the sound of creaking timber. Someone used a mallet to hammer home the chocks under the catapult's front wheels.

Four men appeared, each holding a corner of a net containing a round, leathery object bigger than an ox's head. It was heavy enough to make them stagger slightly. A blue-robed sorcerer followed, clutching a small velvet sack. Lank, bald and bearded, his features were set in the requisite austerity.

Melyobar clapped his hands like a petulant schoolmarm. 'Come on, come on!'

They loaded the leather ball into the catapult's scoop. The sorcerer rummaged in his sack and brought out a thin, square stone, about the size and reddish-brown colour of a fallen oak leaf. He slipped it into the coil of twine binding the ball, then began mumbling an incantation.

Watching with ill-concealed impatience, the Prince remarked caustically, 'Let's try to be a little more accurate this time, shall we?'

He took a glamoured spy tube from the pile on the bench beside him. Holding it to his eye, he saw the farmhouse in close-up, as though it had been moved to within a stone's throw of the palace. He could make out people gathered on its porch. Some of them were waving.

Melyobar squinted as the image flicked, started to fade, and died. The spy tube's magic expended, he tossed it aside with an irritable snort. The tube rolled a few feet and disappeared over the rampart's edge. He snatched another from the table. There were a dozen or so there, each worth the equivalent of a militiaman's wages for a month.

The catapult unit stood to attention while the Prince fiddled with his spy tube. When the farmhouse was parallel, he raised his sword.

'*Fire!*'

The lever was pulled, the arm went up and over with tremendous force. Spinning, the leather ball climbed high, fast. Describing a great arc, it curved down towards the farm building. The people around it started to scatter. Ants running from a boot.

Looking tense, the sorcerer continued muttering, eyes half shut. Melyobar studied the target through the tube. A black dot descending, the missile seemed on a path to take it safely over the farmhouse. The scurrying ants realised this too, and most of them stopped to crane their necks.

When the ball reached a point directly above the roof, and the sorcerer's chanting came to a pitch, it silently burst. A fraction of a second later a muffled boom reached the palace. A mass of purple vapour hung in the air where the ball had been. Then, like a rain cloud, it began discharging its load. A shower of blue liquid fell, pattering on the thatch, the farmhouse garden and the perplexed spectators. Unaffected by the wind, the cloud kept its position. The drizzle became a downpour. People were running again, hands over their heads, as a blue torrent drenched the entire area.

'Better,' Melyobar pronounced. 'Much better.'

The sorcerer relaxed a little. By the catapult, and on the square, the militiamen allowed themselves a slight ease.

At the farmhouse, the deluge stopped. The cloud dispersed. A few remaining purple wisps quickly melted away.

The Prince beckoned the wizard. 'That's more like it! Practice makes perfect, eh? Eh?'

'Er . . . yes, Highness. Thank you, Highness.' He gave an awkward bow.

'Soon iron out the kinks. Shoulders to the wheel and all that.'

'We could carry out your wishes more efficiently, Royal

Highness, if we knew your intentions, the aim you have in mind.' He immediately regretted saying it.

Melyobar's expression darkened. But not, it turned out, with his infamous fury. He leaned closer, his manner that of a plotter. 'Suffice it to say . . .' He looked to left and right to satisfy himself they were not overheard. 'Suffice it to say that my work here will lead to the ruination of –' his voice dropped to a whisper '– *the great destroyer*.'

'I'm sure we all yearn for that outcome, sire.' He chose his words carefully, aware that conversing with the Prince was like entering a house of glamoured mirrors.

'The plan is sound,' Melyobar confided. 'My father, the King, devised it himself.'

'Indeed, sire?' The wizard swallowed. 'How fortunate for us all that His Majesty's great wisdom should be brought to bear on the problem.'

'Quite so. That's something I often tell him when we talk.'

The sorcerer, aware as anyone that the old King was dead, or as good as, nodded gravely. He strove to think of a suitable platitude to respond with. 'I trust His Majesty is in good health,' he returned, desperately.

'In robust health and excellent spirits. And anxious to assist in destroying the foe.'

'Capital, sire. The reaper's days must surely be numbered.'

'No doubt about it, and today I've taken a step towards arming myself against him.'

The wizard stole an oblique glance at the saturated farmhouse. 'Begging your forgiveness, Highness, but with . . . *coloured water*?'

Melyobar gave him a knowing wink and tapped the side of his nose. 'Oh, look. A barn. *Sergeant!* New target!'

9

'It's no good,' Kutch pleaded. 'I can't do this.'

'You can,' the mage insisted. 'Trust me. Concentrate on the exercise and –'

'I *can't*! I thought it was a good idea, but now I see you . . .'

'Seeing me this way was the whole point, remember? Now forget everything else and focus on the task at hand.'

'It's not easy.'

'Since when was anything to do with the potent art easy? Just try. Will you do that for me?'

'I . . . I'll try.'

'Good. I suggest we be still for a moment and centre ourselves. Breathe as you've been taught.'

Kutch wriggled into a meditative position. Back straight, hands on thighs. He was stiff and fidgety.

'Relax.'

'Relaxing's hard work sometimes,' the boy grumbled.

A smile crimped the old man's face, exposing remarkably well-preserved, even teeth. His face was wrinkled and a little weather beaten, and he had a knack of adopting an expression that was simultaneously severe and benevolent. He was Kutch's late master, Grentor Domex, to a T.

Kutch's eyes were closed, but his lashes trembled, betraying his tension. The mage let him be.

The room was quiet and softly lit. It was unmistakably a wizard's den, filled with stone pots and glass jars of herbs and elixirs; ceremonial paraphernalia; ancient books. Everything was in haphazard piles and disordered heaps. There was a temporary air about it that declared its occupant was an itinerant.

When a few minutes had passed, the mage said, 'Open your eyes.'

The boy did so.

'Let's get rid of these, shall we?' The mage leaned over, took the blinkers dangling from Kutch's wrist and dropped them on an adjacent table. 'They're not needed.'

Kutch nodded, but kept a wary eye on them.

'We'll try something different,' the mage decided. 'Look over there.' He pointed to a tall wooden cabinet standing in the middle of the room's clutter. Its doors were half wire mesh. There were sounds of movement inside, but the mesh was too dense to see what made them. The mage performed a swift hand gesture. The cabinet's doors swung open. 'Which is real?' he challenged.

Three pigeons fluttered out, one black, one white, one grey. They spread their wings and took off. The room was small, and the frenzied birds seemed to fill it. They flew in circles, collided with furniture, pecked at the closed window. The noise they made was deafening.

'Centre yourself, Kutch!' the mage called out, oblivious to the racket. 'Focus, focus!'

Kutch struggled to apply his spotting talent. The constant movement, the shrill cooing, the beating wings, all made his head spin. Loose sheets of parchment swirled in the chaos. An earthenware pot fell from its shelf and burst open, splattering the floor with something gelatinous and bright green.

A vial of sparkly, salmon-coloured powder dropped and shattered next to it. Neither had a particularly pleasant odour.

The mage was unconcerned. 'You can do it!' he urged. 'Have confidence in your master!'

'You're not him,' Kutch announced deliberately, barely making himself heard above the din. 'He's dead.'

The mage saw that the boy's eyes were moist, and sighed. He snapped his fingers. Instantly, silence returned. The pigeons hung motionless in the air, frozen in mid-flight. Two of them, the white and the black, lost their definition. Feathers and flesh dissolved into masses of golden motes. The birds' shimmering outlines remained for a second, then faded into nonexistence. Another snap of his fingers freed the real pigeon, the grey. It beat its wings and compliantly swooped back into the cabinet. The doors slammed shut behind it.

'I'm sorry, Kutch,' the mage began. 'I . . . Just a minute.'

He lowered his head. Immediately his features were somehow less certain. They churned, altered, mutated. His flesh took on a pappy, malleable appearance, and flowed like hot candle wax. The image of Kutch's late master departed. In an instant, a new form emerged.

Another old man occupied the chair, but quite different to the one who'd been sitting there seconds before. He too was familiar. But he was no longer Grentor Domex.

Phoenix shook his head, as though clearing it. 'Perhaps I made the likeness too poorly,' he surmised. 'After all, I haven't seen your master for some years and I had to extrapolate his –'

'No, it wasn't that,' Kutch told him. 'If anything, you were too good.'

'I thought that appearing in the guise of your master would put you at your ease.'

'I thought so, too. But it just brought back memories. Not good ones. Memories of his death and . . .'

'I understand. Forgive me.'

'But . . . it wasn't just seeing my master again that flustered me.'

'Oh?'

'Why are you giving me more spotting exercises when what I need is help with these visions I've been having?'

'I look at it as being like treating a lame horse.'

'I'm not a horse. Or lame.'

'No. But the horse you're riding might be.'

'I don't understand.'

'You suspect that your visions are connected in some way with training as a spotter.'

'It's difficult to think what else might be doing it.'

'I agree That's rational. So we have to walk the horse to see if that's where the problem is.'

'So you think it's the spotting, too?'

'I'm just trying to eliminate all possibilities, Kutch.'

'Have you ever heard of other spotters having this kind of problem?'

'No. Then again, the number of spotters is very small, and I certainly haven't known all of them. But there's no reason to believe that spotting's dangerous in that sense.'

'In that sense?'

'Well, we haven't got a lot to go on, you understand, but it does seem that spotters are a bit more prone to certain pitfalls.'

'Such as?'

'Excessive use of alcohol, drug taking, anti-social behaviour, that sort of thing.'

'Why didn't you tell me this at the start?'

'Partly because I didn't know as much about it then as I do now. I've been doing some research, you see. Anyway, the numbers succumbing in that way aren't significant, and I suspect those that do fall victim to the pressure from the use spotting's put to, rather than the spotting itself.'

'You said partly.'

'The other reason was that I judged you to be resilient enough to resist any such snares.'

'How could you be so sure? I mean, suppose the training's started something? Opened a door that can't be closed, or –'

'Magic has dangers, you know that. But I've never heard of anything resembling what's happening to you. Then again, let's not forget that your problem seems unique in more ways than one.'

'Because I'm sharing visions with Reeth?'

'Yes. That's totally outside my experience. It's not as though we're talking about some kind of magical illusion that temporarily dazzles its subject, is it?'

'No. This is different. It's like watching something real. But something Reeth sees too, and has done for a long time.'

'Do you see everything he sees?'

'No. Just . . . just one particular thing.'

'Go on,' Phoenix coaxed. 'You've never really tried explaining it to me.'

'That's because I can't. Not really. What I get is a glimpse of. . .somewhere else, is the best way I can describe it. Another kind of landscape, but not like anything I've ever seen before, or heard about.'

'What's it like?'

'Bad. It's never still. It changes, constantly. As though the land itself is a living thing, forever in flux. And there's a terrible sense of menace. A feeling of not belonging there.' He shuddered. 'Definitely not.'

'It's all right, Kutch. What else?'

'Something lives there. Or a whole mass of somethings, I don't know. Vile, poisonous things that would just love to hurt me.'

'Do you ever see any of this in dreams?'

'No, only when I'm awake. When I was practising spotting,

at first. Then it started when I wasn't. That's what scared me.' His eyes had been downcast. Now he lifted them, and they were wide with dread. 'You know what frightens me most?'

'Tell me.'

'That I'll get to see more of it.'

'We'll have to make sure that doesn't happen.'

'How?'

Phoenix didn't answer. Instead, he asked, 'And this. . .*place* is familiar to Caldason?'

'He says it is. But he sees lots more than I do. It's hard to say what, because he's not keen to talk about it.' He added, hesitantly, 'Though he just told me about something else he'd seen. Something new. I can trust you, can't I, Phoenix? I mean, if Reeth thought I'd been talking about it –'

'You have my word.'

Kutch took a breath. 'He told me that he was responsible for his mother's death.'

'He knew this from one of these visions?'

'Yes. Or thought he did. I was there. He was shouting and screaming in his sleep and it woke me up. We talked about it.'

'And he said he killed his own mother?'

'He didn't really explain it, just said it was his fault. But I can't see how he could be responsible.'

'Let's get this straight. Caldason has visions about his past life. You don't share those. The other sort of visions, about another place, you do share.'

'Yes. And Reeth's visions seem to. . .evolve. They're getting more elaborate for some reason.'

'And they're tied in somehow with these berserk fits he has.'

'He has visions without berserking. But rarely a fit without a vision. At least, that's what he says. It's all so complicated, I don't understand it.'

'It's one of the things that makes him so dangerous, Kutch.'

'I know.'

'I mean, much more dangerous than any ordinary man. Think about it. Imagine you had an infinite amount of time to perfect whatever it was you did. Your magical studies, for instance. I myself have had the privilege of an extended life-span, and it's been enormously beneficial to my under-standing of the Craft. Caldason's become such a good fighter because he's had years to develop his skills, years without his body deteriorating or his stamina lessening. I estimate he's older than me, yet he's still as strong as a mountain buffalo on ramp. But whether his mental faculties have stayed as hardy –'

'He's not a bad man.'

'I'm not saying he is. I think you're right; he has the impulses of a decent man. But even the best of us can act in evil ways when under a powerful influence. Money, lust, pride . . . many things can turn a person bad.'

'Not Reeth.'

'Perhaps. But I can see why he has such a loathing of magic. Assuming magic's the cause of his state. Which I'm not entirely convinced it is.'

'You doubt it?' Kutch was surprised.

'In some ways. Do *you* know of any sorcery that could make somebody damn near immortal?'

'Founder magic.'

'Magic we have access to, I mean.'

'You had access to it. It extended your life. You just said so.'

'I was fortunate in having the chance to study a tiny scrap of surviving Founder lore. One of the very few. Decades I've pored over it. Its gift to me is my extended life, along with some immunity to disease. Wonderful things, but all there is to be taken from it, I'm sure.'

'That proves my point, doesn't it? If you've achieved that from just a little fragment, what might somebody else do with more? With Founder magic, they could do anything.'

'There is no such somebody. I would have known about it. Covenant would have known. And the remaining morsels of Founder knowledge are very rare.'

'Suppose someone's already found the Clepsydra, and has the Source?'

'Then we'd *certainly* know about it. Whoever had it, assuming they understood how to use it, would be running the world. And you're forgetting that if they found it long enough ago to affect Caldason with it, they'd likely have wrung all its secrets out by now.'

'Well, perhaps they're about to. Maybe they've been teasing bits out for years, and making use of each new piece of knowledge as they deciphered it. And maybe Reeth was –'

'No. The best protection the Source has is that extracting its secrets will prove an almost impossible task. Except for Covenant, which has studied practically nothing else for centuries.'

'I hope you're right, Phoenix. For Reeth's sake if nothing else. He's gambling a lot on the Clepsydra being found.'

'Understandable. But I wish I'd never told him about it.'

'You know he's refusing to deliver the gold to Darrok?'

Phoenix nodded.

'I can't blame him. Like he said, he didn't sign on for a war with pirates.'

'I think he'll come round. If he doesn't, there are others in the movement who could carry out the mission. No one's indispensable, Kutch, not even a man with such extraordinary talents as Caldason.'

'I don't know if he'll change his mind or not. He's very unpredictable in some ways. Everybody's worried about Serrah, too.'

'Another troubled soul. Magic isn't *her* problem, that's for sure. We could do without all this, Kutch, with the move not so far off.'

'What can I do?'

'About Caldason and Serrah? Very little, I'm afraid. Except continuing to give them your friendship unstintingly. Which isn't so little after all, really.'

'And my visions?'

'That's something I'm going to have to give a lot more thought to. Meanwhile, follow the exercises I've given you. Meditate. Breathe. And no more spotter training for you for a while, that's certain. Oh, and there's some reading you might find beneficial. I'll give you a list.'

Kutch pulled a long face. 'More studying?'

'There's nothing like the sustenance a good book can give you, boy, believe me.'

'There's nothing like a clean kill to lift the spirits, boy, take it from me,' Ivak Bastorran enthused.

His nephew grunted and nocked an arrow.

They were on a balcony of a building at the paladin compound. Bundled against the autumn chill, Devlor Bastorran sat in a chair not unlike a throne, his bound leg supported by a footstool. Chair and stool had been elevated with wooden blocks, allowing him a clear view over the balcony's low wall. He held a short bow, and a quiver lay across his lap. His uncle stood beside him, spine straight as a spear, hands clasped behind his back.

Several storeys below, neatly trimmed lawns spread out. They ran a considerable distance before reaching a border of mature trees. Beyond the trees stood the compound's lofty walls. Nearest the building there was a natural, grassy amphitheatre of perhaps half an acre, with sloping sides. It was this area that the Bastorrans looked down on.

To their left, and almost out of sight, was an elongated wooden building resembling a stable. Ivak lifted a hand and signalled, and an unseen minion heeded the sign. Bolts were thrown, hinges squeaked. The sound of cracking whips could be heard.

A fawn stumbled into view. It had a whimsical way of walking, its slender, uncertain legs almost crossing with each step. Tan, with white mottling and underbelly, it had the tiny beginnings of horns. Its eyes were dark and soft.

An arrow struck the fawn's neck. The animal went down, so light it seemed to bounce when it hit the green sward. Its legs convulsed, twitched. Were still.

'Too easy,' Devlor muttered, reaching for another shaft.

Three or four rabbits scurried into the amphitheatre. He got one square in the head, the force knocking it several feet.

'Good shot!' his uncle exclaimed.

Devlor didn't bother with the other rabbits. Something more challenging had appeared. A snorting boar charged through; head down, tusks close to ploughing the earth, mad as hell. It took an erratic path around the grassy basin. So much so that Devlor's first shot flew over the boar's back and ran into the ground. The creature turned to look in his direction, clouds of huffing breath issuing from its flared nostrils.

Re-nocking quickly, Devlor fired again. His bolt pierced the squealing boar's forehead. It collapsed and went into spasms. Seconds later the vigour had gone from its eyes and it gave up the struggle.

The animal's death throes were of no interest to the younger Bastorran. His attention was on a stag entering the killing ground. The beast was in his prime, chest thrust out, head raised nobly. His off-white, faintly yellowish antlers made for a magnificent display. With the smell of blood in the air the stag was skittish, and he obeyed the instinct to flee. He ran in circles, tossing his head from side to side, intuiting the nearness of death.

Devlor's arrow winged in and pierced his flank. The stag kept going, leaving a trail of blood on the grass.

'Again, again!' Ivak urged.

The stag headed for the slope and began climbing. But men were stationed at the lip. Yelling and waving pikes, they forced the stag back down. Stumbling, almost falling, it was in a state of panic. It turned, ready to make another assault, when Devlor's second arrow slammed into its side. Its legs buckled and it collapsed, finished.

'Well *done*, boy!' Ivak gave his nephew's shoulder a congratulatory punch. The sort men who otherwise never touched gave each other.

Devlor put on a frigid smile and drew yet another arrow from the sheath.

The prey was still coming, shooed and whipped from behind. A gazelle. A pair of speckled pigs. A slinking fox, three grass snakes, a llama. A trotting buffalo, looking to charge something. Animals that might otherwise be antagonistic, weaving around the bodies of fellow creatures and united in fear.

While Devlor was taking his pick, someone discreetly cleared their throat. Lahon Meakin stepped forward, bowing first to the uncle then, just slightly less deferentially, to the nephew.

'Yes?' Devlor said.

'Begging your pardon, sir, but you asked me to remind you about your meeting with the armourers' guild. The delegation's just arrived.'

'Damn it, yes. I'd forgotten. I'll be there in ten minutes.'

'Very good. I'll send someone to assist you, sir.' Meakin showed them obeisance again, turned and left.

Ivak Bastorran watched him go, sour faced. 'I'll never understand why you couldn't have chosen someone of the blood for an aide.'

'I tried several. Clansmen are better at fighting than admin-
istration, perhaps. None of them was up to muster.'

'I'm sure I could find you a suitable –'

'Thank you, uncle, no. I'm satisfied with Meakin. Best adju-
tant I've ever had. So far I've not regretted taking him from
the army.'

'The army? He's a Bhealfan?'

'Yes. And why not? Should I question his origins when
we have no state to boast of at all?'

'He isn't a paladin born. We don't usually allow outsiders
such familiarity, you know that.'

'There's a limit to the licence I grant him. Be assured I
know what I'm doing, uncle.'

Ivak smiled. 'It's good to see your old spirit returning. You're
healing well, getting stronger. And I'm delighted, of course
I am, but . . .'

'But?'

'I'm worried that you might do something foolish to even
yourself with Caldason.'

'*Even* myself? I should better him, at least. Annihilate him,
for preference. After the hurt and humiliation he subjected
me to, not to mention the affront to the honour of the
clans –'

'I know, I know. And I share your hunger for revenge.
When he came out best from his engagement with you –'

'I think you'll find, uncle,' Devlor replied frostily, 'that it
was the wagon crashing that prevented me from finishing
him. Besides, he caught me on the raw.'

'Of course, and he'll pay for it. Dearly. But you're aware
that certain rules apply to our dealings with the man.'

'Not that you've ever explained them to me, or why we
should adhere to them.'

'All you need to know at this stage is that they're rules
we can't change, and that breaking them could be very detri-

mental to clan influence. I wouldn't like to think you'd imperil our standing with higher authority because of an obsession with the Qalochian.'

'You can put your mind to rest on that.' He spied the buffalo and pulled taut his bow. The arrow he discharged took the beast in an eye, felling it instantly.

'I have your word?'

'Don't worry about it. I promise *I* won't do anything to harm Caldason, uncle.'

10

'How long do you think you're going to be in there?'

Kutch smiled. 'You really don't have to come, you know, Reeth. I'm quite capable of doing this by myself.'

'I'm mindful of what happened the last time you were out alone.'

'You're not going to let me forget that, are you?'

'The streets aren't safe. Best we stick together.' He glanced towards a pair of militia standing on the other side of the road, watching the crowds.

'You're the wanted man,' Kutch reminded him. 'I would have thought you were more at risk.'

The look Caldason gave him dispelled any doubt about his attitude to danger. But he had made concessions to his status as an outlaw; he was wearing a grey, hooded jerkin with the cowl pulled up, and he'd temporarily dispensed with his trademark second sword.

For his part, Kutch had refrained from wearing his blinkers, though he had them ready in his pocket.

They were making their way through the press of people in central Valdarr, with several blocks to go before they reached their destination. Watchmen were out in force, along with militia and regular soldiers. There was no shortage of distinctive red-garbed clansmen either.

'I've never seen so many paladins,' Kutch remarked.

'The word means heroes,' Caldason informed him rancorously. 'Did you know that? It says something about their arrogance that they should have chosen it.'

'Perhaps this isn't the best time to be out and about after all,' Kutch suggested, gauging the Qalochian's mood.

'We're nearly there. No point in turning back now.' He mellowed a little and added, 'Don't worry, there won't be any trouble.'

They pushed on silently for a moment, Kutch gathering mettle to raise a subject.

'Reeth.'

'Hmmm?'

'About what you told me.'

'What was that?'

'That you think you were responsible for . . .'

'My mother's death?'

'Yes.' He was treading softly, nervous of how Caldason might react.

'What about it?'

'It was a vision, Reeth. Can you be sure it was true?'

'I can't swear that what I see in the visions is truth. But I'd swear to them feeling like it.' He turned his gaze to the boy. 'You've had some experience yourself now. Do they seem real to you?'

'Real? Yes. Remember the first time we met, at my master's house? You said something I didn't understand. As you were going into your fit you spoke about it being a dose of reality.'

'Did I?'

'Yes, and I didn't understand it at the time.'

'I meant that this other place I glimpse sometimes seems as real as reality. Sometimes it seems . . . *more* real.'

'I know, it's the same with me. I realise how *genuine* it seems. But . . . suppose it's some kind of really convincing glamour or –'

'You're clutching at straws. The way I used to.'

'What are you saying? That it's *actual*? If that's the case, why were you seeking out my master, and all those other sorcerers you've consulted? You must have thought it was some kind of hex.'

'I don't know what I was thinking, Kutch. Like I said, clutching at straws.'

'Phoenix says we shouldn't close our minds to any possibility until we have proof that what we believe is true. You've no evidence that the visions show the truth.'

'That's what I was hoping the Source could do. Disentangle truth from lies for me, and free me.'

'So why are you throwing the chance away?'

'What?'

'To find the Source you have to find the Clepsydra's hiding place. To get *there* you need the help of the Resistance. Refusing to deliver the gold to Darrok isn't going to make them happy to help, is it?'

There was a flash of anger in Caldason's eyes, hot and deep. 'Did Karr put you up to this? Or Disgleirio?'

'You know me better than that, Reeth. Don't you?'

After a pause, he replied, 'Yes. Sorry.' There was a hardening then. 'I'm thinking of saying to hell with the Resistance and getting there by myself.'

'How?'

'Find the money to charter a ship, maybe. Work as crew if it comes to that.'

Kutch's objections came out in a flood. 'And where exactly would you be going? Has Phoenix given you precise directions? Where would you get a captain prepared to search through a thousand and more islets? And if you found the right one, what if it was guarded by something even you couldn't handle? Would a hired crew fight for you? You're used to doing things alone, Reeth, the way I'm having to learn to. But you can't do *everything* alone.'

At least there was no acid rebuke. Caldason seemed to contemplate the boy's words. But all he said, almost under his breath, was, 'You're not alone.'

They lapsed back into silence after that, and soon got to the district they sought.

It was one of Valdarr's more prosperous quarters, a mix of fine residences and fancy stores. Affluent enough for the tradesmen to afford glamoured signs for their shops. Above a butcher's, a corpulent, illuminated pig incessantly foraged. For the boot maker it was a pair of shoes, endlessly plodding some invisible highway. A purveyor of musical instruments sported a jaunty pipe and drum; the baker had his steaming loaf; an armourer displayed two crimson blades, engaged in an animated duel.

Caldason hoped Kutch wouldn't notice the sign over a bordello further along the street.

The boy touched his arm. 'It's down here.' He led them into a side turning, a less well-heeled thoroughfare than the one they left. There were shops here too, but slightly meaner, many needing a lick of paint and their stock dusting.

Halfway along, they came to a particularly dilapidated storefront. It didn't have a spruce exterior like its main-street neighbours, just peeling grey boards where a window might have been. There was a glamoured sign above its frontage, showing an open book with its pages turning, but it flickered and spluttered fit to expire. The faded letters over its door read *The Wordsmiths' Repository*.

Caldason raised an eyebrow. Kutch said, 'All right, it sounds a bit pretentious, but it should have what I need,' and reached for the door handle.

An old lady shuffled their way. She was warty and little and bent-backed, and her silver hair was trying to escape an ancient, battered bonnet. A tattered shawl of indeterminate colour draped her shoulders. Her ankle-length dress was shapeless, and she wore scuffed, buttoned boots. She, too, was heading for the bookshop.

Kutch opened the door, setting off a tinkling bell that almost masked its creaking, and held it for her. Arthritically edging past, she croaked, 'Thank you, young man.'

He smiled, and made to follow. But didn't.

'You all right?' Caldason asked.

Kutch came out of his reverie. 'Eh? Oh. Yes, I'm fine.'

'What was it?'

'Don't know. A little . . . You know when people say somebody's just walked over their grave? Like that. It's gone now.'

'Sure you're all right?'

'Yes. Come on.' He walked into the shop. Caldason pulled back his hood and went in after him.

They were confronted, not unnaturally, by a great many books. Shelves ran floor to ceiling on every wall, and there were enough large tables to restrict the floor space to narrow aisles. Every surface was laden with books. Fat books with rusty iron hinges, slim books, multi-volume sets, dog-eared pamphlets. Though other colours could be seen, the majority had brown bindings. Some were shiny new, others were practically falling apart. Tomes with gold-embossed spines stood next to fellows whose lettering had worn to anonymity. The smell was glorious, though it was hard to say why, given it consisted of rotting paper, mould and crumbling bindings. It was the odour of antiquity.

The sole break in the shelving was to allow for a door-sized opening into a further room, also stuffed with books. Next to it, a rickety staircase rose to another floor.

There was no sign of the old woman. The only person they

could see was the proprietor, hunched like a vulture on a stool behind his littered counter. He was a needle-faced individual of indeterminate age, bony thin. His wire-wool black hair ended in a widow's peak, and he had tiny, dark, acquisitive eyes. Though he was unlikely to demonstrate it by smiling, his teeth were probably bad.

Kutch took a folded sheet of parchment from his pocket and approached him.

'I wonder if you have any of these?' he said, offering the list.

The bookseller didn't look at it, let alone take it. 'What are they?'

'Books.'

'What *kind* of books?' His half sarcastic, half disgusted tone spoke of the long-suffering patience of a man forced to deal on a daily basis with people he regarded as morons.

'Oh. Yes, sorry. Books on the Craft.'

'Down there.' He waved vaguely towards the far end of the shop.

Kutch caught a whiff of bad breath and took a backwards step. 'Er, thanks.'

'And be careful how you handle the merchandise, some of it's expensive.' Curt dismissal issued, he went back to reading a book he had open on the counter.

Caldason was standing by the staircase. Kutch joined him. 'Seems what I want is down there.' He jabbed a thumb.

'I heard. While you're doing that, I think I'll take a look upstairs.' He indicated a chalk board on the wall. An upward pointing arrow had been drawn on it. Underneath was written:

AGRICULTURE

CARPENTRY

HERBALISM

HISTORY

MARTIAL ARTS

WEAPONRY

NO MORE THAN TWO CUSTOMERS AT A TIME

Kutch could guess which subjects Caldason would be perusing. 'All right. See you when you've finished.'

'Don't forget Serrah's meeting us here.'

'I'll keep an eye out for her.' He moved off.

As Caldason put his foot on the first stair, the bookseller quickly raised his head. He wore an expression reminiscent of a hawk spying prey. 'Tread with care up there,' he snapped, but offered no explanation as to why that might be necessary.

When Caldason got to the top of the shaky staircase he understood the warning, and the two-customer restriction. The sizeable room he came to had an uneven floor, and the boards groaned with every step. Unlike downstairs, here there were just a couple of tables, stacked high. But the walls were equally crowded with books. The only difference being that they were jammed into a series of massive wooden bookcases, the enormous weight bowing the shelves in places. As he crossed the room the floorboards felt springy underfoot. The whole place seemed to creak and wobble.

One part of the room consisted of a shelved alcove, and as he drew level with it he saw the old woman there. She was stooping to look at a herbal laid out on the seat of a chair. Caldason nodded. She gave him an apple-cheeked smile.

He found the combat section, ran his eye along the titles and tugged out a hefty volume. The book was glamoured, and as he flipped the pages its illustrations sparked into life. Painted characters fought with swords, axes and quarterstaffs. Lances raised, warriors rode chargers into battle. He paused at a picture showing a siege, with a battering ram hammering at a castle's doors while defenders rained down arrows from the ramparts.

There was a faint noise. Of movement, rustling and soft commotion. Then the hint of a fragrance mingling with the smell of decaying books. Something sickly-sweet with a sulphurous tinge to it.

He looked up.

Downstairs, Kutch had located several of the books he needed. Their cost was higher than he'd expected, and he doubted whether the money Phoenix had given him would be enough for everything. So he'd started sorting them into vital and not-so-necessary piles.

He froze, letting a book slip from his fingers, and slowly straightened. He was aware of a cognisance, not dissimilar to the feeling he got before a vision, and feared he was about to have one. Several seconds of stilled breath later, he knew that wasn't it. Something else was happening.

He looked up.

Caldason realised the sounds were coming from the alcove. Stealthily, he moved towards it.

Before he got there, a figure stepped out to face him. It wasn't the old woman. But it took no great leap of logic on his part to guess that it had been.

He was looking at someone who appeared to be neither one sex nor the other, though their features inclined a little more to the feminine. She was wiry, hard-muscled and near flat-chested. Her fair hair was severely cropped, and she had a shockingly white complexion. The eyes were arresting; astonishingly big, unblinking, black as coal. Overall, the sight of her was dismaying, and his first thought was that she must be a glamour. Some instinct made him reject the idea. He reckoned her to be magically enhanced in some way, but human.

Before he could speak, she jerked to one side, leaving a ghostly silhouette of herself in the place she'd just occupied. The wafting outline quickly filled with light. In short order it began to solidify, offering brief glimpses of bones, sinew, blood and finally flesh.

A duplicate of the woman stood beside her, and initially seemed identical. They could have been unholy twins, and were even dressed the same way. But he saw that the new arrival did differ slightly, and certainly appeared more masculine.

Then he noticed that they were connected. A gossamer film, shiny and moist to the eye, tender as moonlight, bound them from shoulder to ankle. But only for a heartbeat. It tensed and ripped apart, and each half was instantly sucked into one of the twins' bodies.

They regarded him as though he were a horse they were thinking of stealing. But when the female spoke, it wasn't Caldason she addressed. 'What do you think, Aphrim? One of us or both?'

'Hmmm.' He studied the Qalochian. 'Both to be sure, I'd say.' The creature's voice was a giveaway to the sharp-eared; it had a jot of the inorganic that marked it as glamoured.

'Don't mind me,' Caldason told them, fury building.

'We won't,' the one called Aphrim replied. 'Let's get this done, Aphri.'

The woman nodded and they both drew blades.

Caldason quickly unsheathed his own, cursing himself for having no second sword.

The woman came at him, and fast. He reflexively dodged her swinging blade. She wasn't fazed. Spinning swiftly, she struck out again. This time, steel met steel and they slipped into a frenzied exchange. She was a supple fencer, hard to pin down, and checked his passes unerringly. Caldason was just as adept at blocking her.

For a full minute they traded blows, seeking a path to flesh. Ducking and weaving, blades clattering, each tried to tease an opening from the other.

She took a savage overhand swing at him, fit to crack his skull. Caldason hurled himself clear. Unstoppable, her sword came down hard on a table, its edge cleaving into a book. When she whipped back the blade, the book was still attached. Deftly she flicked it clear and the book flew across the room.

Caldason exploited the distraction. As she turned to him again he lunged forwards, grasped her arm and half pulled, half threw her at the wall. Crying out, she struck one of the bookcases heavily with her back. The case rocked alarmingly. A dozen volumes dislodged and fell, showering down on her. Hand over her head, she scurried clear, and shouted *'Aphrim!'*

Her twin moved in. Caldason spun to face him. But he didn't meet the blade he expected. Something gleaming and hot narrowly missed his bobbing head.

On the lower floor, Kutch was staring at the ceiling. There were thumps and rumbles from above, and dust was filtering through the boards.

'What the *hell*?' the bookseller exclaimed, leaping to his feet and upsetting his stool. He glared at Kutch. 'What are you two up to? What's your game, eh?'

All Kutch could do was gape at him.

'We'll see about this,' the bookseller resolved, making for the stairs.

The noises overhead grew louder, and he hesitated on the bottom step. Then he cautiously began to climb.

Swinging a chain in a hissing circle above his head, the glamour twin was about to cast again. The iron ball at the chain's end glowed cherry red and left a fiery trace in the air. It may have been glamour-generated heat, but it felt real enough.

The chain was loosed; the flaming orb shot in Caldason's

direction. He threw himself aside, barely evading the blistering missile. It hit a shelf of books, scouring their spines as it passed. The acrid smell of scorched leather pricked his nostrils. Aphrim yanked back the chain and quickly had it circling again.

An irate head popped out of the stairwell.

'What in damnation is going on up here?' the bookseller shrieked. He clambered to the top of the stairs and gawked at them, red faced with indignation. 'Hooligans! You're wrecking my shop, you philistines! *Stop it!* Stop it now, or I'll call the watch!'

With a roar, Aphrim swung the fireball at him. It came close enough to blister his nose, without actually striking him. The bookseller instinctively drew back. For a second he stood poised on the edge of the step, arms flapping wildly in a vain attempt to keep his balance. Then gravity took him. Issuing a high-pitched shriek, he fell backwards and disappeared. They heard him thud against every step as he tumbled back the way he'd come.

Aphri tutted and wagged an admonishing finger at her twin. 'You can't play with people like that,' she said. 'They break.'

As one, they returned their attention to Caldason.

Kutch was at the foot of the juddering stairs when the shop owner bounced down them. He descended like a drunken acrobat, in a confusion of flailing limbs and disarrayed clothing, and came to rest in Kutch's shadow.

'Are you all right?' Kutch exclaimed, bending over him.

The bookseller moaned. He sat up painfully, shaking off the hand Kutch extended to help him. Refocusing, he stared at the boy. 'You're trying to ruin me,' he whined.

'Of course we're not. I mean. . .it's just a misunderstanding. I'm sure we –'

The fight resumed noisily upstairs. With surprising agility for a member of a cerebral profession who'd just fallen down a flight of stairs, the man leapt to his feet. 'You'll pay for this!' he raved. 'Just you wait 'til the watch gets here!'

'No, don't!' Kutch pleaded. 'There's no need for –'

But the bookseller was halfway to the door, moving at speed despite a new-found limp. Kutch almost went after him, thought better of it and returned anxiously to the bottom of the stairs. *'Reeth!'* he bellowed.

'Your boyfriend's calling you,' Aphri taunted. She slashed at Caldason and he parried.

'Stay away, Kutch!' he yelled. *'Get out!'*

He was facing both of them simultaneously now. The female tried for a low sweep, aiming at his legs. Caldason leapt over it. When he landed, the pliant floor shook mightily.

Aphri had to retreat to let her partner use his ball and chain. This time, Caldason side-stepped and got himself parallel to it. He thrust out his sword and let the chain wrap itself around the blade. One good tug wrenched the chain from Aphrim's hands. Then, as a man might rid himself of a poisonous snake curled round a stick, Caldason shook off the chain with a flip of his wrist. Sliding along the blade and off, the ball and chain clanked across the floor. Parted from their glamour host, and energy source, they instantly transmuted to flickering sparks and in short order turned to ashes.

The twins weren't happy about it. They charged together, looking to overwhelm Caldason. He deflected both their blades. A flurry of pounding swordplay followed as he engaged them in turn, blade flashing from one to the other. Brisk and furious, the three-way duel allowed no margin for error. One slip would be his last.

He succeeded in wrong-footing them, retreated a few steps and grabbed the side of a bookcase. A powerful heave toppled it. Scores of volumes tumbled from the shelves as the massive slab of furniture came down. It landed with a resounding crash between him and his foes. The impact made the floor shake.

What Caldason didn't reckon on was setting off a domino effect. The cases on either side of the one he'd felled began to sway, disgorging books. A second later they came down, one after the other, smashing to the floor with a deafening reverberation. Nearby, one end of a floorboard flew up like a child's see-saw, exposing the rusty nails that held it down. Another followed, imitating a catapult's arm.

Aphri vaulted each of the obstacles keeping her from Caldason. Aphrim ran to skirt them. They came at him head-on and from the side, and the fight resumed.

The floor was making ominous sounds, the room shuddering.

Then the world lurched crazily.

In a neighbouring street, Serrah and Tanalvah were making their way through the mid-town crowds.

'What's going on over there?' Tanalvah said, pointing to the other side of the road.

A skinny, dark-haired man in a dishevelled state was running along the pavement, waving his arms about and shouting.

Serrah shrugged. 'Don't know. Can you hear what he's saying?'

'Something about the watch, I think. And sandals. It could have been vandals.'

'Big cities. You get all sorts.'

'Perhaps he's one of those poor deluded people you see talking to themselves on the streets sometimes.'

'Could be.'

They walked on. The shouting man faded into the distance.

'You don't think . . .'

'What, Tan?'

'You don't think that man could have had anything to do with Reeth and Kutch, do you?'

'Why should he? What possible trouble could they get into visiting a bookshop? Ah, there it is.'

No sooner had they spotted the shop than a sound like thunder came from it. Clouds of dust billowed from its open door.

Caldason and the twins were still fighting when the floor collapsed. It dropped like the deck of a rapidly sinking ship. Timber, masonry, plaster, thousands of books and three hapless figures plummeted through the ceiling of the ground floor. In a chorus of tremendous crashes the tables and un-secured bookcases fell with them.

A blizzard of countless fluttering pages descended, followed by the fusty grime of ages to garnish the chaos.

An after-the-storm silence blanketed the scene, broken only by the sound of an occasional book late in falling.

'*Whoooaa!* Do it again! Do it again!' Aphri, still on her feet, was grinning, jubilant as a child just off a fairground ride. Her glamour twin was nearby, sitting incongruously on a heap of books, cross-legged, an impassive expression on its face.

Half covered in debris, Caldason lifted his head. He found he was still clutching his sword. Disentangling himself from the wreckage, he got up.

'Still alive?' Aphrim snorted petulantly.

'We must rectify that, my dear,' Aphri told him.

They started to move in on the Qalochian.

'*Hey!*'

All heads turned. Serrah and Tanalvah were scrambling over the rubble towards them, and Serrah had her sword drawn.

'Playtime's over,' Aphri decided. 'Come.' She beckoned Aphrim.

He ran to her, and *in* to her, merging instantly. Aphri twitched ever so slightly as she reabsorbed her twin. Then she turned on her heel and streaked to the door. Tanalvah drew back as she passed, appalled at what she'd just seen. Serrah made to give chase.

'Let her go!' Caldason called out, re-sheathing his blade. 'Chances are she already looks like somebody else.'

'What happened?' Tanalvah said.

'And what the hell *was* that?' Serrah wanted to know.

Caldason ignored them. 'Kutch?' he yelled. *'Kutch?'*

'Here!' a muffled voice responded.

It came from the foot of the staircase, which remained standing, just. They set to clearing the debris, and found him curled up under the protective wooden slats. Reeth and Serrah took an arm each and pulled him out.

'Are you all right?' Tanalvah inquired anxiously.

'Yes, I think so.' He seemed more excited than upset as he dusted himself off. 'I got a peek, from back there. It was a *meld*, Reeth! I've never seen one before. They're really rare.'

'And the woman was wearing a masking glamour, pretending to be old,' Caldason said.

'Neither sounds cheap,' Serrah ventured.

'Far from it.'

'And they . . . she was after you?' Tanalvah asked.

'Yes.'

'Looks like you have a complicating factor in your life, Reeth,' Serrah announced.

'Just what I needed.'

She saw blood on his sleeve. 'You're hurt.'

He hadn't noticed, and hardly gave it a glance. 'It doesn't matter. You know how quickly I heal.'

'Does that make it less painful?' Serrah took hold of the fabric and ripped it apart. He had an ugly gash running along the outside of his arm. Tearing off a portion of her own, much cleaner, shirt sleeve, she proceeded to bind the wound. There was something almost tender about the way she did it.

'I hate to break this up,' Tanalvah said, 'but –'

'Yes,' Caldason agreed, finishing the last knot himself, 'we have to get out of here.' He caught Serrah's eyes and added softly, 'Thanks.'

They headed for the door. Kutch hung back, surveying the mess.

'Come *on*!' Serrah chided.

'But I didn't even get a book,' he grumbled, slinking after her.

11

'A *symbiote*?'

'*Ssshhh!* I wouldn't want the children to hear any of this, Kinsel. They'll have nightmares.'

'Sorry,' Rukanis replied in a softer voice, glancing at the half-open bedroom door across the hall. 'It's one of the drawbacks of being a singer. I'm always projecting to an audience.'

She smiled. 'Fool.'

'Anyway, I think Teg and Lirrin are more resilient than you believe, Tan.'

'Perhaps. But after what they've been through they deserve a break from the world's harshness.'

'Absolutely. But we were talking about what *you* went through today.'

'Oh, I wasn't that involved, not really. We arrived after it was all over. Except for seeing that . . .'

'I think they're commonly called melds.'

'Yes. But they're not common, fortunately.'

'I always thought they were a myth.'

'The one we saw was real enough.'

Kinsel sipped his wine. 'Poor Reeth. He seems to attract trouble wherever he goes.'

In the glow of the glamour orbs, Tanalvah's face took on a harder set. 'His sort always does.'

'His sort? Aren't *you* . . . his sort?'

'No. I'm not talking about the race we share.'

'Oh.'

'Don't look at me that way, Kinsel.'

'It's just not like you. You normally show such generosity of spirit to everyone. It's one of the things I love you for.' He squeezed her hand. 'But you seem to have this blind spot when it comes to Reeth.'

'I'd call it the opposite: I can see all too clearly what he's capable of.' She noticed his expression and sighed. 'All right, maybe I am being unfair. But I've never got over feeling uneasy about him, and a bit frightened, if I'm being honest.'

'I think you misjudge him. Surely you of all people can understand where his combative tendencies come from? It's your mutual birthright, isn't it?'

'I may be of the Qaloch, but I wasn't brought up the way he was.'

'Only because circumstances prevented it.'

'You think blood will out, is that it?'

'I'm saying that Qalochians have been renowned as warriors for centuries. That kind of legacy goes deep.'

'I wouldn't have thought it was one that appealed to a pacifist, dear.'

'It's just an observation. I'm not saying it's good or bad.'

'It isn't about Reeth's heritage, *our* heritage, it's . . . A man like that, a maverick, can ruin things for other people.' She grew more intense. 'I wouldn't allow that to happen to us, Kin. Never. Whatever I had to do to prevent it.'

'He isn't going to ruin anything for us,' he told her.

'Perhaps I do have a bit of Qaloch belligerence in my blood,' she conceded, grinning.

'We're going to be all right. Teg, Lirrin; all of us.'

'You always speak with such passion when you refer to the children, my love.'

'Do I?'

'Yes, you do. And don't be shy about it. I'm pleased that you take their welfare so seriously.' She paused, trying to read his face, then decided to gently probe. 'It's because of your own childhood, isn't it?'

He nodded.

'You never talk about it. You know everything about me and my background –'

'I know how terrible it was.'

'I'm at peace with it. It's gone now, like it was somebody else's story.'

'It's not that I want to keep you out.'

'I understand that. But remember that your past is *in* the past, like mine. And you don't have to tell me about it if you don't want to.'

'But I *do*. We shouldn't have secrets.'

She decided to try drawing him out a little. 'You've said your upbringing was poor . . .'

'Yes. Or rather, that's what it became.'

'How?'

For a moment, she thought he might not reply. But, falteringly at first, he did. 'Back in Gath Tampoor, my father was a public servant, a bureaucrat. A lowly one, admittedly, but he fought all his life to better himself, educate himself, for us, his family. So our life wasn't too bad, certainly compared with many others.'

'But something happened to change it?'

He nodded and took another drink. 'When I was seven or eight years old, my father got a promotion. It was quite a modest advance; he moved one small rung up a very high ladder. But he was so proud. Shortly after, he was approached by somebody who told him a story. The details aren't important, but it was convincing enough to persuade my father to show this man certain documents in his charge. He did this because he thought he was helping someone who'd suffered an injustice, you understand.'

'And it was a lie.'

'Yes. It turned out that the petitioner was more sinner than sinned against. He was a CIS agent. They said my father took a bribe. He didn't. The worst he was guilty of was being naive.'

Tanalvah had never heard him speak so freely of his background, and she saw the pain in his eyes. 'What did they do to your father?' she coaxed tenderly.

'They made an example of him. He was put to work on the land at first. Slave labour, basically. Then one of their wars came along and he was inducted into the army. We never saw him again. That was when my pacifism was seeded.'

'My poor Kinsel.'

'It killed my mother. Well, she was half dead already from overwork, trying to keep us both. Not to mention the effect of the stigma.'

'What became of you?'

'I was made a ward of the state. Which is a fancy way of saying I ended up an orphan in a poorhouse. That was . . . grim. They kicked me out of there when I was fourteen. Onto the streets, literally. If it hadn't been for my singing, and a few kind people who held out a charitable hand . . . Well, I don't know where I'd be now.'

'I can see why you came to support the Resistance.'

'From that day to this I've had a horror of enslavement; any kind of imposition of one man over another, and that goes doubly for the state. Any state. And I've a terror of poverty. Not just for myself; for everyone. But I don't see either of the empires improving things for most people. Quite the contrary. That's why I put so much hope into the new state. For us, and most of all for the children.'

'Thank you, Kinsel.'

'For what, dear?'

'For telling me. For opening your heart. I know it isn't easy for you.'

'Perhaps I have a trace of shame in my blood, the same way you have a little of the martial.'

'There's no need for shame. You've done nothing to deserve it.'

'Knowing that and feeling it are two different things sometimes.'

'You can talk to me about anything, you know.'

'I know. It's one of the many blessings you've brought me.' Tanalvah stretched. 'It's getting late. Big day tomorrow.'

'Ah, yes. The concert.'

'Nervous?'

'A bit. I always am. You're bound to be a little worried that things won't go well.'

'Why shouldn't they? The gods know you've rehearsed enough. You'll be wonderful, and you'll be doing something for the poor.'

'I just wouldn't want to let them down.'

'You *won't*. You'll give it all you've got, Kinsel, the way you always do.' She slipped her hand into his. 'Now let's get some rest, shall we?'

A short walk away, in the paladin compound, restful was the last word anyone would apply to Devlor Bastorran's state of mind.

Ensconced in his private suite, injured leg resting on a padded stool, he was engaged in a tirade. The object of his wrath, a look of indifference on her face, leaned one arm sloppily on the mantel of the fine marble fireplace.

'. . . not to mention an incompetent, idiotic, irresponsible, useless little . . . *freak*!'

'Finished?' Aphri Kordenza said.

'Impertinent *bitch*.'

'Yes. And your point is?'

'Haven't I made myself clear? You *failed*. I gave you a simple commission and you bungled it.'

'Not that simple, considering who we were after. Anyway, there were unseen complications that let Caldason get the better of us.'

'Oh, come *on*.'

'The same happened to *you*. Or so you said. Took you by surprise was the expression you used.'

'All right, all right. I concede the Qalochian's a difficult mark for someone of your calibre.'

'Well, you picked us.'

'I believed your reputation. More fool me.'

'You military types have a saying: the one about time spent in reconnaissance never being wasted. We learnt a lot about the way Caldason operates by going against him. The next time we meet –'

'He's going to be even more on his guard. No, I wouldn't want you tackling him again unless the odds were massively in our favour.'

'Wait a minute. This is a personal thing for us now. We can't let him get away with besting us. It's a matter of honour.'

'I imagine that's something you surrendered years ago. Forget your personal feelings.'

'The way you have?'

'My own sentiments don't come into this.'

'Really?' She glanced pointedly at his bound limb. 'How's your leg?'

'You forget yourself,' he replied coldly. 'Keep up your insolence and the next assignment's going to someone else.'

'Next? I thought we let you down on the first one.'

'You did. But I'm prepared to give you a second chance.

Follow my instructions to the letter this time and you could redeem yourself. Not to mention earning an even larger fee.'

'How?'

'I've seen a way to down a whole flock of birds with a single, well-aimed stone.'

'You've what?'

'Leave the thinking to me, Kordenza. Let's just say that I have an even bigger commission for you, if you've the courage to take it.'

'A bigger target?'

'Yes. But softer, and considerably more lucrative for you.'

'You know how to entice a girl, General.'

'Then sit, and listen while I explain.'

Bastorran laid out his plan, and they talked until the banked fire dwindled to embers.

'There's a certain poetic justice to it,' Aphri granted, 'and I take my hat off to your base ruthlessness. But the risk . . .'

'That'll be kept to a minimum as far as the deed itself is concerned. I'll see to that. Remember, you'll be under my protection, and, of course, you'll have my eternal gratitude.'

'And your money.'

'That too.'

'Doesn't it worry you that you've told me so much? I mean, you've put your fate in my hands.'

'A measure of how much I trust you. Then again, if you breathe a word about this, or try to betray me in any way, I'll not only deny it, I'll have you killed. Both of you. And not pleasantly.'

'Sealed lips are an essential in our business, General.'

'See you keep it that way. Well, what do you think?'

'Sounds good to me. I'll have to talk it over with Aphrim, of course.'

'You will?'

'We *are* partners.'

'Er, where is he, by the way?'

She thrust a thumb at her chest, and answered under her breath. 'Sulking. He lost a favourite weapon today, so he's generating a new one.' Even more quietly, she mouthed, 'Now's not a good time.'

He stared at her for a second. 'I see. You'll talk it over with him soon, though?'

'First thing.'

There was a rap on the door.

'Come!' the paladin barked.

Lahon Meakin entered. He gave his master a respectful nod, and looked askance at the meld. 'Your briefing, sir. But if this isn't a convenient time . . .'

'Perfectly convenient. Kordenza was just leaving.'

She got up. 'I'll be in touch.'

'I'll look forward to it. There's an escort waiting to see you out of the compound. Meakin, the door.'

The aide opened it for her. She passed through without so much as acknowledging his existence.

'Take a seat, Meakin.'

'Thank you, sir.' He chose the severest chair and produced his customary sheaf of notes.

'Tomorrow is an auspicious day, Meakin. Remind me why.'

'Well, sir, the ten for one law comes into force at midnight.'

'About time, too. Ten prisoners executed every time a paladin's killed will exercise the rabble's minds very nicely. What else?'

'On a personal note, sir, you're due to have that binding removed.'

'Yes, thank the gods. I'll finally be mobile again. And able to kick some backsides in person. But it's not entirely personal, Meakin. Whatever affects me has a bearing on the clans. We are indivisible, and don't forget it.'

'Of course, sir.'

'And lastly?'

'Lastly? Ah.' He consulted his notes. 'I don't seem to have –'

'No, you don't. Because this has been kept on a strictly need-to-know basis. I'm telling you about it now, and I expect you to make all necessary arrangements despite the hour.'

'Yes, sir. What will I be preparing for exactly, sir?'

'I've decided to act on certain intelligence that's come our way regarding dissident activity.' He smiled a cat-that-got-the-cream smile. 'We're going to deal the Resistance a blow, Meakin. One they'll not forget in a hurry.'

12

It was a perfect autumn day.

A handful of downy white clouds graced a sky of matchless blue. The crystal-clear air was cold. Trees were gently shedding leaves of red and brown.

The venue for the concert was the city's main park, and a stage had been set up between two large statues of semi-mythical Gath Tampoorian heroes. One was equestrian. It depicted a champion with a lance, slaying a fearsome, many-tentacled beast. The other showed a warrior astride a heap of corpses, sword raised victoriously. Both were recently erected and made of bronze. Only bird droppings marred their sheen.

In front of the stage, a sizeable area was roped off. There were no seats of any kind; the thousands gathered here were expected to make do with the grass and chill earth. Most took this in good part. They were a genial crowd, anxious to forget their daily struggles for a while. Few were overly boisterous, but there was a constant buzz of expectation.

Hawkers of food and drink moved among them. Balladeers and jugglers performed, and street magicians conjured small glamoured entertainments. Uniformed law-keepers circulated too, while their confederates, less conspicuously dressed, listened for sedition. Overhead, spy glamours hovered.

Things were more congenial for one segment of the audience who were housed behind barriers, in a covered stand. Although the concert was intended for the poor, many of Valdarr's elite had turned out. High-ranking administrators, military chiefs, landowners, guildsmen, attachés and sorcerer fraternities sat in their finery alongside empire citizens: attended, fêted and well protected from the common folk.

A broad marquee stood at the rear of the stage. Inside, it was bustling. Musicians and set builders rubbed shoulders with sound wizards and members of the chorus. Of the latter, there were above a score, all youngsters dressed uniformly in white surplices.

Kinsel Rukanis was at the centre of activity. Tanalvah, Lirrin and Teg clustered round him, the children excited and overawed.

'All right, you two,' Tanalvah told them, 'it's almost time for Kinsel to go on. Say goodbye for now.' They scrambled to be lifted for hugs, and to deposit wet kisses. She indicated Kutch, standing to one side with Quinn Disgleirio. 'Go to Kutch. I'll be with you in a minute.' They ran off to join the young apprentice. 'And behave yourselves!'

Tanalvah gave her full attention to her man. He wore a black stage suit, minus the jacket, and a white silk shirt with ruffled front. She smiled. 'You look marvellous, Kinsel.'

'Really?' He started to fiddle with his cravat. 'You don't think that perhaps –'

'No, you're just right. Stop fussing. How are your nerves?'

'Self-evidently not too good.' He returned her smile at last.

'Nothing new there, then. Still, you know what they say. If you didn't have nerves –'

'The performance wouldn't be any good. I know. And I am anxious to give this particular audience a good show.'

'You will. You always do.'

'I'm not entirely happy with the glamoured amplification.'

'Even your voice won't carry to everyone in a crowd that size. See it as a necessary evil.'

'I suppose you're right.'

'I am. Don't *worry*.' She embraced him.

A dresser appeared holding the singer's velvet jacket, and prudently cleared his throat. Rukanis excused himself and stepped aside to try the coat on. Then he began to fret over it, helped by the dresser.

'Tan?'

She turned. Serrah was there. The clothes she had on were out of the ordinary for her: a dull reddish skirt, full-length, with a drab blouse and wrap, topped with a faded headscarf. No weapons were apparent, but Tanalvah didn't doubt at least one was concealed.

'How's it going?' Serrah asked.

'Well, Kinsel's nervous. Not that there's anything unusual in that.'

'There's a hell of a crowd out there.'

'Wonderful, isn't it? Kin can't quite believe it.'

'What did he expect? Given his reputation and the fact that it's free.'

'I don't think he's ever quite come to terms with how popular he is. But then, his modesty's one of his attractive features.' She regarded Serrah. 'It's good of you to come.'

'Everybody says he's a great singer. I thought I'd find out for myself.'

'I'm glad you're here, Serrah. But you won't . . .'

'What? Start a brawl?'

'I didn't mean –'

'Yes you did.' She flashed a smile. 'And I don't blame you. But I'm not out of control, you know. It's just that sometimes I don't quite see the . . . borders.' She paused, then promised, 'I won't do anything to spoil the big day, Tan. I'm just another spectator.'

'And dressed like one.'

Serrah looked down at herself. 'Just a concession to blending in.'

'Well, you make a very fetching peasant.'

'Thanks.' She took in the scene. 'Not long now.'

'Yes. Do you know if Karr made it?'

'No, he didn't.'

'That's a pity.'

'He says he's too busy, as always. But it's his health, I reckon. Not that he'd ever admit to it.'

'You've only got to look at him to see he's ill. Kin's worried about him. We all are.'

'He's not the sort of man to slow down.'

'Someone should tell him.'

'You think nobody has?' She eyed Tanalvah, and added, 'Reeth didn't come either.'

Tanalvah's features hardened, but she said nothing.

'He thought his presence might attract the wrong kind of attention,' Serrah went on.

'*Good*. I'm glad he isn't here.'

'I thought you might say that.'

'He's a complication I can do without, Serrah. Today of all days.'

'You're being a bit hard on him, aren't you?'

'He's bad news. Trouble follows him like a shadow.'

'You could say the same about me.'

'You're different.'

'How?'

'You've lost . . . somebody close.'

'He's lost everybody.'

'And somewhere along the way he lost himself, Serrah. That's the difference.'

'You think I'm redeemable and he isn't, is that it?'

'I'm just saying it's a relief not having him here.'

'I would have thought you, of all people –'

'Oh, don't *you* start. That's Kinsel's line. Because I'm a Qalochian like Reeth, I'm supposed to understand why he's so tormented. Well, I don't. We share a bloodline, not a common history.'

'Your people do.'

'I never knew my people. Maybe that's my loss. But seeing the way Reeth is, I doubt it.'

'I can't believe you mean that.'

'My birthright's brought me nothing except being spat at on the street. It's meant I've been treated with contempt, reviled, abused, seen as less than human.'

'And there's no excuse for that. It's unforgivable. But at least Reeth's trying to do something to restore his dignity.'

'Really? I thought he just wanted revenge.'

'Hitting back at those who caused your people so much grief is how he keeps his self-respect. It's only natural.'

'It might be natural to you and him; you're warriors. But that isn't how I've lived my life, for all that I'm a Qalochian.'

'I'm sorry, Tan, but I think you're being unfair to Reeth.'

'I know you're close to him, Serrah, but –'

'I'm not sure that's the way I'd put it.'

'However you put it, be careful. I've no idea what your relationship is with him, but don't get yourself hurt.'

'Relationship?' she came back stiffly. 'I don't know what you're talking about.'

'Perhaps you don't. Sometimes others see what we're doing better than we do ourselves.'

'Just a minute. Are you suggesting –'

'Serrah, I'm sorry. Kinsel's about to go on, and the children need me. We'll be watching from the wings. Where will you be?'

'Around.' She turned abruptly and strode off.

'Serrah!' Ignored, Tanalvah cursed softly and went back to Kinsel.

Serrah marched past Kutch, Disgleirio and the children without a word.

'You all right, Serrah?' Disgleirio called out.

'Yes,' she replied, cold as ice. 'Perfectly.'

Kutch and Quinn exchanged a look.

The audience had begun to applaud and cheer the moment Kinsel walked on stage.

He was in excellent voice, and every song drew a thunderous response. The crowd was enchanted, roused, transported by the music. His lays of chivalry stirred their blood, and the lyrical ballads brought them to sweet melancholy. He led them into shadow and back to the light, by way of wonderment. The purity of his singing inspired rapture and tears.

His most appreciative audience was in the wings. Tanalvah, with Teg in her arms and Lirrin clutching her skirt, stood entranced. Every so often, Kinsel favoured them with surreptitious smiles and winks.

He had scoured orphanages and foundling workhouses to choose each member of the chorus himself. His diligence, and days of rehearsal, had paid off. They shadowed him perfectly, snug as a silk glove on a rich woman's hand. Swarms of glamoured sound boosters, made to look like birds or bloated, unseasonable wasps, drifted above the crowd relaying the music to every corner, as distinct as it was to those in the front row.

At last Rukanis reached the climax of his repertoire with songs of great deeds. His voice soared as he intoned fables of gallantry and unrequited love. And the bronze statues on either side of the dais came to glamoured life.

To the left, the conquering hero stretched as though from a long sleep. The enemies he had downed rose too, and battle recommenced. On the right, the warrior awoke, his horse rearing. The monster's tentacles lashed and contorted and a thrust of the champion's spear caused yellow ichor to spurt from the creature's scaly flesh. It wasn't to Kinsel's taste, but it was a crowd-pleaser.

As he drew to a close, a magically generated rainbow arched over the heads of the audience, its hues more vivid than Nature's own. It looked solid, as though a multicoloured bridge had been thrown across the breadth of the park. As thousands craned to see, a network of jagged cracks appeared on the rainbow's surface. Then it began to crumble. Red, blue and green chunks came away, breaking up into even smaller fragments as they fell. The people below cried out, and many covered their heads. But what showered down on them was an abundance of flowers. Beautiful, radiantly coloured blooms of every imaginable genus. Within seconds of falling they transmuted into a froth of minute golden stars and returned to nothingness. Only their exquisite perfume lingered.

Kinsel brought his last song to a booming, triumphant finish. The crowd roared. They rained the stage with real flowers, singly and in bouquets and bunches. People chanted his name and let off dazzling red and white glamour flares. They whistled, clapped and released synthetic doves, shiny as platinum.

Grinning, he took his bows and retreated.

In the wings, Tanalvah and the children clustered round and hugged him.

'You were wonderful,' she said.

'I was?' He looked slightly bewildered, as though the possibility had never entered his head. 'Truly?'

'*Yes*. It was an amazing performance. A *great* performance.' She showed good-natured annoyance. 'Oh, Kinsel, sometimes

I . . . If you don't believe me, listen to *them*.' The clamour from the audience still hadn't died down. She smiled warmly. 'Now get out there and bow some more.'

He kissed her cheek and went back on.

One person in the cheering crowd took no notice of his reappearance. Standing near the front, Serrah was watching two men as they elbowed towards the stage. They were dressed almost identically in blacks and greys, and they were armed with matching swords. But it wasn't only that. It was something about their bearing and the way they moved. It was the set of their faces, and their darting, alert eyes. She had an instinct about them, and had learned to trust her instincts.

The men reached the stage and made for a gap at its side that led to the tent at the rear. There were guards at the entrance, but after a few words they stood aside. The men went in.

Serrah began pushing through the crowd to follow them.

Backstage, things were even more chaotic than before the concert. Musicians, choristers and the rest had been joined by hangers-on, well-wishers and VIPs with their entourages.

Kinsel loosened his collar and dabbed at the perspiration on his forehead. Tanalvah had one eye on the children, whose excitement was beginning to shade into boredom.

'You know,' Kinsel ruminated, 'I just might do this again.'

'Good. I thought you'd enjoy it once it was over.'

He laughed. 'I think you're getting to know me too well, my love.'

An assistant approached. 'Master Rukanis, sir? As you instructed, we're letting through some of the people who want to meet you. Could you do it now?'

'I'd love to. Want to come along, Tan?'

She shook her head. 'No, I'll stay here with these two. They're getting a little cranky.' Teg and Lirrin turned butter-wouldn't-melt, angelic faces up to her.

Kinsel went off with the assistant. 'It would have been nice to meet as many people as want to meet me,' he lamented.

'You'd be here for the rest of the week,' the helper replied.

'I know. But you've picked a representative group?'

'As good a mix as we could find.'

At the far end of the tent, where there were two openings to the outside, a line of forty or fifty audience members was snaking in. They were as diverse as promised. Youths, elderly couples, middle-aged patrons of music, street beggars, parents with babes in arms. As soon as they saw Rukanis they started cheering.

Guards kept them in check as he stepped forward, smiling, to shake hands and converse. Scraps of parchment and glamoured graph-sticks were thrust at him. He signed his name in silver, gold and crimson, and wrote inscriptions for the excited, chattering group. Adolescent girls giggled as he autographed the backs of their hands. People tugged at his sleeves. Babies were lifted to have their cheeks pecked.

Two unsmiling men in dark clothing moved towards him through the crowd.

Tanalvah no more than half watched this from her elevated position at the back of the stage. Her attention was on the children.

'When are we going home?' Lirrin yawned. Her heavy-eyed young brother, propped against her, was beyond even grumbling.

'Not long,' Tanalvah promised, ruffling the girl's hair. 'Just as soon as Kinsel gets back.'

Serrah strode up to them.

'Serrah! I'm so glad you came back. I wanted to say I'm sorry for –'

'Don't worry about that.' She was scanning the lively scene inside the tent. 'I think we might have a problem.'

At the look on Serrah's face Tanalvah instinctively drew the children to her. 'What is it? Is it Kinsel? Has something happened?'

'It's just a hunch.' She looked down and saw Kinsel signing autographs and talking with admirers. 'Those two.' She pointed. 'The ones dressed alike.'

'In the black and grey? What about them?'

'It could be nothing.'

'If Kinsel's in danger, he needs me.'

'*No*. Stay where you are.' Serrah's tone forbade argument.

'Is something bad going to happen to Kinsel?' Lirrin piped up, sensing the adults' alarm.

'No, darling,' Tanalvah assured her, almost calmly, 'it's all right.' To Serrah she mouthed, *'Isn't it?'*

Serrah didn't answer.

They watched.

Kinsel finished signing his name for somebody and handed back the paper.

'Kinsel Rukanis.' It wasn't a question, more a flat statement.

He looked up. Two men, clad darkly, stared at him. Their faces were sober. 'Yes,' he replied tentatively.

'You're going to do exactly what we tell you,' one of them said. He spoke softly, but his manner was professional, and threatening.

'Who are you?'

'We have the authority of the state. That's all you need to know.'

'And we're not here alone,' the other man added.

'Am I being arrested?'

'You're to be taken into custody, yes.'

'On what charge?'

'This isn't a debate,' the first man informed him coldly. 'Our orders are to take you quietly, if possible. But it makes no difference to us. If you want to be difficult, an awful lot of people here are going to get hurt. It's your choice.'

Kinsel didn't doubt he meant it. 'I understand.'

'Good. Now you're going to tell your minders that you have to leave. Don't make a meal of it. Then we're going out of here with no fuss. Got that?'

'Yes.' He wanted to ask to see Tanalvah and the children, but knew that would be a mistake.

'Just do as we say,' the second man told him, 'and no blood need be shed.'

On the stage, Kutch and Disgleirio joined the women.

'Have you –' Quinn began.

'Yes,' Serrah said, 'we see them.'

Tanalvah was growing more distraught. 'They're taking him away. Do something!'

'It isn't just those two,' Serrah pointed out. 'There are others down there.'

At least a dozen similarly dressed men had made their way into the tent.

'And no doubt they'll be plenty more about the place,' Disgleirio reckoned.

'They can't do this,' Tanalvah protested, her eyes welling.

'They're government,' Serrah said, 'they can do what they damn well please.'

'Do you think they're after all of us?' Kutch wondered, looking troubled.

'They only seem interested in Kinsel,' Quinn replied. 'If this was some kind of general raid we'd know it by now.'

'Why are you standing here *talking*?' Tanalvah demanded. 'Help him!'

The children were distressed and crying, too. Kutch did his best to comfort them.

'There are a lot of civilians here, Tan,' Serrah reminded her, 'and it's a good bet those bastards don't give a damn about them. If we wade in –'

'If you won't do something, I will!' Tanalvah spat.

Serrah grabbed her arm and held on tight. 'If you move, or scream, or do anything to attract their attention, so help me I'll knock you down.' She backed the threat with a clenched fist.

Tanalvah stared at her for a moment. Then she began to break down. 'Oh gods, it's my fault. I made him do this. I –'

'*Shut up*. Get a hold. This isn't helping Kinsel. Or the kids.' She turned to Kutch. 'You're going to stick with Lirrin and Teg. You stay with them whatever happens. Right?' Kutch nodded. 'As for Kinsel, all we can do for now is find out where they're taking him.'

'I'll do that,' Quinn offered.

'All right, but be careful. Go.'

He slipped away.

Down in the tent, Kinsel was leaving, flanked by his two escorts. Their associates followed at a distance, keeping a watch on the crowd.

'It wasn't supposed to be like this,' Tanalvah muttered.

Serrah looked at her. 'What?'

All she got was another blank stare.

'We have to get you away from here, Tan. And not back to your place either. Kutch, stay close. Come on, all of you.'

Once his captors had got Kinsel a reasonable distance from the concert area, they stopped. One of them produced a pair of glamoured hand shackles.

'That won't be necessary,' Kinsel promised.

'Orders,' the man grunted. He clamped the bracelets on Kinsel's wrists. They tightened of their own accord, and would stay that way, unbreakable, until the counter spell revoked them.

They resumed walking at a brisk pace, trailed by their accomplices, who amounted to at least a score by now. A number of them went forward to clear the way of curious citizens leaving the park. There were plenty of other people about, and not a few of them recognised Rukanis. But no one felt confident enough to brave his escort and approach him.

Disgleirio followed, hanging well back, trying to look like any other citizen and using the occasional tree for cover.

Kinsel was marched to a road abutting the park. There was a heavy security presence. An assortment of uniformed men and women prowled the area, but the majority were red-jacketed paladins. Curious bystanders were being kept well away.

A small fleet of carriages was parked in the road. The grandest was harnessed to four coal-black steeds, and its windows were blinded. He was taken to it, bundled in and deposited heavily on one of the leather seats. Then the door was slammed. He found himself facing a young man in the uniform of a high-ranking paladin officer. The man favoured him with a triumphant smile.

'What a pleasure it is to meet you at last,' Devlor Bastorran said.

13

By the time they got to the nearest safe house there was an air of barely suppressed panic.

Serrah did her best to comfort Tanalvah, leaving Kutch to look after the children more or less on his own. None of them felt secure, and Serrah was at a window or door every few minutes to check on the outside world. There was no sign of Disgleirio.

Within the hour, Caldason arrived.

'Everybody all right?' he asked as he slipped in, doffing his hood.

'Yes. Well, physically.' Serrah nodded towards Tanalvah, hunched in a chair by the hearth, staring into the yellow-blue flames of a log fire. 'She's still in shock. I'd leave her be for now.'

He nodded. 'And Kutch?'

'Upstairs with the kids. He's fine.'

'What about you?'

'Me?'

'How do you feel?'

'I'm all right, Reeth. What did you expect, that I'd run amok or something?'

'No. From what I've heard you dealt with it in exactly the right way. But just lately you have been a bit...'

'Unpredictable? Apt to fly off the handle? Like you?'

'Well...'

They exchanged sheepish smiles.

'It's funny, but having to take charge back there kind of centred me. Otherwise ... well, maybe my reaction would have been different.'

'It's not so strange when you think about it.'

'Perhaps. Anyway, what do you mean by "from what you've heard"?'

'There were other Resistance people at the concert, and they've been spreading the word. I figured out where you'd be.'

'Do you think Kinsel's arrest was part of a general clamp-down?'

'There doesn't seem to be any more activity on the streets than usual. I reckon they were targeting just him.'

'That's what I thought.'

'Where's Quinn?'

'I was going to ask if you knew. He was trying to find out where they were taking Kinsel. I hope he hasn't shared his fate.'

'He can look after himself.' He glanced at Tanalvah. She hadn't moved, and seemed unaware of them. 'I was with Karr earlier. He's on his way, taking a roundabout route, same as me.'

'Good. Reeth, that meld you had a run-in with.'

'What about it? Her...them...'

'I think "it" will do. Could it be connected in any way? With Kinsel, I mean.'

'Can't see how. I don't know what the hell that was about.'

'Yes, could have been anything, I suppose. You've made a lot of enemies.'

'That's a habit we share.'

She was about to answer when Kutch entered the room.

'Reeth! Am I glad to see you.'

'How are the children?' Serrah asked.

'Sleeping. What's happening, Reeth? Are they rounding up everybody in the Resistance?'

'We don't think so. But it's as well to take precautions.'

'Including abandoning places like this,' Serrah added, 'though I'm sure Kinsel didn't know about this particular house. But we're going to have to make some big changes to how we operate.'

'Why?' Kutch said.

'Oh, come on, Kutch.'

'What?'

'Serrah means that we'll need to be extra careful now Kinsel's in their hands,' Caldason explained, 'because he'll be made to talk.'

'He'd never do that.'

They turned. Tanalvah had lifted her head and was glaring at them, eyes red-rimmed.

'He wouldn't do it,' she repeated. 'Kinsel wouldn't betray anyone.'

'Of course he wouldn't,' Serrah agreed, 'not willingly. How are you feeling, Tan?'

She ignored that. 'He's strong. I know he isn't like you. He's not a fighter. But he has a . . . *moral* strength.'

'Nobody doubts he has guts,' Caldason said. 'Or that he'll try to hold out.'

'He won't inform. He's too principled for that.'

'It's not a question of choice, Tan. Particularly as I think I know who's –'

Someone rapped a signal on the door.

Hand on sword hilt, Caldason went to the spy-hole, then drew the bolts.

Karr and Disgleirio came in together. The patrician looked white and exhausted.

'We ran into each other on the way,' Disgleirio told them.

'Was anybody hurt?' Karr wanted to know, sounding short of breath.

'No,' Serrah assured him. 'Shaken, but otherwise all right.'

Karr moved over to Tanalvah. 'This must be a terrible time for you, my dear.' He took her hands. 'We're going to keep you safe, you and the children. And we'll do all we can to help your man.'

'I told Kinsel it doesn't matter. I said no cause is worth your life.' She looked up at Karr. 'I don't think he believed that. Any more than you do.'

'I deserve your blame. I should have –'

'No. If I blame anybody, it's myself. I was the one who . . . talked him into giving the concert.'

'Doling out guilt won't help Kinsel,' Serrah announced. 'What's important is, what do we know? And what can we do?'

Karr nodded. 'You're right. In that respect, Quinn has something to tell us.'

'Well, it's short and not so sweet,' the Righteous Blade man reported. 'The carriage they put him in went straight to paladin headquarters.'

'Could we get him out?' Kutch asked.

'Maybe if we attacked with an army,' Caldason allowed, 'though I doubt it. And the chances of Kinsel still being alive when we got to him are slim.'

That sent them all into a reflective silence.

Disgleirio cut through it. 'There's something else. Guess who rode in the carriage with him? Devlor Bastorran.'

'The young pretender himself,' Karr mused, 'and your greatest admirer, Reeth.'

If Caldason appreciated the joke he didn't show it. 'How did he look, Quinn?'

'I only caught a glimpse of him. There was no sign of bandages or dressings, and his leg was out of plaster. He walked a little stiffly, but looked hale apart from that.'

'So, the paladins were behind this,' Karr concluded. 'Or at least the younger Bastorran.'

'It might not be that simple,' Serrah said. 'I think at least some of the men who arrested Kinsel were CIS agents.'

'You're certain?'

'Not entirely. But I worked with them long enough to be pretty sure.'

'I don't understand,' Kutch admitted. 'What does it mean?'

'The Council for Internal Security is one of the most powerful and feared arms of the Gath Tampoorian government,' Karr clarified. 'But by tradition and treaty it's only supposed to operate within Gath Tampoor itself.'

'You're naive if you think it's never meddled in any of the empire's colonies,' Disgleirio said. 'The pretence that it doesn't was only ever to do with agencies not being seen to step on each other's toes. It's just internal politics.'

'True. But if they're acting *openly* here in Bhealfa, and working closely with the paladins, we've moved to a new level.'

Caldason shrugged. 'More evidence that the gloves are off. We knew that.'

'But hardly good timing when we're so close to the move,' the patrician reminded him.

'How does this do Kinsel any good?' Tanalvah broke in.

None of them had an answer.

They talked on, pooling their knowledge, arguing, considering plans. And doing their best to comfort Tanalvah when tears overcame her.

Eventually night began to fall and the curfew loomed. Karr left for home, promising to send people to keep a discreet eye on the safe house. Disgleirio went off to check the look-outs stationed near the paladin headquarters, and to increase their number. Kutch, suppressing yawns, was sent upstairs to sleep by the children.

'I'm going to scout the area before curfew,' Caldason decided. 'When I get back I'll stay the night.'

'All right,' Serrah said. 'Be careful.'

He let himself out and she secured the door behind him.

Tanalvah still sat forlornly by the dying fire, seeing who knew what in the dancing flames. Serrah tossed on another log and sat next to her.

'It sounds a stupid question,' she confessed, 'but how are you?'

'I've lost him, haven't I? The only man who ever respected me. The only man I . . . loved.'

'Listen to me, Tan. We're going to do everything we can to get him out of this situation. You heard what Karr and the others said; no effort's going to be spared to bring Kinsel back to you.'

'I also heard them say he's in a fortress, and in the hands of ruthless men. I don't fool myself, Serrah. It's over.'

'It is as long as you have that attitude.'

'Where there's life there's hope, eh?'

'Well, yes. It sounds trite but it's true.'

'I'm finding it hard to keep any hope going right now. I can't see . . . I can't see a way out of –'

'It's easy for me to say, Tan, but this isn't the time to go to pieces. Kinsel needs you, and so do Teg and Lirrin.'

Tears began coursing down Tanalvah's cheeks. 'The children . . .'

'At least they're going to be safe.' She reached over and squeezed her hand. 'You can rely on that. I swear it.'

'I know. If it wasn't for you, we wouldn't have had the brief happiness we were lucky enough to have.'

'You can have it again. We'll work something out.'

'I know you'll all do your best. But –'

'What?'

'There's something you don't know.'

'If it's something that might help Kinsel you must tell me, Tan.'

She gave a short, bitter laugh. 'It doesn't help. Far from it.'

Serrah passed her a kerchief. Tanalvah began dabbing her wet cheeks with it.

'What is it, Tan?'

'Serrah, I . . . I'm pregnant.'

Serrah was speechless for a moment, then said, 'You're sure?'

Tanalvah nodded.

'How long?'

'A couple of months.'

'Oh gods, Tan.'

'You know the ironic thing? I prayed for it. I begged the goddess every day to bless us with a child of our own, to make our family complete. The gods work mysteriously. They give with one hand and take away with the other.'

'What's happened to Kinsel is the work of men, not gods.'

'I think the goddess knew what was going to happen to him. She gave me this child as compensation, a way of balancing things.'

'If it helps you to think of it that way, go ahead. But don't lose sight of the possibility that you may still have both; Kinsel and the child.'

'You have more optimism than I do at the moment.'

'Yes, at the moment. You've had a tremendous shock. Things will look different soon.'

'I hope you're right. But . . . don't tell anybody. About the baby. Not just yet. I don't think I could take much more sympathy right now.'

When Caldason got back, Tanalvah was slumbering on the fireside couch.

'You look tired yourself,' he told Serrah.

'It's been a long day.'

'Get some sleep. I'll look out for Tanalvah.'

'Sure?'

'Go ahead. If you're needed, I'll call.'

She left to rest in another room.

He quietly hefted a chair to the hearth. Placing his swords on the floor beside it, he sat.

All was silent for a while.

'Reeth?'

'I thought you were asleep.'

Tanalvah shifted on the couch. 'The way I feel at the moment I might never sleep again.'

'I feel that way myself sometimes.'

'You have demons waiting for you in sleep. I know what that's like now.'

He said nothing.

'Tell me, Reeth: what gives you your strength?'

'What do you mean?'

'The capacity to go on. Your will to survive.'

'I have no choice.'

'Because of this . . . immortality thing?'

'I could end my life if I chose. There have been times when I've tried.'

'But not too hard, it seems.'

Again he didn't answer.

'So it's simply revenge that gives you the resolve to carry on?' she ventured.

'Don't underestimate it. Revenge can be a worthy sentiment.'

'There was a time when I would have argued with that.'

'But not now.'

'After what's happened to Kinsel, I've thought of nothing but vengeance.'

'Then you understand.'

'We're not the same. Don't try to make out we are.'

'It's just a matter of degree. You want retribution for your personal hurt. I seek vengeance for my tribe, and our entire race.'

'How very noble of you.' It was an intentional barb.

'You're of the Qaloch. I would have thought you'd look favourably on what I'm doing.'

'Just being born of Qalochians doesn't make me one. Not really.'

'You're wrong. Blood will out.'

'I've had no experience of being a member of the race we share, except its negative effects.'

'That's hardly the fault of the race. Unless you believe in blaming the victims.'

'The Qalochians are history's victims. Can you fight history?'

'History's made by people. I can fight *them*. Or at least the ones who wronged us, and go on wronging us.'

'So you're fighting the world, then. You're ambitious in your enemies, I'll give you that.'

'You don't know much about our past, do you? Or our culture?'

'Beyond the fact that we're a warrior race, what else is there?'

'So much, Tanalvah. And it's fading with every year that passes. Can you speak the Qaloch tongue?'

Tanalvah shook her head.

'Language was one of the first things they took away from us, because they understand the power of words. There was a time when many places in this land bore Qalochian names. But no longer. And where they can't abolish language, they twist it. So invasion becomes liberation, and they call slavery freedom. These things go unnoticed when we lose touch with our customs and beliefs.'

'I have beliefs,' she came back indignantly. 'I worship Iparrater, defender of –'

'The downtrodden. I know. She's a Rintarahian deity.'

'So you're a believer in the old Qaloch gods, are you?'

'I follow no gods.'

'You would do well to.'

'Who would you suggest? Mapoy, patron of bathhouses, perhaps? Ven, the god of rag pickers? How about Isabelle, goddess of shoemakers?'

'You're mocking me.'

'No. I just wonder why you honour petty foreign deities rather than Qaloch gods.'

'What would be the point? The gods of the Qaloch have forsaken us.'

'And your new goddess hasn't?'

'What do you care, Reeth? You've left no room for faith in your withered heart.'

'The gods have done nothing for me. If there are gods. I walk my own path, as well as any man can.'

'You're asking for ruin when you scorn the powers that gave you life, Reeth.'

'Life? Life's just the difference between what we hope for and what we get.'

She stared at him coldly. 'If you really believe that, I'm sorry for you.'

There wasn't a lot more to be said. Tanalvah turned away, and eventually she slept, or pretended to.

Caldason kept watch until first light, when Serrah relieved him.

Then he drifted into sleep himself.

*   *   *

He was on the edge of a field, the golden corn as high as his chest.

It was hot. The sun beat down like a hammer and heat contorted the air. There was hardly a breath of wind. The drone of bees and faint birdsong were all that broke the silence.

A flurry of movement caught his eye, far off, near the other end of the cornfield. Something moved through the crop, heading in his direction. He couldn't see what it was, just the corn rustling as the commotion progressed. When it got to about a third of the way across, he noticed something else.

A party of horsemen, five strong, appeared at the field's farthest edge. They plunged in, living ships breasting an ocean of gold. He could hear shouting, and saw the riders whipping their mounts unmercifully.

Their unseen quarry ploughed on, cutting a path that came nearer and nearer to where he was standing. The pursuing horsemen, crashing heedless through the stand, were closing the gap.

Suddenly, a figure burst into the open, scattering stalks, leaves and corn pollen. Reeth recognised the old man he had seen so often before. Then he realised that the man carried a child, perhaps three or four years old. The youngster, too, was familiar, though he had no idea why.

Child hugging his chest, the elderly protector, running with surprising speed and agility, dashed past him. Then he knew that he had been cast once more as a powerless observer, invisible to the actors in this particular drama.

He turned to follow the old man's progress. Now he had the cornfield at his back, and was looking towards grassland with rolling hills in the middle distance. The old man was sprinting to meet another, larger group of riders, obviously allies, galloping towards him. They came together. With a deftness belying his years, the old man scrambled onto a riderless steed, hoisting the child up with him. Then he set off across the plain, hell for leather. But the others remained, forming a defensive line.

At that moment the five pursuing horsemen came out of the corn behind Reeth. Two thundered past on his right, two to his left. The fifth, disconcertingly, rode through him.

He watched as the two groups, screaming murderously, met with a clash of steel.

There was a flash, bright as lightning, and the scene dissolved into pitch black.

Now he stood on the lip of a low cliff, overlooking a fast-flowing river. Here and there, smooth rocks poked out, turning the water to white foam.

A boat appeared, bumpily riding the current downstream. It was a rudimentary craft, made of tanned hides stretched over a wooden frame. There was no sail; it relied on oars for motive power, and it had a primitive rudder.

Six people occupied the boat. Four were oarsmen, though the speed of the river made their paddles redundant. They used them to fend off the half-submerged boulders that threatened to rip open the hull.

At the stern, hand on the tiller, sat the old man. Huddled next to him was a boy; unmistakably the same child he had seen carried from the cornfield, now around eight or nine years of age. But whereas the boy had taken on some years, the old man looked exactly the same.

On the opposite bank, a gang of men, perhaps a score in number, came into view. They were on foot, running to keep up with the bobbing, scarcely controlled boat. There were archers among them, who at intervals loosed arrows at the boat. Its erratic course was such that few of their shots came near. The boy, despite his tender age, occasionally fired back. His bolts flew with greater accuracy, causing the outraged mob to duck.

A moment later the boat was washed round a bend and out of sight.

The blast of light came again. Darkness closed in.

He was standing in rough, boggy terrain, and it was night. But ahead of him several buildings were on fire, illuminating the landscape. Pungent wood-smoke stung his eyes and scorched his throat.

It was a scene of chaos, with people running in all directions, and it took a second for him to make sense of things. A small battle was going on, a raid on a modest settlement by the look of it, and the defenders had just begun to rally. He saw raiders un-horsed and speared where they lay. Knots of men belaboured each other with broadswords. Savage hand-to-hand fighting went on all around.

He looked about, expectant. The old man caught his eye first. He was unchanged; moving through the mêlée, barking orders.

Then he saw the boy. Though youth would be a better description. He must have been fifteen or above, and now he sought no one's protection. Giving as good an account as any, and better than most, he not only fought but directed others. He moved with a fluid assurance, cutting down foes, cheering on his comrades, showing no quarter.

In the middle of the slaughter the youth turned and peered his way. It seemed that their eyes met, giving the lie to his observer's invisibility. And in that moment of contact, real or imagined, the disembodied onlooker realised, or rather had confirmed, the youth's identity.

It lasted just an instant.

The searing, unbearable light came then, swiftly followed by a darkness that was all-consuming.

14

He could have had a palace. He chose a tent. He could have dined on banquets, but preferred army rations. He could have dressed in finery, but favoured humbler garb. He could have taken the lives of the vanquished, but dispensed mercy. He could have had his pick of riches and women, but kept to modesty and abstinence. He could have embraced tyranny, but showed forbearance.

For these and other qualities, his followers loved him. Almost enough to hide the fear they felt.

The warlord Zerreiss – Shadow of the Gods, the Velvet Axe, the Man Who Fell From the Sun, and bearer of a dozen other sobriquets not assumed but conferred on him – was perfectly unexceptional in appearance. Many found this surprising in one who had achieved so much. As though Nature should honour conquerors with a special aspect. But the truth was that in almost every respect he was ordinary. His physique was average at best, and his face, once seen, might immediately be forgotten.

Except for the singular vigour that animated it; a curious, indefinable potency that gave him an extraordinary presence.

For all that the world called him a barbarian, Zerreiss was

not a tyrant. But he was despotic. To many, this might seem a fine distinction. He was no tyrant in that he waged war as a last resort and strove not to waste lives unnecessarily. He was despotic in being resolute in his hunger for territorial expansion, and in his insistence that the gift he came to bestow, as he saw it, had to be accepted. It was only when thwarted in this regard that he made a rare display of a harsher side.

In the valley below, his army prepared for another siege, dependent upon an offer of clemency. They faced a formidable redoubt: a fortress of massive proportions, shimmering with myriad glamoured lights and magical discharges. Well soldiered, amply provisioned, it had never been taken. But his horde was in good cheer. They knew their warlord held the key to victory.

It was snowing. Winter always came much earlier in the northern wastelands, and as yet the weather was mild compared to what was due. But the onset of freezing conditions was a good reason to get the job over and done with. As no one doubted he would.

Zerreiss came into his command tent like any other man: no grand entrance, no fanfare, no retinue. Yet his appearance galvanised the generals and adjuncts working there.

He called over his two closest aides.

'Has there been word on our proposal yet, Sephor?'

'Not so far, sir,' the much younger of the pair replied. 'Should we send in another envoy?'

'No. They have a lot to chew over. Let's leave them to it for a while.' He turned to the other man. 'Wellem.'

'Sir?' The old campaigner instinctively came to attention, though Zerreiss seldom demanded shows of obeisance.

'Everything's ready in respect of our troops and their needs?'

'All done, sir. They only await your order.'

'Good. Let's hope I don't have to issue it. And how goes tracing the magic sources in these parts, Sephor?'

'You were right, sir, about energy lines in the area. It seems at least three cross where the city stands. No doubt it was founded for that reason.'

'The usual pattern. Wretched Founders,' Zerreiss grumbled. 'They have a lot to answer for.'

'So we'll probably be facing a full complement of magical munitions,' Sephor added. 'Or would have, depending on the outcome, of course.'

'I think you can rely on the outcome.' He looked to his other aide. 'Tell me, Wellem, how do you think those below will respond?' It was the sort of question the warlord was fond of asking, and his temperament was such that he encouraged candid replies.

'No surrender. That's what I'd say, sir, if I were in their position.'

'That's the answer I'd expect from an old campaigner, my friend. What are your reasons?'

'Well, apart from the obvious reason that they find themselves under attack from someone they haven't offended, I reckon they'd see no need to accept change. From their point of view you're here to take something away, not to give them anything.'

'A fear of the unknown, in other words. The standard response.'

'Let's hope we get the standard outcome, sir.'

'In the end we will,' Zerreiss assured him. 'Though I wish it were possible to reach that goal without bloodshed.'

'That's war, sir,' Wellem offered.

'As you say.' Their master's tone was genuinely regretful. 'Do you know the story of the Sythea?'

They did, of course; the ancient fable was well known in the northern lands. But it pleased him to occasionally put things in allegorical form, so they feigned ignorance.

'The men of the Sythea,' he began, 'who lived deep inside

the Bariall caves, always held that they were in a state of grace. They had shelter and warmth in their underground burrows, and fungus to eat and water to drink from subterranean rivers. They even had some light from glowing minerals and phosphorescent lichens. The Sythea were dimly aware that another world existed far above them and the occasional hardy soul ventured out, never to return. But these troglodytes weren't concerned with other worlds. Why should they be? Their domain had everything they needed, and they believed themselves and their dingy warrens to be protected by their underworld gods. Do you know what happened to change that?'

Of course they did; they'd heard the story many times. 'A flood, sir,' Sephor dutifully replied.

'A flood, yes.' Sometimes Zerreiss seemed for all the world like a children's tutor or priest-scholar in the way he spoke to people. But somehow he had the knack of not making it sound patronising. 'Their underground rivers and lakes swelled because of unusually heavy rainfall on the surface, though of course they didn't know that. The water level kept rising and they were forced to move higher and higher, until eventually they had no choice but to leave their caves and risk the alien surface world. This was a cause of great fear to them, and many stubbornly clung on to what remained of their underground kingdom. Eventually, they perished. But others, bolder or more desperate, did venture out. Those who braved the surface, near-blinded by the light, found a world of wonder and fecundity. And of course the legends say that they became men as we know them. Some believe that the gods of this world sent the flood to force them from their caves so that the true race of men could begin.' He paused, almost theatrically. 'I am the flood.'

'Not a god?' Sephor ventured, half humorously. It was a measure of his master's tolerance that he could make such a comment.

Zerreiss smiled. 'No, not a god. Though some would try to see me that way. An instrument of the gods, perhaps, if such things as gods exist. Don't look so shocked, Wellem. You know my views on this matter.'

'Yes, sir. It's the way I was brought up, I suppose. Sorry, sir.'

'I'll have no one apologise for what they believe, my friend. You have never seen me suppress any faith in the lands we've taken, nor will I start now. I believe that in time people will come to their own conclusions about the truth or falsity of these things.'

'That does you credit, sir.'

'You know, commanders of old had aides whose job it was to whisper in their ears that their victories and triumphs, like life itself, were all transient. If not actually illusions.' He smiled again. 'Don't worry, I won't require that of you two. I have no need of such. That voice has always been here, in my head.' He lifted a hand to his temple. 'I stray from the point. But I think you see what I was getting at with the story of the Sythea. The people of the city below are troglodytes, through no fault of their own, and see no need to come out of their comfortable caves. Our mission is to bring them into the light. The true light.' He let that soak in, then said, 'Why do you follow me?'

Had the question been asked by a true tyrant, his minions would have been quaking for fear of giving a wrong answer. But this was Zerreiss.

'Because you are a great conqueror, sir,' Wellem said.

'Exactly what I'd expect from an old soldier.' He looked to his other, younger aide. 'Sephor?'

'Because you are just, sir, and seek to make your peoples' lives better.'

'I want to bring them into the light, yes. But I say you follow not me, but what I have, what I *am*. Not the man but the tinder he carries inside, let's say.' He seemed pleased with the analogy. 'We are firm in our resolve? As one in the legitimacy of our crusade?'

'Yes, sir!' they chorused.

'Then I'm blessed.' He turned a benign grin on them. 'To more mundane matters. What do we know of the two ships the empires sent our way?'

'They're making a race of it, sir,' Sephor reported. 'It's difficult to say which will enter your waters first.'

'When they do, we must be ready for them.'

'Do we meet them as friend or foe?'

'I've yet to decide on what response would be appropriate.'

'With respect, sir,' Wellem said, 'would it do to antagonise Gath Tampoor or Rintarah?'

'I think the question is better put the other way about: would they be wise to antagonise me?'

'Perhaps they simply need assurances of the limit your influence will extend to, sir,' Sephor suggested.

'We push further south.'

'Yes, sir. But where do we stop?'

'Stop? We've hardly begun.'

The arrival of a messenger put paid to the discussion. He was blue with cold and caked with snow. Shivering, he stamped his boots while delivering a salute. 'We have tidings, sir.'

'You look perished, lieutenant,' Zerreiss told him. 'A warming drink for this man!' He moved closer and asked, 'What's their decision? Yes or no?'

'They refuse to surrender, sir.'

Zerreiss sighed. 'Then it comes to my intervention again.' He walked to the open tent flap and looked down at the city and the great fortress it suckled. Its shimmering lights and the driving snow made it all seem unreal somehow. His aides joined him. 'Let's be done with this,' he decided. 'Make ready the troops. We move to the endgame.' He lifted his hands.

What happened next had those around him thinking that perhaps he was a god after all.

As yet, whatever the warlord did had little effect in the temperate south. Besides, they had pressing problems nearer to home.

In a run-down, near lawless quarter of Valdarr, not far from the docks, a secret hide-out had been hastily established. It was in a deconsecrated temple that had seen its congregation go down along with the area. A new, empire-built place of worship in an adjoining, more salubrious neighbourhood had taken the rest. Now it was boarded-up and dusty, and ideally situated for Resistance purposes.

In one corner, Phoenix and Caldason stood before a wall-mounted, luminous map. For once, the sorcerer wasn't trying out a magical disguise.

'See it?' he said, pointing to one of numerous specks off Bhealfa's northern coast.

'Just about. And you're sure that's the place?'

'There's nothing totally certain about it,' Phoenix admitted. 'But Covenant's been studying the mystery of the Clepsydra for years, and all the probabilities indicate this islet.' He tapped the map with his finger.

'Probabilities,' Caldason repeated.

'It's the best we can offer, short of going there.'

'Which I hope you're not thinking of doing, Reeth,' Karr said. He'd approached without them noticing. 'At least, not unless you're part of a Resistance mission.'

'We have an agreement, don't we?'

'We do. But I know how frustrating it must be for you having to wait.'

'I asked Phoenix to show me where the thing might be

because I'm curious. But there's a limit to my patience, Karr. Do you have any idea when I'll get to go?'

'No, frankly. What with the move, and now what's happened to Kinsel. And there's still the question of getting the gold to Darrok.'

'I thought that might be on your mind.'

'Well, at least you don't go into a sulk whenever it's mentioned. I suppose that's some kind of progress.'

'I'm thinking about it.'

Karr brightened. 'I'm glad to hear that.'

'But don't take anything for granted. Like I said, I can only be patient for so long.'

'Shouldn't we be getting on with the business at hand?' Phoenix reminded them.

'Yes, of course,' Karr agreed.

They moved off to the main part of the hall, where there were more people, some on benches, a few making do with the floor. Caldason shoved in next to Serrah. Kutch was there, too, along with Quinn Disgleirio. Phoenix joined Karr's indefatigable administrative officer, Goyter, carrying her inevitable wad of documents, at the side of the room.

The remaining twenty or so people were all known to Caldason to a lesser or greater degree. They consisted of high-ranking members of Covenant, the Righteous Blade and several other groups affiliated to the movement. No more than half of them sat on the United Revolutionary Council, as care was taken never to have every important operative present in the same place at the same time.

Karr went to the front of the group, and addressed them without preamble.

'We're all far too busy to spend too much time here, quite apart from the security considerations, so I intend keeping this as brief as possible. I don't have to tell you that we've taken on a massive task. The coming move has to be one of the biggest endeavours in recent history, and so far things are going more or less to plan. Which is remarkable considering the pitfalls we've encountered, not least the fact that the authorities are bearing down ever harder on the civil population.'

'He doesn't look any healthier, does he?' Serrah whispered.

'A little worse, if anything,' Caldason replied.

'The purpose of this meeting is two-fold,' the patrician continued. 'First, it's for you to report on the progress of your particular areas of responsibility. That way, we can all get an idea of the larger picture. Second, it's an opportunity for you to meet your counterparts, exchange ideas and maybe help each other out with any problems you're encountering. We'll keep it simple. There's no need for names, just remind us of your position or function and tell us how you're doing. Got that? Good. Who's first?' About half those present raised a hand. 'Yes, you.' He pointed at a heavily built, full-bearded man in the front row.

'Shipping,' the man declared bluntly as he got to his feet. 'Our fleet's up to about two-thirds of what we'll need, though it's as ragtag a navy as you'll ever set eyes on.' There was some laughter at that. 'We could use more ships, naturally, any class; and we're especially short on experienced seamen to handle them.' He sat down.

'We're doing what we can about that,' Karr assured him. 'We've increased the parties we have out buying and stealing vessels, and we're looking into the possibility of building our own. They only have to be capable of the one crossing, so that shouldn't prove too difficult. Now . . .' He looked around. 'You.'

A thin, bald, middle-aged individual stood up. 'Transport, including supply of horses, mules, oxen and other working animals. We're fortunate in having a renewable resource, and we've already got a number of breeding herds ready to go. A good stockpile of wagons, too.'

He sat, and a mature woman near the front got up. 'Food and water,' she announced. 'We're renewable too, of course, and as far as drinking water goes we know the island is well provided with springs and wells. We've got good stocks of most dried foodstuffs, but I am a bit worried about a possible food gap.' She half turned to explain to the audience. 'That's the period of time that might exist between the food we take running out and the first harvest. I think my colleague in charge of agriculture may have something to say about that.' She nodded to another woman, who took the floor.

'I'm fairly confident about the prospects for farming. The island's central plains are fertile; the soil's good and well drained, though naturally there's no accounting for un-expectedly bad weather. There are some gaps in our seed stores, and I'd be pleased to hear from anybody who could assist with that. And I could do with more people to help with the crops and animal husbandry, not to mention experienced fishermen.'

Karr picked another speaker.

'Gives you some idea of the scale of the thing, doesn't it?' Kutch remarked in a hushed tone.

Caldason nodded.

It was the turn of a short, muscular man with mousy, shoulder-length hair. 'Armourer,' he explained. 'I also speak for fletchers, sword-wrights and the weapon-making broth-erhood generally. We have substantial arsenals secreted. Blades are ample, as are bows, arrows, spears and axes. Shields, chainmail and helms we could use more of. That's down to a shortage of suitable materials rather than skilled labour.'

'Buildings and island fortifications,' the next man stated. 'We have a materials problem too. Wood is plentiful but it won't last long once we get started. There's some stone out there we can quarry, and we can adapt the existing buildings, but we'll have to consider importing it. The workforce isn't too big a headache because a lot of the requirement's for menial labour. And I'd guess that if nothing else they'll be plenty of people about.'

'You should be able to count on it,' Karr agreed, 'gods willing. Quinn, what about you?'

Disgleirio rose. 'The Fellowship of the Righteous Blade is handling island defences, martial training and general security. We're meeting our targets on all those. But let me remind you that we'll be forming a people's militia as soon as the island's secure. That's anybody who can lift a weapon, basically, and it'll be Blade members who instruct them. Beyond that, we'll be building a standing army as fast as we can. So spread the word that we're willing to consider fit, motivated men and women.'

He was replaced by a chubby, weather-beaten man with black hair and a goatee. 'I speak for artisans. That includes blacksmiths, wheelwrights, carpenters, glass-blowers, potters and the rest. Our trades are well represented in the Resistance ranks. Like others who have spoken before, the problems we see are the supply of materials to work with, and fuel for our stoves, braziers and furnaces.'

Phoenix talked of magical provisions and the part Covenant would play. Goyter, in charge of logistics, appealed for more clerks, and scholars with a head for numbers. And there were others, covering every imaginable aspect of state-building from scratch. They related their achievements and shortcomings, their needs and difficulties.

At last, everyone had spoken, and Karr took charge again.

'Many of you are wondering when the move will happen. Of necessity, we have to keep that flexible. All I can say is that the most favourable time will be chosen, and that you'll be given as much advance warning as possible. We already have people on Batariss, smoothing the way. So, in a sense, the exodus has already begun.' He paused and looked them over. 'Now that I've given up the political forum to devote myself unstintingly to the cause –' there was clapping and a few shouted compliments '– I'll be working as hard as I can to bring nearer the day of our departure.'

Serrah and Reeth exchanged apprehensive glances amid the applause.

'To less happy matters,' Karr went on, stilling it. 'Many of you will have heard that a great supporter of our struggle, and a man I count as a dear personal friend, Kinsel Rukanis, has been arrested. We don't know what charges, if any, will be brought. I'm sure that your thoughts and prayers will go out to him and his loved ones. Kinsel is a man of honour, who would never dream of telling what he knows about our activities. But . . . realistically, he's being held by determined and unscrupulous enemies well versed in cruelty. We must assume the worst and act accordingly. Before you leave here tonight you'll be told of certain safe houses to be avoided, contacts it would be best not to approach, and any other information concerning Kinsel's knowledge of us you'll need to know about. I'm sorry to end on a sad note. Now, please, take this chance to mingle, talk and exchange ideas.'

As everyone began to mill about, Serrah and Reeth approached Disgleirio.

'Any word on Kinsel?' Serrah asked.

'Nothing. And not for want of trying. I've got more ears to the ground than . . . well, than I can usually spare. But they've got him sealed up too tightly. How's Tanalvah?'

'About as you'd expect. She's with some good people at the moment, and well guarded. I'll go there myself after this.'

'What do you think his chances are?' Caldason said.

'Of what?' Disgleirio replied. 'A quick death? A long prison sentence? I don't mean to be facetious, but there are a limited number of options in a situation like this.'

Serrah looked unhappy about that. 'We can't just give up on him.'

'Nobody's suggesting that. It's a question of what's possible.'

'Lots of things are possible given the will,' Caldason told him.

Phoenix came by at that moment and Disgleirio collared him.

'Tell these two what you told me earlier.'

'What was that?' Realisation dawned. 'Oh, *that*. It's not the sort of thing I like making a fuss about, Quinn.'

'What is it?' Serrah asked, curiosity whetted.

The sorcerer didn't answer, so Disgleirio did. 'Phoenix here is shortly to celebrate his hundredth birthday. That makes you and him contemporaries, doesn't it, Reeth?'

The Qalochian regarded him stony-faced.

'Er . . . Congratulations, Phoenix,' Serrah said, hoping to move things along.

'Thank you. Now if you'll excuse me, I have many people to talk with.' He moved off.

'I believe he was *embarrassed*,' Disgleirio reckoned. 'That must be a first for the old boy. But I have to say, Reeth, that you're wearing a lot better than he is.'

It was probably intended as friendly mockery, but from the look on Caldason's face, Serrah wasn't sure he saw it that way.

She need not have worried. The guards had let in a messenger, and he made straight for the Righteous Blade man. They had a whispered conversation before Disgleirio dismissed him.

'Well, we have some news,' he told Serrah and Reeth. 'It seems somebody very important just arrived from Gath Tampoor.'

'Who?' Serrah asked.

'We don't know yet. But it warranted a fast chartered ship and a very heavy escort to paladin HQ.'

'You're assuming this has something to do with Kinsel?'

'It's a fair assumption. Some top official arriving so soon after such a high-profile arrest; it's hardly likely to be a co-incidence, is it? And we've heard nothing about an official visit being due.'

'Any hunches?' Caldason wondered.

'Only nagging worries.'

'Such as?'

'Suppose they've brought in a really skilled interrogator, or a master torturer?'

'I would have thought they had enough perfectly able ones here already.'

'Know what I think? I think Karr's underestimating the damage Rukanis could do. He knows quite a bit about our operation and if . . . *when* he talks, he could take us all down. We should do everything we can to prevent that.'

'What are you saying, Disgleirio?'

'He's been an asset. Now fate, or betrayal, has turned him into a liability. I don't want to sound hard-hearted about it, but if we can't rescue Rukanis . . .'

'Go on.'

'I'd recommend assassinating him.'

15

It was a matter of pride to the paladin clans that no prisoner had ever escaped from their Valdarr headquarters. Not that there had never been attempts at both break-outs and break-ins. But all had ended in failure and the deaths of everyone involved.

Important captives weren't held in ill-lit dungeons deep in the bowels of the central fortress, as might be expected. They were hidden in plain sight. There was an extensive clearing in the grounds, an area in which not a tree, a rock or even a single blade of grass had been left standing. Its perimeter was guarded day and night by sentries with kill dogs on slip-leashes. The second line of defence was deadlier still: a range of protective spells of the highest order. Glamours that would raise ear-splitting alarms as they injured, mutilated and killed at any hint of an unauthorised approach.

In the middle of the clearing was a building. It was a windowless, single-storey structure built of stone, with a flat roof and one robust door. No attempt had been made to beautify the exterior, which was uniformly weathered grey.

Inside, there were just six chambers. Four were cells. The

other two housed what were euphemistically referred to as persuasion suites.

Currently, the building had only one occupant.

Kinsel Rukanis had been deprived of food, water and, crucially, sleep. He had been interrogated with little respite, and some violence had been shown to him, though it was more rough handling than actual abuse. Most of his captors' questions were about who he knew in the Resistance, and its organisation. So far, he'd refused to answer any of them.

For the last couple of hours he'd sat uncomfortably on a hard wooden chair, his wrists bound, facing an increasingly agitated Devlor Bastorran.

'You do know that this attitude isn't helping your case, don't you?' the paladin said.

'I'm doing my best to answer your questions.'

'You've failed to answer a single one of them!'

'I can only address questions on things I have knowledge of. If you will persist in asking about matters beyond my –'

'Oh, come on, Rukanis! We both know you're up to your neck in terrorist activities.'

'I resent that accusation,' he came back heatedly. 'Terrorism's something I would never –'

'We have evidence, and witnesses.'

'Then produce them. Charge me and take me to trial. As an empire citizen I have that right.'

'Under the new emergency powers the rights citizens shall be accorded are at the discretion of legally designated law enforcers,' Bastorran chanted.

'How am I expected to prove my innocence under such conditions?'

'As far as we're concerned, the question of your innocence or guilt is already settled.'

'If that's the case, why should I co-operate?'

'Because things will go easier on you if you do.'

'Show me a law I've broken. Cite me one example of –'

'This isn't so much about anything you've done. It's your friends in the so-called Resistance whose activities interest us. Tell us about that and you'll find us much more accommodating. But carry on obstructing us . . .' He left the threat hanging.

'I'm afraid I can't help you.'

'Afraid? You don't know the meaning of –'

There was a light tap on the open cell door. Visibly irritated, Bastorran swung round to see his aide, Lahon Meakin, hovering there. 'Yes? What is it?'

'Your pardon, sir, but you asked me to let you know when our visitor was ready to see the prisoner.'

'Ah, yes.' He turned back to Rukanis. 'One moment.'

He left the room with his aide, slamming the door behind them.

Kinsel sagged in his chair. He didn't know how much more of this he could take, and there were ominous signs that they hadn't even started to flex their muscles yet. And now somebody else seemed to be involved, though he was damned if he could think who.

The door opened again, breaking his chain of thought.

Devlor Bastorran came back in, accompanied by an almost skeletally thin man, probably in his sixties. He was totally bald and clean-shaven, with lips that were a colourless slash, and sharp, intensely blue eyes. His expensive clothes had a discreet quality often associated with the rich and powerful. The man seemed vaguely familiar to Kinsel, but he had no recollection of ever meeting him.

'You have a caller,' Bastorran announced as though ushering in a guest at a social event. 'This is Commissioner Laffon, of the Council for Internal Security.'

Kinsel didn't know what to say. This was a very important man; the head of the CIS himself. And if everything he'd heard about him was true, a man whose reputation wasn't entirely without blemish.

'Thank you, General, that will be all,' Laffon told Bastorran.

The paladin looked offended at being dismissed as though he were a mere lackey. 'You may want someone to stay with you and the prisoner,' he suggested.

'I'm sure that won't be necessary.'

Bastorran nodded curtly and left, leaving the door half open. Laffon pushed it until it was just ajar. Then he grinned widely at Kinsel and moved forward to grasp his bound hands. 'I am *so* pleased to meet you.'

Kinsel was taken aback. 'You are?'

'Oh, yes. I'm a great admirer of your singing talents. I've seen you perform several times back in Merakasa.' He sat on the seat Bastorran had recently vacated. 'So, how are you?' he asked.

It seemed such an absurd question the singer wasn't sure how to respond. 'Um. Well . . .'

'Aggrieved, no doubt. Angry and vexed at finding your-self dealt with in this way. That's very understandable. We must clear up this awful mistake.'

'Mistake?'

'Yes, of course. That's what it is, isn't it? I mean, a respectable man like yourself, a man of your stature, would hardly associate with unsavoury elements.'

'I can say in all truth, Commissioner, that I don't mix with anyone unsavoury.'

'Quite so. I was sure this must all be a terrible misunder-standing. Not least because of your well-known support of pacifism.'

'I've never made a secret of the fact that I believe in non-violence.'

'And I admire you for that, I really do. I wish I had your moral fibre. The thing is . . . Well, not everyone feels the way you do. It's very regrettable, but it's the world we live in.'

'I'm aware of that. What's it to do with me?'

'The accusations against you centre mostly on the company you're said to keep. You say you're above reproach in this regard, and of course I completely accept that. But given the large number of people a man like yourself must meet, isn't it possible that certain of them might have taken advantage of your . . . shall we say innocence?'

'*No.* I mean . . . how could they?'

'Don't underestimate your own importance. You've had access to echelons of society most people are excluded from. Wouldn't you concede the possibility that you might have dropped the occasional indiscreet word about what you'd seen and heard? Or have you never been tempted, perhaps, to carry out a small task for friendly acquaintances?'

'I'm a singer, not a politician or a street fighter. And certainly not an odd job man or message carrier.'

'Ah. Messages.'

'I beg your pardon?'

'You just said message carrier. I didn't mention it, you did. I wonder why.'

'Well, from what you were saying, it just seemed natural to assume . . .'

'You see? That's how easy it is.'

'What do you mean? What's easy?'

'Forgetting little things in a busy life. I asked if you'd ever undertaken any chores, and you mention carrying messages.'

'No, that's not what I meant. You make it sound as though I've done something to be ashamed of, and I haven't.'

'Then nothing's lost by you passing on some names,' Laffon returned triumphantly.

'You're twisting my words, making me out to be some kind of criminal.'

The Commissioner looked appalled. 'I wouldn't dream of

suggesting such a thing. I'm sure you've never done anything to endanger the security of the state . . . intentionally.'

'What does that mean?'

'We can never be entirely certain what the intentions of others might be. When it comes to state security, that's a job for the professionals. All you have to do is supply a list of names –'

'Why should I be part of subjecting other people to this sort of treatment?'

'So there are other people, then?'

'I was speaking hypothetically.'

'Do these hypothetical people have real names?'

'I can't help you, Commissioner.'

'You might think that certain people you know are innocent, and perhaps they are, but that needs to be properly investigated.'

'Any names I gave you would be purely as the result of pressure. There really wouldn't be anyone deserving of your attention.'

'Let us be the judge of that.'

'I want an advocate present before I say anything else.'

'That isn't possible.' Laffon sighed. 'Look, Rukanis, there are hard, violent men in this world.'

'That's rather a statement of the obvious, isn't it, Commissioner?'

'What may not be so obvious to you is that many of them are paladins, and it's the paladins who are holding you at the moment. There's a limit to the influence I might have in this case.'

'My understanding is that the clans are soldiers of fortune in the empire's employ. You have authority over them.'

'Ultimately, yes. But what with the officialdom that bedevils us these days, and the fact that this is a protectorate and not Gath Tampoor itself . . . well, it could take some time to establish who has supremacy. While it was being sorted out, you'd remain in their custody. Whereas, if you co-operate fully with me now, I might be able to get you transferred to the custody of the CIS. I'm sure you'd find my department much more reasonable in these matters.'

'You'll forgive me for doubting that.'

Exasperation showed on Laffon's features. 'You're failing to appreciate how grave your situation is, Rukanis. You don't know how much we've learnt about your activities.'

'I thought you said it must all be a mistake.'

'You don't understand, do you? This isn't a question of your innocence or guilt, or whether you've been naive. It's about doing what we tell you.'

'In all conscience, I can't.'

'Few of us can afford the luxury of a conscience in these troubled times. Speak, man. Tell what you know and avoid any . . . unpleasantness.'

'I've already said –'

'Very well,' Laffon replied stiffly as he rose from the chair. 'I wash my hands of you.'

He went to the cell door and hammered on it twice with his fist. The door was opened.

Outside stood a tall, muscular man wearing the traditional black garb and mask of the torturer's trade.

Tanalvah shuddered.

'What's the matter?' Serrah said.

'A chill ran up my spine.'

'Well, it is getting colder.'

'It wasn't that.'

They were sitting side by side on a horse blanket, bundled against the crisp air, on the crest of a hill.

'You're not in this alone, Tan; I do wish you'd understand that. We're all here to support you.'

'I know you are, and I'm grateful. But we can't say the same about Kinsel, can we? I keep thinking of him, there alone, suffering who knows what kind of . . .' She couldn't go on.

Serrah tried to take her mind off it. 'At least you have the children, and they're safe.' She nodded to where Teg and Lirrin romped with Kutch. Caldason stood a little further away, looking down at the city. It was coming to dusk, and the metropolis had begun to glow with magical energy. They would have to head back soon.

'You're right,' Tanalvah conceded, 'and I'm being selfish.'

'How?'

'I have the children. They're mine now, and I love them as though they were my own. But you lost your only child, and you have no one. Forgive me being blunt. I hope bringing it up doesn't grieve you too much.'

Serrah shook her head.

'I only mention it,' Tanalvah went on, 'because you're one of the few people who can understand how I feel. Tell me, were you haunted by how things might have turned out if you'd acted differently? Did you reproach yourself?'

'Of course. Endlessly. I should think everyone does in that situation.'

'Then you know how I feel. There were things I did wrong, and things I shouldn't have done, and now Kinsel's paying for it.'

'The last thing you need is to blame yourself.'

'You don't know.'

'Tell me,' Serrah gently coaxed.

'I can't.'

Serrah had thought her friend was on the verge of opening up, but she didn't try to push her. 'All right. I'll be around if you ever want to talk about it. But, Tan, what you mustn't do is add guilt to your burden. Believe me, I know.'

Tanalvah nodded, but looked far from convinced.

Two small whirlwinds arrived, in the form of a pair of excited children. They wanted Tanalvah to join them, and pulled at her hands until she stood and went with them to Kutch.

Serrah watched them for a while, then Caldason strolled back and sat down beside her.

'Look at them,' she said. 'I wish I could be like a child and block out the lousy things in life. How do they do it?'

'I don't know; it was never like that for me. But it's a good thing they can. How is Tanalvah?'

'Isn't it obvious?'

'It's hard to form an opinion when she avoids talking to me.'

'Don't blame her for that. She's just about hanging on, I'd say. And now she's letting guilt get to her.'

'What does she have to feel guilty about?'

'Nothing, I'm sure. But she thinks she does.'

'You didn't tell her what Disgleirio said about wanting Kinsel killed?'

'Of course not! What do you take me for?'

'Sorry, I should have known you wouldn't.'

'It got me thinking about him though. Disgleirio, I mean. I find it hard to fathom the man. You think you know where he stands, then he comes out with something like that.'

'Perhaps it's not so surprising. The Fellowship of the Righteous Blade are zealots, in a way. They're focused on their goal and tend to see anything in their path as some-thing to be swept aside, no matter how ruthlessly.'

'And that makes them unique, does it? I can think of at least one other person with a similar outlook.'

He had to smile. 'I just stabbed myself in the foot, didn't I?'

She smiled back. 'Don't worry about it. It's one of my specialities, too.'

'The Blade's a patriotic group. I reckon having to accept they're not going to get their country back would be a bitter potion for a man like Quinn. Signing up for Karr's dream of a new state must seem like second best.'

'They're monarchists, aren't they?'

'I imagine so. They've sworn allegiance to all the old institutions, so that must include the Crown.'

'Doesn't that make them Melyobar supporters?'

'I suppose it does, in theory. You can see why they gave up on it and threw in their lot with Karr.'

That made them smile again.

She sobered. 'He's not looking any better, is he?'

'Karr? No. He's clearly exhausted, but there's something else underneath it. An ailment.'

'There's a way you could lift some of the weight off his shoulders, you know.'

'Let me guess. Delivering the gold?'

'It does make sense, Reeth.'

'He didn't put you up to this, did he? Or any of the others?'

'You know me better than that. I just happen to think it's the right thing. Earlier on, I got talking to Tan about the move, and she said it had to go ahead, that it's what Kinsel would have wanted. He's given up everything for the cause, including his life, probably. It seems to me we should be willing to take the same risk.'

'As a matter of fact, I've been thinking along similar lines.'

'Whoa, that was too easy! I thought you'd need battering into it.'

'No, I really have been thinking about it as something I could do. Though I'd much prefer it to be an expedition to the Clepsydra.'

'Karr says delivering the gold brings us a step nearer to that. I believe him. The Resistance, and Covenant in particular, seem no less keen to find the Source.'

'If I do go to the Diamond Isle, I'd like to have you along.'

'No, I don't think –'

'Hear me out. You're getting better, more stable, stronger in yourself. You're not entirely right yet –'

'Oh, don't stint your words, please.'

'But you were an asset to the band, and you could be again. I think we worked well together.'

'Thanks. So do I. But I'm not sure the Council would sanction it. Besides, after what's happened to Tan, I think I ought to be here.'

'She'll have plenty of people to look after her.'

'Reeth . . .' She looked over at Tanalvah to make sure she was out of earshot. '. . . I'm going to break a confidence. Tanalvah's with child.'

'Oh. Kinsel's?'

'Of course it is!' She adopted an expression of mock disgust. '*Men*. So you see, if anything happened to him and I wasn't here for her –'

'I understand.'

'Don't tell anybody. I promised.'

'But would you reconsider coming if Kinsel got out of the mess he's in?'

'If he were to do that . . . yes, perhaps I would. But let's face it, Reeth. That would take a miracle, wouldn't it?'

16

The citizens of Jecellam, capital of Rintarah's extensive empire, lived ordered lives. Theirs was a culture where many everyday activities were centrally directed. Most people were reasonably happy with this, unless they found themselves in conflict with the state's will. Which was more easily done than the majority of them suspected.

As a result of being part of a rigidly controlled society, the average citizen expected to be housed, fed and protected by the state. They didn't expect more than a nominal voice in how that state was run. They expected to be left to their own devices in the matter of accumulating wealth, property and magic, as long as they didn't exceed the very strict limits imposed. They certainly never expected to have any contact with, or even a glimpse of, the elite that ran everything.

In the unlikely event of an ordinary person being allowed access to their rulers' high-walled domain, they would encounter many things that seemed wondrous, even for a world drenched in enchantment.

One of the more modest spectacles was an impossible garden. It was unfeasible in two respects. First, it contained a profusion of flowers that simply shouldn't have been blooming at

such an intemperate time of year. Second, there were plants
– exotic, beautiful, bizarre – unknown to the most know-
ledgeable of horticulturists. Another peculiarity of this acre of
abundance was that it occupied a perfectly defined circular
plot. Outside an apparently invisible line, everything was
dormant or withered, as would be expected in this season. It
was as though a totally transparent dome encased the entire
growing area, and different weather conditions prevailed inside.

The garden was being tended by a tall, gangling old man.
He had faultless skin and a copious head of hair, but both
looked markedly unnatural. On his knees, trowel in hand,
he appeared in his element. But woe betide anyone who
mistook him for a menial. Despite his humble gardening
clothes and the soil under his fingernails, he was by far the
most powerful man in Rintarah.

He was Elder Felderth Jacinth, head of the empire's ruling
Central Council.

Not far from his garden stood one of the many flagpoles
scattered about the grounds. The ensign it bore showed
Rintarah's emblem: an eagle with spread wings, framed by
lightning bolts. An approaching figure glanced at the flag as
he walked the path that wound to the improbable garden.

When he stepped through the imperceptible barrier he was
met by a wave of warmth and exquisite perfume.

'Good day, brother.'

Jacinth looked up. 'Rhylan. It's not often I see you here.'

'I thought you might have been at the strategy meeting.'

The ruler climbed to his feet and patted the dirt from his
hands. 'They function just as well without me at these routine
gatherings,' he told his younger sibling. 'I preferred to spend
time here.'

'I've never understood the attraction this holds for you,
Felderth. It's not as though you use the Craft to raise these
plants. You don't even get servants to do the work.'

'It's important that I do it myself. It gives me a chance to think.'

'And to partially quench your thirst for true creation? Given that's largely a memory for us now.'

'Or a dream of what's to come again.'

'Indeed.'

'Another thing about being here, working with the soil, is that I gain some empathy with the common people.'

'Why ever would you want to do that?' his brother wondered.

'Because they've gone wrong somewhere. Or we have. The masses don't have the deference they used to. Some of them even dare to take up arms against us.'

'Then we must meet such insolence as we always have, with force.'

'We bear down on them ever harder, and make punishments more severe, and it only seems to inflame them. We know Gath Tampoor is doing the same, with no better results.'

'Think how much worse it might be if we didn't. Society hasn't collapsed. We don't have anarchy.'

'I find myself more in sympathy with those who think it might be best to simply eradicate the masses that serve us and start afresh. As Nature dampens down life to make ready for a new season.'

Rhylan looked to the summer garden. 'Unlike you. You've suspended the seasons here.'

'Which is exactly what we should have done with those we rule.'

'How do you mean, brother?'

'Our interests would have been best served by keeping them tightly yoked. Instead we've allowed them to develop greater and greater leeway. So much so that they now presume to challenge us.'

'They don't have an inexhaustible supply of lives to throw
away in their cause. We will endure.'

'But that isn't all, is it? We've rarely had so many impon-
derables facing us at the same time. Not only are increasing
numbers resisting our rule, there's also this business of the
northern warlord and his expansion. We've had no word
from the expedition we sent. Doesn't that concern you?'

'You've changed your tune on all this. Not long since you
were practically dismissing such problems as insignificant.'

'I'm beginning to think that perhaps I was wrong. I edge
towards the doubters' camp, Rhylan.'

'I still think Gath Tampoor is more culprit than victim as
far as the disorder's concerned, as you used to. And it wouldn't
surprise me to find that they were behind Zerreiss in some
way, too. It's the old, old story, brother; the struggle between
the empires carries on, it just takes different guises.'

'That's enough of a worry in itself.'

'Don't underestimate the strength we can bring to bear
against them. Rintarah is no sickly weakling. Our might is
incomparable.'

'Yet in respect of the insurgents in our midst, we're like a
bear that's trodden on an ants' nest. For all our might we
haven't rooted them out.'

'We will. You forget who we are. What we are.'

'You make no mention of the most worrying development;
the disturbance to the matrix. There was a particularly severe
episode just in the last few days, as you know.'

'Again, why shouldn't this be Gath Tampoor's doing?'

'Because *we* can't do it. It's beyond the powers we now
have, and we've no reason to think they're any more
advanced.'

'What, then?'

'There are two possibilities, both of which I find troubling.
One is that some unknown, unsuspected power is respon-

sible for interfering with the magic's flow. In some ways that might be the worse option, as it implies something we didn't anticipate.'

'And the other possibility?'

'I fear that Caldason might have become aware of his capabilities.'

'Now we get to it. That damnable situation has been a thorn to us for far too long. But why should he have woken to himself now and not before?'

'Who knows? That may not be as important as recognising that he *has*.'

'He can't have entirely realised his potential, or we'd certainly know it.'

'Perhaps not, but he could be progressing by degrees. As a man might learn some new skill.'

'With respect, Felderth, what I see are several unrelated events. Thugs making trouble on the streets, as ever was; a barbarian warlord, latest in a long line of ten-day wonders; and an anomaly in the matrix, which in itself isn't entirely without precedent. None of it necessarily adds up to a threat to us. I repeat: remember who we are.'

'Take this,' his brother said, plucking a red rose from its stem, 'and see in it the fate of our rule if you're wrong.'

Rhylan took the flower and breathed deep of its gorgeous aroma.

But the instant he stepped outside the barrier the rose turned black and crumbled to dust.

The constant glow of magic that emanated from any heavily populated area usually outshone the night sky. But this evening the luminescence was less bright than normal, perhaps because the colder weather meant fewer people on the streets. And the rooftop of the safe house where Caldason and Serrah sat was on the edge of Valdarr, well away from the frenetic centre. Consequently they had a rare view of the stars.

'And how do your people account for them?' Serrah asked.

'The Qaloch tell several stories of how the stars were created.'

'There isn't one accepted version?'

'No. Qalochian religion and myths aren't carved in stone the way they are in most other places. There tend to be various versions of our legends.'

'Which do you like best?'

'About the stars? My favourite's the one about Jahon Alpseer. Ever hear of him?'

She shook her head.

'He's one of the Qaloch god-heroes who presided over the birth of the world. Back then, there weren't any stars, because the gods saw no need to hang other lamps than the Sun and Moon. That was mostly because they were too busy fighting a constant war against an equally powerful race of demon deities. The prize they fought over was the fate of the human race, which is to say the Qalochian race, as it was our story. The demons wanted to exterminate the small number of men and women the gods had made; they feared this new life-form would multiply until it threatened their power.'

'What happened?'

'Well, quite a lot, actually. But the climax of the story tells how Jahon faced the lord of all the demons, Pavall, in a duel they fought across the sky. Jahon was getting the worst of it, because Pavall was a night demon who could conceal himself in shadow and strike out of the darkness. So Jahon used his sword, which was made of ice incidentally, to pierce holes in the black veil that shrouded the world. The holes let in the great light from outside, exposing Pavall, and Jahon slew him. Jahon left the holes so that no other demons would ever be able to hide in darkness.'

'It's a charming story. A bit . . . martial.'

'Yes, it's typically Qalochian. These days, at those rare times when Qalochians meet, it tends to be told ironically.'

'How do you mean?'

'Well, the way things have worked out, we say that Pavall must have won after all.'

'Oh. Gallows humour.'

'Don't knock it. What is it they say? Better to laugh lest you cry.'

'That isn't restricted to Qalochians, Reeth. Though there's been precious little to laugh about lately. But let's not get into the whole Kinsel thing again. Thinking about it's too depressing.'

'You looked a bit downcast when we came away from the hill. Was it something Tanalvah said?'

'Yes, but it wasn't about Kinsel. She mentioned Eithne.'

'I thought that was a subject you didn't like talking about.'

'There are times when it's a taboo with me,' she admitted. 'But they tend to be triggered by something I wasn't expecting, like when I was in the temple. Generally I can live with it, though I can never make promises about the future. I was doing a pretty good job of not thinking about Eithne until Tan brought it up.'

'There is one thing I'll confess to being curious about,' he ventured carefully. 'It's not really about your daughter, but —'

'Spit it out. If it's too close to the heart I'll tell you.'

'Eithne's father.'

'Ah. A flesh wound rather than a direct hit.'

'You can tell me to mind my own business.'

'It's all right. There's not much to say about him, actually. He was like me. Well, he was in some ways; mostly he wasn't. I mean we were alike in being professional fighters. Only with him it was the army. He was really ambitious and rose fast. Fought in a number of campaigns and gave a good account of himself. Then the fool went and got himself knifed in a brawl in a tavern. No, it didn't kill him. He ran off with the healer who nursed him through it. She was older than me, too, a bit. Eithne was five or six when it happened. He didn't want to be tied down with a child, you see. At least, that's what he said.'

'I'm sorry.'

'No need. I was too young, and we wanted different things. It didn't take me long to realise I was better off without him. Though I've often wondered whether it would have gone better for Eithne if she'd had a father around.'

'Maybe I shouldn't have got you talking about this. It must be painful.'

'No, not at all. Talking can help, in fact. That's something I've taken a long time to understand.' She brightened. 'Let's make a pact. From now on, either of us can ask the other about anything. And if it's something we don't want to talk about, we just say. That way we can stop tip-toeing.'

'All right.'

'Good. Now, about the gold consignment.'

'I walked into that, didn't I?'

'It's the best service you can give to the Resistance right now, Reeth. Besides, it occurs to me you might be better off out of Bhealfa for a while.'

'Why?'

'Don't look at me like that. I know you can take care of yourself, but a couple of things have been bothering me. First, do you remember finding your file when we torched the records office? With all the pages torn out? I've seen how bureaucracies work, when I was with the CIS, and I'm telling you that kind of thing doesn't happen without authority. Somebody very powerful has an interest in you, and they didn't want anybody seeing the contents of that file, least of all you.'

'I have to admit that has been puzzling me. What else?'

'The meld. She might or might not be connected to it, but if there's even a slim chance she is, it starts looking as though you're attracting some unhealthy attention.'

'It wouldn't be the first time. I'm officially an outlaw, you know; I'd expect there to be records on me.'

'I bet if we'd gone through every file in that place, yours would have been the only damaged one. It *means* something, Reeth. Though I'm damned if I can think what.'

'I don't know that it adds up to a need for me to leave the country.' He held up his hands. 'All right, all right. It's true I'll probably go anyway –'

'Great!'

'– but I'm not a man to run, Serrah. Not for anything.'

'I know *that*. It's one of your more endearing qualities.'

'Thanks.'

'Don't get smug about it. You have less endearing ones, too.'

They smiled at each other.

A trapdoor in the roof lifted and a head appeared.

'Quinn?' she said.

Disgleirio climbed out. 'There's news.'

'About Kinsel?'

He nodded. 'They're going to put him on trial, and soon.'

'That's something, I suppose,' Caldason argued.

'Not really. He's to be allowed no defence witnesses and no one to speak for his character, and the whole thing's going to be in private with a single judge presiding.'

'A show trial,' Serrah murmured. 'A veneer of justice with the verdict decided before they start.'

Disgleirio shrugged. 'What else did you expect? There's another piece of news, and I think it should interest you especially, Serrah.'

'Tell me.'

'We know who the VIP from Gath Tampoor is. It's your old boss at the CIS. Commissioner Laffon himself.'

The blood drained out of her face and it took a moment for her to say anything. Then she whispered, 'I think any chance Kinsel might have had just died.'

17

'We're not likely to find out anything by hiding here.'

'Give it a chance, Reeth, it's been barely an hour.'

'I don't know what you expect to achieve. The Resistance have plenty of people watching the place already.'

'Like I said, when I heard Laffon was here I just had to do something.'

'You don't believe he'd walk out of there unaccompanied, do you?'

'If he did he'd be dead before he got ten paces,' Serrah vowed.

'All right, we'll stay a little longer. But I don't know how safe this place is. Paladins are bastards but they're not stupid; they're bound to check buildings this close to their HQ. Disgleirio's men have already had a couple of narrow squeaks.'

'If it looks like getting awkward we'll be out of here. Promise. Now keep your eyes open.'

The empty house they'd broken into was opposite the immense walls of the paladin's bastion, and almost faced its main gates. Serrah and Reeth had arrived not long after dawn, and now the streets were starting to fill with people.

'What *do* you think's going to happen, Serrah?'

'Nothing, probably. But don't you ever feel you have to act rather than sit around waiting? Look, you go. I'll stay here a while and –'

'No, you're right. We might as well be here as anywhere else. But don't build your hopes up.'

Another hour passed. There were comings and goings across the road but they all seemed routine. Then a closed coach was let out.

'For all we know, that could be him,' Reeth said, 'and we can hardly go over and demand to look inside.'

'Yes, I suppose so,' Serrah sighed. 'I guess this was a stupid idea after all. But I –' Something caught her attention.

'What is it?'

'Over there. The small gate next to the main ones. See what I see?'

He peered through the gap in the dusty window drapes. 'It's her, isn't it?'

'You could hardly make a mistake about it; she's pretty distinctive.'

A striking figure was leaving the grounds. She was athletically built and pale as snow, and her fair hair was cropped.

'Interesting that she should be coming out of there, isn't it?' Reeth said. 'Let's get after her.'

'Wait.' Serrah dug in her pocket and brought out two die-sized orange cubes. 'Face charms.'

'Oh, no. *Must* I?'

'Yes. The meld knows what you look like, and she got a look at me, too. She'd spot us in a minute without a disguise.'

'I hate these things.'

'I'm not crazy about them myself.'

He took the cube marked with an M, leaving the one with an F on her palm. 'These are really expensive. Where did you get them?'

'I couldn't get the real thing. They're counterfeits. So they won't be as reliable as a genuine spell. Won't last anything like as long either, so bear that in mind.'

'Great.'

'Hurry up! She'll be gone soon.'

He crushed the cube in his fist, then opened his hand. The pile of sandy dust flew from his palm and straight to his face, like a swarm of tiny airborne bugs. It settled as a fine, even coating, covering everything except his eyes and mouth, and instantly began creating the illusion. Serrah did the same, and in seconds their appearances were transformed.

'Brunette suits you,' he told her, 'though I'm not so sure about the green eyes.'

'Right. Now let's –'

'How do I look?'

She let out an exasperated breath. 'Your Qalochian features have softened quite a bit. The blond hair looks all right, I suppose, but I don't think much of the beard.'

Automatically, his hand went to his chin, but of course it felt just as smooth as always.

'Can we *go* now?' she insisted.

By the time they'd slipped out of the house the meld was halfway down the road. They followed at a safe distance, trying to look casual. Which wasn't easy for Caldason, who felt self-conscious about the face charm. But nobody seemed to take any notice of them.

The meld turned into some of the centre's busiest streets. Crowds made it easier for Reeth and Serrah to stay concealed, but increased the chances of losing her. They started to close the gap.

'This damn thing's beginning to itch,' Reeth complained, fighting back the temptation to scratch his face.

'So does mine. Try to ignore it.'

They were led up one steep lane and down another, then across a square. A block later they were in a busy street market.

'Do you think she's actually going somewhere or just wandering?' Reeth said.

'She seems to be walking with a purpose. Let's get a bit nearer.' She upped her pace.

The market sold everything. There were stalls with vegetables, fruit, cheese, meat, fish, bread and wine. Others were stacked with clothing, boots, saddles, chainmail, pottery, woven baskets, lucky charms and cheap glamours. Live lobsters were on sale, along with rabbits, cockerels, goats, kittens and venomous snakes. Healers held kerbside surgeries; soothsayers read fortunes from cards; people had their hair cut. Musicians strolled, plucking strings or blowing horns; jugglers flung their clubs; street jesters performed. Livestock bleated and everybody haggled.

Inevitably, there were glamours too. Creatures repulsive and comely materialised in flashes or expired in flaming shards every few minutes. Large and small blasts of magical radiance pulsed out on all sides. The din was fierce, and the air was scented with a thousand smells, pleasant and otherwise.

With the market growing busier, and the prospect of their quarry disappearing from sight, Reeth and Serrah had to follow at close quarters. They were almost near enough to reach out and touch the meld's shoulder, should they be sufficiently foolish to do so.

'The wretched thing's tingling now,' Reeth whispered, jabbing a thumb at his face.

'Mine too. Don't think about it.'

At that instant the meld stopped and turned. Reeth grabbed Serrah's arm and pulled her to one side. Their heads went down and they pretended to be engrossed in a display of cheap jewellery. From the corner of his eye, Reeth was aware of the meld looking their way. A long moment later she resumed walking.

'Think she spotted us?' Serrah asked.

'Don't know. But at least she's not running. Come on.'

They continued to trail her. The meld kept to an easy stride, occasionally glancing at the wares on sale, but mostly concentrating on weaving through the crowd. Emboldened, Serrah and Reeth began closing the gap again.

About six paces separated them from the meld when she stopped again. Once more, she spun around and stared. By this time her pursuers had drifted to the middle of the street, well clear of the stalls on either side. They froze.

'Shit,' Serrah muttered. 'Look disinterested.'

'Any idea *how*?'

The meld took a step towards them, then noticeably started.

'Reeth. *Your face.*'

His features were liquefying. In seconds his eyes reverted to their original colour, the shape of his cheekbones went back to normal, his whiskers fell away.

'Lousy fakes!' Serrah cursed as her own disguise began to fade.

The meld turned on her heel and ran to the right. But as she moved, a near-identical duplicate dashed to the left. The two figures were joined by a membrane, a glistening film resembling a wet spider's web. When they were separated by a couple of yards it ripped apart and the halves were each rapidly sucked back into their bodies.

Now two foes were advancing on Reeth and Serrah, and all four of them went for their blades. The crowd, dense as it was, shrank away.

'Watch that one!' Reeth warned, pointing at Aphrim.

'Watch your own!' she tossed back.

Aphri and Aphrim moved in.

The female came at Reeth fast. Their blades clattered together and the pounding began. Her passes were quick and surgical. He matched her for skill and gave as he got. They bobbed and leapt, whipping the air with steel.

Where Aphri was agile, Aphrim was strong. The first time their blades met, Serrah felt the shock from wrist to shoulder. She withdrew nimbly from his next stroke. As he regrouped she was under his guard and swiping. He blocked, and set her bones shaking again.

With Reeth and Aphri it was keen-edged precision. She engaged him with a series of probing nips, interspersed with wide, unpredictable swings. He ducked. Her blade sailed over his head and sliced a rope supporting a wooden cage of chickens. The cage fell and burst in a turmoil of squawking and feathers.

Reeth battered at the meld, forcing her back. Then he struck her blade a glancing blow. It was no more than a metal kiss, but she'd over-stretched, and lost balance. She staggered, slipped and crashed into a greengrocer's barrow, bringing it down. While she lithely recovered, rolling a yard and springing to her feet in one fluid move, the grocer's stock disgorged. There was an avalanche of apples, cauliflowers and onions. Potatoes, turnips and oranges bounced in all directions. Some of the crowd scrabbled for them, or trod them underfoot. People slipped and fell on the mush as the stall's owner bellowed impotent oaths.

Caldason and the meld squared off again. The crowd was shouting and brewing minor fights of its own. Caldason knew it was a bad place for a brawl. Law enforcers were going to be drawn like flies, and soon.

Serrah and Aphrim had fallen into a slog of hack and slash. He was given to vicious downward swipes, using his sword like an axe, and one nearly cleaved her. Instead his blade ploughed through the wooden support of a stall selling beer. The counter pitched forwards, hurtling half a dozen barrels to the ground. Two smashed instantly in foaming amber explosions. The others rolled into the crowd, bowling one man off his feet and triggering fistfights for the spoils.

Taking the chance to pull back, Serrah tensed for Aphrim's fresh assault. But his next move baffled her. He tossed his sword

aside, as though discarding a broken toy and, staring at her, he
opened his mouth wide. For one crazy second she thought he
was going to poke his tongue out at her. But what shot out of
his mouth was a glittering red orb the size of a grapefruit. It
flew at her, swift as an arrow, leaving a fiery trail in its wake.
At the last moment she dropped and it soared overhead. The
glowing ball smashed into a clothes stall and detonated in a
huge gout of flame. The stall and its stock went up immediately, throwing out a wave of heat and acrid black smoke.

This was too rich for the blood of many in the crowd, and
there was a disorderly retreat. But the press of people was
so great they could only withdraw about twenty feet. The
fire spread from the burning stall to an adjacent sweetmeat
booth. A few hardy souls appeared with buckets of water
and tried to douse it.

Slowly, warily, Serrah advanced towards her opponent.
Aphrim stood in the same position, absolutely still, his face
impassive. She was tensing for a charge when his jaw gaped
and he spat another fireball. This one came lower than the
last, and would have impacted at her waist if she hadn't
swerved. The fireball zipped past on a downward trajectory
and hit the road, shedding sparks, then rocketed on, straight
at the crowd. There was panic. People yelled, screamed and
struggled to get out of the way.

Reeth and Aphri's duel had spilt back into the road. The
flaming globe was set to miss them by several feet as it sailed
towards the mob. Reeth took a chance. Back-footing Aphri
with a rain of blows, he threw himself to one side, swinging
his sword in a high, broad arc. The flat of his blade met the
flying orb like a bat slapping a ball. He acted on instinct; for
all he knew the globe would explode on impact.

But as Reeth came heavily to ground, the orb was deflected
onto a new course. It travelled at a right-angle to the crowd,
speeding in the direction of the houses lining the market.

Nobody moved an inch, not even Aphri, and everyone was transfixed in silence as they tracked its progress.

A small comet towing a vivid crimson tail, the missile headed for the upper storey of a brick and timber warehouse. With a precision it would have been hard to improve on if actually aimed, it flew through the only window with open shutters. There was a second of utter quiet, followed by an echoing blast and an eruption of flame. Smoke spewed from the window. People began blundering out of the street-level door, red-eyed and coughing. Behind them, the interior of the warehouse was blazing.

The spell was broken. Renewed uproar swept the market. Reeth climbed to his feet, but Aphri had gone. He looked round and saw her running. Aphrim had bypassed Serrah and was on the move, too; dashing his twin's way. To Reeth, Aphri looked like someone racing towards a life-sized mirror. The two figures collided, but only one carried on. Bystanders shifted fast to let the meld through.

Serrah jogged over to Reeth. 'Do we go after her?'

'No. Look.'

Militiamen were shoving aside the spectators, and red tunics appeared.

There were those among the onlookers who might have tried to stop Reeth and Serrah from getting away. Whether they stayed their hands through fear, gratitude or greater hatred of the law-enforcers, the crowd parted and let them pass.

Minutes later, they were several blocks away.

'I can't say that exactly added to our sum of knowledge,' Serrah lamented. 'Apart from the fact that those two are dangerous.'

'Actually, we learnt something valuable. We can be pretty sure the meld's connected in some way with the paladins.'

'Like I said, Reeth; it might be a good idea to get out of Bhealfa for a while.'

18

Of all the major cities of the known world, Merakasa, capital of the western empire of Gath Tampoor, was one of the most colourful and vibrant.

Like its eastern counterpart, Rintarah's Jecellam, Merakasa housed a city within a city. This nucleus, or unlanced abscess as some saw it, was the leadership's citadel. It was a self-contained metropolis that provided everything the ruling clan needed to keep them isolated from their subjects. So that with the exception of ceremonial occasions, or affairs of national importance where their fleeting, distant presence was unavoidable, the empire's masters could live in shadow.

But it was necessary now and again for the elite to come into contact with the lesser mortals who served them. This could be to dispense rewards or punishments, or where news concerning their far-flung interests was best heard directly from the mouths of their representatives.

Today it was the turn of Andar Talgorian, Imperial Envoy to the Sovereign State of Bhealfa. Though the term 'sovereign' was misleading.

Whether he had been summoned to Merakasa for reward, punishment or the imparting of news was something

Ambassador Talgorian never entirely knew in advance. Which made his job all the more exciting. Exciting in the sense that a drowning man thrown a lead weight as a life-belt might use the word.

This wasn't the only reason the Envoy always found an audience with the Empress an unnerving experience. She was a disquieting presence. Partly this was due to the power she wielded, and the knowledge that his life was worth no more than a capricious snap of her fingers. Partly, he had to admit, it was her appearance.

He couldn't begin to guess how old Bethmilno XXV was, beyond very old indeed. Like her Rintarahian counterparts, whom Talgorian had never seen, she sought to disguise the ravages of age. So she caked her face in white rouge, and coloured her lips in pigment redder than blood. Her eyelashes, eyebrows and suspiciously full head of hair were all densely blackened. That all this looked so synthetic was due either to the artlessness of her maids or to the fact that her great age was beyond masking.

He sat opposite her in a grand reception room on the palace's ground floor, where one entire wall was occupied by casement windows, affording a panoramic view of the estate. A subterranean power channel ran beneath the chamber. He knew this because the imperial household kept the tradition of marking out these conduits of magic, and a tincture had been used to show its course across the floor. The incongruous gold line, ramrod straight, passed almost exactly through the centre of the apartment. He thought despoiling the room in this way took respect for custom too far.

But the outrage to Talgorian's aesthetic sense was forgotten when, midway through their conversation on security matters, the Empress declared, 'It might well come to war.'

The Envoy was taken aback. 'Excellency?'

Feigning patience, Bethmilno spelt it out. 'With the other side.' She almost always referred to Rintarah as 'the other side'.

'Forgive me being dull-witted, Excellency, but we've been fighting against Rintarah with proxy wars for a very long time.'

'I'm referring to *open* war; a direct confrontation.'

'May I be so bold as to ask what has brought you to consider such an option, ma'am?'

'Impatience, Ambassador. I grow weary of this eternal game of cat and mouse with them.'

'Would not stepping up our present activities be sufficient, Excellency?'

'How?'

'Perhaps by offering more assistance to the insurgents within Rintarah's borders?'

'It may have escaped your attention, Ambassador, that giving money to their terrorists amounts to handing it to our own. Besides, I regard the so-called Resistance as a disorganised rabble, and of doubtful use as a weapon against the other side.' She anticipated his rejoinder, and waved it away. 'I don't say they aren't a problem. But they could never overthrow even the smallest of our protectorates. Essentially they're just an irritant.'

Begging to differ was more than Talgorian dared. So he fell back on diplomacy. 'Quite so, your Highness. Although even an irritant can tie up valuable resources, and on occasion inflict real damage. As we've discovered in Bhealfa.'

'Yes, it does seem a particularly troublesome little island.' She shot him an accusing look that chilled his backbone. 'But I anticipate a lessening of their activities now that I've ordered our law enforcers to bear down more heavily on the insubordinates.'

He wanted to believe that would happen.

'And in that respect,' she went on, 'authorising the Council for Internal Security to operate beyond our shores strengthens our hand immeasurably. I could wish we'd done that long since. Commissioner Laffon himself is in Bhealfa at the moment, as you know, and proving as loyal a servant as ever.'

Talgorian noted her approving tone, and judged it prudent to show his solidarity with someone she favoured. But he kept it low-key. It didn't do to be *too* closely associated with a man who might yet fall. 'A commendably industrious worker, Excellency. The Commissioner has already been instrumental in at least one high-profile arrest.'

'Indeed. And if he succeeds in Bhealfa, as I have no doubt he will, the CIS will have my blessing to extend its operations to all other protectorates.'

Making Laffon even more powerful, Talgorian thought. But his only response was a smile.

'However, we drift from the point,' the Empress continued. 'Some of my advisors –' by which she meant her family '– have expressed concern about the progress of this new northern warlord, Zerreiss. For myself, I have yet to be entirely convinced that he represents any kind of threat to our interests, though one or two factors have given me pause.' She meant the upheavals in the essence, but naturally wouldn't mention that to Talgorian. The knowledge required to read the matrix was available only to those of her blood, and was never to be revealed to outsiders. 'We must be alive to the possibility, no matter how remote, of a pact between the warlord and our enemies.' She fixed her stern gaze upon him. 'What word is there of our expedition to the northern wastelands?'

It was a question he dreaded. 'As of yet, your Imperial Highness,' he replied carefully, 'we've had few tidings from them.'

'None, you mean. And what about the party sent by Rintarah? Have we heard how they're faring?'

'Information concerning their progress is equally –'

'So nothing about them either. We need information, yet we're working in the dark regarding this man. And I don't like working in the dark. Efforts to make contact will be redoubled.'

'Excellency.'

'And if that yields no fruit, I'll seriously consider the option of sending you personally to the northern wastes to assess the situation.'

Talgorian suppressed a shudder. 'I understand, Excellency.'

'Should the barbarian and Rintarah unite,' the Empress said, 'the consequences could certainly include all-out conflict. But even that has its compensations. A distraction for the populace in a time of strife isn't necessarily a bad thing.'

'But . . . *war*, Excellency?'

'I said that it *might* come to war.' She huffed an exasperated sigh. 'As a diplomat your impulse is towards compromise and negotiation. But there are times when the silken tongue must give way to steel.'

He bowed his head low in the customary show of obeisance. Her will was law.

'My spies tell me that fool Melyobar continues to squander Bhealfa's resources on harebrained schemes,' she added.

Talgorian looked up. 'It's always been our policy to allow certain conquered rulers to remain in place as puppets, as your gracious Majesty knows. It's proved a cost-effective way of administering protectorates.'

'It's a close-run thing in this case. His excesses have come near to draining the coffers. Perhaps it's time to rethink the whole issue of titular rulers of our colonies.'

'It is worth considering that peoples taken into the empire's embrace, ma'am, are generally more manageable if their own leaders remain in office. They tend to respect the monarchs they know.'

'What respect can the rabble have for a madman?'

Talgorian was mindful that hereditary rulers could be touchy about suggestions of insanity, despite what they might say.

'Mad, Excellency? That is perhaps a *little* harsh.'

Prince Melyobar had spent the morning chatting with his dead father.

Not that he was dead as far as the Prince was concerned, albeit the many experts who had been consulted remained undecided on the matter.

Melyobar's discussion with his technically late parent, King Narbetton, had proved very beneficial. He now knew what further elements were needed to ensure the success of his plan. A plan that would result in the exposure and inevitable death of Death.

At the moment, the Prince was nervous. A case could be made for him being in a constant state of nervousness, but under the present circumstances he was even more jumpy than usual. He always was when forced to bring his moving court to a standstill, however briefly. And the pausing of Melyobar's travelling abode was such a rare event that once word got out, people came from far and wide just to watch. This added to the Prince's trepidation, and ever more elaborate defences had been put in place to protect him from his ultimate enemy. For who was to say that the reaper wouldn't use the commotion to slip through unnoticed?

The royal palace was stationary, but continued to float despite its immensity, hovering at roughly the height of a farmhouse roof. In order to help guarantee the Prince's safety, he had ordered all the other magically impelled castles and villas of his courtiers to continually orbit the palace. The result was a gigantic merry-go-round, covering many acres of verdant countryside. An arrangement which, if viewed from the air, looked like a queen bee circled by anxious drones.

Beyond the circling mansions and chateaux a vast temporary encampment had sprung up, girdling the whole affair. Here the thousands of court followers had billeted themselves, resembling an army preparing for battle. An instant town of tents and lean-tos, herds of horses and idle wagons. For many of its occupants, being still was an uncommon experience. For some, born on the move, it was completely novel.

At the motionless palace itself, a walkway had been erected, running from its lower levels down to the ground. Its elevation was gentle, and it was wide enough to allow two wagons to travel abreast. The function of the gangplank was to take on cargo. Normally, provisions of all kinds were loaded in transit, and many elaborate contrivances and procedures had been devised to achieve this. But occasionally the unusual nature of certain cargoes defeated the cunning of the Prince's engineers.

Melyobar sat on a throne placed at the top of the walkway, looking over everything being brought aboard. He had an aide at his side and a bevy of minions dancing attendance. As the cargo was led, steered, carried and dragged past him, and identified by the aide if required, the Prince indicated acceptance or refusal. All the items, without exception, were in pairs.

Two thoroughbred horses were nodded through, followed by a couple each of donkeys and oxen. A bull and a cow were herded past, along with sheep, goats, pigs and boars.

'Let's take all useful beasts as read, shall we?' the Prince decreed.

'Very good, your Majesty,' the aide confirmed, scribbling a note.

All variant breeds of horses, sheep, goats and the like were consequently hurried by. But Melyobar's definition of a useful animal was by no means consistent.

'Are all dogs to be considered acceptable, Majesty?' the aide wondered, as a yapping, barking horde approached.

'Yes. *No*. I don't like those.' He pointed to pairs of bull-dogs and pugs, which were promptly hived-off. 'Ugly brutes.'

Cats he said yes to, as he was fond of them. But he saw no benefit in accepting mice or rats. Frogs, too, were vetoed.

He had no doubt that those who served him burned with curiosity about the menagerie he was gathering. But of course none dared question him on it. Besides, it was none of their business.

'What's that?' the Prince demanded of a soldier carrying a straw-lined box. The man showed it to him. Two tortoises dozed inside. 'I'm not sure these things serve much purpose,' Melyobar remarked.

The soldier looked to the aide. 'That's a no,' the aide mouthed at him. The tortoises were taken to the reject line.

A stag and a deer went past. Then a variety of fowl were shown. Melyobar was keen on the eagles and hawks, and a diversity of songbirds were admitted. A cockerel and a hen were let in, naturally, but the Prince dithered over the owls. Eventually he nodded, but was firm about partridges, which he thought ungainly. Swans and geese went through. There was some doubt about ducks, until he was reminded that they provided eggs, as did quail. Pigeons and doves passed the test.

A batch of exotics from far-flung lands appeared, causing no little excitement. Two tigers, well manacled and with three handlers apiece, were paraded.

'Excellent for sport,' Melyobar declared.

He was no less enthusiastic about a lion and lioness. When a pair of crocodiles slithered into view, however, he was less eager. 'Can't see how you could do much more than club them to death. Not much sport in that.'

'Quite so, Majesty.' The aide waved the crocodiles aside, and wrote himself a memo concerning alligators.

The coming of the elephants was an awesome sight. Their

legs were shackled in robust iron, and each had a skilled rider on its neck. None of that mitigated their sheer size, and the Prince cricked his neck staring up at them.

'Extraordinary,' he allowed. 'But have they a use?'

'Indeed, sire. As beasts of burden they're unsurpassed. And it is said their appearance on a field of battle has a most salutary effect.'

He was convinced.

The camels made him laugh, and they were admitted on that basis. He was baffled by a couple of giant, slow-moving lizards, green-scaled, with flicking tongues.

'If I wanted grotesques,' he decided, 'I could have glamours conjured.'

The lizards were taken way.

Snakes he likewise forsook, but was persuaded to relent in the case of several species whose venom, his head apothecary explained, had healing properties.

He kept the monkeys, which he found amusing, and likewise two saucy parrots. Insects he universally refused, seeing this as an opportunity to be rid of them. Though he did hesitate when a pair of exquisitely marked butterflies were produced. They fluttered in a charm-warmed glass container to preserve them from the autumn chill.

'Such creatures are problematic, Majesty,' his aide said.

'They are?'

'Insects require other insects on which to feed. I don't believe it's possible to be selective about them, Majesty.'

'What about the birds? They eat insects, don't they?'

'Ah. You're absolutely right, of course, sir; some do.' He wrote himself yet another note. 'I'll look into that.'

'Yes to rabbits,' Melyobar announced as they were carted on in a wooden hutch. 'But definitely no more than two, mind!'

Moles he thought useless for all but irksome tunnelling. But badgers were let aboard, as were the brown bears. Baiting was one of his favourite pastimes, and he had to think of future leisure.

Then they began toting barrels and tubs of fish to him. Most he agreed to, but he turned away those he didn't like the look of. So pike, eels and catfish found no home. Crabs and lobsters he wanted because he relished their taste.

He glanced at the seemingly endless line of animals and their handlers making their way up the gangplank. And now a line of rejects was working its way down on the other side. In the confusion it was hard to keep predators and prey apart, and there was a deal of snapping, slashing and biting. The noise and smell was growing intense. A clean-up crew had its work cut out shovelling away droppings.

'Are there many more?' the Prince asked.

'We've barely begun. You did order two of everything, Majesty.'

Hunting parties were scouring the land for mating pairs. He had agents purchasing specimens from zoos and private collections, and bartering with merchants as they returned from foreign climes.

His father's instructions had been quite explicit. Animals were to be acquired two by two, to serve the Prince's needs in a world in which there was no death. Or, indeed, many other human beings. Melyobar determined to marshal his stamina and see it through, for the sake of the plan. And for his salvation.

An unseemly honking and a fleshy slapping sound broke his reverie. A walrus waddled over for its audience, its mate close behind. Attendants walked ahead of them, holding out fish to keep them moving, while others doused them with buckets of water.

The walrus turned its whiskery face up to the Prince and they locked gazes.

He thought its eyes were very sad.

19

It was the morning of Kinsel Rukanis' trial.

Under the circumstances, Caldason thought it odd that Karr should have chosen this day to invite him to share a secret. He wouldn't be drawn on what it was, and made Reeth swear not to mention it to anyone, without exception. But in the carriage, on their way to a destination Karr wouldn't reveal, he took the opportunity to castigate the Qalochian.

'I have to tell you I'm not happy about the brawl you and Serrah got into. With the meld.'

'We didn't have too much choice.'

'Yes, you did. As I understand it, you went looking for trouble.'

'Then you understand it wrong, Karr. We weren't looking for the meld.'

'No, you were carrying out some half-baked little scheme of your own, you and Serrah. Spying on the paladins, of all damn things, without even telling us, let alone asking permission.'

'Permission?' Caldason smouldered.

'I know authority's not something you take to very well,

Reeth; *any* kind of authority. But when you've thrown your lot in with the Resistance you have to accept some measure of discipline.'

'It was a spur of the moment thing, I admit that. But we just wanted to do something about Kinsel.'

'We all do, Reeth. But you and Serrah have no monopoly on compassion; Kinsel's a friend of mine too, and I've known him a lot longer. Do you think I find it easy having to sit back while he's put through the mill?'

'No, Karr, I don't.'

'We don't need unnecessary attention at the best of times, and certainly not now, with the move looming.' He was looking tense and flushed.

'All right,' Reeth conceded. 'Message received. Now take it easy, Karr. Don't get worked up about it. You look ill.'

'Why does everybody keep worrying about my health?' the patrician came back heatedly.

'Because *you* don't. You're pushing yourself too hard, man.'

'I've little choice with everything that's going on at the moment.'

'There's always a lot going on. Delegate.'

Karr didn't answer. He stared out of the carriage's half-blinded window. It was a crisp autumn day, chill but pleasantly sunny. There were plenty of people about, and road traffic was building up.

'You're not indispensable,' Caldason appended. 'You've told me often enough that nobody is.'

Karr returned his attention to him. 'I don't have the stamina I used to. My brain's all right, more or less, but once I had energy to spare, and now . . . well, it's just not there when I need it. Getting old's a bastard, Reeth.'

Caldason had never heard Karr utter an oath before, even a mild one. 'I know a bit about growing older. In a way.'

Realisation dawned. 'Of course. Sorry. I don't think of you

that way.' He gave a little laugh. 'It's hard to come to terms
with the idea that you're older than me.'

'Imagine how I feel. But you're right. Age takes people
and twists them out of shape. They look in a mirror and start
seeing a stranger. It's life's last great act of treachery. I've seen
it happen to so many. By rights, it should have happened to
me long since. You've no idea how hard it is, Karr, watching
the people around you disfigured by the years, before they
wither and die.'

'I can see why you shun attachments.'

'But it's not always possible. Sometimes you can't help
being drawn in.'

'That's the thing about people, Reeth. The more you're
with them, the more you can't help caring. Tell me . . .'

'What?'

'In my head I'm still a young man, still the idealistic youth
who first got involved with the movement all those years
ago. It's my body that increasingly fails to respond, not my
intellect. How . . .'

'How's my mind? Do I feel like an old man? No. I'm more
or less the same inside as I was when I was young. A bit
wiser, hopefully. And from what I can make out from other
people, that's the norm. It's another trick Nature plays on
us.'

They were silent for a while, watching the anonymous
streets roll by.

'Where *are* we going?' Caldason said.

'Just an ordinary private house. It's not far now.'

'Want to tell me what this is all about?'

'Do you recall our first day here in Valdarr? When you
and Kutch and I arrived together in Domex's old wagon?'

'What about it?'

'Remember that storm, and how the lightning struck the
energy line and fractured it?'

'It's not the sort of thing you're likely to forget.'

'No, it isn't.'

'What's that got to do with where we're going?'

'You're about to find out for yourself. We're here.'

The carriage drew to a halt in an undistinguished side street, lined with unremarkable houses. It wasn't a poor area, but nor was it particularly well-heeled. They got out. Karr nodded to the driver and the carriage left them.

'Let's not linger,' he said.

He led Caldason to the front door, and delivered a rapid series of knocks. Shortly, a spy hatch slid open and they were scrutinised. Then the door was unbolted and they went in.

The man who admitted them nodded but didn't speak. He was dressed like an ordinary worker, and was presumably a Resistance man. Caldason hadn't seen him before, and Karr made no introductions.

'Would you be good enough to let them know we're here?' Karr asked.

The man nodded again and pointed to an open door. They went through it and found themselves in a dusty, neglected room containing not much more than a worn table and a couple of chairs. The window was shuttered, and light came from a few candles.

'It shouldn't be long,' Karr explained. 'They have to be reasonably sure it isn't dangerous.'

Caldason raised a quizzical eyebrow at that, but Karr didn't elaborate.

A moment later the man came back and beckoned them. They were taken along a corridor to another door. This opened onto a staircase that snaked to the cellar, and they were left to make their own way down.

The cellar was quite large and brightly lit by a number of glamour lamps. There were two men and a woman there, all in their middle or late years, and all dressed in the blue ceremonial robes favoured by Covenant. Karr exchanged greetings with them, but again no names were offered. In one corner a wooden rail had been set up around a sizeable hole. It looked deep.

'May we approach?' Karr asked one of the blue-robed figures.

The man nodded. 'But with care. And be ready to draw back if we tell you.'

'I understand. Come on, Reeth.'

They approached the hole.

'I think you'll find this familiar,' Karr reckoned.

The pit was deeper than the height of a tall man, and its sides were smooth. At its bottom a small pond of a substance resembling quicksilver had formed. The liquid flowed in from a cavity on one side of the excavation and out again through a similar recess on the opposite side. The silvery pool was agitated. It swirled and bubbled, and kaleidoscopic, vari-coloured patterns played across its glistening surface, not unlike oil on water. Waves of intense cold rolled off it, though the cellar itself somehow maintained a normal temperature.

'Remember what the sorcerers call it?' Karr said. 'Magic's chariot. This was exposed when the owners of the house were extending the cellar. Like the channel we saw exposed by lightning, this one's unusually close to the surface. Anyway, fortunately for us, the people who lived here are sympathetic to our cause and got word to us. We moved them out and took over the place.'

'Fortunate? How is this of any use to the Resistance?'

'It could be of immense value, if a theory our friends in Covenant have proves correct. But I'll let them explain it.' He called over the man who had just spoken to them.

The Covenant member wasted no time on a preamble. 'For years we've suspected that the energy lines have a number of functions. Well, more than suspected; we've grown sure of it, based on the extensive research we've undertaken on the Founders. One possibility in particular has long intrigued us: we think the energy lines can be used as a communication network.'

Caldason had been staring into the pit, transfixed by the shifting patterns. Now he looked up.

'I don't pretend to understand all the esoteric details,' Karr admitted, 'but it makes sense. We know the grid is everywhere; it almost certainly covers the whole world. It's not beyond the bounds of reason to imagine feeding in a message of some sort at one point and having it come out at another.'

'Nor would it necessarily take too much time to transmit,' the Covenant man went on. 'There's every reason to believe it could carry information almost instantly.'

'You really believe that's possible?' Caldason remarked.

'For the Founders, entirely possible. From what we've learnt, it could have been one of their minor miracles.'

'Think of it,' Karr enthused; 'the ability to send and receive messages anywhere in the world, providing you're near a line. Which, of course, everyone is.'

'And *you* could use it that way?' Caldason asked.

'That's probably a way off, to be honest,' the sorcerer replied.

'But Covenant's made a discovery,' Karr added. 'It seems somebody's already employing it for that purpose.'

'Let's get this straight,' Caldason said. 'These channels, the energy lines, are like...' he groped for a parallel '...a network of rivers. And if you have a boat, you could go anywhere in it.'

The sorcerer smiled. 'That's rather well put. Except the boat would move faster than any wind could drive it.'

'But you're saying someone's already using this network for sending messages?'

The Covenant man nodded.

'It looks like it,' Karr confirmed.

'Who?' Caldason wanted to know.

'That's the big question. But logically, it's going to be an elite, isn't it? Those who rule us. Whether that's the leaders of Gath Tampoor or Rintarah, or the state on a lower level, like the government here in Bhealfa. . . well, it's a moot point. But I think a resource like this, with all its potential, is probably going to be jealously guarded by the highest. It would give them such an edge.'

'So, making use of it ourselves isn't really an option if somebody is already using it?'

'Right. Not much privacy. But that led us to think about another way of turning this to our advantage. If the grid's being used to send messages, maybe we can intercept them.'

Caldason addressed the sorcerer. 'It's within your power to do that?'

'In theory, yes. But it's by no means easy.'

'What does it involve?'

'No disrespect, but unless you're a practitioner of the Craft yourself –'

'Which I'm certainly not.'

'Then I'm not sure I could explain how we'd go about it. One way of looking at it, I suppose, although it's a gross simplification, would be to think of that energy channel as a silken cord. The spells we'd cast would cut into it like a blade to let the information it carries bleed out. You might say we'd be hacking our way in.'

'Reeth's a fighting man,' Karr revealed. 'I can see he appreciates the comparison.'

Caldason glanced into the turbulent, freezing pit. 'These channels are dangerous, aren't they? The only other time we've seen one like this it caused havoc.'

'Yes, potentially very dangerous,' the sorcerer agreed. 'But we've bound it with a number of powerful containment spells. They should hold off any detrimental effects that might arise.'

'I hope you're right.'

'Don't worry, we're confident of it. Now, if you'll excuse me, I have to . . .'

'Of course,' Karr told him. 'And thank you.'

The man moved off to join his colleagues and occupied himself with something out of earshot.

Karr and Reeth turned back to the pit, their hands on the wooden rail. The liquid below carried on seething.

'Think they'll be able to do it?'

'I don't know, Reeth. But it's a prize worth going all out for.'

Caldason made no reply. His gaze had slipped to the agitated quicksilver pool.

'Reeth?'

He didn't seem to hear. His knuckles were white on the charred rail.

'*Reeth!*'

'Hmm? Oh. Sorry.' He shook his head, as though clearing it. 'I was . . . I guess I was away with the fairies for a minute there.'

The quicksilver spring staged a minor eruption, like a scaled-down volcano about to spew lava. It spat little globules of mercury that stuck the pit's walls, then rolled back down to the pool. An even more intense wave of cold came off it.

Karr tugged at Reeth's arm. 'It might be best to come away. Let's leave this to the experts.'

They retreated. The sound of the quicksilver's small upheaval quietened.

'Do you reckon they know what they're doing?' Caldason whispered.

'If Covenant doesn't, nobody does.' He glanced the way of the huddled sorcerers. 'Well, I hope it took your mind off Kinsel, if nothing else.'

'A little. But that isn't why you brought me here, surely?'

'I wanted you to see the stakes we're playing for. And, I admit it, I hoped that being let into our confidence even more might help you make up your mind about the gold shipment.'

'Always a reason behind everything, eh, Karr?' He didn't mean it critically. 'Well, I think I've more or less decided what I'll be doing.'

'Is it a decision I'll be pleased about?'

'Depends if you want that gold delivered or not.'

'Good.' He beamed.

'Karr.'

'Yes?'

'It's to do with Kinsel. Disgleirio said something to Serrah and me about . . .'

'Assassination? He made the same suggestion in Council.'

'What was the consensus?'

'It was unanimous. We don't operate that way. How could we? If we lose our humanity, our souls, in fighting the oppressors, how are we any better than them? Frankly, Reeth, I find it difficult enough sanctioning the death of an enemy, let alone one of our own.'

'You don't think Disgleirio or the Blade might act autonomously?'

'No. We made it clear to him that wasn't acceptable.'

'I suppose I can kind of see his point. What with the CIS operating in Bhealfa now, and their expertise in getting people to talk –'

'Kinsel didn't break under their interrogation, or any torture they might have applied. He couldn't have. No one's been betrayed. We would certainly have known by now if they had. For courage like that I think we owe him more than assassination, don't you?'

'Can we get anyone in there?'

'The courtroom? Not a chance. And I've had every inch of the route from there to the paladins' headquarters thoroughly checked. We can't see a chink, no matter how hard we try.' He sighed. 'Poor Kinsel. I'm afraid he's on his own.'

20

There was no necessity to bring him in chains, but they did. Rukanis supposed it was to give the impression he was a dangerous man, deserving of punishment. But as he looked about the court from his place in the dock, saw the faces and sensed the atmosphere, he knew they need not have bothered. He doubted anyone here could be further prejudiced against him.

He had been tortured, and there were times when he'd come close to betraying others. Somehow, he had found the strength to resist. Even when they threatened to tear out his vocal cords and still his voice forever. He felt proud of his defiance, and thought it a triumph of sorts, though his body ached atrociously with every breath.

The courtroom's public gallery was empty, and the desk where defence advocates normally sat was unoccupied. The officials of the court numbered just three. A single judge, enthroned higher than everyone else and looking stern; his clerk, seated below; and a scribe to write down the proceedings.

Three people sat at the prosecutor's desk. He knew all of them. Ivak Bastorran, the chief of the paladins himself, alongside his nephew and prospective heir, Devlor. And Commissioner Laffon, looking like a perched vulture. A pair of guards, one on each side of Kinsel, completed the cast.

The court wasted no time in beginning its proceedings.

Unrolling a vellum scroll, the clerk rose, cleared his throat and launched into the formalities. 'You are Kinsel Rukanis, a singer by profession, and citizen of the Gath Tampoorian Empire, officially resident in the city of Merakasa?'

All Kinsel could do was stare at him. It was as though he'd forgotten how to talk.

'You must answer,' the judge grated harshly.

Kinsel swallowed. 'I am.' His voice sounded feeble and uncertain.

'The charges will be put to you,' the clerk continued, 'and you will enter a plea. Do you understand?'

'I protest,' Kinsel managed. 'I've been allowed no legal representation and –'

'*Silence!*' the judge bellowed, hammering his bench with a gavel. 'This is not the time for speeches. You will answer the questions the clerk of the court puts to you. Read the indictment against the prisoner.'

'Kinsel Rukanis. You are charged that on diverse dates and in concert with person or persons unknown you did deliberately and with calculated malice conspire to pass on, disseminate and otherwise broadcast certain confidential information in your trust, to the detriment, potential harm and embarrassment of the Empress, her servants and people. You are further charged with consorting with others with a view to plotting violent and disorderly acts directed at legally constituted authorities and various law enforcement agencies serving those authorities. You are lastly charged that you did scheme, conspire, offer aid to and generally abet designated enemies of the state to commit certain treasonable acts designed to disturb the peace of the realm with the object of undermining and ultimately overthrowing the said state. How do you plead?'

'The charges are meaningless. They imply anything you want them to.'

'You will respond as directed!' the judge thundered. 'Do you plead guilty or not guilty?'

'I've suffered ill treatment. Torture. My rights have been –'

'The accused will be quiet or be silenced. *Guards!'*

Kinsel's warders moved in and painfully tightened his chains. They shoved him to the rail at the front of the dock, knocking the wind out of him.

'How do you plead?' the clerk repeated.

Kinsel sighed. 'Not guilty.'

'The prisoner will be seated.'

His shackles were sharply jerked, causing him to come down heavily on a wooden chair fixed to the floor.

'The prosecution may summarise the state's case,' the judge directed.

Laffon got to his feet and, for the sake of the record, identified himself to the court. He added that under the newly instigated anti-insurgency laws the statutory right to act as prosecutor in cases relating to terrorist offences had been conferred on his office.

So it was that one of the supposed victims of conspiracy was also the gatherer of evidence against Kinsel, and his main accuser.

'Despite the range and breadth of the charges against the prisoner,' he began, 'this case is essentially quite simple. It is our contention that the accused has long conspired with revolutionary and criminal elements whose sole aim is to bring about the downfall of our gracious Empress' legally constituted government.' He paused to let that soak in. The scribe's quill scratched against his sheet of parchment.

'We do not seek to weary the court with reams of

evidence,' Laffon went on, 'damning as that testimony undoubtedly is. Let one or two examples of this man's treachery suffice. Your Honour, I beg leave to present the state's first witness.'

'Proceed.'

'I call Ivak Bastorran, High Chief of the Paladin Clans.'

Bastorran stood up.

'I see no necessity to insist on protocol,' the judge told him. 'You may give your evidence from where you are, Chief Bastorran. Please be seated.'

'Thank you, Your Honour.' Bastorran sat again.

'I understand all witnesses have been sworn-in prior to this hearing,' the judge said.

'That is so, Your Honour,' Laffon confirmed.

'Then let's get on with it, shall we?'

Laffon turned to the paladin and smiled. 'I think we can keep this fairly brief. Be so kind as to look at the man in the dock and tell us whether you recognise him.'

'I do.'

'And how do you know him?'

'As a public figure, naturally, whom I have in fact met on several occasions. Social functions, that kind of thing. I also know of him in my official capacity as a law enforcer.'

'Perhaps you could elaborate on that.'

'His name has featured in reports compiled by paladin operatives assigned to combating terrorist activities. I'm also aware that other law enforcement agencies have taken an interest in him for similar reasons.'

'And how frequently has his name appeared in these reports?'

'Oh, on numerous occasions. There are copious references to him in our files. The paladins have long harboured grave suspicions about him.'

'How would you characterise the accused?'

'As a fellow traveller at best, and at worst an active partici-pant in illegality. But up to now he's proved both too cunning and too well shielded by his dissident cohorts for us to bring charges against him.'

'Do you regard him as a danger to the state?'

'There's no doubt about it. And I base that opinion not only on the evidence, but on the experience I've gathered during the many years in which it has been my honour to lead the clans.'

'Thank you, Chief Bastorran.'

'The accused may question the witness,' the judge announced.

Kinsel was startled. No one had told him he would have an opportunity to question his accusers. The guards hoisted him to his feet.

'Well?' the judge said. 'This is a busy court and we don't have all day. Speak or lose the privilege.'

Kinsel took a breath. 'You say, Chief Bastorran, that accu-sations have appeared about me in various reports. Can you tell me what the nature of these reports is?'

'I can't answer that question on the grounds of state security.'

'Would it not be possible, then, to produce these reports here in court so that the judge might see for himself the allegations they contain?'

'Again, state security forbids such documents being made public.'

'But surely there's no one here who could be considered a security risk. Why can't –'

'*Overruled!*' The judge underlined his decision with a rap of the gavel. 'The records are secret for sound reasons. The accused will pursue another line of questioning or withdraw.'

'The people who compiled these reports,' Kinsel said. 'Couldn't they attend court to –'

Laffon was on his feet. 'I object, Your Honour. The accused is asking the same question differently expressed.'

'I agree with you, Commissioner. Your objection is upheld. The accused must confine his questions to areas other than those covered by matters of state security.'

'If I had an advocate,' Kinsel complained, 'perhaps the right questions would be asked.'

'That is not germane. Be seated.'

The guards dumped Kinsel back in his chair.

'Call your next witness, Commissioner.'

'Thank you, sir. I call Devlor Bastorran, General-in-Chief of the paladin clans. Tell me, General, from your knowledge of the state's anti-terrorist efforts, can you corroborate what your unc – what High Chief Bastorran has said about the accused?'

'I can.'

'You know Kinsel Rukanis to be a man the security services have taken an interest in for some considerable time, and whom you suspect to have been involved in insurgency?'

'I do.'

'Can you add anything to the portrait, so to speak?'

'Yes. Rukanis' name has been mentioned on several occasions by people under interrogation. These were felons and enemies of the state who were subsequently found to be culpable in matters of terrorism.'

'In what context did these criminals refer to the accused?'

'As a co-conspirator, a comrade-in-arms. Someone as deeply involved in deeds of civil insubordination as they were. But also as a man whom it was hard to gather evidence against. There were even hints that he might be protected by people in positions of influence.'

'That's an interesting line of inquiry, General. But one for another occasion, I think. So, to sum up, you're saying that your assessment of the accused accords with that given by Chief Bastorran?'

'I am saying that. The man's a menace to decent folk going about their lawful business.'

'Thank you, General.'

The judge glared down at Kinsel. 'Questions?' he snapped.

'These people you claim named me under interrogation. Can you produce any of them in court?'

'Regrettably, no,' Devlor Bastorran responded, his face a picture of contriteness. 'You have to understand that they were hardened revolutionaries and outlaws. Some were sentenced to long prison terms in various of the colonies. Several had the death sentence passed on them. Quite justifiably in my opinion. And one or two of the others, sadly, resisted questioning to the extent of deliberately forfeiting their lives.'

'If their . . . *interrogation* was anything like mine, I'm not surprised.'

The judge's gavel pounded his bench again. 'The accused will refrain from making frivolous and irrelevant comments.'

'If you can't bring any of these people here, General,' Kinsel said, 'at least name them.'

'Can't be done, I'm afraid. That could compromise ongoing investigations. It's a matter of —'

'State security, yes. But perhaps you *could* tell the court who the persons of influence were who supposedly protected me?'

'Objection!' Laffon stated. 'It must be obvious even to the accused that such sensitive information couldn't possibly be exposed to public gaze.'

'Where are the public?' Kinsel argued. 'I see none here.'

'We'll have no facetious remarks,' the judge barked. 'You're right, Commissioner. Questions on this subject will not be pursued.' He eyed Kinsel. 'Do you have anything else to ask? Anything sensible, that is?'

'I . . .'

'I thought not. Do you have any further witnesses, Commissioner?'

'Just one, Your Honour. He's waiting outside.'

'Well, bring him in, bring him in.'

'Call Aido Brendall.'

The name meant nothing to Kinsel. But as the clerk directed the man to the witness stand, he recognised him. He was probably in his thirties. His build was average, his clothes unremarkable and his features nondescript. Except for one thing. He had a black leather protuberance in place of a nose. It seemed to be padded, and was held fast by narrow ties that ran round to the back of his head.

'You are Aido Brendall, a corporal with the harbour watch patrol?' Laffon asked.

'I am, sir.' It came as no surprise to anyone that his voice had a distinctly muffled quality.

'I'll not beat about the bush, Corporal. It's evident to all present that you've suffered an injury. Tell me, did this come about whilst carrying out your duties on behalf of the citizens of Valdarr?'

'It did, sir. I was disfigured in the line of duty.'

'And was it not the case that several of your colleagues actually lost their lives in the same incident?'

'They did, sir. Two of 'em, and a grievous loss to the watch patrol they were, sir.'

'I believe a member of the paladin clans was also murdered that night.'

'Yes, sir. Died heroically, he did.'

'Please tell the court, in your own words, how this tragedy occurred.'

'There's not a lot to tell, sir. It was last summer, and my unit was patrolling the central docks when we got word of an illegal entrant getting off one of the ships. A woman, it was, along with a couple of children. Quite young they were, those kids. Anyway, we spotted her and gave chase. We had a paladin assigned to our unit that night and he came along too. We caught up with the illegal, and she'd been joined by a man.'

'Can you identify that man?'

'Yes, sir. It was him.' He pointed at Kinsel.

'You're sure?'

'I'm not likely to forget, sir, seeing as what happened next.'

'Do carry on.'

'Well, we confronted him and the woman with the kids, and the next thing we know *another* woman turned up. I reckon she knew 'em. Was one of 'em, if you ask me. Because when we ordered her to stand aside, she attacked us.'

'And as a result of that unprovoked attack, your two comrades and the gallant paladin officer gave their lives, and you were left badly wounded?'

'Yes, sir. Scarred for life, sir.'

'What part did the accused play in the assault?'

'He egged her on, sir. No doubt about that.'

'You saw him as the one behind the attack? The driving force, so to speak?'

'I don't reckon the one who did all the damage would have tangled with us otherwise, sir.'

'To sum up: the accused, whom you have just identified, was deeply involved in an altercation that saw the deaths of three brave defenders of the peace and the severe injury of another, namely yourself?'

'That's just how it was, sir.'

'I think the testimony of this witness, a man who puts himself at risk every day in order to preserve the peace and safeguard the good citizens of Valdarr, gives the lie to the accused's protestations of innocence. Thank you, Corporal.'

'Your witness,' the judge rumbled, nodding at Kinsel.

'You've told the court that you confronted five people that night. Two women, two small children and a man.'

'You should know; you were the man.'

'I want to establish something. Your group consisted of three harbour watchmen and a paladin, all of you trained fighters. In the case of the paladin, a highly experienced swordsman, I imagine. Is that right?'

'That's right.'

'When the fighting began, did either of the children join in and attack you?'

'That's ridiculous. Of course they didn't.'

'Did both of the women attack you?'

'Just the one.'

'And what about the man? Did he take part in this brawl?'

'You know you didn't.'

'So the fact is that four very experienced law enforcers faced one woman, who killed three and dealt you a serious injury?'

'Well . . . yes. But she was good. By which I mean she was wild. Deranged, possibly. There was no reasoning with her.'

'Did you *try* to reason with her? Or did you simply order her aside so you could get at the non-combatants? Isn't it possible that –'

'Objection, my lord!' Laffon was up again. 'It seems the accused is trying to imply a justification of self-defence for this terrible event. And if he is, isn't that as good as admitting that he was present?'

'I'm inclined to agree,' the judge replied. 'Also, the exact circumstances of the incident are secondary to the fact that three law-keepers were killed. There can be no justification for that, and anyone present, in whatever capacity, must be seen as an accessory. This line of questioning will cease. Does the accused have any more questions?'

Kinsel wearily shook his head and sank back onto his chair.

The harbour watchman was dismissed. Then the judge instructed Laffon to deliver his final arguments.

'Your Honour, I do not propose wasting the court's precious time on a lengthy summation of the prosecution's case. The facts speak for themselves. We have heard from the two highest officials of the esteemed paladin clans, and they left us in no doubt of their conviction that Kinsel Rukanis is a dangerous and manipulative individual. In respect of the evidence of Aido Brendall, the court was presented with the testimony of a dedicated and courageous public servant who related how the accused was involved in a vicious act of violence. And you will have noted, Your Honour, that Rukanis did not deny being present at the docks the night murder and mayhem were doled out. My lord, the fact that Kinsel Rukanis is a man of some notoriety makes his crimes all the worse, for such as he should always set a law-abiding and patriotic example. One element of the accused's personality has not been mentioned in court today, but is well known. I refer to his espousal of pacifism. This, too, has a bearing on the issue of patriotism. For how can a man be called a patriot if he does not believe in fighting for his country, and who, indeed, encourages others to embrace his skewed doctrine? What distorted view of the world is it that sees cowardice and contempt for one's homeland as virtues to be championed? For such a philosophy, if it can be dignified with so noble a title, and for the evidence we have heard today, there can be only one verdict.'

'The accused may speak in his defence,' the judge directed.

Kinsel turned weary eyes upon the judge. 'Is there any point?'

'The people must be satisfied that the due process of law has been observed. I won't have it said that a defendant in my court was not allowed to put his case.'

'My lord, I'm sure that's what the people say already. The difference between me and all here is that I regard my fellow citizens as possessing the intelligence to decide between true justice and a sham. And I believe, passionately, that genuine justice is the birthright of every man and woman, whatever their walk of life, and however their hopes and aspirations are seen by their rulers. I didn't expect a fair trial. I wasn't disappointed in that.'

'A pretty speech, and one not designed to wring sympathy from this court. The scribe will strike that portion of the proceedings from the record, and say only that the accused turned down the opportunity to speak on his own behalf.'

The scribe gave him a small bow and scored through what he had written.

'I see no need to retire and contemplate the evidence presented here,' the judge declared. 'The facts seem clear cut to me. However, as no direct evidence has been presented that portrays you as an actual participant in violence, I am minded to be lenient.'

A tiny spark of hope was ignited in Kinsel's breast.

'Nevertheless, the charges *are* grave, and a law lord must always be aware that the punishments he hands down should act as a deterrent to others. Kinsel Rukanis, I find you guilty as charged. By virtue of the powers invested in me by the constitution of Gath Tampoor and its protectorates, I sentence you to be delivered into the custody of the naval branch of the correctional system. You will serve an indefinite term of hard labour as part of a galley crew. And may the gods show you mercy for the wrongs you have committed.'

It was a false hope. Being condemned to work as a galley slave was as final as a direct death sentence. The only difference was that working the galleys meant a death more lingering, more prolonged than one by the rope or block.

'It is the wish of this court that the sentence be carried out without delay. Take the prisoner away.'

All Kinsel could think of as they manhandled him from

the dock was Tanalvah and the children. And of the child she carried, that he would never see.

As he was led past the Bastorrans and Laffon, he saw that they were in good spirits.

21

'We're all taking a hell of a risk,' Caldason whispered.

'It's for Tan,' Serrah told him. 'This is probably going to be the last glimpse she'll have of him. How could we begrudge her that?'

The street was lined with people. Not packed six deep as they would be for an eminent visiting dignitary or a festival day, but a substantial turnout nevertheless, especially during an hour when most should be working. Enough of a crowd for those who didn't want to attract attention to hide themselves in.

Reeth and Serrah, hooded and soberly dressed, stood on the kerbside. Tanalvah and Kutch were situated nearby. Around them, mingling in the press, were a score or so Resistance members who had volunteered to act as bodyguards if the need arose.

'Shouldn't be long now,' Serrah reckoned. 'But I still can't see why we couldn't have planned some kind of ambush.'

'Look around. Not only are there a *lot* of uniforms about, you can bet there are as many plainclothes agents on duty. And the way these people work, they'll have somebody in the wagon with Kinsel ready to cut his throat at the first sign of trouble.'

'The bastards would do it too, wouldn't they? I feel so *help-less*, Reeth.'

'That must be the least Tanalvah's going through. Maybe you should go to her.'

'Yes, I was just thinking that. I'll swap with Kutch.'

He nodded and she slipped away.

Once Serrah had sidled up to Tanalvah, she said, 'Kutch, why don't you go and stand with Reeth now?'

'I'm all right here, Serrah.'

'*Kutch.*'

'Oh. Right. See you later, Tanalvah.'

She gave him a soft smile and he wriggled into the crowd.

'Silly question, Tan, but how are you?' Serrah asked in an undertone.

'It's funny, but I've kind of gone beyond rage and despair and all the rest of it. I just feel numb.'

'You're still in shock. So perhaps being here isn't the greatest idea in the world.'

'No, I want to be here. I need to be. You understand that, don't you? You wouldn't make me leave?'

'Of *course* not. It's why we're all here with you.'

'You know, I'm really proud of Kinsel.'

'Naturally you are. I know that.'

'I meant especially proud of him because he didn't crack under . . . torture.' There was a tiny catch in her voice when she came out with the word.

'We don't know that he was tortured, Tan.'

'Please, Serrah; I'm not naive. It's good of you to try to protect me, but I know what these people are capable of. I had enough experience of their sort when I was a whore back in Rintarah.'

'Sorry.'

'But the important thing is that Kinsel didn't give any names. Nobody suffered because of him.'

'He's a very courageous man.'

'Yes. But not everybody believed that, did they? They said he'd break down and put lots of people in danger.'

'Not everyone thought he would.'

'Perhaps. But some were so convinced they even had the idea that he should be killed to shut him up.'

'Oh, you know about that, do you?' Serrah didn't think to ask how she knew.

'Yes, and I think I know who made the suggestion. I was terribly hurt when I heard about it. But I don't blame him.'

'That's very forgiving of you.'

'It's like Kinsel always said; you have to think about the greatest good for the greatest number. He said it so often I started to think our little family weren't part of that greater number. He had a tendency to see things in terms of what was right for the world before he thought of himself. And maybe before he thought of his own.'

'Tan . . .'

'No. It's the way he is, and one of the reasons I love him.'

'I'm sure . . . I *know* he loved you and the children more than anything.'

'Yes, he did. And I take comfort from that. But, you know, I have a feeling that everything's going to be all right.'

'You do?'

'Yes, honestly. I believe we'll all be able to look back on this as though it was a bad dream, and that we'll be together again.'

'You're taking strength from your faith, is that it?'

'Some. But that's not the reason I feel this way.'

'Tan, don't expect some kind of miracle. Life's not like the stories the wordsmiths tell.'

'It should be. I think people deserve a happy ending.'

'If anybody does, it's you.'

'And I'll do anything I have to, to make that happen.'

Serrah was growing concerned. 'What is it you think you can do?'

'There are ways, Serrah. There's always a path if you have the courage to walk it. That's part of the philosophy attached to my lady Iparrater.'

'Ah. I see.' But somehow Serrah didn't think Tanalvah had been entirely referring to religion.

Not far away, Reeth and Kutch were sending surreptitious glances in the direction of the women.

'Do you think Tan's going to be all right, Reeth?'

'Hard to say. She's suffered a terrible blow. Then again, after all she's been through, she has strength.'

'And the kids. Serrah says that having to care for Teg and Lirrin should help keep Tan on an even keel.'

'I expect she's right.'

'People tend to sacrifice a lot for their children, don't they?'

'Yes. Everything, sometimes.'

'I don't remember a lot about my mother,' Kutch confessed. 'But I'm grateful to her.'

'She sold you.'

'Well, yes. Only I reckon what she was really doing when she let Master Domex take me was giving me the best future she could. Like when my brother went into the army. I don't know whether he really wanted to be a soldier. I think he just wanted to take the pressure off my mum, give her one less mouth to feed.'

'Do you miss your brother?'

'I'd like to see him again. I often wonder what happened to him.'

'Why all this talk of families, Kutch? You don't normally speak about it very much.'

'It's what's happened to Kinsel, I suppose, and Tan. It's

sad, isn't it, Reeth? They all came together like a family, and now they're split again. It doesn't seem fair.'

'Life isn't always fair. You must have realised that by now. There's no law that says the good come out on top.'

Kutch fell silent and thought about that. At length, he said, 'What's going to happen to Kinsel, do you think?'

'What's going to happen to him? Nothing too pleasant, I'm afraid.'

'Well, it's not like they sentenced him to death.'

'They did. A slow, painful death. People don't come back from the galleys, Kutch. If they're lucky they meet their end quick and clean. In an accident at sea or something. They have plenty of those. Otherwise . . .'

'Oh. Do you think Tan knows that?'

'Of course she does.'

'Only, I thought she was taking it quite well.'

'She's being brave. Or she's in shock. Maybe both.' He tilted his head to one side. 'Hear that?'

'What is it?'

'They're coming.'

Distantly, but growing louder, the crowd could be heard. The nearer the convoy came, the more it was obvious that it wasn't getting a uniform reception.

'Why's the crowd making that funny noise?' Kutch wondered.

'It's not one noise. Some of them are cheering, some are booing. I guess feelings about Kinsel are pretty mixed.'

The lead wagon in the convoy came into sight and the roar increased.

'Why are they doing it like this, Reeth?' Kutch asked. 'Taking him through the streets, I mean. They could have done it quietly, couldn't they?'

'They're displaying a trophy, and sending a message. The message says no matter how high you might be, or how well liked, you're not above their vengeance. It's intended to warn off others who might be tempted to stray into the Resistance camp. But I'm not sure they've got it right. Listen to the crowd.'

There was no doubt now that the bystanders were split. Cheers and boos went up in equal measure. Bizarrely, lots of people were clapping, but Caldason didn't think it marked approval of what the authorities were doing. Some catcalled, spat and even threw things, but many more simply stood silently, their expressions morose. Here and there, people waved, and that couldn't be called a gesture of ill-will. Kinsel's popularity seemed intact as far as a goodly portion of the crowd was concerned.

Several wagons passed, loaded with militia. Cavalrymen and paladins acted as outriders. Then, in the middle of the convoy, the wagon holding Kinsel came into view. It bore a cage and Kinsel stood inside, hands clutching the bars. He wore an impassive expression. People hurled rotten fruit. Others tossed flowers.

In an instant, the wagon passed.

'Come on,' Caldason said.

The crowd, strangely quiet, had begun to disperse. Reeth and Kutch pushed their way to Serrah and Tanalvah.

'Let's not hang around here,' Caldason suggested.

'I think he saw me,' Tanalvah said, eyes shining.

'I'm sure he did,' Serrah told her, slipping an arm around her friend's shoulders. 'But we have to leave now; it's not safe to stay on the streets.'

Two Resistance men, known to them all, appeared and said they had a carriage waiting.

'You go with Tanalvah, Kutch,' Serrah told him. 'Reeth and I will catch you up.'

They watched as Tanalvah, the apprentice and the Resistance men got into the carriage and left.

'I don't like the way she's been acting, Reeth. It's not natural.'

'What's natural in a situation like this? She's in shock.'

'That's what I thought, but . . . I don't know, this is something different.'

'What are you trying to say?'

'Shit, Reeth, she reminds me of . . . well, of *me*. The way I got a couple of months ago.'

'You think she might try to harm herself?'

'Maybe. Mind you, there are the children, and I think that should give her pause. Unless . . .'

'You don't think she'd hurt them?'

'Unlikely. *Very* unlikely. But you can never really be sure what people will do. Believe me, I speak from experience.'

'So it'd be best if you could be with her as much as possible.'

'That's what I figure. Damn it, Reeth! Why do you have to be going off to deliver the gold tomorrow?'

'*What?* After all the trouble you went to persuading me? And Karr getting everything organised so fast? I can hardly call it off now, can I?'

'No, of course you can't. It's lousy timing, that's all. And . . .'

'Yes?'

'I just wish I was going with you.'

Once the convoy was away from the more populous parts of the city it picked up speed. The authorities had seen to it that the roads ahead were cleared, and there were foot patrols on every corner.

Finally the caravan rattled into the port area. The same harbour where, in what now seemed a dim and distant summer, Kinsel had first laid eyes on Tanalvah and the children.

His wagon drew up outside a large building with barred

windows and guards at the door. The cage was unlocked and, accompanied by a pair of wardens, his ankles shackled, Kinsel was taken in.

There were another fifty or sixty convicted men inside, huddled miserably on a line of benches. They wore manacles, with long chains running through them, so that all were bound together. Kinsel was shoved towards the nearest bench. A guard barked and its occupants slid along to make room for him. Then a smith knelt and fussed with the manacles, and Kinsel became part of the chain-gang.

It was cold, and the shapeless convict uniform of rough cloth Kinsel now wore offered little protection. The place was silent apart from the rattle of chains and occasional wheezing coughs. They were waiting for something, but nobody explained what. Half an hour later, he found out.

A muscular barrel of a man swaggered in. He was completely bald, save for a pencil-thin, black moustache, and his tanned skin looked oiled. He sported leather breeches and a sleeveless leather jerkin, unbuttoned over a hairless, bare chest, despite the season. On his upper right arm there was a tattoo of the Gath Tampoor dragon emblem. His boots were thick and heavy, and he had wide, studded bands on both wrists. A large and elaborate gold buckle secured his belt, from which hung a sheathed knife with a curved blade. He carried a coiled, barbed whip.

'The basic facts of your new life,' he announced, his voice deliberate and penetrating. '*I* am your overseer. *You* are scum. You call me sir, or master, or god. Or better yet, you don't call me at all. My word is law; your lives are worth less than a peck of salt. You jump when I say so. You work until I tell you to stop, which isn't often. If I tell you to plug a hole in the keel with your arse, you do it. If you're called upon to fight, you will do so with savagery and at the expense of your own wretched lives if I think it's necessary.' He was walking along the line, scrutinising the faces of his charges. Very few met his gaze. 'Everyone on board without shackles is your better, and to be obeyed without question. But your first allegiance is to me. If you displease me in any way or fail to obey an order quickly enough, you will be punished. That ranges from a flogging to losing a foot; from having your eye taken out with a hot brand to feeding the sharks. Where we're going is none of your business. What we do once we're there is nothing to do with you.' He'd reached Kinsel, and obviously knew who he was. 'We don't go in for favouritism.' He was staring at him. 'Nobody cares who you were in your old life, which from this minute is over, done with, forgotten. High born or low, it's all the same to me, and this.' He held up the whip. 'Oh, and if you survive for thirty years the Empress gives you a pardon. Don't get too excited; nobody's earned one yet.' He was on the move again. 'You'll be pleased to hear that we're catching the night tide. Your sea voyage begins within the hour. I'd like to say that I hope you'll enjoy it as much as I will. Only I know you won't.' He turned and strode out.

A group of men arrived with buckets. They went along the line doling out ladles of brackish water and small hunks of stale black bread.

Ten minutes later, the chain-gang was on the move, shuffling out of the building with encouragement provided by the whips of the overseer's deputies. They were herded to the gangplank of a ship of the line, then led below decks.

The ship's hull was fitted with benches, port and starboard. Each bench seated two men. They were beaten into them and their wrists shackled to the great oars that projected from slits cut into the hull. Their ankles were chained to sturdy rings set in the floor. Kinsel found himself next to an elderly looking, bone-thin man with broken teeth. When they were all in place, the overseer appeared.

'As this is your first time,' he announced, 'we'll begin nice and easy. Get your hands on those oars!'

A drummer began to pound out a rhythmic beat.

Kinsel took hold of the oar, and felt a tear forming in the corner of his eye.

22

Night had fallen on the city.

In a quiet residential street in an unremarkable quarter of Valdarr, a carriage was discreetly parked in the shadow of an overhanging tree. The carriage was defended by elaborate counter-eavesdropping charms, and its driver had been sent on a meaningless errand.

Inside the carriage, behind drawn blinds, two people were deep in conversation.

'We'll go through it again,' Devlor Bastorran insisted.

'If we must,' Aphri Kordenza replied wearily, 'but I understood the first three times. I'm not stupid, you know.'

'I need to be sure you're clear on every detail. This is an extremely risky operation.'

'We're used to risky situations. Trust me.'

'Get this one wrong and it'll not only go badly for me, it'll go *very* badly for you. Both of you. Get it right and you'll have everything you want.'

'You'll arrange to have our condition made permanent?'

'That's what we agreed.'

'And you'll pay for it?'

'I said I would.'

'Soon?'

'Yes, yes, *yes*! You have my word. Now can we please run over it again? Good. What time do you have be there?'

'A little before midnight.'

'Right. Allowing enough time to get in, do what you have to and get away. You've *got* to be out of there before the chimes. Understood?'

'Perfectly.'

'The room has two ways in. You've no need to worry about the entrance inside the house. The one you're concerned with is the emergency exit. You get into that through the door in the alley at the rear of the building. It's the only door there, and besides it'll have a guard stationed outside.'

'And I'm to kill him.'

'Yes, and don't botch it. Leave him alive and we're both finished. Because you're going to approach him with this.' He held up a rolled parchment bearing a red wax stamp. 'My personal seal. This will win his confidence and allow you to get near enough to do the job. What two things must you be sure to do at this point?'

'Kill him conventionally with a blade; no magic. And get the seal back.'

'That's vital. Leave it at the scene and it's our death warrant.' He slipped a hand into his tunic pocket. 'Then you use this key to open the door. Drag the guard's body inside and lock the door behind you.'

'And that's when I separate from Aphrim.'

'Right. You leave him to guard the entrance in case anybody else comes along. That's very unlikely because there are only a couple of copies of these keys, but I want to cover every eventuality. So, you're in the building. What next?'

'I go up the flight of stairs and there's another door.'

'Which you open with *this* key.' He dangled it in front of the meld. 'Do it quietly. When you're through that door you'll find yourself in a small curtained alcove. Beyond the curtain is his private study. The outer door, the one that leads to the rest of the house, is going to be locked, so you won't be disturbed. Chances are he'll be working at his desk, and that has its back to the alcove. So you should be able to approach without him knowing, providing you're stealthy enough.'

'I do stealth very well.'

'If he isn't at his desk, you'll still have the element of surprise. But should he see you coming and put up a fight, don't assume he'll be easy to take.'

'I'll be prepared for that.'

'I can't emphasise enough that he has to be dealt with just like the guard; no hint of magic. When you've done the deed, mess the study up a bit. Make it look as though there's been a fight, assuming there hasn't, of course. Then smash the door you came through, from the far side. It's got to look as though someone's battered their way in, *not* used a key. His study's in a fairly remote part of the house and it's wood-panelled, so you're all right making a certain amount of noise, but don't overdo it. Oh, and make sure the lock's turned when you break the door. If somebody notices it's unlocked *and* broken, that's going to give it away. Tell me what happens next.'

'Down the stairs to Aphrim, and we do the same to the door there; smash it.'

'That could be the most dangerous point. If somebody should walk past, or you attract attention breaking the door –'

'We'll kill them.'

'Yes. It's important nobody gives your description. Obviously that would ruin the plan. But again, no magic.'

'You can count on it.'

'I hope so. I wouldn't want a repetition of the brawl you had with Caldason and that woman.'

'That wasn't of our choosing. They were following us.'

'And that's worrying. If they followed you from my HQ they'll suspect we're connected.'

'Doesn't do them any good though, does it? Who are they going to tell who'd believe them? Anyway, by then Caldason's going to have a lot more to worry about.'

'I suppose so. Here.' He handed over the keys and the seal. 'And I want them back, as we arranged.'

'Of course.'

'One other thing. If you were thinking of using them to try a little blackmail on me, forget it. Not only would you not get the reward, I'd have every paladin in the city out looking for you. With orders to kill on sight.'

'Wouldn't dream of it. Once this job's done, Aphrim and I are going to be out of your hair forever.'

That was exactly what Devlor Bastorran had in mind.

A reception was being held at Ivak Bastorran's palatial town house.

The guest list was select and the hospitality lavish. Many of Bhealfa's most influential families were represented, and there was more than a smattering of the great and good from Gath Tampoor who were stationed in the colony. A small orchestra played in the mansion's ballroom, and couples in the latest imported fashions had taken to the floor.

In an adjoining reception room, Ivak and Devlor Bastorran, resplendent in their dress uniforms, greeted guests, a trickle of whom were still arriving, despite the lateness of the hour.

'It was an excellent idea of yours,' Ivak said, 'to honour Laffon like this.'

'I see it as politic, uncle. Now that the CIS has been given the go-ahead to operate outside Gath Tampoor proper, he's likely to be an even more powerful man. He certainly seems to have found favour with the Empress. It doesn't hurt the paladins to be on good terms with him.'

'Well, I'm glad you're here to think of this kind of thing, Devlor. These diplomatic shenanigans aren't my forte. Never have been.'

'Quite so, uncle. But the credit really belongs to you, for allowing your home to be used tonight.'

'I can see you're going to be a great asset to the clan leadership one day, my boy.'

'Thank you, uncle. I'm looking forward to it.'

'But not too soon, what?' He laughed.

'As you say, sir. Ah. Here comes the guest of honour himself.'

Laffon joined them, a crystal wine glass in his hand. Devlor thought it typical of the man that it contained nothing stronger than water.

'It's a wonderful gathering, gentlemen.' He flashed them a rare smile. 'Thank you again. It was good of you to arrange this at such short notice.'

'We've been intending to do it from the moment we heard you were coming,' Devlor lied. 'It seemed appropriate to have you here following Rukanis' successful prosecution, in which you played such a vital role.'

'Hear, hear,' the older Bastorran added.

'You're too kind,' Laffon replied, lifting his glass to pallid lips.

'Of course, this should be seen as a double celebration,' Devlor said.

'How so?' Laffon asked.

'Apart from Rukanis' guilt being established, we have cause to commemorate your other triumph, Commissioner, in respect of the CIS being given so much greater responsibility in the war we're all fighting against the terrorists.'

'The Empress did my organisation a great honour in

bestowing such trust on us. We'll all be doing our best not to let Her Highness down.'

'Gods bless her,' Ivak declared, taking a swig from his brandy glass, which he then deposited on the tray of a passing servant.

'I'm sure there's absolutely no danger of you or your esteemed organisation disappointing the Empress,' Devlor said. 'And it goes without saying that the paladins will always be keen to co-operate with you in every way we can.'

'As will the CIS with the paladins,' Laffon returned in a show of equally transparent insincerity. 'I very much look forward to our working as closely together in future as we just have in respect of the Rukanis case.'

At that point, Devlor's aide, Lahon Meakin, approached, bowed and begged their pardons. He whispered briefly in the younger Bastorran's ear, and as quickly withdrew.

'I do apologise,' Devlor told them, 'but a trifling matter requires my attention for a moment. If you'll excuse me . . .'

'Certainly, my boy. The work goes on, doesn't it? There's no rest for the upholders of the law. You go ahead. I'll keep the Commissioner here company.'

Devlor smiled and exited.

The message Meakin had delivered to him, as earlier instructed, was merely a reminder that midnight was a little more than a quarter of an hour away. And midnight, as paladin tradition dictated, was the hour when an honoured guest was toasted.

Devlor walked out of the reception room, nodding and smiling at guests he passed, and into an adjacent chamber which in turn led to the hallway where the front door was. He lingered there for a moment, exchanging the odd word, then retraced his steps back to the reception room.

Laffon and his uncle were still engaged in conversation.

'Everything all right, my boy?' Ivak enquired.

'Perfectly, uncle. Only I'm afraid it's necessary to take you away from our guest for just a moment.' He looked to Laffon. 'A small decision has to be taken in respect of the wine we'll be having later. It's very much a matter for the head of the household.'

'Of course. I quite understand.'

'Surely you can take care of it, can't you, Devlor?' Ivak said, piqued at the prospect of being dragged away.

His nephew glared at him. 'It really would be best if you could come yourself, uncle.'

'Oh, very well. Excuse us, Commissioner.' He was led off grumbling.

Devlor took him to another, less crowded room.

'Uncle, the fact is I told a little white lie back there.'

'You did? You don't want me to select the wine?'

'No. This has nothing to do with wine. It's a matter I thought best dealt with away from prying eyes. A messenger just arrived with this.' He turned his jacket to one side, revealing an envelope poking out of his inside pocket.

'What is it?'

Devlor leaned in and whispered, 'It bears the seal of the Empress herself.'

Ivak's eyebrows rose. 'A message from the imperial court?'

Devlor nodded. 'Under the circumstances I thought it best to be discreet.'

'You were absolutely right. Hand it over, it could be urgent.'

'And possibly sensitive. It's certainly going to be of a private nature. Perhaps it would be best perused in your study, with the door locked. Just to be on the safe side.'

'Yes, good idea.'

'Here, slip it into your pocket; there's no sense in letting everybody know about it. You get on. I'll make your excuses.'

They parted at the foot of the staircase.

Devlor returned to Laffon. He invited several others to join

them. Then one or two more. Before long, the younger
Bastorran was at the centre of quite a group, amusing them
with his fund of anecdotes and stories of clan exploits.

Two floors above, his uncle had secured his study door
and was sitting at the desk. When he took the envelope from
his pocket, he noticed something odd about it. It bore a wax
stamp, but the wax was flat and unadorned. There was no
imperial seal, as Devlor had told him. Puzzled, he reached
for a paper knife and slit open the envelope. Inside was a
single sheet of vellum. He unfolded it and found that it was
completely blank.

It was unlike his nephew to play stupid tricks on him. He
felt there had to be some kind of mistake. Perhaps Devlor
had accidentally given him the wrong envelope. But why he
should be carrying around a sealed envelope containing a
blank sheet of paper was beyond Ivak's understanding. There
was nothing for it but to go back downstairs and get it sorted
out.

As he rose from his chair he heard a faint noise behind
him, and started to turn.

He almost managed it.

Downstairs, Devlor was finishing an elaborate tale about
a paladin campaign from a century before when Meakin
appeared at his shoulder and politely coughed.

'Yes?'

'It's almost midnight, sir.'

'Nearly time to toast our guest. Uncle's the one for that.'
He looked about the room. 'Where is he?'

'I'm afraid I've no idea, sir.'

'Ah, I remember. He said he was going up to his study.
Probably engrossed in some paperwork or something and
forgot about his guests. That'd be typical of Uncle Ivak.'

'Would you like me to go for him, sir?'

'No, don't worry yourself, Meakin. I'll pop up there myself.

You all keep yourselves amused,' he told the guests, 'charge your glasses, and I'll be back down with him in a minute.' He headed for the stairs, walking casually and exchanging smiles with everyone he passed.

When he got to the first landing, and was sure he couldn't be seen, he flew up the steps two at a time. Arriving at the study door he rapped on it and called his uncle's name, just to be sure the meld had done her job. There was no reply so he got out his spare key and let himself in.

Kordenza *had* done her job, and a thorough one at that. His uncle was slumped over his desk. He had multiple stab wounds in his back and there was blood everywhere. There was no question that he was dead. Devlor went over, snatched the envelope and blank sheet of vellum, which were speckled with crimson, and stuffed them in his pocket.

Items of furniture had been overturned, and various bits of bric-a-brac were scattered around. The meld had made it look as though there had been a fight, as instructed. He moved to the alcove, where the curtain had been left open, and saw that the door beyond was smashed. Way down at the bottom of the back stairs lay the body of the guard. So far, so good.

Now it was his turn, and there was no time to waste. He unsheathed the ceremonial sword he wore, and which he'd had sharpened to a razor keenness the day before. Steeling himself, he ran it swiftly across the outside of his left thigh, cutting through uniform fabric and skin. Blood began to flow. Changing hands, he did the same with his right arm. Then he gulped a breath, raised the blade to his cheek and slashed it. Not deep enough to leave a scar, but sufficient to draw blood copiously. He was proud of not crying out when he did it.

After a quick look around to make sure everything seemed right, he ran to the door.

'*Murder!*' he yelled from the landing. '*Help! Murder! Call out the guard!*'

Within seconds there was a thunderous sound on the stairs as a mob ascended.

He slumped against the doorframe, sword dangling from his fingers, blood dripping from his wounds and streaming down his face.

Meakin appeared, with Laffon close behind. Following them came a mix of guests and paladins, weapons drawn.

'*Sir!*' his aide exclaimed. 'What happened?'

'Murder,' Devlor croaked, letting the sword fall from his grasp. 'In there. Murder.'

Laffon plunged into the study, three paladins at his heels.

Meakin stayed with his master. 'You're hurt, sir. Let me see.'

'I don't . . . think it's . . . too . . . bad.'

'Let's get you sat down, sir.' He steered Devlor to a high-backed chair standing against the landing wall, and carefully began tearing the cloth away to expose the wounds.

Laffon reappeared. 'What happened?'

'When I . . . got up here, the door was . . . locked. No . . . reply. Fortunately I had a key. Found . . . Uncle Ivak.'

'Take it easy, sir,' Meakin said.

'No. Must . . . catch him.'

'Who?' Laffon asked. A number of shocked, white faces were staring down at Devlor now.

'We fought. I got in . . . a couple of . . . blows, I think. But he . . . took me . . . unawares. Must go . . . after him.'

'Three men have just gone down those back stairs in pursuit,' Laffon told him. 'And it looks like there's another dead man at the bottom of them.'

'The . . . guard. Poor devil.'

'But who *was* it, Bastorran? Who did this?'

'Caldason. The outlaw . . . Reeth Caldason.'

'He did this?'

'Yes, and nearly did for . . . me, too.'

'I don't think these wounds are too serious, sir,' Meakin reported, dabbing with a cloth. 'Lots of blood, but not too deep, thank the gods.'

'I'll be . . . all right. Just a . . . shock.'

'Was he alone?' Laffon said.

'Far as I could . . . tell, yes.' Bastorran's breathing was more regular, and a little colour was coming back to his cheeks.

'Funny thing, someone battering their way in like that. You'd think your uncle would have been alerted and put up a fight, or raised the alarm.'

'Perhaps Caldason did have somebody . . . with him. But I only . . . saw him.'

'Well, it's a damn audacious thing to do.'

'That's what these people . . . are, Commissioner. Brazen. Reckless. And they've taken my . . . uncle, the bastards.'

'If this just happened, hopefully they haven't got far. We could catch them yet.'

'You know what this . . . is about, don't you, Laffon? Rukanis. It's revenge for that damn *traitor*.'

'The timing certainly seems indicative.' He stared at him. 'You sure you're going to be all right?'

'I'll be fine. I've taken worse knocks than this.' He was calming. 'But suppose this is part of a . . . general uprising? The first blow of many?'

'I suppose we should be alive to that possibility. You're the Clan High Chief now, Bastorran. What do you want to do?'

'Come down hard on them. *Really* hard. Make them pay. Do I have your backing?'

Laffon glanced at the open study door. 'You do.'

Somewhere outside, a bell was chiming midnight.

23

At dawn the following morning a number of covered wagons converged from different directions on a hidden cove on Bhealfa's south-eastern coast. Their journeys had been risky, both in terms of what the wagons carried and because they'd had to defy the curfew to arrive so early. But sound planning and good luck served them well, and they made their rendezvous without incident.

Resistance planners had been working for years on the logistics of moving thousands of people and all manner of cargo from diverse parts of Bhealfa to the new island state. Having six wagons reach the same patch of seashore at approximately the same time was child's play by comparison. So it was that they all rode onto the beach within a space of less than a quarter of an hour.

A ship was anchored not far offshore. The sea was choppy and the vessel rolled slightly as it breasted the foam-flecked waves. In the grey sky, dark rain clouds were forming, and clumps of grass on the edges of the sandy beach were flattened by a brisk wind.

Caldason, Serrah and Kutch disembarked from various of the wagons, along with most of the three-score strong band of Resistance fighters Reeth captained. They were met by the ship's skipper and a handful of his crew, who'd ferried themselves across in a large rowboat.

The last wagon to arrive bore Quinn Disgleirio and the remainder of the band.

He hurried to the others. 'Have you heard the news?'

'What news?' Serrah said.

'We've been travelling all night without a stop,' Caldason explained.

'Well, we *had* to stop,' Disgleirio told them. 'Nearly lost a wheel about halfway here, not far from a village. They'd even heard about it there.'

'Heard *what*?' Serrah repeated.

'Ivak Bastorran's dead.'

'Gods.'

'Yes, and that's not all. He was murdered, right in his own house in Valdarr. While some kind of party was going on, would you believe?'

'Was it anything to do with us, the Resistance?' Serrah asked.

'They're saying it was. Actually . . . prepare yourself for a shock, Reeth. The paladins say it was you.'

'*Me?*'

'The old man's nephew, Devlor, not only swears you did it, he claims he was wounded fighting you off.'

'That's insane. What's supposed to have happened?'

'The story they're putting out is that last night a lone assassin killed a guard and battered his way through two locked doors to get to Ivak. Then he, or you as they'd have it, stabbed him in the back a number of times.'

'A knife in the back doesn't sound like your style, Reeth,' Serrah said.

'No. I would have wanted to see his face while I did it.'

'*Could* it have been the Resistance?' Kutch wondered. 'And maybe they mistook somebody else for Reeth?'

'It had nothing to do with us,' Disgleirio stated adamantly. 'We would have known.'

'And Devlor Bastorran's unlikely to mistake someone else for me,' Reeth said. 'Not after our last meeting.'

'Good luck to whoever it was, I say,' Serrah decided. 'And what if you are blamed for it, Reeth? You would have done it given the chance, wouldn't you? Though not in the back like a sneak.'

'That's all very well,' Disgleirio told them, 'but there's the repercussions to take into account. The top man in the paladins gets murdered and somebody known for his hatred of them gets the blame. They link you with the Resistance, Reeth, and it gives them just the excuse they need to crack down even harder. Not good news when we're coming up to the move.'

'The more I think about it,' Reeth said, 'the more it stinks. Everybody in the Resistance knows a killing like this is only going to make life more difficult for us. If you ask who stands to benefit most, maybe they should be looking nearer to home for the killer.'

'Shit,' Serrah hissed. 'Devlor.'

'He's the likeliest suspect.'

'Well, yes. But I meant: shit, now he's in charge. What with that and Laffon turning up here . . .'

'Things are going to get rough.'

'I said you were better out of it for a while, Reeth.'

'There's nothing we can do about any of this now,' Disgleirio stated. 'Let's just concentrate on the mission in hand, shall we?' He scanned the rough track leading down to the beach. 'I wonder what's happened to Darrok?'

'Why *is* he sailing with you, Reeth? I thought he was going to make his own way back to the island.'

'Last-minute change of plan, Karr said. Probably can't bear to be parted from his gold.'

'Talking of which,' the skipper put in, 'we really should

be loading it. We've got the morning tide to catch.'

Disgleirio nodded. 'How do you want to handle this, captain?'

'Bring the wagons further down the beach and get your men to start chaining the gold into our rowboat. My crew are waiting to stow it, and I'll get them to send over more boats to speed things up.'

'Fine,' Reeth said. 'Let's get it organised.'

It took over an hour to transport the crates of gold to the ship. As the last rowboat set off, the lookouts Caldason had positioned signalled an arrival. Shortly, two carriages pulled in.

'Looks like your man finally got here, Reeth,' Serrah reckoned.

'Just when the hard work's finished. Good timing.'

The occupants of the carriages disembarked. It was the same party who had attended the meeting in Valdarr: four bodyguards, one of them female, clad in black leather and bristling with weapons. And leading them, their charge, Zahgadiah Darrok, seated on his hovering disc.

'Good morning,' Darrok grated.

'You took your time,' Caldason replied. 'Much longer and we wouldn't have been here.'

'Oh, I'm sure you don't mean that.'

'Really? Ever hear the expression time and tide wait for no man? It's true, Darrok, even for you.'

'Well, we're here now. Where's the gold?'

'The last of it is just going on board.'

Darrok looked out at the ship. 'That's a fairly compact vessel.' There was a note of criticism in his voice.

'She's a brig,' the skipper informed him. 'Two-masted, square-rigged. Built to be swift. My crew's well armed, but speed's her best weapon. You might find it a little bit cramped on board, but the journey's going to be shorter.'

'You do know there are pirates in the waters we'll be navigating?'

'I know it very well, Master Darrok. Me and my crew have had more than one run-in with them. It's the reason Patrician Karr picked me for this trip. The buccaneers in those parts go for bigger, heavier craft because they rely on force to overcome their prey. I've found the best defence is not letting them get near enough.'

Darrok looked satisfied. 'I bow to your superior knowledge, captain.'

The skipper glanced out to sea. 'The boats will be coming back any minute. Get yourselves ready to embark.'

Everyone set to picking up their gear.

'Well, this is it, Reeth,' Serrah said. She surprised him with an embrace and a warm kiss to the cheek. 'Look after yourself,' she whispered.

'I will,' he replied softly. 'And do me a favour, will you? Keep an eye on Kutch.'

'Don't worry, I'll see he's all right.'

They parted, and after a look that lingered just a second longer than mere friendship might dictate, Serrah moved off to wish the band members good luck.

Caldason bid farewell to Kutch warrior style, their right hands firmly grasping each other's forearms. The young apprentice was noticeably touched by such an adult gesture.

'Behave yourself, Kutch. Do as Serrah says. And try to keep away from those damn blinkers.'

The boy smiled. 'I will. Come back to us soon, won't you?'

'You won't know I've been away.'

Caldason's goodbye to Disgleirio was brisker, more businesslike.

'Here they come,' the skipper called out as the rowboats reached the shore.

The wagons and carriages departed, then almost another hour passed getting everybody and their kit over to the ship.

'You weren't joking when you said conditions were

cramped,' Darrok complained to the skipper as he scrutinised the crowded vessel.

'You've got a cabin. Mine, in fact. The rest of your people are just going to have to rough it in with you, or down in the hold with the rest. It's no more than I'm asking of my own crew.' He turned to Caldason. 'I might be able to find a cabin for you, too, if you want it.'

'Don't bother. I'm happier sleeping on deck.'

'Really?'

'I always prefer the open air if I can get it.'

'Let's hope the weather holds, then.'

'If it doesn't, I'll join the others below deck.'

'Suit yourself, Master Caldason. My suggestion to you all is that you try to get some shuteye now. You look as though you need it, and it'll stop you getting under my people's feet.'

'Good idea,' Darrok agreed. 'I'll see you later, Caldason.' He glided off, his bodyguards in tow.

'You might find the stern the best place to settle down,' the skipper suggested to Caldason. 'I'll have somebody bring you a blanket.

'Thanks.'

Ten minutes later the ship was underway, and Caldason settled down to rest in a corner of the deck. He didn't feel particularly tired. His mind was occupied with thoughts of Ivak Bastorran's assassination, and the mission ahead.

But soon the ocean's gentle rocking lulled him, and he closed his eyes.

It was unlike anything he'd experienced before.

He was looking at a landscape he didn't recognise. It was blanketed in thick snow. What he could see of the terrain was harsh and unwelcoming. Here and there, clumps of mean, colourless scrub poked through the whiteness. Some tall, craggy rocks were exposed, with sickly lichen clinging to them. A few skeletal, half-dead trees were framed against a slate sky. The cutting wind swirled snow flurries all about.

It was murderously cold. But he knew this without actually feeling it, the way a cook knows a boiling cauldron is scalding hot without needing to touch it. To him, the cold was an abstract thing. Beginning to look around, his eyes adjusted to the gloom.

He saw the city.

It sat on a mountain plateau a great way off, but still appeared large. And it was swathed in sparkling lights.

The instant he saw it, he began moving towards it. But not of his own volition – he was literally drawn.

He found he was some distance above the inhospitable waste, and moving rapidly. The land beneath flew by, a wilderness of white, punctuated by laden pine trees and rock formations crackling with frost. He saw frozen rivers, and a solid lake with a surface turned milky by the layers of snow. At one point he spied a paralysed waterfall, its motion stilled, glistening.

Travelling ever faster, he came to a vast plain that ran to the edge of the city. Encamped on the plain was an immense army, its numbers beyond count. Innumerable tents spread over many acres. Myriad campfires twinkled like burnished rubies.

Then he was hurtling straight at the city's fortified walls. With a stomach-turning lurch he swooped over them, and was looking down on the patchwork of buildings and streets they shielded. There were thousands more people here, engaged in a frenzy of activity.

As he descended he saw that the city's inhabitants were marching, building, gathering, rallying, swearing oaths, defending the walls, strengthening the gates, handing out weapons, hiding their children in cellars, sharpening blades, nocking arrows, boiling vats of oil, loading trebuchets, nailing shut their windows, vowing suicide pacts.

With no more mass than a feather, he floated to the ground. The streets were bathed in light. Dazzle and gleam seeped from every side, in stark contrast to the bleakness outside. Walking unseen, unsuspected, he took in the atmosphere. He knew the patriotism, felt the hope and despair, smelt the fear.

A faint rumble quivered the ground, giving pause to everyone around him. It faded. Another, stronger vibration followed. Men looked to the angry skies; mothers clutched their babes. A further shock came, more powerful yet. Buildings shook, pottery fell and shattered, the coloured glass in a temple window cracked from side to side.

There were cries, screams, entreaties. People ran. Horses bolted. Wagons overturned and spilt their loads.

Then, one by one, and in batches, all the lights started to go out.

He plunged into darkness too, a total, all-embracing absence of light that felt like a tightly stitched shroud. Faintly, he heard the sound of a thousand, thousand throats roaring in triumph from outside the walls.

He fell helplessly through endless black velvet. The drop lasted a second, or perhaps all eternity.

Sensation flooded back. He was on the top of a flat, snow-covered hill. Ahead of him, there was a large marquee.

A man stood at its open flaps. He looked unremarkable. There was nothing particularly distinctive about his build, his clothes or his bearing. He possessed the sort of face that, once seen, was quickly dismissed from memory.

Yet he shone with an indefinable quality that made him fabulous.

They looked deep into each other's eyes. And the world ceased turning.

Caldason sat up, fighting for breath.

It came back to him that he was stretched out on the deck of a ship pitched by waves. A mixture of sea spray and drizzle had soaked him through. His lips tasted salty and his bones ached.

He leaned back his head and let the soft rain caress his face.

The warlord woke suddenly from a troubled sleep.

'Your pardon, sir,' someone said, 'but are you well?'

Zerreiss sat up. His bedclothes were tangled, and the fur that covered him slipped from the camp bed. 'Who's there?' he mumbled groggily.

A lamp was lit, bathing the tent in a friendly orange glow. Sephor, the younger of his closest aides, blew out the taper. 'It's me, sir. Forgive the intrusion, but you cried out.'

'I did?'

'Several times.'

He massaged the bridge of his nose with thumb and forefinger. 'I've no recollection of it. What did I say?'

'Nothing I could make out, sir.' Sephor was pouring a cup of water. 'Or would you prefer wine?' he asked.

'No. Thank you, water will suffice.' He accepted the cup and drained it. 'What time is it?'

'The dawn won't be here for another two hours.' He studied his master. 'Are you all right, sir?'

'I had a dream. It was unlike any I've had before.'

'A dream? That's not like you, sir.'

'Even I can have dreams and be stirred by them, Sephor. The same as any other man.'

'I meant I've not known your sleep disturbed like this before. We're used to your dreams being waking ones. Those you put into practice. If you understand me, sir.'

'I do.' Zerreiss smiled at him. 'And you put it well. But you're right; it's not like me to have dreams that rouse you from your bed. My apologies, Sephor.'

'No need, sir. It's what I'm here for.'

The warlord shivered. 'It's chilly.'

'I'll stoke the brazier.' He busied himself feeding the fire.

'Do you have dreams, Sephor? Silly question, of course you do. I mean, do you have dreams that make an impression on you, and linger after you wake?'

'I suppose I do, sometimes. But they tend to be nightmares rather than dreams. Was yours a nightmare, sir?'

'That's a good question.' Zerreiss pondered it. 'Some say dreams are just meaningless dramas played out in our minds as they wander unfettered in sleep. Others think there are gods who send us dreams as omens or portents of things to come.'

'What do you think, sir?'

'I think there might be another kind.'

'I don't understand, sir.'

'I'm not sure I do either, Sephor. But the dream I had tonight has left me with a very distinct feeling.'

'Sir?'

'There's somebody I need to find. If he exists.'

24

'Kutch. *Kutch!* Wake up!'

'Uh. Hmm?'

Serrah shook him. 'Come *on*! Wake up. *Kutch!*'

His eyes snapped open. Even in the gloom she could see he looked terrified.

'You were shouting,' she said.

He sat up, then moved to her like a frightened child, hugging her tightly. She felt him trembling.

'*Whoa*. It's all right,' she soothed. 'I'm here. It's all right.'

'Oh, Serrah.'

'What was it, a nightmare?'

'It . . . it was . . .' His voice wavered, as though he were near to tears.

'Breathe. Go on, take some deep breaths.' She gently stroked his hair. 'It's all right now.'

'It wasn't a . . . nightmare.'

'Was it another of those visions? Like the ones Reeth has?'

He nodded.

'It's gone now. You're safe.'

'Am I?'

'Yes.'

He disentangled himself, looking embarrassed. His eyes were moist. 'I'm sorry, Serrah.' He swallowed. 'You must think I'm a terrible baby.'

'Don't be silly, of course I don't. Let's have some light, shall we?' She leaned over and snapped her fingers at the glamour orb by his bed. It began emitting a soft glow. 'Better?'

He nodded again, starting to pull himself together.

'Here.' She handed him a tumbler. 'Want to talk about it?'

'It's . . . difficult to explain.' He took a sip of water. 'It wasn't like the other visions I've had.'

'How was it different?'

'Before, it wasn't in dreams. I saw things when I was awake. When I was spotting. But it was different in other ways, too.'

'Tell me.'

'I saw . . . it was another place, like the times before. Only it wasn't the *same* place. There was snow, and a war or something. And there was a man . . . or maybe two men, and . . . It was all mixed up, Serrah.'

'Take it easy.'

'At least this looked like somewhere that could exist. The other times, it was a *strange* place. Really scary.'

'Perhaps it *was* just a dream. An ordinary nightmare. That's possible, isn't it?'

'No. It was too real. Dreams aren't like this. It had the same . . . feel as before.' He shook his head. 'I can't explain.'

'You don't have to try. Not now.'

'I haven't had any of these visions for a while, and I thought . . .'

'What?'

'I thought that because Reeth wasn't here . . .'

'You wouldn't get them?'

'Sounds crazy, doesn't it? But because I was seeing the same thing he does, I thought it was him doing it somehow.' He sniffed and gave a crooked smile. 'As if you could catch dreams the way you caught a fever or something.'

'That's no crazier than any other explanation I can think of. Reeth's been seeing these things for years and he can't figure it out himself.'

'I don't want them coming back, Serrah. They frighten me.'

'I know. Look, lie down again. Get some rest.'

'You won't leave me?'

'No, I'll be right here.'

The sun was getting ready to come up. Through the room's half-open window shutter she could see a gash of red on the horizon.

When he seemed calmer, she said, 'I was talking to Karr today. About the move to the isle.' She kept her tone light, conversational.

'Did he have any news about Reeth?'

'No, not yet. But he did say that he's thinking of asking him to stay on there, at least for a while.'

'Why? I thought he was coming straight back.'

'That was the plan. But Karr needs somebody like Reeth, somebody he can trust, to train people to defend the island. Now we know there are pirates out there, it's a good idea.'

'What do you think Reeth will say?'

'I don't know. Karr hasn't asked him yet. He's going to send him a message glamour about it. To be honest, Kutch, I wish Reeth *would* stay over there. Now the paladins are saying he killed their chief, I think it's better for him to be away from Bhealfa.'

'What about the expedition to find the Clepsydra?'

'It wouldn't affect that. Karr told me it could just as easily go from the island. It might be easier, actually, with all the paladin activity here.'

His face fell. 'Oh, I see.'

'Karr said something else. He said, if I wanted to, I could go to the island too, to help Reeth.'

'Will you?'

'If Reeth decides to stay there, yes, I'd like to. I didn't go with the band in the first place because . . . well, originally because Karr didn't want me to. He thought I was too unstable, and he was right. But I'm getting over that. Then I thought I'd better stay because of Tanalvah, but she seems to be holding up pretty well. She's found a strength from somewhere, and there are lots of people looking out for her now. And frankly, Kutch, I'm a doer. I like being where the action is. There's work to be done here, sure, but it's kind of routine and –'

'You want to be with him, don't you?'

An expression came to Serrah's face Kutch hadn't seen before. She looked almost shy. Her face coloured slightly and there was a sparkle in her eyes. 'It's only been a few days, but . . . I miss him being around. I expect you think that's stupid.'

'No! I think it's great. Only . . . what about me?'

'Oh, *Kutch*. As if I'd . . . I promised Reeth I'd look after you, and I'm not going back on that. What I'm saying is, I rather hoped you'd come too.'

'Me? Come with you? *Yes!*' He punched the air.

'I'll take that as an acceptance, shall I?'

'I don't want to stay here by myself, and we'd be going to the Diamond Isle eventually anyway, wouldn't we?'

'I'm not trying to put a damper on it or anything, but you might like to think this through, Kutch. You *could* stay here, if you wanted, and Karr and the others would make sure you were all right. Plus, I won't lie to you, it could be dangerous.'

'I want to go, and if things get chancy I'd rather be with you and Reeth.'

'Would it be all right with Phoenix?'

'Why shouldn't it be? He's not my master. Not really.'

'There's one other thing. It's all right for me to go off where

I please, and the same applies to Reeth. Bhealfa isn't my home. Nowhere is, now that I can't go back to Merakasa. But you were born in Bhealfa; your roots are here.'

'I made up my mind about that when I first heard Karr's plan. I knew that if I was asked to go, I would. There's nobody here for me now.'

'All right, if you're certain. I'll talk to Karr about how we're going to handle it. But don't get too excited. Reeth might say no and come back, as he intended.'

'In which case he'd still be around, wouldn't he?'

'Yes, he would.' She smiled. 'Feeling better?'

'Lots.'

The rising sun sent bars of golden light into the room.

'Here,' Serrah said, handing over a warm, freshly baked loaf.

'Hmmm. Smells great.' Kutch tore off a chunk and began chewing.

'Straight from the ovens upstairs. Hiding under a bakery has a few advantages.' She sat by him and helped herself to some. Kutch seemed so much more cheerful than she was afraid he might be after last night's drama.

It was nearly midday, and with the move looming, the Resistance's cellar den was busier than ever. There were fifty or sixty people working there, and the place was stacked with crated provisions ready for shipping.

'We'll talk to Karr in a minute,' Serrah told him. 'Before that I'd like to have a word with Tan.' She nodded to the area where a dozen people were assembling small glamour munitions. Tanalvah was seated at the end of a bench, slightly apart from the other workers, engrossed in her chores.

'Go ahead,' Kutch replied, his mouth full. 'I've got enough to keep me busy here.' He had crumbs round his lips and speckling his shirt.

'So I see. Back soon.'

She headed Tanalvah's way, only to be intercepted by the matronly figure of Goyter. 'If you're thinking of joining Tanalvah, young lady, you'll need these.' She held out an apron and a pair of white gloves.

'I don't intend handling anything, Goyter.'

'Humour me.' She thrust the gloves and apron at her.

Serrah quickly put them on. As she walked away she smiled and said, 'Thanks for the "young lady".'

She arrived at Tan's side. 'Can I join you?'

'Of course.'

Serrah took a seat. 'What's that?'

Tanalvah was using a little scoop to carefully transfer a heap of rust-coloured powder into paper twists.

'Dried dragons' blood. I don't know if that's actually what it is or if it's just what they call it. Were there ever really such things as dragons? I don't know.'

'Me neither. What does it do?'

'It ignites when it comes into contact with water. But only salt water, apparently. The paper we wrap it in dissolves in water after a few minutes. Use enough powder and you've got an explosion.'

'Useful. I can see the need for gloves.'

'Yes. Get just a speck of this stuff wet and it goes off with quite a bang.'

'So, how are you finding working here, Tan?'

Tanalvah stopped what she was doing. 'It keeps me busy. I'm grateful for that.'

'You don't find it a bit . . .'

'Menial? Boring? What else can I do, Serrah? Whoring skills aren't greatly in demand with the Resistance.' Had her tone not been light, the words would have sounded bitter. 'Actually, there's a possibility I might be assigned to the counterfeit magic division, helping to raise funds. If I can sell my body I should be able to peddle cheap love potions.'

'Everyone's been treating you well?'

'They've been very good. Quinn tends to avoid me, but that's understandable. We've got a rota going for looking after the children, too.'

'And you're feeling all right? Be honest; are you coping?'

'Don't look so sombre. What you're seeing is more or less how I feel.'

Serrah wasn't entirely convinced of that. 'It's only been a couple of days, Tan. Sometimes the full effect of these things takes a while to –'

'I told you; I know it's going to be all right. I can feel it, here.' She laid her palm over her heart.

Serrah nodded. She reckoned Tanalvah was taking refuge in self-deception. But she was loathe to question something that seemed to be working.

'I know why you're asking, Serrah.'

'You do?'

'Karr sounded me out. About you going to the Diamond Isle, and what I thought about it.'

'What did you tell him?'

'That you should go if you want to. There's no need to linger here on my account.'

'I'd stay, Tan, if you wanted me to.'

'I know you would, and I'm grateful.'

'Anyway, it's not certain yet. We still have to hear what Reeth thinks about it.'

'You want to be with your man. I understand that.'

'Slow down. Reeth and I aren't a couple or anything. I just –'

'Let's not worry about words. You need to do a certain thing because your instincts tell you it's right. That should be enough.'

'It seems so unfair, when you can't be with Kinsel.'

'But I believe I will be. No, don't give me that look, Serrah. I mean in *this* life. I'm not planning to leave it just yet.'

'Good. And remember that I'm only going ahead. We'll be seeing each other again soon.'

'Gods willing.'

'Yes. Look, Karr's waiting to talk to me. If I go, I'll see you before we leave.' She leaned over and kissed Tanalvah's cheek, then left her.

Serrah took off the apron and gloves, dropped them on a chair and beckoned Kutch over.

The patrician sat at a desk at the far end of the cellar, sorting through piles of documents.

'I've made up my mind,' Serrah told him. 'If Reeth decides to stay on the island, I'll join him. Kutch wants to go, too.'

'You're happy about this, Kutch?'

'Yes. I'd like to be with Reeth.'

Karr nodded. 'It's dependent on what he says, of course, but I've already sent a message. So hopefully we'll have a reply soon.'

'He should be arriving at the island any time now, shouldn't he?' Serrah asked.

'Depending on the tides, yes.' He jabbed a thumb at the mass of papers covering his desk. 'I'm just arranging another shipment of men and arms. With a bit of luck you two could be on it. You'll be a great asset to us over there, Serrah.'

'Thanks, I'll do my best.'

'About Tanalvah . . .'

'I was just about to mention her myself.'

'She'll hold together, you think?'

'She says she will, and she seems to be functioning fairly well. I don't know how much of it's a sham.'

'I can't tell either. I'll see she's kept occupied, and of course we'll keep an eye on her.'

'She has this belief that Kinsel's going to be all right. There's nothing rational about it, but it's become a sort of credo for her.'

'I won't try to disillusion her. We all need something to hang onto when times are dark.'

'They must be dark as hell for Kinsel. I wonder what he's holding onto.'

25

Kinsel Rukanis was astonished at how quickly he lost his grip on the passing of time.

His captivity had lasted only days, perhaps a week, yet it could have been years. His existence was almost entirely restricted to the paltry light below decks, and he rarely knew the difference between day and night.

The labours of the condemned were unceasing, bar when they were taken aft to perform their bodily functions in a squalid, stinking privy. Rest meant dozing fitfully at their oars, too weak and apathetic to care about the rats scurrying around their feet. Seldom were they allowed the luxury of a few hours' sleep on the flea-ridden straw in the hull's cells. Their hands were blistered. The fetters left weeping sores on their wrists and ankles. They were given bad food and not enough of it, and water that was barely drinkable. And all the while they had to endure exhaustion's handmaiden, brutality.

Kinsel had already seen two of his fellow convicts die. One collapsed at his oar and only after beatings and a dousing failed to stir him was it found that his heart had burst. The other was accused of some small infraction of the rules and died under the lash. Both bodies were unceremoniously dumped overboard.

But there was something even more shocking to Kinsel. For the first time in his life, and to his shame, he felt a hatred of another human being so intensely that the prospect of murder looked attractive. The object of his malice was the overseer. Kinsel had never known a man so lacking in common decency. His only pleasure was to inflict suffering on his helpless charges. If he smiled it was because of another's pain. For Kinsel, who had always believed in at least the possibility of redemption for even the basest, this was profoundly depressing.

He was determined to maintain his pacifism. To weaken on it would be too great a sacrifice of his principles. But the overseer knew Kinsel's reputation as a man of peace, and made it his business to break his will. So far, his weapon had been ridicule, backed by the whip.

On the eighth or ninth day of the voyage, or possibly some time during its second century, the overseer's deputies came for Kinsel. They deposited him, blinking and half naked, on the freezing deck. Most of the crew seemed to be there, watchful and expectant. A fellow convict was present too, looking cowed and bearing signs of a thrashing.

'Here he is,' the overseer mocked, 'the man who wouldn't lift a hand to defend his country!' There were jeers from the onlookers. 'A man who'd stand idle as our homes were razed and our women defiled, and call it *honour*!' He made it sound like a curse. 'Who dresses his cowardice as virtue and his treachery as an ideal!' They were booing. 'Did I say a man? He's not deserving of the name!' He approached Kinsel. 'But I'm going to give you the chance to be one.' The overseer pointed at the other galley slave. 'That one broke the code, and I've a mind to mix punishment with a bit of entertainment.' The crew cheered and clapped. 'Here's the bargain.

You'll settle this for us. You fight or I'll kill him,' he told Kinsel. Then he turned to the other man. 'You kill this . . . *peace-lover*, and you live. And if you reckon you can get out of it by neither of you fighting, think again. I'll have you both put to death.'

Kinsel was numb. He raised his eyes to the man he was expected to fight. His name wasn't known to him; because the rowers were forbidden to speak, none were. But Kinsel recognised him as someone he'd managed to pass a few drops of his water to, when he was parched in the night and near choking. Perhaps that had been noticed, and was why the overseer matched them. The man looked as wretched and unfit as Kinsel himself, and no more willing.

An order was barked and the chains were struck off Kinsel and his would-be opponent.

The overseer thrust a sword at Kinsel, hilt first. 'Take it. *Take it!*'

He had only ever held a sword once or twice before. He didn't even like to have one on stage as a prop. It was heavy, and its metal handgrip was cold. He had no idea how to use it, but supposed that would add to his persecutors' amusement.

The man he was supposed to fight looked as though he'd handled a sword in the past. But he seemed to find his just as weighty, probably from pure fatigue.

Sluggish as Kinsel's mind was, a succession of thoughts rapidly went through it. The first was to use the blade on himself, but he knew they wouldn't allow that. He thought that perhaps he might merely wound the man. But they'd insist on him finishing the job, and in any event it assumed a skill he didn't have. It occurred to him to turn the blade on the overseer. That he instantly dismissed as an absurd notion. The only feasible choice was to let the other man kill him and end it here.

He was roughly shoved forward, and so was his opponent. The crowd began to roar and egg them on.

Kinsel threw down his sword.

It was illogical, but totally instinctive. He simply couldn't face someone while holding a weapon in his hand. The other man just stood with his mouth open, the tip of his sword resting on the deck.

The onlookers were incensed, and howled their frustration. But no more so than the overseer. He gave in to an apocalyptic fury.

'You *bastard!* Pick it up! *Pick it up, I say!*' The order was emphasised with a wild swipe of his coiled whip across Kinsel's chest.

He flinched and swayed, but didn't move.

The overseer struck him with the whip again, even harder, and its barbs bit. '*Pick it up and fight, you swine!*'

Kinsel felt as though a score of white-hot pokers had scoured his flesh. But still he refused to obey.

'To hell with it!' the overseer raged. '*Kill 'em both!*'

Rough hands were laid upon Kinsel, and the man he'd refused to fight was similarly grabbed. Ropes and whips were produced.

Somebody was shouting, loudly. The words couldn't be made out above the commotion.

'*Quiet!*' the overseer bellowed. '*Quiet! Shut up, you scum!*'

The mob fell silent. Save one shrill voice. '*Ahoy! To the west! The west!*'

All eyes went up to the lookout's nest, then over to the direction in which he was frantically pointing.

A ship was coming at them, bow on, moving with speed. It was at least as big as the galley, and its sails were full to bursting.

'*Gods!*' the overseer cried. 'We neglected the watch! *Battle stations! Put on speed!*'

He laid about the crew with his whip and boot, yelling orders.

There was chaos. Men ran in all directions to hoist ropes, break out weapons and a dozen more chores in defence of the ship. Several of the overseer's deputies pounded below decks to whip the rowers. A frantic drum beat started up.

Kinsel and the other slave were forgotten. Men who seconds before had been intent on killing them, let go and scattered. The convict and Kinsel held each other's gaze for a moment, incredulous. Then the convict picked up his sword and was swallowed by the confusion. Kinsel left his where it was.

He looked west and saw that the ship heading their way had moved much nearer. Its speed was such that it could only be a matter of minutes before it reached them. Kinsel estimated that it would narrowly cut across their path, or possibly strike the prow. He made for the stern, ignored by everyone and hobbling painfully.

The galley began to move forwards, but lazily, from its almost standing start. It might have been better if it hadn't. Whereas there was a chance before that the oncoming ship would miss them, now they were putting themselves directly in its path.

Kinsel got to the rear of the galley. He glanced out to sea. The attacking ship was a stone's throw away and he could see a host of men crowded at its bow.

Then it rammed the galley, hitting amidships with a tremendous impact. Kinsel was knocked from his feet. He heard the oars on the injured side splintering and breaking apart. The lookout, halfway down the rigging, was dislodged and fell screaming into the ocean. All around, men were shouting and running with blades in their hands.

He started to get up, then flattened again when a shower of arrows homed in. Several embedded themselves in the deck close by. Others found living targets, felling crewmen not ten paces distant. He crawled, keeping low, looking for a place to hide. Almost bumping into a great coil of rope, thick as his arm, he wriggled behind it.

Kinsel didn't know how long he crouched there, listening to the yells and screams, and the clashing of steel. Not being able to see was worse than knowing exactly what was going on.

But when he heard a terrible chorus of shrieks from below deck, and knew they could only be coming from the rowers, chained and at the mercy of their attackers, he had little doubt which way the wind blew.

After a while, the sounds of fighting began to fade. Then they ceased all together and silence descended. In a way, that was worse still. The only noises he heard now were creaks that he prayed were the natural movement of the galley's timbers. He dared to nurture the hope that their attackers had fled and left the ship drifting.

That hope was dashed.

Suddenly, rough pairs of hands seized him and he was hoisted to his feet. The men surrounding him weren't from the galley. He expected no more than death. With luck, swiftly.

'We've got another one!' somebody shouted.

They dragged him, laughing, to the front of the ship. Short as the journey was, he passed an awful lot of corpses on the way. The vast majority were galley crew, including the rower the overseer had wanted him to fight.

He was thrown on his knees near a man who couldn't have been anything but their commander. Tall and large of frame, he had black curly hair and a full beard. His face was rugged, weather-beaten and pock-marked. He wore a blue frock-coat that reached his ankles, thick breeches and scuffed black boots that came to his thighs and still had turned-over flaps of soft leather a foot long. There was more gold on the man than Kinsel had ever seen any one person wearing. Every finger, and even his thumbs, bore at least one ring. Not content with a single chain about his neck, he had several, at least two of them with fat pendants. He sported gold bracelets, an ostentatious brooch, and a belt buckle large enough to tether a horse with.

But the captain, as Kinsel took him to be, had his attention elsewhere at that moment.

He was staring at the overseer, who stood bound between two smirking captors. Kinsel saw something in the overseer's eyes he hadn't seen before, and which he had so fervently wished for. Fear.

'I do not appreciate resistance,' the captain was telling him, 'but have considerably less respect for a man who hides and lets others fight for him.'

Even in his terror, Kinsel appreciated the black irony of it. But as he himself had been found quaking like a craven deserter, he didn't think his prospects good.

The captain snapped his fingers. 'Bring brandy,' he ordered. 'The good stuff.' A subordinate trotted off to obey.

Kinsel was puzzled. Was he going to toast the overseer?

Soon, the minion returned with a full bottle, pausing only to draw its cork with his teeth.

The captain approached the trembling overseer, bottle in hand. 'Your health,' he saluted, and took a generous swig. Then he poured the rest over the man's head, shoulders and body, liberally soaking him. The drenched overseer spluttered. His expression alternated between outraged, bewildered and frightened.

Another snap of the captain's fingers had a lackey producing something from his pocket. The overseer saw what it was before Kinsel did, and set to wailing and struggling in his bonds.

The captain struck flint, or perhaps it was a glamour brand,

and there was a tiny flame in his hand. He touched it casually to the writhing overseer's jerkin, then stepped back.
Flames immediately engulfed the man. His whole body
became a roaring fireball. The two men guarding him had
moved away too, leaving the overseer to burn. He shrieked,
staggering about the deck. His skin began to sear and peel,
and the sickly smell of roasting flesh was given off.
Blundering in agony, the desperate overseer tottered to the
rail, swayed for a second and plunged over, screaming.
There was a distant splash. He'd ignited a little fire on the
rail where he'd touched it. One of the men took off his hat
and absently beat it out.

'Who can doubt my generosity?' the captain said. 'I even
provide cooked food for the sharks.'

His men doubled with mirth.

'What about him?' he mouthed, waving a hand Kinsel's
way but not really looking at him.

'Just one of the rowers, captain,' someone explained.

'Be done with it. But don't waste any more brandy on
him.'

Firm hands forced Kinsel forwards so that his neck was
stretched. A sword was drawn and raised high.

'*Wait!*' The captain strolled over, foppishly brandishing a
gold-embossed dagger. 'I believe I know him.' He put the flat
of the knife under Kinsel's chin and lifted his face for a proper
look. 'My word. *Up!*'

They hauled Kinsel to his feet.

'I'm Kingdom Vance,' the captain announced, 'merchant
adventurer. Are you by any chance Kinsel Rukanis?'

Kinsel was too horrified to speak. He could only manage
a stiff nod.

'Of course, I could be wrong,' Vance reflected. 'And you,
naturally, could be grasping at a straw. If you're the man I
think you are, and want to keep your head, there's one way

to settle the issue. All you have to do is prove it.' His dark eyes bored into Kinsel's.

'Sing,' he said.

The voyage had been more than long enough for Caldason, and he was anxious for dry land again. That, the skipper told him, would appear any time now.

The cramped conditions on the brig hadn't done much to improve anyone's temper. Darrok's way of weathering the trip was simply to stay in his cabin for long stretches. Caldason couldn't help noticing, as everyone did, that Darrok's red-headed female bodyguard spent most of her time in there with him.

At the moment, with landfall imminent, most people crowded the decks, anxious for sight of their destination. Caldason stood with the skipper and Darrok, who had parked his disk on a capstan to conserve the magic that powered it. The trio were talking about nothing in particular, and their eyes were more often on the sea than each other.

'Look at that,' the skipper said.

'What?' Darrok asked, scanning the horizon.

'There.' The skipper pointed skyward.

A bird was flapping their way. It moved rapidly, and the nearer it got the more obvious it was that it was big. Eventually it reached the ship and circled overhead. It was white, with enormously long wings and a hooked beak.

'Well, I'll be . . .' the skipper exclaimed.

'What is it?' Caldason said.

But before he got an answer the bird descended and landed on the rail close by. It was so large it hardly had room to perch. Caldason noted that some of the crew viewed the creature anxiously.

'Just a minute,' the skipper said, and slowly made his way to it.

They watched as he spent a minute in the bird's company. Then he returned.

'It's for you,' he told Caldason.

Reeth walked along the deck, stopped by the huge bird and seemed to engage it in conversation.

'What's going on?' Darrok wanted to know.

'It seems Dulian Karr has a twisted sense of humour,' the skipper replied. 'That or a total ignorance of the ways of the sea. It has to be one or the other to send a messenger glamour in the form of an albatross.'

A couple of minutes later the ungainly bird took off again. Once more it circled above, then headed back the way it had come. Caldason watched it go, then rejoined them.

'It looks as though I'm going to be on the Diamond Isle longer than I thought,' he said and seemed contented at the prospect.

'Well, I hope you're going to like it here,' the skipper came back, 'because there it is.'

On the horizon, between sea and sky, a thin, dark strip of land had appeared.

26

'I suppose this place is technically yours now,' Darrok said.

'Not mine *personally*,' Caldason replied, 'and more than just technically. Now the last of the gold's been delivered, the island belongs to the alliance of interests Karr heads.'

'Oh, come on, Caldason. Talking like a legal advocate hardly suits you. Be honest. You mean the so-called Resistance.'

The Qalochian didn't answer.

'Suit yourself,' Darrok returned in his distinctive rasp. 'I don't give a damn personally, now I've got the gold.'

'It's true what they say about you, then? That riches are your only motivation.'

'Is it true what they say about you, too? That revenge and bloodletting is all that drives you? Things are rarely what they at first seem, my friend. You of all people should know that. And if money was all I cared about, I'd turn you in for the reward the paladins have put on your head. Didn't know about that, did you?'

'It comes as no surprise. Aren't you tempted?'

'No. And the bounty's big.'

'How big?'

'*Very*. Though nowhere near as much as the money I'm

getting for this island. I'm not entirely driven by a lust for riches, Caldason, despite what people think. That gold represents my retirement and future security. Not only mine; quite a few other people rely on me for their livelihoods.'

'I had no idea you were a benefactor,' Caldason came back dryly.

'I am in a way, given that I see money as just a means to an end.'

'Doesn't everybody?'

'Most use it less wisely than I do.'

'What, for feeding their families, that kind of thing?'

'I feed a lot of families. More than you ever have, I'd wager.' He offered the wine flask. 'Sure you won't have a drink?'

'No.'

'Pity. It's an excellent vintage.' He sipped from his glass appreciatively.

They sat in one of the many rooms in Darrok's spacious, beautifully appointed hillside mansion. His hovering disk was lodged in a hollow on a specially made, reinforced chair that meant he was at the same height as guests. A large window stood close to where they talked, and through it the landscaped grounds could be seen.

'Impressive house, isn't it?' Darrok said. 'Don't get the impression the whole island is like this, though. I'm afraid most of the rest is rather run down. It's just my bit that's so agreeable. I say mine. The house is yours too now, isn't it? Sorry, Karr's alliance of interests'. The deal was the island and everything on it, after all. I expect you could live here yourself if you asked nicely enough. They must owe you a favour.'

'It's not my style. I never did go for overblown ostentation. I think it reveals a bit too much about the insecurities of its owner. Sorry, ex-owner.'

Darrok ignored that. 'I'll miss this place. I won't miss the island; it's been a thorn in my side for too long. But I'll be sad to see the back of this house. I've put a lot of work into it.'

Caldason scanned the special furniture, extra wide door frames without the doors, and a dozen other refinements. 'I can see it's been designed for a man lacking legs.'

'Originally, yes. Then later I had it adapted some more when I got the disk.' He affectionately patted the side of his seat-cum-transporter.

'It must cost you a fortune to run that thing.'

'I can afford it.'

'Darrok, how did you lose your legs? You said it was Kingdom Vance, but you didn't explain how. Or is it something you prefer not to talk about?'

'You'll find there are few things I'm not prepared to talk about, Caldason. Yes, it was Vance.'

'You survived one of his raids?'

'Not exactly. It was more in the way of a falling out with him.'

'A falling out? You mean you were . . .'

'A pirate, yes. Though I preferred to think of myself as being on a slightly higher level than mere crew. As his partner, in fact. But in the event he saw it differently.'

'What happened?'

'I spent three years in the business. And I use the word advisedly; it was a business as far as I was concerned.'

'That's a novel way of describing it.'

'But it's true. Piracy's a very elementary form of barter. You take possessions from people in exchange for letting them keep their lives. It's not dissimilar to taxes. Nobody wants to pay them but governments make you. It's certainly no worse than what the empires' rulers do, where people have to follow their laws at the ultimate expense of their lives.'

'Let's take the self-justification as read, shall we?'

Darrok grinned. 'Me and Vance worked well enough together for a while, though we had different attitudes to buccaneering. That thing about taking possessions but sparing lives, for instance. He too often wanted both. But the real difference between us, what led me to this chair, was to do with money.'

'There's a surprise.'

'Vance's way was to spend as fast as he got it. Mine was to hoard most of what I made. I saw piracy as a stepping stone to other things, not something I'd be doing for the rest of my life. Which would probably have been quite short, incidentally.'

'It looks as though it almost was.'

'Anyway, we hit a lean period. Even pirates have them, believe it or not. Vance started agitating for a share of my nest-egg. I wasn't keen, let's say, and things quickly came to the crunch. He persuaded the rest of the crew to take his side by offering them a portion of my money. To cut a long and rather unpleasant story short, it inevitably ended in violence.'

'What kind loses a man his legs?'

'The kind where you find yourself having to jump over-board. Then being sucked under the keel of a ship in shallow water with a rocky bottom. That's how I got this rather fetching voice, too.'

'How do you mean?'

'The surface of the water was ablaze at the time. Vance is nothing if not thorough. I inhaled a goodly measure of searing oil.'

'And you *survived* that?'

'I hear you're a pretty good survivor yourself. Maybe you're as bone-headed stubborn as I am. Anyway, I washed up here, on Batariss. The Diamond Isle. I was lucky. There were some people here inclined to help me, and they had healing skills. They couldn't salvage my legs, what was left of them, but they did save my life. I was able to reward them for that later, and quite lavishly, I might add. I was doubly lucky, as a matter of fact. The then owners of this place wanted to sell up, and I used most of my savings to buy it. It wasn't exactly what I had in mind as a career move, but the options for half a man can be somewhat limited. It's provided a good income until the last couple of years.'

'And Vance?'

'He thought I was dead, and was *very* pissed off because he hadn't got the location of my hoard out of me first. But that was nothing compared to how he felt when he found out I was alive and must have used the money to buy this island.'

'So this is personal? His interest in the island, I mean.'

'He'd probably be haunting these waters anyway. But me being here has certainly twisted the knife for him. The way Vance thinks, this should all be his by rights, and he's madder than hell about it.'

'That isn't going to change once you've gone, is it?'

'I don't know. There's a good chance he'd try to find me. But it's just as likely he'd want to plunder this place first. If ever a man was ridden by greed, it's Vance.'

'Where will you go?'

Darrok smiled. 'You'll forgive me for not answering that. But I will say that I've got another island in mind, a very long way from here. I've acquired rather a taste for having my own little principality.'

'Not a kingdom?'

'That's a word that doesn't figure in my vocabulary too much these days.' They swapped smiles. 'But I'm not ready to go just yet. I still have arrangements to make concerning shipping out the gold. Quite complicated arrangements. My staying a bit longer won't be a problem for you, will it?'

'It's all the same to me. I don't suppose Karr and the others will mind much either. Besides, you can familiarise me with the island in the meantime. If I'm going to be staying here a while, that could be useful.'

'Let's start now. A quick tour before the sun goes down. Are you game for it?'

Caldason was.

They rode in an open carriage, with Darrok at the reins and Caldason beside him. Darrok's hover disk was loaded in the back. He hadn't brought any of his bodyguards, not even the redhead who'd occupied so much of his time on the trip from Bhealfa. Caldason took that as a vote of confidence on Darrok's part. Presumably he didn't think Reeth was going to cut his throat as soon as they turned a corner.

The carriage was travelling along a less-than-perfect road towards a cluster of buildings.

'We can't do it all with the light we have left,' Darrok explained. 'The island's only a fraction of the size of Bhealfa, but it's still pretty big. You'd need at least a couple of days to explore it all. But you probably know that.'

'I've never been here before, but I've seen maps. That's given me a rough idea of the geography. Do you still have visitors?'

'Paying guests? Not really. As I said, the last few years have seen poor pickings. Did you know the history of this place goes back a couple of centuries? As a resort, that is?'

'I think somebody mentioned it. It was quite exclusive in the early days, wasn't it?'

'Up until, oh, seventy or eighty years ago. When people started to drop the name Batariss and took to calling it the Diamond Isle. Its days as a grand resort are long in the past. Not that it went right down after that. It was a slow decline.'

'What brought it about?'

'A combination of things. Fashion, mostly. People were less interested in coming. Probably because, as the affluent got richer, they were able to afford more and more glamours for private use. They just didn't need to come here to experience what they already had at home. And it's expensive to maintain something like this. It got to the point where all the money coming in was going straight out again on repairs and the like. The final nail in the coffin, in recent years, has been the pirates.'

'Did you ever prey on people visiting here when you were one?'

'It would be ironic if I had, wouldn't it? But no, there was little point. Not if you wanted to make a good amount from every raid. It was better to go for merchant ships, or maybe some of those fancy cruise ships the very rich patronise. Of course, they're usually better protected, but the rewards are worth it. That was my philosophy, anyway. Vance, on the other hand, had to be argued out of attacking everything that floated. Not that my way always paid off. I remember one time we boarded a merchantman and found it was a chandler's vessel. Had about a hundred thousand candles on board, which are not the easiest goods to shift quickly. Especially as most people prefer glamour lighting these days. Vance got so worked up about that one he torched the ship and sank it.'

Caldason found himself dismissing his preconceptions about this man and warming to him. Notwithstanding he'd been a rogue in his time, and not necessarily someone he would have approved of.

They came to something that looked like a small village, except all the buildings were more or less identical, and they were dilapidated.

'These used to be luxurious chalets,' Darrok said, 'hard as it is to picture now. A retreat for the wealthy and influential. You couldn't let them out as pigsties these days.'

The tour continued, taking in further clusters of buildings. There were areas where gambling parlours were situated, and a whole row of brothels, hidden prettily in a shallow valley so as not to offend the more strait-laced visitors. They passed a circuit for chariot races, and a sizeable boating lake being choked by uncontrolled vegetation.

Oddest were the so-called jest fayres, where glamour power had been used to offer novelty rides, distortion houses, gambling dens, monstrosity shows and the like. The architecture of these attractions was fantastical, bizarre and not a little tacky. They looked all the stranger for being semi-derelict and overrun by weeds.

'It's going to be dark soon,' Darrok said. 'We should be getting back. I'll show you the rest of the island tomorrow. Are you sure you won't take up my offer to stay at my house?'

'Thanks, Darrok, but I think it's best if I lodge with my band.'

'You don't want to erode their morale by leaving them in the rather shabby guest block I've provided while you bed down in luxury.'

'Something like that.'

'You're probably right. Make do with it for a couple of days and I'll see your men get something better.'

They headed for the billet. As they went past another collection of tumbledown buildings, Darrok remarked, 'It's amazing how quickly Nature reclaims its realm. Some of these places were in use just two or three years ago. Most of the island's always been relatively unspoilt, actually. No more than a tenth at most was ever built on. But I don't suppose a jumble of old buildings are going to be of much interest to your people. I gather they intend using a fair slice of the island for agriculture.'

'That's the plan.'

'Oh, I think that's just part of it, Caldason, if the truth be known. No need to look uncomfortable, my friend. You might think I'm solely a materialist, so it might surprise you to know I'm not unsympathetic to . . . well, to whatever it is you intend doing here.'

'Is it that transparent?'

'I hope not, for your sakes.'

'This . . . plan we supposedly have. How do you view it?'

'Totally hypothetically, of course, given that I have no idea what it is?'

'Of course.'

'I'd say it was . . . inspiring, marvellously idealistic. Noble, even.'

'And what would you say its chances were?'

'Realistically? Oh, about the same as an ice crystal's in hell.'

'Ah.'

'But what's life without its challenges?'

27

'I'm so glad you could make it, Commissioner,' Devlor Bastorran said as his aide ushered Laffon into the paladin's office.

'Your message left me little choice. I hope the matter you referred to is urgent enough to warrant our meeting at such a late hour.'

'I'm sure you'll think so once I've explained everything. Please, make yourself comfortable. Can I have Meakin bring you something? Refreshments? A drink?'

Laffon held up a bony hand. 'Thank you, no, High Chief. All I require is the briefing you promised.'

'Very well. On the night my uncle was so tragically cut down, and since, you and I have spoken about the need for our two organisations to co-operate on affairs of state security.'

'We have. Though I must say the flow of information so far has been somewhat less than I was hoping for.'

'If we're being candid, I think I could say the same from my side. But what I have to tell you tonight is solid, reliable and has a very significant bearing on the activities of the terrorists. It demands co-operation between the CIS and the paladins, to the great advantage of both.'

Laffon steepled his fingers. 'Go on.'

'We've been cultivating spies in the dissidents' ranks for some time now.'

'We both do *that*, Bastorran.'

'Yes, but with respect, we now have a particular source more centrally placed than any hitherto known. That's not supposition, it's fact.'

'This is a new contact?'

'Yes.'

'And you have no reason to suspect their motives?'

'If you mean are we being fed misinformation or lured into some kind of trap, no, I don't believe so. And may I say, Commissioner, that our recent harsher clampdown on the dissidents, and high-profile arrests like that of Rukanis, have contributed in no small way to a flow of higher grade intelligence. I believe our stance has been vindicated, and that we'll see more informants like this one coming forward.'

'That would be gratifying. Do continue.'

'This source has supplied us with names, addresses and other data concerning those calling themselves the Resistance. Not everything by any means, but enough to strike a substantial blow against them. Possibly enough to disrupt their activities for the foreseeable future.'

'I repeat: can you trust this information? The kind of resources we'd need to devote to any action based on it would be considerable.'

'I know that. And, yes, I trust the source. The person in question has an important personal stake in telling us the truth.'

'Very well, I'm prepared to accept that. What do you propose?'

'Acting, naturally, and as quickly as possible. We need to mount a number of raids on the addresses I've been given. They must be simultaneous in order to have maximum impact, and ideally they should be combined paladin-CIS operations. Pooling our expertise and manpower will greatly increase their effectiveness.'

'That can be arranged. As the CIS is still in the process of securing a headquarters here in Valdarr, I suggest we use yours as our base of operations.'

'Our facilities are at your disposal.'

'I'll get my people over here immediately to start planning.'

'Excellent.'

'I'll need to avail myself of several of your messengers, if I may. But in a moment. I have something I need to speak to you about first. Privately.' He shot a pointed look Meakin's way.

'Certainly. Meakin, go and make the arrangements for the Commissioner to send the messages he needs to get out. Then come back here afterwards.'

'Yes, sir.' The aide left.

'Is this related to the subject in hand, Commissioner?'

'In some respects it is. It concerns this very substantial reward you've offered for the capture of Reeth Caldason.'

'What of it?'

'Now that you've assumed control of the paladins, I imagine you've been made aware of the special guidelines concerning this man?'

'I have. My uncle left a sealed briefing.'

'We're concerned that offering such a large reward might breach those guidelines.'

'I don't see why it should.'

'I think I might beg to differ on that.'

'A man murders the top official of the paladin clans. How can we not offer a reward in order to catch him? What kind of message would it send out to the rabble if we didn't? That it's permissible to assassinate who they like, no matter how

exalted, in the certainty that our efforts to catch the perpe-
trators will be feeble? And do note, Commissioner, that our
reward stipulates his capture, not his death.'

'A fine distinction, and not one likely to be noticed by the
average street rowdy or bounty hunter who might be tempted
to collect it. Look, I understand how you feel, particularly in
view of the personal loss you've suffered. But I still think we
have to tread very carefully in respect of Caldason. May I
remind you that the guidelines in question came down from
the highest possible authority?'

'And I intend lobbying that same authority to have them
rescinded. Because, frankly, I see no sense in them.'

'It isn't always given to us to reason why, Bastorran.'

'Commissioner, in view of the other matter I've laid before
you, can I respectfully suggest we return to this subject at a
later date? We have plenty to occupy us tonight.'

'As you say. We'll speak about this another time, then.
Where's that man of yours?'

On cue, Meakin knocked and came back into the room.

He conducted Laffon to the messengers' block, and in due
course returned to his master.

'Sir, speaking of messages, we've had several from Aphri
Kordenza, demanding to see you. She's getting quite insistent, in fact.'

'Insistent be damned. This isn't the time. Stall her. We have
much bigger fish to net, Meakin.'

'Information from spies can't always be relied upon,' Disgleirio
maintained. 'Do we have any independent confirmation?'

'Not as yet,' Karr replied, 'but our informants in the dock-
yards have proved very trustworthy in the past. All we know
is that the galley Kinsel's on failed to make port when
expected. The delay's getting to the point now where adverse
weather can't be blamed. Not that any has been reported.'

'That doesn't mean the vessel's been lost. It might be acting on new orders and making for somewhere else.'

'Yes, there are several reasons why we shouldn't necessarily be too alarmed just yet. But we must be alive to the possibility that something's gone wrong. In which case –'

'Tanalvah.'

'Yes. After all she's suffered, Kinsel's loss would be a most grievous blow. It's going to extinguish any hope she has of ever seeing him again, no matter how unrealistic that hope might be. That's why I've asked you here too, Goyter. If the worst has happened, we'll need you to lend a hand in getting Tanalvah through it. After Serrah, you seem to be the one she's come to rely on most since the trial.'

'Of course I'll do whatever I can for the poor girl,' his aide said. 'Though, to be honest, I'm not sure I'd do anything like as good a job of it as Serrah. Those two seem to have formed a bond.'

'Karr, in view of this, shouldn't Serrah's departure be delayed, or even cancelled?' Disgleirio suggested.

'On balance, I think not. She and Kutch are at a safe house now, ready to go out to the island at first light tomorrow. I'm loathe to change that. After all, what can she do here? If Kinsel's lost, he's lost. I don't want to sound hard-hearted about it, but Serrah's of more use to us out there, helping to pave the way, than trying to deal with a hopeless situation here.'

'Perhaps we should at least get word to her,' Goyter submitted. 'Doesn't she have a right to know?'

'I'm inclined to reject that idea, too. Knowing that Kinsel *might* be lost isn't a piece of information she can do anything about except fret over it. That's hardly going to improve her efficiency. Yes, I know; it's a harsh way of looking at it. But decisions have to be made for the greater good. The nearer we get to the move, the more that's going to apply, I'm afraid.'

'In that case,' Disgleirio said, 'isn't there an argument for not telling Tanalvah herself what we've learnt?'

Karr sighed. 'I've wrestled with that one. Do we tell her now of the possibility that her lover's perished? Or do we hold back until we know for sure? Bearing in mind that if his ship has gone down, there's likely to be a public announcement of some kind, and we wouldn't want her finding out that way.'

'Further investigation seems to be in order, then.'

'Yes. What I propose is a compromise. Whether we know more or not, I'll break the news to her this time tomorrow. Meanwhile, we'll use all the contacts we have. In fact, I intend having a word with Phoenix concerning the project to tap into the matrix. They keep telling us how near a breakthrough they are; perhaps they can throw some light on things.'

'It seems to me they're nowhere near being able to intercept messages on the grid. Assuming that really is what it can be used for.'

'It's worth a try, Quinn. After all, what have we got to lose?'

'Exciting, isn't it?'

'Not too exciting for you to get some sleep, I hope. We've got a long day tomorrow.'

'Aren't you just a little bit thrilled at the idea of going somewhere new, Serrah?'

'I'm getting too old for thrills. No, that's a lie, isn't it?' She grinned. 'Yes, of course I'm looking forward to seeing the Diamond Isle. Things have been hectic around here but a little dull at the same time. For me, anyway.'

'And seeing Reeth. That's something worth being glad about, isn't it?'

'That goes without saying, Kutch.'

'You haven't told me what's actually going to happen tomorrow. You know, what we have to do.'

'There's nothing particularly complicated about it. The ship that's taking us is called the *Stag*. It's not actually going to be at the docks; it's anchored offshore. We have to meet with a rowboat crew that's taking us over. A couple of days after that, we'll be on the island.'

'I can't wait. I've never been on a ship before.'

'Then that's something else you've got to look forward to. But if you don't get some sleep you won't be in a fit state to appreciate it. We've got a very early start, remember. This safe house isn't that far from the harbour, but I'm leaving nothing to chance. We're out of here at dawn.'

'All right.'

She blew out the candle. Before closing the door, she said, 'Sleep well, Kutch. From tomorrow, everything's going to be different.'

28

At dawn, the occupants at upwards of forty addresses across Valdarr had a rude awakening. Houses were surrounded, doors kicked in, suspects dragged away. Not all went meekly. There was resistance, from individuals facing hopeless odds to heavily armed groups determined to die rather than be taken. Many had their wish granted.

Some resorted to arson to protect the Underground's secrets, and in several cases perished along with the evidence they sought to destroy. A few took their own lives by blade or poison rather than fall into the hands of state torturers. There were instances of hopelessly outnumbered dissidents taking ramp in order to meet the enemy in a drug-induced frenzy.

Not everyone was taken unawares. The well prepared, overly cautious or just plain lucky escaped. So that the news, and a measure of panic, began to spread. Soon, there was disorder on the streets. The Resistance, disarrayed in any event, had no need to stoke the fires of civil disobedience. That was done for them by the law-enforcers. They made occasional mistakes and targeted the wrong premises, subjecting innocent citizens to open brutality. And once the disturbances began to grow, their typically heavy-handed attempts to restore calm only widened the turmoil.

But ill judgement wasn't restricted to one side. A significant minority in the Resistance ranks, privy to the movement's plans and being only human, with human fears and frailties, took a decision that was to engender even greater chaos.

'What's going on out there?'

'I can't see, Kutch.' Serrah tried leaning even further from the window, then pulled herself back in. 'It's no good, I can't make anything out. But it sounds like something big.'

'It couldn't be a war, could it?'

'I think we would have heard about one coming before now,' she replied aridly.

'I only asked because of my vision. There seemed to be some kind of war going on in that.'

She instantly regretted her slightly acerbic tone. 'No, it's not a war,' she repeated more gently. 'Even if you've become a prophet somehow, wars send a long shadow ahead of them. They don't just happen spontaneously.' *But civil wars can*, she thought, and decided not to share that with him. 'It's just some kind of trouble on the streets.'

'What are we going to do?'

'Good question. What we should be doing is getting to the harbour, of course. Look, we don't know how widespread this is, or what might have set it off. What I suggest is that we make for the port, and if things look too bad we'll think again.'

'All right.'

'And let's forget our luggage, shall we? We don't need to be slowed down, and carrying bags might attract the wrong sort of attention.'

'I've got books in mine. The ones Phoenix gave me to study.'

'See? There's a bright side to everything.' They exchanged

smiles. 'Seriously, leave them. They'll only hold us back. I can get you more books later. Just cram a few essentials in your pockets for now.'

'That's fine by me.'

Serrah hesitated before saying the next thing that came to mind. 'Kutch, I want you to take this.' She reached inside her shirt and tugged a small dagger from its sheath.

His eyes were wide. 'Why?'

'Just in case.'

'You've never wanted me to carry a weapon before.'

'We've never been in a situation like this before.'

'I wouldn't know what to do with it.'

'You hold it like this.' She showed him. 'Nothing fancy; if you need to use it, you stab with it. Straight and hard. Do it just the way you would if you were delivering a punch. All right?'

'I suppose so.'

'Here. Take it.'

He gingerly accepted the weapon. 'Where do I keep it?'

'In your boot, maybe? No, slip it into your belt. This way.' She did it for him. 'Don't worry, Kutch, I'm sure you won't have to draw it. It's just insurance. You can give it back to me when we're on the ship.'

'What do you think we're going to run into out there?'

'I don't know. That's why you've got the knife. Now let's get going, shall we?'

As soon as they stepped onto the street she knew the situation was serious. The atmosphere was grim. There were knots of people hanging about, and it was obvious their mood was unhappy. Stern-faced paladins, militia and army regulars were out in force. Every direction Serrah and Kutch looked they saw columns of black smoke rising into the sky. And in the background there was a constant hum of human noise. Shouts, jeers, marching boots, chanting, the odd scream.

It seemed to be emanating from nearer the city centre. Fortunately they weren't going that way.

'Shouldn't we stop to ask somebody what's happening?'

'No, Kutch. Just keep your head down and your pace up. We're honest citizens going about our business.'

They seemed to be the only ones looking as though they were.

When they turned into another street they found the same scenario. Ugly crowds and edgy peace-keepers. Burnt-out houses. A shop that had obviously been looted.

A block later, they found themselves walking towards a place they knew. It was an ordinary enough dwelling, but one they both recognised as being part of the Resistance's circuit of safe houses. There were a dozen or more militia-men and paladins outside, and a four-man crew was pounding at the door with a battering ram.

'Isn't that –' Kutch began.

'Yes. Keep walking. Don't look that way.'

She got him around a corner and into a lane that was comparatively quiet. Then she pulled him to the side of the pavement.

'I think what we just saw proves it,' she told him. 'There's obviously some big clampdown going on, bigger even than the last couple of weeks. They're targeting the Resistance. And it looks as though people aren't too keen on it.'

'What do we do?'

'I think we should push on to the port.'

'What about the others? Karr and Quinn, and . . . oh, Tanalvah and the children!'

'Listen to me, Kutch. We'll just have to hope they've managed to go to ground. Because there's nothing we can do to help any of them in a situation like this. I reckon the authorities might even be trying to stamp out the Resistance all together.'

'They couldn't do that. Could they?'

'They'd have their work cut out, admittedly. But they can do a lot of damage in the process, including to innocent people.'

'We can't just leave our friends.'

'Don't think of it as abandoning them. Chances are they'll be all right. They're smart, and they've got experience of handling tricky situations.' Serrah looked at him, and thought of how she hadn't been able to protect her daughter, or do anything about Kinsel. As long as it was in her power, she'd be damned if she was going to let anything happen to this boy. 'We have to look after ourselves,' she told him softly. 'Come on.'

They resumed their journey.

Five minutes later they came out of a side street and found themselves heading for a roadblock. It was manned by a paladin and an army regular, and they were turning back pedestrians as well as road traffic.

'Shit,' Serrah cursed.

The paladin saw them and started to gesture.

'He wants us to go back,' Kutch said.

'We're not going back.' She increased the pace.

'He looks pretty angry, Serrah.'

'We're not stopping.'

'But –'

'We're *not*. Just keep up with me and ignore anything he says. But move aside when we get to him.'

The paladin was shouting now, and waving furiously for them to turn around. They couldn't hear exactly what he was saying. Then they got into earshot.

'Are you two morons, or what? I'm ordering you to turn back. This is a restricted area. *Now get the hell out of here!*'

Serrah's response was to smile sweetly and keep walking towards him. Kutch did as he was told and started to move away from her slightly.

'Are you deaf as well as *stupid*?' the paladin raged. His hand edged towards his sheathed sword.

Serrah covered the distance between them in three quick strides. Something metallic flashed in her hand. What happened next looked to Kutch like a punch. Then he remembered what Serrah had said about using a knife. He felt sick.

The paladin sank to the ground, a deeper red staining the crimson of his tunic. His eyes were frozen in shock.

'Come on!' Serrah snapped.

They ran at the roadblock. The army man, turning from bullying somebody else, saw them coming. Then his eyes flashed to the dying paladin sprawled on the pavement. He whipped out his sword and dashed for Kutch and Serrah.

'If this one gets near us,' Serrah instructed, 'keep away.'

She still held the bloodstained knife. On the move, she swiftly drew back her arm and lobbed it. The soldier ducked and the blade flew harmlessly over his head.

'Damn it!' Serrah spat. 'Be ready to run, Kutch. I won't let this last long.'

The soldier came at her just as she got her own sword out. She blocked his opening swing, returned one of her own and saw that deflected by the edge of his blade. A brief flurry of swordplay ensued. It ended when she hammered his weapon aside and drilled his chest. The soldier went down like a dropped sack of turnips.

'Let's get to that ship!' she yelled.

They skipped over the fallen man and began jogging.

'Serrah!' Kutch cried. 'We're being followed!'

She looked back. Two or three uniformed men were running after them. Grabbing Kutch's hand, she pulled him level and they sprinted.

They were aided by two factors. The streets were teeming and they were far from the only ones running. Uncertain whether they'd shaken off their pursuers, Serrah dragged

Kutch into an alley. They bundled down behind a heap of discarded crates, panting heavily.

'We'll...stay here...for a bit...then move...on,' Serrah explained.

They had been crouched there for a couple of minutes when a small child of perhaps five or six years toddled into sight. He saw them, and smiled shyly. Serrah smiled back, and so did Kutch. They began to make tiny shooing gestures, in hope of persuading the child to move away.

Without warning, the child opened his mouth and screamed, *'They're here! They're here!'* He waddled back to the street, waving his arms and pointing to the alley, shouting all the while.

Kutch and Serrah scrambled to their feet and fled.

They went another four blocks before they stopped running.

Near the harbour now, the streets seemed unusually full. But the crowds weren't like the ones they'd seen earlier, with knots of people looking for trouble. Here, men, women and children were moving with a purpose, and many toted baggage. There was an atmosphere of barely suppressed hysteria.

The destination they shared was the same one Serrah and Kutch were trying to reach.

'What's going on?' Kutch wondered.

Serrah got an inkling of what had happened. 'We've been betrayed,' she whispered.

At that moment they rounded the corner of a warehouse and looked into the face of chaos.

The paladins had to arrange for an unmarked carriage. It needed a determined escort to get through the chaotic streets. But at last it arrived at clan headquarters and was waved through the gates.

Its sole occupant wore a long coat, buttoned to the throat, with a generous hood that completely hid their features. It could have been a monk from a reclusive order being taken on a pilgrimage.

The visitor, accompanied by two burly, well-armed guards, was taken through a concealed door into a restricted area. They walked endless corridors, negotiated a number of check-points, had their credentials looked over by sentries. Eventually they came to a small, windowless room, lit by a single glamour orb. The only pieces of furniture were two plain chairs. Instructing the visitor to be seated, the guards withdrew.

A moment later, Devlor Bastorran entered.

'It was good of you to come,' he said.

'Did I have a choice?'

'I'm afraid necessity forced my hand on this occasion,' he explained as he took the other chair. 'There's no need to keep that on in here,' he added. 'After all, we have no secrets, do we?'

The visitor threw back the hood. 'Bringing me here was dangerous. Why couldn't we have met somewhere less obvious?'

'Have you seen the state of the streets today? Oh, yes, of course you have. Silly of me.'

'Why am I here? I've done what you wanted.'

'We need to talk.'

'We've talked. Now I want you to do what you promised.'

'In good time. But before that, we have to talk some more.'

'And if I refuse?'

'In that event, my side of the bargain may prove a little more difficult to honour. So let's be sensible, shall we?'

'What do you want to know?' Tanalvah Lahn said.

29

There must have been a thousand people in the road ahead of them.

The side streets and byways of the harbour probably held several hundred more, and they were still coming. Their mood was one of mounting desperation.

Kutch stared incredulously. 'Who *are* all these people?'

'I recognise some of them,' Serrah said.

'You do?'

'Yes. You probably would yourself, given long enough.'

He looked around, baffled. 'Would I?'

'Maybe there are criminals here trying to avoid the clamp-down, and a few ordinary citizens, fed up with endless oppression. But I reckon the majority are Resistance, or at least sympathisers. I've seen familiar faces.'

'Resistance? *Our* people?'

She nodded, a finger to her lips. 'Keep it down. Not every pair of ears is going to be friendly.'

'I don't understand,' he whispered. 'Where are they going?'

'Where do you think?'

It slowly dawned on him. 'They're not supposed to do that!'

'No law says they can't go to the Diamond Isle if they can pay their passage. Not yet, anyway.'

'Those ships in the harbour; they can't all be heading there.'

'No. The crowd's going to try to make them. They'll offer money at first, and if there aren't enough skippers willing to take it, or too few ships to carry everybody, things will turn nasty.'

'But who's organising this? Who's in charge?'

'You still don't get it, do you, Kutch? Nobody's in charge. It's broken down, gone off half-cocked.' She saw his bewilderment and took pity on him. 'The authorities have been cracking down ever harder. Today they've come down harder still. There must be people in the Resistance who think the stables are being cleaned out once and for all, that the movement's about to be crushed. Who knows? Maybe they're right. But it only took one or two who knew about Karr's plan to say, "Save yourself. Get to the Diamond Isle. It's a haven." The word would have spread, and this is the result.'

He was appalled. 'Can't it be stopped?'

'The genie's out of the bottle. I'm sure there are Resistance people here who've kept their heads and are trying to preach reason. I can't see them holding back the tide.'

'But the Resistance . . . our people . . . they're not supposed . . .'

'Not supposed to be like everyone else? Our side may be right, but that doesn't give us a monopoly on acting rationally.'

The press of people was building up. Serrah grasped his wrist and led him back the way they'd come. They got to a slightly less crowded area. That wasn't going to last.

'This is a really dangerous situation,' she said. 'There are just a few uniforms in this place, and they can't do much. The only reason there aren't a lot more is because they're so occupied elsewhere in the city they haven't realised what's

going on here yet. But they will. Then they'll blockade the
harbour, and the gods know what else. Think about it from
their point of view, Kutch. What do you see? A great swathe
of the state's enemies, all conveniently gathered together in
one place with the sea at their backs. Ever heard of spearing
fish in a barrel?'

'You said somebody betrayed us. How do you know?'

'The paladins, CIS, militia and the rest wouldn't just pick
on houses at random. They had to have something to go on.'

'Who would do such a thing?'

Serrah shrugged. 'Like I said, no monopoly on reason. Or
loyalty.'

'We'll have to stop here in Bhealfa,' Kutch moaned. 'We'll
never get through all these people, never see Reeth again.'

'Only if we stay in this mob.' She looked around. Her eye
lighted on something. 'How do you like heights?'

'Heights?'

'For a start, yes. Come with me. Keep close.'

She elbowed them to the warehouse they had passed
earlier. They battled to its far side, where one wall formed
half of a narrow alleyway. There was a door.

'Block the view from the road, Kutch.' She produced a
knife and slipped it into the lock. 'Let's hope nobody's in.'
The knife jerked, there was a click. One shove and the door
creaked open. 'Get in, quickly.'

It was dark inside, and apparently unoccupied. They
weaved through stacks of crates tall as a house, looking for
windows. There were none. They found a staircase. Two flights
took them to the top floor, where there was a window, but
it was shuttered. Serrah's knife proved useful again, and she
flung the shutters wide. Beyond the barred window was a
clear view of the ocean.

'Thought so. This warehouse backs onto the water's edge.'

'Now what?'

'We can't get through these.' She tested a bar. 'We'll have to try the roof after all.'

'Roof?'

'But how?' Serrah mused, scanning the place. 'There!'

A trapdoor was set in the ceiling.

'Help me move some of those boxes,' she said.

They hurriedly made a small step pyramid. The trap had only a simple bolt. Palms to the wood, they heaved it free, revealing a square of blue-grey sky. There was no problem scrambling through and onto the flat roof.

The salt air was windy but the view was impressive. In front of them, a vista of rippling ocean. To their right the harbour complex and the mass of people milling about it. Further on, a long jetty stretched from the shore, with two ships tied up at its end. The jetty thronged with even more people looking like worker ants from this distance, besieging the ships. Plenty of other vessels were moored all along the harbour wall. They were being stormed, too.

'That should be the *Stag*.' Serrah pointed to a three-master at anchor in the middle of the bay.

She took Kutch to the edge of the building. When they looked down he grabbed her hand, palm sweaty. She squeezed it.

Two floors below, the top of the harbour wall abutted the warehouse, forming a wide stone ledge. Then there was a respectable drop to the water. The building had basic ornamentation on its facade, consisting of tiers of bricks projecting edgeways.

'We can use those to climb down,' Serrah decided. 'Kutch?'

His attention was on the sky. She followed his gaze.

Four or five black somethings were flying in a line towards the harbour. The distance was too great to make out what they were, but they certainly weren't birds. They were far too big.

Serrah went over to the other side of the roof, Kutch in tow. Convoys of wagons clogged the streets leading to the harbour entrance. Many were uncovered, and they saw distinctive red uniforms.

'It's starting, isn't it?' Kutch said.

She nodded. 'And the gods know how that crowd's going to react to the arrival of a small army. They're only one notch down from full-blown panic as it is.'

They could clearly make out five objects in the sky now, and there were more further back.

'Glamour squadron,' Kutch confirmed, suppressing a shudder.

Their various distinctive shapes identified them as fire-spitters, manslayers, berserker-drones, fangdivers, trackers and gargoyles.

'They're not stinting on the firepower,' Serrah remarked.

Suddenly, the racket the crowd was making took on a different quality. A spreading roar washed over it. Down below, troops spilled from the wagons. On the edges of the crowd, fighting had already begun.

Then a louder noise caught their attention. A flying glamour that looked like a cross between a serpent and a spider was dive-bombing the jetty. It belched fireballs that exploded on impact. People were ablaze and leaping into the dock and the rigging on one of the ships was burning.

Another creature, blimpish and prickly, struck nearer home. Its fire came down on the heads beneath in glutinous sheets.

As with any crowd, many in it were armed. Some had conventional weapons like bows. Others carried glamour munitions. Arrows flew and the flash of magical discharges began. But those wanting to fight were hampered by the crush of humanity. People were jumping or falling from the harbour wall. Swimmers could be seen, and several over-loaded rowboats had been launched. A further ship, much closer than the jetty, had burst into flames. They saw crew running about its decks.

'Standing on a roof might not be the brightest idea,' Serrah figured. 'We should –'

An airborne glamour swooped low overhead, confirming her fear. They dropped flat. The soaring glamour, pyramid-shaped, striped like a tiger and with huge eyes on stalks, flew over the trapped crowd. It showered them with razor-sharp ice crystals.

'The *Stag* isn't going to wait much longer,' Serrah said.

They crawled back to the harbour-side edge of the wall. Several ships were approaching from the open sea, flying Bhealfan and Gath Tampoorian military ensigns.

'As I feared. They're going to block the harbour mouth. We've got to get out to the ship, fast.'

Then they spied a galley rounding the spit, oars churning the water to white foam.

'You don't think . . . ?'

'No, Kutch. Kinsel's a long way from here.' Serrah looked down the wall. 'It's not too great a height. Take it easy, use those jutting bricks for foot and handholds. You'll be fine.' She clocked his expression. 'Don't think. Just *do* it.'

They eased themselves over the edge and began their descent. Taking it steady, gingerly putting a little pressure on each brick before trusting it with their weight, progress was slow.

Something went past them at speed, wriggling through the air, giving off a deafening wail. Kutch started. The brick he'd just laid his foot on dislodged and plummeted, shattering below.

Serrah, alongside him, grasped his wrist. 'Easy, easy. You all right?'

He nodded, panting.

They started moving again, even more slowly. With their

faces to the wall they could hear the turmoil but not see anything, which made it seem all the worse. Both of them half expected one of the flying glamours to swoop in and crisp them.

Finally they reached the top of the harbour wall. Incongruously, with the sounds of pitched battles and death all around, seagulls were bobbing serenely on the waves.

'The *Stag*'s not that far out, fortunately,' Serrah judged.

'How do we get to it?'

'What did you expect, a waiting boat to ferry us across?'

'Well, yes; I was kind of hoping there would be.'

'Competition's a bit too stiff for that. We're going to have to swim. Damn, I forgot to ask: you *can* swim?'

'Well, yes. Only not that well. I'm not particularly fond of water.'

'You're about to make friends with it. Get your boots off.'

She did the same. Very reluctantly, she ditched her sword, too.

They stood with their toes curling over the lip of the wall.

'There's no other way but jumping,' Serrah told him. 'We'll go in feet first. Then use nice, easy strokes to get to the ship. We're not in a race. Don't worry, I'll be with you. Ready? On three. One . . . two . . . th –'

The cold water all but knocked the wind out of them. There was a second's confusion as they resurfaced and got their bearings. Then, side by side, they started to swim.

Only once did they have to alter course, when a patch of burning oil drifted into their path. And they saw several floating corpses, terribly burnt or mutilated. Serrah had just started to worry what effect the cold might have on them when she stretched her hand and touched the slimy hull.

There was a tense moment when it looked like the crew weren't going to allow them aboard. But when Serrah called out her name, and it was recognised, they let them climb the netting that draped the ship's side.

Once they'd struggled over the rail, the skipper said, 'Five more minutes and we wouldn't have been here. As it is we're going to have to outrun the blockade they're bringing in.'

'Think we'll do it?' she asked, scraping strands of wet hair from her face.

'I reckon.' He turned away to bark orders.

A crewman cloaked them with blankets. Serrah and Kutch leaned on the rail, getting their breath back and dripping.

'You did well, Kutch,' she said. 'I'm proud of you.'

He gave a weak smile. 'We were luckier than those still on shore.'

The port area was all chaos and fiery confusion.

As the ship lifted anchor and the crew prepared to sail, Serrah noticed that they weren't the only people to have been picked up. Further along the deck a bedraggled, pasty-faced group of ten or twelve people were huddled together.

Heaven help us, she thought, *if this is all that's left of the Resistance.*

30

The air stank of charred flesh.

Dulian Karr pressed a cloth to his lower face as he picked through the wreckage. Disgleirio, rummaging at the opposite end of the cellar, hadn't bothered.

There were four corpses scattered across the flagstone floor, all horribly burnt, their blue Covenant robes little more than brittle ash. One had been a woman, but they couldn't tell which.

In the corner, the fenced-off pit gently bubbled, like a cooking pot. Its sides were caked in a gritty, sooty substance, and at its bottom the flow of quicksilver was down to a sluggish trickle. The whole cellar – floor, walls and ceiling – looked as though it had been subjected to intense heat. But no other part of the house had been affected.

'We're not going to get anything from this,' Disgleirio decided. 'Everything's been incinerated.'

'I'm afraid you're right, Quinn,' Karr agreed. He looked even paler than usual, and there was a faint bluish tint to his lips. His breathing was laboured even when he wasn't exerting himself. The events of the last few hours had done nothing to improve his vitality.

'I don't know what you hoped to find out anyway,' the Righteous Blade man added.

'A clue as to what might have happened here. Perhaps a hint that these poor devils had been able to pluck some kind of message from the matrix.'

'It's obvious, isn't it? Whatever it was they were doing here went badly wrong. They weren't up to meddling with Founder magic, whatever they thought.'

The patrician sighed. 'That might be, I suppose. Though I wish we could have Phoenix's opinion.'

'If we knew where he was. Let's leave this. There's no purpose served wasting our time on something we don't even understand. There are much more pressing matters to deal with.'

'Very well.'

'I think we should –'

'*Ssshh*. What was that?'

'What?'

There was a tiny sound. Disgleirio heard it this time. It was unmistakably a groan. They realised that it came from the man lying farthest from the pit, and hurried to him.

'My gods,' Disgleirio muttered, 'he's alive.'

The man was terribly burnt. What remained of his flesh was almost black. But his seared lips were trembling.

'I think he's trying to say something.' Karr wanted to touch the man, to comfort him, but knew any contact would only add to his agony. Instead he lowered his head close to the sorcerer's quivering mouth. There was another attempt to speak.

'What's he saying?' Disgleirio whispered.

'I can't tell. Wait.' There was a throaty rasp. Then the death rattle sounded. 'He's gone. I don't know how he managed to last this long.'

'To pass on a message, perhaps? Did you catch what he said?'

'Yes. It was just one word. *Surge.*'

'Surge? Was that all?'

'Yes.'

'Do you know what it means?'

'I'm afraid not. Again, we'd need Phoenix or someone with similar knowledge to help with it.'

'There's nothing more we can do here, Karr. We should be turning our efforts to what's more important.'

'You're right.'

They closed the scorched door behind them and tramped up the stairs. Karr took each step like a much older man.

When they reached the ground floor they went into its biggest room. There were several edgy Resistance fighters there, along with Goyter, Karr's aide. Karr shook his head in response to her unspoken question. Then he walked slowly to a chair and sank into it with a sigh.

'Are we sure this place is safe?' Disgleirio said.

'You keep asking that, Quinn,' Karr replied wearily, 'and I can only give you the same answer. I don't know. It's one of the most secret hideaways we have. In theory it should be secure. But with what's happening now, who can say?'

'It turns on whether the one who betrayed us knows about it, doesn't it?'

'We are positive it was treachery?' Goyter wondered.

'It had to be,' Karr confirmed. 'And by somebody who knows an awful lot about us.'

'All the more reason to make finding new safe houses a priority,' Disgleirio suggested.

'Goyter, has there been any word on Tanalvah?' Karr wanted to know.

She looked grieved. 'None. Her or the children. I pray they're all right.'

'Or Serrah and Kutch?'

'Nothing.'

'So many have gone missing. They couldn't all have been caught in the harbour massacre, could they?'

'Nowhere near,' Disgleirio reckoned. 'But naturally everyone's gone to ground.'

'I wonder how many got away?' Goyter said. 'From the harbour, I mean.'

'Impossible to say,' Karr answered. 'But not a large number, I fear.'

A thought occurred to Disgleirio. 'Do you think Gath Tampoor and Rintarah are experiencing anything like this? Or any of their other colonies?'

'We know they've had equally tough crackdowns recently. But if you mean are they having a day like this, that would assume an informant who knew the workings of the Resistance not only here but everywhere. There are very, very few people in that position. And I'd personally vouch for all of them.' He gave a little intake of breath, and his hand went to his forehead.

'Are you all right?' Goyter said, looking concerned.

'Hm? Yes. I'm fine.'

'You were overdoing it even before all this happened,' she commented sternly. 'I dread to think of the effect it's having on you.'

He flashed her a feeble smile. 'You worry too much, Goyter.'

Disgleirio picked up his thread. 'I mentioned the empires because I was wondering if Resistance people from elsewhere might have got to the island.'

'That's a two-edged sword, isn't it? If they did, it means the movement's suffered treachery on a universal scale. If they didn't, the Diamond Isle's going to be poorly populated from our point of view. Neither prospect appeals.'

'It's going to be a hell of a job picking up the pieces after this.'

'There may not be any pieces left.'

'What do you mean?'

'Think on it. This break in Resistance discipline we've witnessed has exposed the whole plan, hasn't it? The empires would have to be very dim indeed not to realise what we intended. Now there has to be a temptation on the part of both Rintarah and Gath Tampoor to seize the Diamond Isle, in order to put a stop to any idea of a dissident state. I'd put money on the possibility of an invasion by one or the other of them.'

'With hardly any of our people out there to fend it off.'

'Exactly. You know, I intended showing you all something today. It's quite ironic, really.'

'What is?'

'Will you pass it over, please, Goyter?'

'Are you sure there's any point? In view of what you've just said?'

'Yes. It was intended to be an inspiration. Now it could well serve as a small memorial to a shattered dream.'

'If you insist.' Goyter leaned over and lifted something that had been lying on the floor beside her chair. It proved to be a square of folded green cloth. She got up and took it to him. He stood, then opened it out for them to see. It was a flag. The motif was a scorpion, its curled stinger raised, ready to strike.

'It was approved by the Council just last week,' Karr explained, 'as the new state's emblem. I don't think the imagery will be lost on you.'

'Small but deadly, eh?' Disgleirio commented approvingly.

'Yes. It says we may be tiny but we ... we ... pack a ... sting.' He swayed, eyes rolling, jaw agape, and fell. The flag covered his chest like a shroud.

'Gods!' Goyter exclaimed. 'Dulian! *Dulian!* Do something, Quinn!' she demanded.

Disgleirio and the fighters rushed to him. They loosened

his collar. Disgleirio felt for a pulse. 'Get him a healer,' he pronounced. *'Quickly!'*

Autumn was shading into winter.

In the chill of a breaking dawn, four people stood on the crest of a hill, looking out to sea. To be exact, three stood and one sat on a curved hovering dish, suspended by magical energy.

A ship was nosing its way into the little harbour down below.

'I wonder how many more this will bring?' Serrah wondered.

'That reminds me,' Zahgadiah Darrok said. 'I've had some figures compiled.' He reached into a pouch, extracted a sheet of paper and unfolded it. 'Taking into account the pathfinders who were already here, plus your band, Reeth, and all those who've made their way over since the troubles, we come to a total of two thousand, four hundred and sixty seven. That doesn't count any of my people, of course.'

'It's not a lot compared to how many were supposed to get here, is it?' Kutch said.

'No,' Caldason agreed. 'But a small number can make a big difference, if they're properly motivated. A lot of those who braved the journey have shown they are.'

'I can't help thinking about the others,' Serrah admitted. 'Tanalvah, Karr, Phoenix. Kinsel, of course. Even Quinn. How must they be faring, do you think?'

'Hopefully they'll get through. They're all survivors in their way.'

'Like us,' Kutch piped up.

Caldason smiled. 'Yes.'

'My mind's just as often on whoever betrayed the cause,' Serrah added, her face darkening. 'If I ever . . . *when* I find out who it was, I'm going to take a great deal of pleasure paying them back.'

'That may never happen,' Darrok told her. 'My experience of life has been that sometimes it's better to let the past go. Concentrate on the future. Try to make your dreams come true.'

'I'm not sure about dreams. I think we're witnesses to one dying.' She lightened the mood. 'How about your dreams, Reeth?' She slipped an arm around his waist. 'When will you be pursuing them?'

'Soon, I hope. But it'll involve another voyage.'

'Well, next time I'm going with you, no matter what.'

'Me, too!' Kutch added.

'We'll see.'

'Until then,' Darrok said, 'it looks like this place is going to be your home.'

'Perhaps,' Caldason replied. 'But that might not be in our hands.'

'Everything's in our hands,' Serrah told him. 'We'll learn to dream our own dreams.'

Red as blood, the sun rose on the Diamond Isle.

Stan Nicholls is best kown for the internationally acclaimed Orcs: First Blood series. His journalism has appeared in *Locus, SFX*, the *Guardian*, the *Independent*, the *Daily Mirror, Time Out, Sight and Sound*, and *Rolling Stone*, among many others. He currently lives in the West Midlands with his wife, the writer Anne Gay.

www.stannicholls.com